"Hot and romantic, with an edge of
—Shayla Black, *New*

"An angsty backstory made beautiful by a hero who doesn't know how perfect he is. Don't miss this Ranch treat!"
—Carly Phillips, *New York Times* bestselling author

"[A] steamy, sexy yet emotionally gripping story."
—Julie Cross, author of the Tempest novels

"I dare you to even attempt to put it down."
—Cassandra Carr, author of *Burning Love*

"Unique and emotional." —*USA Today*

"Thoroughly pleasing . . . The romance is as sweet as the action is hot, and there's something deeply satisfying about the way this couple comes together." —*Publishers Weekly*

"Get ready to crank up the A/C—this is a scorcher!"
—*RT Book Reviews*

"Loren does an incredible job portraying the BDSM lifestyle in a sexy and romantic way . . . Loren should definitely be put on the must-read list." —The Book Pushers

"Like a roller-coaster ride . . . When you hit the last page, you say, let's ride it again." —Guilty Pleasures Book Reviews

"Roni Loren's books are masterful, story-driven, sensual and very erotic . . . Definitely one of my have-to-get-as-soon-as-possible series!" —Under the Covers Book Blog

Titles by Roni Loren

CRASH INTO YOU

MELT INTO YOU

FALL INTO YOU

NOT UNTIL YOU

CAUGHT UP IN YOU

NEED YOU TONIGHT

NOTHING BETWEEN US

CALL ON ME

OFF THE CLOCK

WANDERLUST

LOVING YOU EASY

Novellas

STILL INTO YOU

FOREVER STARTS TONIGHT

BREAK ME DOWN

NICE GIRLS DON'T RIDE

YOURS ALL ALONG

LOVING YOU EASY

RONI LOREN

BERKLEY
New York

BERKLEY
An imprint of Penguin Random House LLC
375 Hudson Street, New York, New York 10014

Copyright © 2016 by Roni Loren
Penguin Random House supports copyright. Copyright fuels creativity,
encourages diverse voices, promotes free speech, and creates a vibrant culture.
Thank you for buying an authorized edition of this book and for complying
with copyright laws by not reproducing, scanning, or distributing any part of it
in any form without permission. You are supporting writers and allowing
Penguin Random House to continue to publish books for every reader.

BERKLEY is a registered trademark and the B colophon is a trademark of
Penguin Random House LLC.

Library of Congress Cataloging-in-Publication Data

Names: Loren, Roni, author.
Title: Loving you easy / Roni Loren.
Description: Berkley trade paperback edition. |
New York : Berkley Books, 2016. | Series: A loving on the edge novel ; 9
Identifiers: LCCN 2016025988 (print) | LCCN 2016028867 (ebook) |
ISBN 9780425278574 (softcover) | ISBN 9780698184237 (eBook)
Subjects: LCSH: Sexual dominance and submission—Fiction. | Bondage (Sexual
behavior)—Fiction. | Virtual reality—Fiction. |
BISAC: FICTION / Romance/ Contemporary. | FICTION / Contemporary
Women. | FICTION / Romance /General. |
GSAFD: Romantic suspense fiction. | Erotic fiction.
Classification: LCC PS3612.O764 L69 2016 (print) | LCC PS3612.O764 (ebook) |
DDC 813/.6—dc23
LC record available at https://lccn.loc.gov/2016025988

First Edition: September 2016

Printed in the United States of America
1 3 5 7 9 10 8 6 4 2

Cover art: Fiber optics © alexskopje / Shutterstock.
Cover design by Annette DeFex.

To my husband, kidlet, and family,
thank you for your endless encouragement and love.

To my friend Dawn for being my sounding board and
first reader for this book. It might've been
burned in a bonfire before it was
done if you hadn't helped me push past the roadblocks.
Thanks for being such a bossy cheerleader!

And finally, to my readers, thank you for continuing
on this journey with me. I look forward to
many more trips to come! ☺

PROLOGUE

I know how to recognize dangerous men.

My mother taught me from an early age what to zero in on. The way a man looked at you. The way he spoke. The way he tried to get you to do something or see his point of view. The way he made you feel when he came close to you, that visceral, bone-deep sense that there was danger present. *Your instincts know, Cora. Don't ignore them.*

It'd been a lot to teach an eight-year-old.

I doubt Mom wanted me to have to face that kind of fear so early on, but when you're a detective and there's a killer on the loose with a vendetta against you, you do what you have to do. My mom never caught the killer, and I never forgot the lesson.

So even though he's only a form on a screen, a cartoon really, I know the instant that he strides into the game what Master Dmitry is. I know what my body is trying to tell me even as I sit in the safety of my bedroom on the other side of a screen. *Danger. Back away.*

But I don't. I can't.

Dangerous men scare me. And I'm fascinated. After years of being mostly ignored, of failing at the dating game, of making high art of being put in the friend zone, I want to know what it's like to be someone else. To not play it safe. To be desired.

I use my wireless controller and have my character, Lenore, flip her hair to catch his attention. She's so unlike me, Lenore. All flowing blond locks and epic curves. Feminine with a capital *F*. She's the girl the guys fantasize about. I want to be that girl for a little while. Feel what that's like.

He turns and faces me. His hair is long and the color of the deep ocean, pulled back with a leather band. He's chosen to wear all black. Most of the dominants in the Hayven game wear the same, but somehow it looks more fitting for him, like he was made to only wear that color. He hasn't designed his character to be overly muscled. He doesn't look like a comic book superhero like most of the male players in Hayven, but he's tall and broad and intimidating. Quietly powerful.

"So, you're Lenore."

The deep voice in my headset makes me jump. I know the sound is affected by the voice changer the game has. Hayven has layers of identity protection. That's why I've chosen this game, why I can be someone else without worry. But still, the sound of him in my ear is enough to send goose bumps prickling my skin. I lick my lips, force the word past my lips. "Yes."

He doesn't correct me, tell me to call him *sir*. I like that. I like players who don't make assumptions.

He steps closer. We're in the public part of the game. You can create whatever environment you want in the private spaces, but the main part of the game has zones—the park, the island, the city, the forest, and the main house. Right now we're in the forest. A place with towering trees and limited moonlight. There's a map in a small box in the corner of my screen where a few red dots glow, indicating other players are nearby, but I can't see anyone. That's why I was here. I was looking for others to watch. That's what I do. Harmless fun. But with Dmitry moving toward me and the first-person style of the game, I feel like I'm suddenly alone with this man. Red Riding Hood to his Wolf. I'm looking through Lenore's eyes and there's nowhere to run.

"You're popular around here," he says, that deep voice a stroke against my ear, the sound intimately close in my headset. Despite the name, there's no accent.

Popular. Ha. There's a word that's never been used to describe me before. Unless it was to designate most popular girl to play against in a video game battle or most popular chick to invite to guys' poker night. But I remind myself that he's not talking about me. Tomboy. Proud geek girl. He's talking about Lenore. Pretty, voluptuous Lenore. "I do all right."

The night sky is black behind him until a streak of lightning cuts across it, making the leaves of the digital trees turn to a thousand silhouettes. The gamemasters are brewing a storm, playing with the many toys this game has. Dmitry doesn't appear to notice. If anything, he looks as if he's called the lightning himself, his presence making everything feel electric. "Why do you think you're so popular? Besides being beautiful. There are lots of beautiful women here."

Yeah, no shit. No one's going to make an ugly avatar. Hello, beauty of video games. But I don't know how to answer the question. I'm not sure why I get a lot of friends or attention in the game. Maybe it's because I'm involved but mysterious. I'm a watcher, a tease, not a participator. "I'm here a lot. People get to know me."

His blue hair is blowing in the wind now, a few strands pulling free of the tieback. "You're here on Valentine's Day."

The words hit me like icy drops of rain, yanking me briefly out of the game world and back into reality. Like I need a reminder. Like the TV isn't playing a marathon of every romantic movie ever made. Like the dudes at my shitty job didn't spend the day incessantly talking about how they're *so getting laid* tonight because they threw a box of chocolate or some flowers at a girl. Like the guy I've been sleeping with for three years didn't balk when I asked him if he wanted to do something tonight.

Why? It's not like we're dating, Cora. We're just great FWB. You're like a bro with a vagina. Sex without the drama of things like Valentine's Day. Which made me realize a) I thought I had a boyfriend and didn't, b) I've been sleeping with a guy who uses chat abbreviations in actual speech, and c) he actually said *bro with a vagina* like that was an okay thing to call me. I'm not sure which one disturbs me more. Probably that I let this "bro with a penis" in my bed. For three years. It's too pathetic to even cry about. Okay, maybe I cried a little.

"I'm not a romantic. Hallmark holidays aren't my thing." I ignore the half-empty heart-shaped box of Russell Stover candy I bought at the Walgreens on the way home.

"Guess we have that in common, then." He's close now. If this were real life, the wispy dress Lenore is wearing would be whipping in the breeze, brushing against his skin. He looks like he wants to rip it off. I kind of want him to, until he lifts his hand.

My fingers, so in tune with the controller by now, automatically shift to make Lenore take a step back. My heartbeat has picked up speed. The danger signals are going off in my head, the virtual world playing tricks on my real brain.

"Why are you scared to play, Lenore?" The voice caresses my senses, startles me with its quiet edge as he lowers his hand.

"What? I'm not. I just . . . like to watch."

"I know. I've watched you watch. I've also watched you deftly deflect any offers. You're good at the tease. Good at playing the less-experienced dominants and keeping them panting after you."

My throat tightens and I reach for my beer to take a sip. I've seen glimpses of Dmitry in the game. But if he plays, he does it privately. And he doesn't seem to have any regulars he talks to either. He's like a shadow. That guy at the bar who comes in, drinks, and leaves. But somehow he knows. He knows that despite the submissive designation on my character, I've never actually played that role in the game. "You watch, too."

"Yes, I do. But I also study. There's a difference. I've studied you." He steps closer and this time my fingers are frozen against the controller. There's so much that I don't know. I don't know what he really looks like. I don't know how he smells or if his real voice is that deep. But somehow with his words in my ear, the soft sound of his breath, my body reacts anyway, knows there's a real man on the end of this phone line. My skin is warming, my blood pumping, arousal and a hint of fear twining together. He reaches up and brushes hair away from Lenore's face. I shouldn't feel a tingle against my brow where his fingers would be, but I do. "I'm tired of watching."

"Oh." My voice is small, an afterthought. My persona as Lenore the Confident Vixen slips out of my reach as my real self invades.

"I think you are, too."

I close my eyes, the words filtering through my blood, my defenses rising, trying to put up some sort of fight against my galloping libido. "Why would you think that? You don't know me."

"I know enough," he says with utter calm. "I know that you're smart and that anytime someone gets you close to participating in the game, you make jokes, get sarcastic, and protect yourself. You've got a sharp wit and a smart mouth, Lenore. I bet in your life, you're a force, a successful woman with a lot on her plate. You don't give in to men. You don't give in to anyone."

The truth of the words rattles me. This man doesn't know me, but somehow it's like he's peering through the computer screen and seeing my life.

"And that's exactly why you crave this so much. Why you're here so often. You want to know what it's like and it terrifies you."

My throat is dry, the words sticky against my tongue. "This is just a game."

"It's been a very long time for me, Lenore, and I know this is a game. Believe me. But ignore the window dressing on the screen. What's real is that I'm here and you're here. Whatever roles and labels we have in real life aren't with us right now. All that's left is this: what we want to do right now, alone, with no one else watching or judging. No one will know what happens tonight except us. You can let go. You're safe."

Safe.

My mother would say that word is its own kind of lie, but I want to believe it. Right now, I do. The truth tumbles out of me. "I don't know how to do this."

"Close your eyes." The words are gentle but commanding.

I can't do anything but listen. My lids fall shut.

"All you have to do is listen to my voice. You can always say no at any point, but trust that I've got your pleasure in mind. I can give you what I know you're craving when you watch. All I ask is that you're honest with me, in your reactions and in what you're telling me you're doing. And I'll give you the same." He pauses for a long second and when he speaks again, his voice has grit in it, his own need sneaking through. "Give me tonight. I want to hear what you sound like when you surrender to it, how you sound when you come."

I swallow hard and something tightens low in my belly. I knew all along where this was leading. From the very moment he walked into my corner of the game. That's what Hayven is about ultimately—sex. And I'd be lying if I said I didn't use what I watched in Hayven for fantasy fodder. But I've never taken the step of sharing that experience with another player. It seems a little too . . . far. Too personal. Like it stops being a game and becomes part of my life. And maybe a piece of me had thought it would be like cheating on Kevin—Kevin who was never my boyfriend. But there's no more Kevin and the temptation is beating through me like a wild drumbeat.

"Don't you want to know what it's like? To give up the power for just a little while? To let go of any responsibilities and just listen and act?" His voice is like a dark, winding river, rumbling against my senses, dragging me into the current. "To let me bring you to your edge? To know you're bringing me to mine?"

I inhale deeply, keeping my eyes closed, and focus on just his voice. Not the game. Not Lenore. Not the romantic comedy playing in the living room. Not the fact that everyone else I know is on a date tonight. Just the unfamiliar sound of a sexy dominant man making irresistible promises in my ear. *Let me bring you to your edge.*

Your instincts know, Cora.

I've spent my life avoiding dangerous men.

I won't tonight.

In the tell-no-secrets safety of my bedroom, I say yes.

ONE

four months later

BigMan232: I need you naked and at my feet tonight. You've been a bad girl. Time to pay up.

Cora kept her phone in her lap as she surreptitiously read the message lighting the screen and tried not to roll her eyes. *Ugh, get a clue, dude.* She clicked Ignore and Block. She thought she'd done that the last time BigMan had contacted her in the Hayven game but apparently not.

She quickly checked her inbox to make sure she didn't have a message from the guy she really wanted to hear from, but there was nothing there. *Bummer.* He'd been quiet the last few days.

"You better not be working over there, cupcake," Grace said from across the table, her voice barely cutting through the din of voices and music at the party. She popped a stuffed mushroom into her mouth and gave Cora the cocked eyebrow of challenge.

Cora pressed the button to make the screen go black. "Not working."

"Liar." Grace leaned forward on her forearms, her silver bangle bracelets jangling against the table and her poker-straight blond hair turning gold under the soft lights of the winery's gorgeous cedar and glass event space. "Well, cut that shit out. This is called a networking party for a reason. No hiding in our phones. We're here to drink loads of local wine and to mingle."

"The wine I can do. But mingle? Have you met me?" She held her hand out across the table. "Hello, I'm Cora Benning, your mingle-averse best friend."

Grace ignored Cora's outstretched hand. "Mingle-averse."

"Yes. It's a thing, actually—like an allergy."

"Uh-huh," Grace said, deadpan.

Cora gave her a grave look. "I should've made you aware ahead of time. I could break out in hives or something, or you know, go anaphylactic on you—throat swelling, eyes bulging. Not pretty. Really, I should be carrying an EpiPen with me just being around all these strangers who require small talk. This is why I went into IT. Medical safety."

Grace tossed a balled-up napkin at her, missing left. "Well, you're going to have to get over it, smartass. You're the one who wanted to start her own company. And part of that is putting yourself out there and meeting new people. *Mingling. Mixing.*"

Ha. She loved that Grace framed it as Cora wanting to start her own company instead of the truth—that she'd quit her last job in an unplanned blaze of non-glory only to find out afterward that she had no decent job options that didn't involve working overnight at a call center. Yay for expensive college degrees that apparently meant diddly without a recommendation from your previous employer.

"You need bigger jobs than setting up virus protection for Marv's Auto Parts or helping your mother out at the police station—which, by the way, she should be paying you more for. You've been getting intern pay for how many years now?"

Cora shrugged. "You know I don't do the police stuff for the money. It's a good cause."

Plus, she'd never admit it to her mom but she loved the challenge of working on cases. In a different world, she may have gone into the field herself, but her mom had always warned her away from it. *Too dangerous. Crappy pay. Find yourself a fancy office to work in, Coraline. Capitalize on that brain of yours.*

"Yeah, the good cause of keeping your mother off your back. But I promise you, if they contracted that work out to someone else, they'd be paying whoever it was a helluva lot more. Playing Good Samaritan doesn't pay the bills. Your landlord isn't going to care that you're doing good deeds when you can't make rent."

Cora groaned and took a big sip of her wine, trying to focus on how delicious the Water's Edge Tempranillo was and not on the cold splash of reality Grace insisted on giving her. Last thing Cora needed to think about was the dwindling number in her bank account. She'd had a decent savings when she'd left her job at Braecom, but she'd had to lean on that to get her business started. And though the part-time gig at the police station helped provide some steady income, it wasn't enough to sustain her once her little nest egg dried up. She needed to land some bigger accounts.

However, that didn't mean she'd suddenly developed the ability to mingle. Business meetings? Presentations? She could handle that stuff. But small talk with strangers? *Ugh.* She'd only been half-kidding about the hives. "I can make business contacts by email. I'm better in writing. Or on the phone."

Where I can control things and not have to be charming.

"No, babe. That's called spam and is the chickenshit way of going about it. You're better than that."

Cora rearranged the food on her tasting plate. Cubed chorizo and smoked Gouda became little Monopoly-style neighborhoods, the spicy mustard a moat in between. She resisted the urge to level the whole gourmet town with a sweep of her hand. Grace didn't get it. The woman sparkled at these functions. She could talk to a wall and make it interested. Cora could make that same wall feel awkward and want to excuse itself to grab a drink.

When she felt Grace's stare burning into her, she looked up and attempted a deflecting smile. "So I'm a chickenshit. Exactly when did I hire you as my business coach? Because this motivational talk is really helping. I mean, I feel like I need a poster with a dude jumping off a cliff into the open sea or something. Or maybe that one where the cat sees the lion in the mirror." She held up her hand and curled her fingers like a claw. "Rawr."

Grace pointed at her. "Don't get snippy with me, Benning. I'm acting as your benevolent and helpful mentor, which means I'm not above kicking your ass. I don't want you living on ramen by the end of the year or worse, going to back to Braecom to beg for your job back."

"Not gonna happen."

No fucking way. She'd sell hot dogs on the street before she returned to Braecom. When her boss had gotten wind that she'd been sleeping with Kevin, *Cora* had gotten a talk about how to conduct herself professionally. A week later, he'd told her that she was no longer being considered for the supervisory position she was in line for because the rest of the guys on the team wouldn't respect her as an authority figure.

And what had Kevin gotten? Her promotion. Fucker.

"It's not as bad as you're making it out to be," Cora said, trying to sound upbeat and swallow past the bitterness the memories dredged up. "I have prospects. The other day, I had a lady offer me two grand to hack into her ex-boyfriend's Instagram. I think there's a business opportunity there. Cora Benning—*Avenging Hacker for Victims of Cheating Assholes*." She spread her hands like she was seeing the words on a sign. "Though we may have to play with the company title. That may be too much to put on a business card."

Grace snorted. "Yeah, let's try to focus on things that *won't* land you in handcuffs. You don't need to go to the dark side to make money."

"But it wouldn't *really* be the dark side. I mean, technically yes, but it'd be for a good reason. Only shitty people would be harmed. It'd be like *Dexter* or that show *Cheaters*, hacker style." She gave Grace a bright grin, knowing it'd only piss her off.

"Okay, Robin Hood of Hackerville. Let's not give your mother a reason to throw you in jail, all right? You just need to get out there and rub elbows with people who actually have cash and could use your services—the *legal* ones. You're a badass, mother-fucking, white-hat hacker. They need you."

"Now *that's* what should be on the business card. *Badass motherfucking hacker.* I'd get loads of business."

"Not if you don't *speak to anyone ever.*"

Cora deflated at that, her mood souring further. "Come on, Grace. I'm a start-up. The people here are big deals. We're at some hoity-toity winery for God's sake. That big-ass cowboy who was welcoming everybody when we came in? Yeah, that's Grant Waters, the owner. He's got so much money that he's lost count. These people walking around? They own corporations and yachts and shit. They've already got a team of IT security on their payroll. They're here to drink expensive wine and network with other CEOs, not people like me. I appreciate you getting Jonah to snag us an invite to this, and I love you for thinking I'm at this level, but I need to start smaller. Like way smaller."

Cora's phone vibrated in her lap again, and she forced herself not to check it. Grace knew she was always online but assumed Cora was just a workaholic. She'd die of shock if she found out her best friend was a regular player in a kinky online game. And then Cora would promptly die of embarrassment. *Yes, my sex life is now one hundred percent online. No, that's not pathetic at all.*

"You don't know that these people don't need you," Grace insisted.

"But I do." Cora glanced out at the milling crowd. There were no tuxes or sparkly cocktail dresses. From the outside looking in, these people didn't look important with a capital *I*, but she knew better. In the dot-com world, the more casual someone looked, the more money they probably had. The thought of pitching to any of them made her stomach knot, especially after the trauma of the job interviews she'd had right after leaving Braecom. You could only hear "not the right fit" so many times before you started to wonder if you'd accidentally been assigned to the wrong planet. She looked back to her best friend. "Plus, let's not pretend you finagled an invitation to this party for my benefit. You're here to meet hot Internet moguls."

Grace put a who-me? hand to her chest. "Is it so wrong to have a two-pronged reason for being here? That's called being efficient. And I don't see how that would be bad for either of us. Your on-the-rebound dry spell has gone on for way longer than is healthy."

Cora stabbed a toothpick through the Gouda tower she'd built on her plate. Was it really being on the rebound if the relationship hadn't actually been a relationship? "I'm not in a dry spell. I'm on hiatus by choice."

Truth. Sort of.

"No. You're avoiding." Grace lifted a hand when Cora tried to protest. "Since the Kevin incident and quitting Braecom, you've used starting up your business as an excuse to shut down your social life. That worked for the first few months, but I'm not buying that excuse anymore."

Cora sniffed. "Exactly when did I have this booming social life?"

"You used to at least go out after work sometimes. And you'd let me drag you to bars. And before Kevin, there was that guy you saw for a while—Nick, Nelson."

"Neil? You're going back that far? We went on three dates in college. He liked to talk about dorm room beer-making. And smelled like old bread."

She flicked a hand. "Details. Now you shut me down anytime I ask for anything that involves you going out after seven. I bet if this hadn't been work-related tonight, you would've canceled on me. You would've turned down *free wine* and *fancy cheese.*"

True. She almost had. And really, turning down free fancy cheese *was* probably on her personal checklist of The-Girl-Ain't-Right signs. But she'd agreed to go because she'd wanted to see Grace, and she knew Grace wouldn't let her get away with inviting her over just to hang out and watch movies again. "I have a lot going on."

"I know you do. But you can't let all that stuff shut down your whole life." Grace gave her a pointed look. "It's my duty as your best friend to not let you become a crazy, sexless cat lady because some asshole wronged you. It's in the handbook."

Cora smirked. "I'm allergic to cats. And I've had sex. You're cleared of liability."

She cocked her head in that take-no-bullshit way she'd perfected. "*Had* being the operative word there. *Had*, Cora. I get that you needed some time. But don't let what happened with Kevin turn you into a hermit. You thought you had something with him and you didn't. He was a jerk about it."

"He called me a bro with a vagina, Grace."

"Okay. Fine. More than a jerk. A complete asshole. But I don't think this is even about him. That night we had too many margaritas at Rosa's, you told me the sex was *sufficient*. Who the hell wants to have sufficient sex? You never got stars in your eyes when you talked about him. He was cute and convenient. And safe. And he saved you the trouble of being out in the dating world. That's what you're mourning. Not him."

A bitter taste crossed Cora's tongue, and she had to take another sip of wine to clear it. She wished there was some magical app where you could just wipe a certain time in your life out of your head. One click and it went into some unrecoverable trash bin. But that trash bin would be overflowing by now. Reading too much into her hookups with Kevin had just been the final dating mistake in a long list of them.

In the end, it'd been a good thing. She'd finally accepted her place in the dating pecking order. She was and had always been a tomboy and a geek, never quite comfortable in the skin she'd been given until she'd accepted that "proper girl" trappings and behaviors were not for her. But that had set her up to be the girl to hang out with, the buddy. She was the one they'd sleep with if they had no one else better lined up. *Sufficient.* Nothing more. Not the woman anyone lusted over. Not the girl anyone fantasized about.

And really, after accepting that, the loss of her dating life hadn't been all that tragic. Dating had always been painful and awkward for her. The sex . . . uninspiring. These last few months, taking that off the table completely, had been a weird kind of relief. She had friends to hang out with. She had Dmitry and Hayven. She knew how to take care of her sexual needs. Not everyone needed to pair off like little plastic pegs riding in the car in The Game of Life.

"I'm not in mourning or unhappy, Gracie," Cora said, hoping her friend could hear sincerity in her voice. "Truly. You don't have to fix anything. I'm fine. I don't need a guy right now. I'm a busy girl and a wizard with a vibrator. Who needs more than that?"

Grace's lip curled, her silver nose ring catching the light. "A wizard? Does that mean your vibrator is magical?"

"Hey, they don't call it a wand for nothing." Cora held up her toothpick and waved it around. "I'm working on my sex Patronus. I'm thinking mine will be shaped like a naked Chris Pratt riding a T-Rex."

That earned a laugh, but concern lingered in Grace's eyes.

Cora sighed and dropped the toothpick onto the plate. "Look, seriously, I'm fine. Why don't you go and circulate? Do what you came here to do. I promise I'll finish my wine and work up some liquid courage to do the same."

Grace's green eyes went catlike, skeptical. "Yeah?"

"Sure. Drunk, chorizo-breath Cora will leave great impressions wherever she goes. All introverted tendencies will transform into glittering wit and brilliant sales pitches."

"Cora." She said it in the tone Cora's mother used when she'd catch her playing video games instead of doing homework.

Cora shooed her with a flick of her hand. "Go. I swear I will leave this table once I'm done with my wine and will attempt to interact with fellow humans."

Grace considered her for another second but then pushed her chair back and stood. She jabbed a purple-nailed finger Cora's way. "I expect a fistful of business cards to be handed out, Ms. Benning."

She saluted. "Yes, ma'am."

Cora watched her friend go and then stared into her wine, wondering how long she could make it last. Maybe she could sneak a refill and drag this out. She took a teeny-tiny sip and let it roll around in her mouth, pretending she actually knew how to do this whole wine-tasting song and dance.

"Is this seat taken?"

Cora glanced up to find a well-dressed guy with a nice smile looking down at her. His hand was on the back of the chair Grace had vacated, and Cora was almost too surprised to speak. She swallowed the wine, half-choking. "Uh, yeah, I mean, no. It's not taken."

His grin went wider. "Great. Thanks."

She took a breath, mentally preparing for a conversation with a cute stranger. She *was* still capable. *Maybe.* "So, some party, huh?"

Wait. *That* was her opening line? Maybe she *had* been hanging out in her house too long. Why not just ask about the weather while she was at it?

But the guy didn't hear her anyway. Because instead of sitting down, he picked up the chair and walked away, bringing it to another table that was overflowing with laughing people.

The air whooshed out of her and heat flooded her face. Oh. Right. Of course.

She stood, her chair scraping hard against the floor, and drained the rest of her wine. Sitting alone at a table with one chair in the middle of a party was just a little too high on the pathetic scale, even for her. She left her empty wineglass and looked for a wall she could decorate with her presence.

She found a contender, one where the lighting was low and she could blend into the background. She started the excuse-me-pardon-me dance across the room. But as she made her way through the crowd, her phone buzzed. She grabbed it from the outside pocket of her purse, thankful to have something to make her look busy and not like she was escaping.

Dmitry: I've been thinking about you all day.

They were just little black letters on a screen, but God, did it unknot something inside her. Warm, sweet relief filtered through her. She typed back as she walked.

Lenore: Same here. Long, long day.

Dmitry: Plans tonight? Your dance card looks crowded.

She smiled. In Hayven, she never had a shortage of offers, especially since others knew she was now actively playing with the mysterious Dmitry. But she rarely watched anyone else's scenes anymore. Since that first night with Dmitry, she'd developed a bit of an addiction for the man. He'd gone easy on her the first time, had led her through a scene where he told her exactly how to touch herself and for how long. He'd teased her for an hour before letting her come. It'd been simple. But it'd been one of the best orgasms of her life. And it'd made her forget all about being alone on Valentine's Day.

After that, the boundaries had nudged farther out. He'd sometimes give her instructions. They'd be waiting for her on her phone when she woke up in the morning. *No panties today. No touching yourself until you talk to me again.* Somehow he could set her off balance with the simplest commands. There was something about having a secret that only the two of them shared that was intensely sexual. So even when she was alone during the day, she knew he was out there, pulling those invisible strings, maybe thinking about her like she was thinking of him. There was an odd sort of comfort in that. An intimate connection without the angst. Someone waiting for her to get home even though he wasn't there physically. In a short few months, Dmitry had become a touchstone for her in her day.

Not that he still didn't intimidate the hell out of her sometimes.

Her instincts about him being dangerous still flared up. When he went into full dom mode, he was formidable as hell. But in the conversations in between, she'd found him to be smart and interesting and funny. They could play the game and push limits. But they could also have a normal conversation outside of the game. They'd become . . . friends.

And he used full English instead of text speak, which was odd and surprisingly refreshing. No FWB Kevin anymore.

Lenore: You're the only one I want on my dance card. But I'm trapped at a boring work thing right now. Short of a zombie invasion, I'm stuck for a while. Will be home later, though.

Dmitry: Boring work thing? Since when is international espionage boring?

She laughed as she squeezed through a group of people and then coughed over it when she realized how loud the laugh had come out.

Lenore: That's your guess? International spy? That's what I had YOU pegged for. Well, after I ruled out Batman.

It was a game they played, guessing each other's job. They knew neither would ever tell the truth. The beauty of the thing was in the anonymity. They didn't want to know. Neither wanted the illusion shattered.

Dmitry: You got me. I'm currently hiding in the coat closet of a drug kingpin, gathering intel. *Types quietly*

She could almost picture that. She had no idea what Dmitry looked like in person, but his game persona would be fit for a spy.

Lenore: *looks at closet* Shit. You found me! Sorry that I have to kill you now. It's been fun. *bang*

Dmitry: *catches the bullet between his teeth and spits it out*

Lenore: Oh no! You ARE Batman.

Dmitry: *captures you, strips you naked, and ties you to the bed*

Her stomach dipped, the scene turning vivid in her head. This was how things went with Dmitry. Their conversations could go from playful to hot in a few short exchanges. She reached the wall she'd been planning to park herself against. If she stayed there, she'd have a nice view through the picture windows that lined the left side of the room. She could make the excuse that she wasn't avoiding the party but was enjoying the moonlit rows of grapevines and admiring the looming, cedar-and-stone building in the distance, presumably Grant Waters's massive ranch home. But her face felt warm, and she was afraid that if Dmitry continued down this texting path, it would show all over her expression.

So instead of stopping, she slipped into a darkened hallway off the main room. The noise of the party softened instantly. Two doors labeled Storage were on the left, but no one was around and nothing looked to be in active use. The quiet was more than a little welcome, and she let out a breath she hadn't known she'd been holding.

She glanced down at her phone.

Dmitry: *spends all night touching you and not letting you come*

She licked her lips, her temperature kicking up a few notches more, the words and the wine blending together in her blood. She should probably go back to the party, tell Dmitry she'd talk to him later. She'd made a promise to Grace and was supposed to be mingling. Instead, she moved deeper into the dark and stepped between two stacks of plastic storage crates. Only the dim blue light of her phone screen filled the space.

Lenore: *struggles but secretly likes having your hands on me*

Dmitry: You like the idea of being captured?

The question wound through her like sweet temptation. Never before would she have considered that a desirable scenario. She'd spent half her life being scared someone would grab her. Her mother and the cases she'd worked had put that fear in Cora. It was a legitimate fear. But playing that kind of game with someone she could trust? Facing that nightmare scenario and twisting it into something sexy? She'd never be able to trust someone that implicitly, but virtually, she could go there in her head.

Lenore: Only if you're the captor.

Dmitry: Mmm. I'd like to watch you struggle for my touch. I'd make you ride your edge until you beg. I bet you're beautiful when you beg. I know you sound sexy when you do it.

Goose bumps chased over her skin. Since she couldn't picture the real man, she pictured the version of him from the game. She imagined him knotting the ropes around her wrists and ankles, touching her everywhere, searching fingers and hot skin, making her want all the things he could give her.

Dmitry: Are you struggling now, L? Are you getting wet at this boring work thing?

She shifted in her shoes. Her blood was pumping, the place between her thighs growing warm. The dark felt like a cloak around her. Safe. Secret.

Lenore: Yes. It's not feeling so boring now.

Dmitry: Where are you? Meeting? Your desk?

Lenore: At an event, stepped into a hallway.

Dmitry: Are you wearing a skirt?

She frowned. Never. She'd never felt comfortable in the things, despite her mother's repeated attempts to get her to wear them. She glanced down at her pinstripe dress pants and white silk tank top. Grace had given her a thumbs-up on the outfit, but Cora doubted Lenore would wear such a thing.

Lenore: Dress

Dmitry: Perfect. Part your knees. Pretend I'm there with you running my hand up your thigh.

Despite the fact that she wasn't really wearing a dress, she stepped a little wider, imagining his hand gliding up her legs and along her overheated skin, causing her to shiver. Her nipples became obvious points beneath her shirt.

Dmitry: Did you do it?

Lenore: Yes.

Dmitry: Picture my fingers beneath your dress, trailing up your thigh, pulling your panties to the side. Can you feel them, teasing you, not quite giving you what you want yet?

Sensation traced over her skin and she tilted her head back against the wall. God, she longed for that feeling, wished she could will him into existence right in front of her.

Lenore: Yes.

Dmitry: Tell me what you need.

Lenore: You. Your touch.

Dmitry: I bet you do. You've been good for me, so I won't make you wait. I can feel how slippery you are against my fingertips. I slide my finger lower and push inside.

Cora shuddered, her breath quickening.

Dmitry: You're so wet for me, L, and I can feel you tighten around me. You need this so badly. You want to beg for more, but you have to be quiet. No one would know what I was doing to you. The event would just go on around you. You'd wear a nice polite smile while I fucked you with my fingers and made you come all over my hand.

A gasp slipped past her lips as her inner muscles clenched hard. She was steps away from a crowded party, but she could almost feel his hand on her, thick fingertips finding her sex and pushing inside her. She closed her eyes and pressed her thighs together, trying to put pressure where she needed it most. Her pulse pounded in her ears, and her nipples turned sensitive against her bra. She wanted to touch, to get relief. Her fingers curled against her thigh. Maybe she could just press the heel of her hand . . .

"So I think it's time for our very important business meeting."

Cora's eyes popped open, and her breath caught at the sound of the unfamiliar male voice. She automatically clutched her phone to her chest, blocking the light.

A woman laughed. "Oh, is that what you're calling it?"

Two shadowed forms came into view and passed by Cora as they headed toward the back of the hallway. The fine hairs that had escaped the twist in Cora's hair fluttered against her face as the couple kicked up a breeze in their wake, but neither noticed her. She was just another shadow.

Cora squinted. There was enough light that she could make out the height of the man, the petiteness of the woman, but not much else. They were walking close together, obviously sneaking away for something and in a hurry. Cora glanced toward the entrance and the rectangle of light that led back to the party. She needed to bail.

"Keep it up with the laughing," the man said, his voice low but ringing with authority. "See how long it takes me to shut you up."

Cora stiffened and her attention swung back to the couple.

But the woman made a sound like she'd just taken a bite of the best chocolate. "Look forward to it, sir."

Sir. The word rang through Cora. Reverberated. *Sir.* It meant a very specific thing to Cora. But this couldn't be that. Her mind was just stuck on Dmitry and the game. This was probably some assistant and her boss sneaking off to make out. She needed to leave, make it known that they weren't alone. *Hello, innocent bystander here! I was just leaving. Don't mind me!*

And she was all prepared to do that until she heard the sound of a zipper and shift of fabric. She turned her head automatically toward the noise, the harsh unzipping like a beacon.

The woman's breaths were sharp in the darkness—quick, anticipatory. *Sexual.*

Cora tried to pull her attention from them, tried to make her feet work.

Look away, Cora. Look away!

The man's voice sliced through the silence like a bullet. "Suck it."

Cora froze.

And she didn't look away.

TWO

"Suck it."

The two utterly male words filled the dark space and hit Cora like a knee to the gut, stealing her air. The command wasn't directed at her, but, God, she wasn't sure she'd ever heard anything hotter. *Suck it.* It should've sounded stupid. Juvenile. It *so* didn't. Her free hand pressed flat against the wall, and she tried to stop breathing altogether.

There was a rustle of movement—the woman getting to her knees, no doubt, and the man showing her what to suck.

Cora decided then and there that she was a bad, bad person because goddamn, she couldn't make herself leave now. She couldn't look away. It was the Hayven game manifesting in real life, and she had a front row ticket.

She blinked a few times, trying to focus her vision. Now that she hadn't looked at her phone for a minute, her eyes were adjusting to the inky darkness. The couple was a few yards away from where Cora had tucked herself between the stacks of plastic crates. She wouldn't be completely hidden from their view if they looked her way hard enough, but both seemed too involved to bother. The woman was on her knees and had her back to Cora, a long curling ponytail snaking down her spine, and the man had his head down, his focus on what was about to happen. The moment before impact. The moment before pleasure.

Cora held her breath. The whole *room* seemed to hold its breath. Like air had ceased to move. A still, heavy quiet.

Then, her phone vibrated against her chest, nearly causing her to yelp and give herself away. She cringed and pressed the phone harder against her shirt to make sure no light peeked out before she could hit the button to darken it. Her gaze stayed fixed on the view in front of her, her heart pounding in her ears. Thankfully, her companions didn't notice anything was amiss. They were too wrapped up in the moment.

The man dragged his palm along the side of the woman's head and then wound her ponytail around his fist. Once. Twice. Deliberate. Menacing.

Sexy as shit.

Cora couldn't see the man's open fly, but his rough grip on the woman's hair had Cora's scalp tingling, imagining what that must feel like.

"Open wider," he commanded. "You've been begging for this for how long? Now you're going to take it all. Hands behind your back."

The woman moaned and leaned forward, taking him into her mouth and linking her hands together behind her back like some sort of reverse prayer. Her head bobbed as she went to work on him—slow and sensual, taking her time like she was savoring every moment. A hypnotic pace. One Cora was sure she'd never used with a guy.

But as compelling as that view was, Cora found her gaze tracking upward, seeking out the one running this show. The one called *sir.* The man was tall, broad-shouldered—black hair, maybe. She couldn't make out much else. But there was an air of authority about him, this cool composure, like he was somehow doing a favor for this woman even though he was the one getting head. Like he was almost . . . bored.

Cora couldn't move. She barely breathed. She'd given blow jobs before. But she'd never gotten much pleasure from it. It'd always been a favor in hopes that the guy would return the effort. But it felt like she was witnessing something altogether different here, something much more intense, something that might actually turn her on. A challenge. *Suck me and see if you can break me.* What would make a man like that lose his cool?

Her gaze fell on the hard grip of his hand, watched the knuckles flex with the force of how hard yet controlled he was fucking the woman's mouth now. In. Out. Deep. Steady. *Yes. Like that.* She could imagine his thoughts. His inner commands. *Suck it like you love it. Take my cock and swallow every inch.*

It was something she could imagine Dmitry saying. A rush of warmth settled between Cora's thighs, turning her panties from damp to embarrassing. She was throbbing there. This shouldn't flip her switches. She shouldn't be watching. But seeing one of the scenes from her game played out in real life was damn riveting. She'd never witnessed real life dominance. Hell, she hadn't known it existed until a few years ago when she'd been interning at the station and had stumbled upon some kinky videos on a suspect's computer. The guy had turned out to be innocent of anything, but her curiosity had been piqued.

She'd watched her fair share of naughty videos since then, but porn had never pulled it off for her. And the one time she'd considered bringing up the idea of kink to Kevin, she'd chickened out. She hadn't been able to imagine being that vulnerable with him. There was naked and then there was *naked.* And she would've been mortified if he'd laughed at the suggestion or teased her about it. So, she'd turned to Hayven to explore on her own in a low-risk way.

But as much fun as she had with Dmitry, virtual couldn't mimic this. This was different. Raw. *Dangerous.* The woman had to be scared they'd get caught, but she was going to obey. What did that level of edge bring to the sex? Cora imagined it brought a lot, based on how she was feeling just from watching. And even though there was no kinky equipment or elaborate setup, some part of her knew without a doubt what she was witnessing. This man was a dominant. This was a scene.

"This is the only time you're going to get this cock," the man said, gravel in his voice. "Better make it count."

The woman moved faster. Wet, hungry noises drifted from the darkened corner, making it sound like *she* was the one about to come even though he only had a hand in her hair.

Lord, to be so openly sexual and unashamed about it. Most people would probably judge this woman. She was being used, treated like a whore. But Cora could feel it, the mutual pleasure of this. This was a woman who was getting exactly what she craved and loving it. An unexpected wisp of jealousy wound through Cora.

"You're going to drink down everything I have," the man said. "And then you're going to go out there and kiss your boyfriend on the mouth. I wonder if he'll be able to taste what a filthy girl you are."

Cora's belly dipped. *Fuck.* The woman's *boyfriend* was at the party?

Cora should be appalled.

She couldn't stop watching.

Her phone vibrated again. She held it tight, but this time, it grazed her silver necklace, making the faintest of noises.

Oh, shit. No. No! She shifted it quickly, silencing it completely, but when she glanced up, the man's head had lifted.

He was staring her way, his gaze narrowing and then locking on her as his vision probably adjusted. *Click.* His face was half in shadow but she could see enough. Dark hair, angled jaw, full mouth, Asian. Gorgeous.

She was frozen in the headlights of that look. An apology

hovered on her lips. Her feet were ready to run. But he had her pinned. He may as well have had a hand pressed to her chest, forcing her to stay there against the wall.

"That's right," the man said, holding Cora's gaze as the woman continued to pleasure him. "Take it all in. Every bit of it."

Cora's mouth went chalky dry. He was talking to her now, not the woman. Taunting Cora. Bringing her into the game. *Take it all in.* Even without the words, his eyes said as much.

Panic surged. She'd wanted to watch but only while she was invisible. Being seen left her naked. Exposed. Embarrassed.

"You like it a little too much, don't you?"

The words wrapped around her like barbed wire.

You like it too much. She wanted to react, to flip him off, to show him that he hadn't gotten to her. That she wasn't some player in this game.

But then he smiled, this sexy half-smile that made every erogenous part of her clamor to attention.

No. *No.*

This was fucked up. She yanked her gaze away and tugged off the heels Grace had loaned her. She would not embarrass this woman and let her know someone had been watching. But Cora had to get the hell out of there. Forcing herself not to give one last look, she hauled ass on bare feet out of the hallway and into the blinding light of the party.

The sudden brightness and noise were an assault on her senses, and it took a second for her vision to recover. Her pupils were blown, her breath was too quick, and her back was covered in a fine sheen of sweat. She quickly slipped her shoes back on, her legs unsteady and her hands shaky, adrenaline beating through her. She needed to get out of there before the couple exited and she ended up face-to-face with Mr. Exhibitionist. But she'd ridden to the party with Grace, and as Cora scanned the crowd, she didn't see her friend anywhere.

She started walking anyway. Anything to get her far from that hallway. Her phone buzzed and she glanced at the screen. Dmitry had sent a few messages and there was another from BigMan telling her that he demanded she speak with him tonight.

What the hell? The blocking system on the site was turning out to be a major fail. She deleted that one and checked Dmitry's. His last read, "You OK?"

She quickly typed as she walked.

Lenore: Yes. Sorry. Work.

Dmitry: No problem.

No problem. She wished. She had nothing but problems right now. She tossed her phone into her purse and strode forward, looking to get lost in the crowd. Until she could find Grace, she needed to blend in. The guy in the hallway probably hadn't seen her all that well. She'd been backlit. Her face should've been in the dark, her body a silhouette. But she wasn't going to take any chances. She reached up and pulled the clip out of her messy twist, letting her brown hair fall loose around her shoulders and changing up the outline of what he would've seen.

She inhaled through her nose, trying to calm herself. She should be okay. The party was crowded and blending in shouldn't be a problem.

She moved through the main part of the room, grabbing a glass of wine off a passing waiter's tray and scanning faces for Grace. Usually her friend was hard to miss, but Cora didn't see her blond head anywhere. *Dammit.*

She spotted a table in the farthest spot from the hallway. Two women were sitting there, but there was a chair free. She headed that way and retrieved her phone from her purse so she could text Grace.

The women looked up when she reached their table. Cora smiled. "Hi, do you mind if I sit?"

The older of the two women waved a hand. "Not at all, please do. We were just about to go to the bar anyway."

"Oh, you don't have to get up. I—"

But they were already up and gathering their things.

God. She was apparently wearing people repellant tonight. She resisted doing a sniff test to make sure her deodorant was working and then plopped down in one of the chairs. The last thing she wanted to do was sit at a table alone again, but she needed to text Grace, and standing around with no one to talk to looked even more conspicuous. She set down her wine so she could type two-thumbed.

Cora: Where r u??? #911

The message sent, but as Cora stared at the screen, no little dots popped up to indicate that Grace was responding. "Come on, where the hell are you?"

She opened up her favorites list, ready to call Grace until she answered, but before she could hit the button to dial, a hand planted on the table right next to Cora's wine, rattling the glass.

She startled but didn't look up. That hand was all she could focus on. Because somehow, she knew. Tan skin and long fingers, the edge of a colorful tattoo peeking out from a shirt cuff.

Cora prayed for a trap door. An eject button. An invisibility cloak.

None appeared.

In one fluid motion, the chair across from her was pulled out and dragged closer. Her guest slid into the spot. Uninvited. Unapologetic. His mere presence demanded she respond. There was a sense of . . . provocation. Almost a dare. Cora forced herself to look up.

Shit. The curse almost slipped out.

It was worse than she'd thought—the looking. The guy could've just stepped off the red carpet. Charcoal suit, plum-colored T-shirt, a mess of perfectly styled jet-black hair, and a face that was so beautiful it'd almost seem feminine if not for the hard angle of his jaw and the shadow of stubble. This was a guy who knew he looked good and wasn't afraid to use it like a weapon.

He gave her an unreadable smile. "This seat taken?"

Her throat felt like it'd narrowed to nothing, but she forced words out. "Seems a little late to ask."

The man's coal eyes sparkled, like he was in on some eternal joke. And he was. He knew. Somehow in this sea of people he'd picked out the girl from the dark. He knew she'd just watched him get off in the hallway, and she couldn't play it off.

"I'm sorry." She blurted—too loud, too sharp. One hundred percent without grace. Fantastic.

He leaned back in his chair, grabbed a drink off a passing waiter's tray, and hooked an ankle over his knee, looking like he could literally be comfortable anywhere with anyone. "You were there first. Maybe I should apologize. Though, what you were doing all alone in the dark has got me curious."

She cleared her throat, trying to tap the brakes on her body's railroading response to this man. He was a stranger, but they'd shared this intensely sexual moment. Her wires were crossed, her body confused. "I was just trying to find a quiet place to make a call. But I . . . couldn't get a good signal. Then . . . you walked in with your . . . a woman."

He smiled and his gaze strayed toward the bar. Cora couldn't help but follow it. It's like he'd put his hand on her head to make it turn. At the bar, a woman with a long ponytail and blue maxi dress was in the arms of a man with salt-and-pepper hair. They were kissing—a little too passionately for this kind of party.

And Cora couldn't help it—she had the thought. *Can he taste this man's come on his girlfriend's lips?* The thought tripped a wire inside her. One it shouldn't. Her cheeks burned. "If you're worried that I'm going to say anything, I'm not. Not my business."

"You're right. It's not." Her companion looked back to her, a secret smile playing around the edges of his mouth. "But it wouldn't matter if you did. He already knows. He was the one who set it up."

Cora's lips parted. On some level, she knew that kind of thing happened. She was no innocent. But she couldn't hide her knee-jerk reaction or shake off the sense that this man was toying with her. "Then why did you come over here? If you're not worried about me outing you?"

He frowned, a line appearing between his dark brows. "I don't recognize you. Have you been to one of Grant's parties before?"

She straightened. Technically, she wasn't crashing this thing. Grace's boss had been the one to get the invite and had let Grace come on his behalf with a plus one. But Cora suddenly felt one hundred percent out of her league and like she'd been left out of some joke. Not that she was going to let this guy know that. "No. Haven't had time to get to one before now."

"Well, then I'm over here because things seen out of context by those who don't know what they're looking at can be miscon-strued and get people in trouble. From the outside looking in, what happened could look . . . non-consensual. I needed to make sure you understood."

"You needed to cover your ass. Got it," she said, unsure why it came out with a biting edge to it. "You're good."

His eyebrow arched and he shifted forward in his seat, bracing his forearms on his thighs and pinning her with that gaze. "Plus, I thought I should know the name of the woman who chose to stay and watch while another woman sucked me off."

The words hit her like a stun gun. *Zap!* And all she could hear in her head was him saying, *Suck it.*

Suck. It.

She should be offended, disgusted. They should not be having this conversation. Instead, her heart tried to pound out of her chest and her skin went tingly. "You don't need my name."

"Mmm." He nodded. "True. But you want to tell me anyway. Just like you wanted to stay longer and watch it all."

The words were so self-assured that she would've laughed if they hadn't rung through her like the truest of truths. "I—"

"Cora! There you are!"

The familiar voice came from behind her, snapping Cora out of the spell she'd fallen under. *Grace.*

Mr. Exhibitionist gifted Cora with a smirk and leaned back out of her space.

Grace swooped around on her left, her eyes meeting Cora's, question marks there. Cora knew this look. It was the do-you-need-me-to-rescue-you-or-should-I-be-your-wing-woman? look.

Cora bolted up out of her chair. "Hey, oh my God, I've been looking everywhere for you! I needed to talk to you about. . . . that thing." Her voice was so high and unlike her normal tone that she may as well have sucked helium.

Sucked. The word twined around her girl parts, set things aflame.

Fuck.

She grabbed Grace's hand and sent an over-the-shoulder look to the man who'd knocked her completely on her ass, but he was already getting to his feet.

He tucked his hands in his pockets, and though there was an affable expression on his face, his gaze held something intent when it met hers. "Nice meeting you, *Cora.*"

For a second, she didn't know how he knew her name, but then she remembered Grace had said it. And before she could respond, he turned on his heel and strolled back into the crowd.

Grace watched him go and then spun around, putting her back to him. She gave Cora this wide-eyed look of wonder. "Holy shit, who the hell was that? And why did you let me rescue you from him?" She peered over her shoulder for one last look. "Jesus. He's like . . . whoa."

Cora let out a long breath, one she may have been holding since Mystery Man had sat down. But she couldn't stop watching him walk away. The man could wear a suit. "I don't know his name. It's . . . a long story."

Grace shook her head. "Not long enough. Tell me you gave him your card."

"I . . . forgot."

"Cora! You need to go—"

She grabbed Grace's arm before she could go after the guy. "No. Stop. I'm done."

The hope on Grace's face crashed into a petulant scowl. But it wasn't going to work this time. There was no way Cora was willingly having another conversation with that man. She'd barely survived the first. Talk about bringing a knife to a gunfight.

Hell, she hadn't even had a knife.

She'd brought a spork.

Online, she was daring. She was kinky. She was brave. But tonight had proven what she'd always known. She was no Lenore.

And never would be. She had no idea how to handle men like that or how to play in those shark-infested waters.

She pulled out her phone and messaged Dmitry.

Back to her reality. The virtual one.

The safe one.

THREE

Cora waved as Grace drove off and left her standing in her driveway. The neighborhood was quiet at this hour, and the porch light on Cora's duplex had burned out again, so it was just her and the moonlight. The silence was like a balm to her nerves after the loud party and the pop music Grace had been blasting in the car during the hour-long ride from the winery back into Dallas. She wished she could sit out here and absorb it for a while, but that would be a little crazy at midnight.

Cora dug in her purse for her keys and headed up the walk. Dmitry had told her that he'd be up late and had a small window of time to play tonight, so she didn't want to miss that chance. After what she'd witnessed at the party, her body was still on a hair trigger, and she could use a little bit of his brand of relaxation. Anything to distract her from the forbidden images that kept replaying in her head. Images of the man from the hallway sending the other woman away and inviting Cora into that darkened corner with him. Of his hands and those tattooed arms holding her in place. Of Dmitry joining them and doing all those things he'd said in his texts. Reality and fantasy merging and putting her on her knees, captive for the both of them.

God. She shook her head. She really had gotten herself wound up tonight. Her fantasies were venturing into crazy town. She needed an orgasm, a shower, and some sleep. Stat.

She jogged up the sagging front steps of the house, careful not to make too much noise. Faint blue-gray TV light flashed behind her neighbors' curtains, so Josh and Carlos were probably still up, but she didn't want to risk bothering them.

She made it to her door with only the squeak of a floorboard. But once she got there, the keyhole was nearly impossible to see in the dark. She stabbed around with the key a few times. It was like trying to thread a needle with her eyes closed. "Goddamn piece of shit. Come on—"

But she didn't get the rest out. One second her lips were poised for another curse, and the next a hand was clamped over them.

The shock of it jolted through her like lightning, making everything freeze in some suspended state of disbelief. In that blink of inaction, her attacker's other arm wrapped around her, trapping her back against him.

Her brain finally kicked in at that. Cora screamed behind the hand, and she swung her leg out, banging her foot against her door in a futile attempt to make noise. All her childhood nightmares flooded her. Boogeymen. Kidnappers. Killers.

"You're just causing more trouble for yourself," the deep voice said behind her as he dragged her backward and out of reach of the door. "Calm down."

Cora screamed again, but the sound was muffled and useless. She tried to force the panic down, tried to focus. But it was like a giant swirling ball of fear knotting around her thoughts. All she could think about was the Taser her mother had given her. The damn thing was in her purse, but she couldn't move her arms to get to it.

His grip tightened. "I told you we needed to talk. But you didn't answer me tonight. What was I supposed to do? You tease me and then ignore me? It's not nice to ignore a master, Lenore. I told you I would punish you. Now I can do it in person."

Lenore? The name screamed through her head like a siren wail.

Oh, shit. Shit! This was someone from the game. Dmitry? No. She hadn't teased and ignored him. *BigMan.* It had to be. He was the only person she'd ignored tonight.

Her mind raced, things crashing together inside her head. This couldn't be happening. The site was anonymous. She didn't tell anyone her real information. She was *so* careful.

But she couldn't think about any of that now. She needed to free herself, and her writhing and screaming wasn't working. Based on the thick arm wrapped around her, he hadn't been lying with his screen name. She tried to think of some of the self-defense moves her mother had taught her. There were ways to get free of someone bigger than you, but she couldn't think, couldn't remember. And with his hand over her mouth, she couldn't even talk her way out of it.

So she did the only thing she thought might work.

She let the fight go out of her body and sagged like a sack of stones in his arms. He was here for Lenore. She was supposed to be submissive. She prayed he would buy it.

"That's it," he said, his words gentling. "I know you like these kinds of games, but we can't be so loud, babe. That could get us in trouble. Your neighbors won't get it."

She nodded enthusiastically behind his hand. *Yes. I'm totally on board with you, psycho asshole.*

"Do you think you can be a good girl?"

Instead of screaming again like she wanted to, she whimpered. The sound was pathetic and pitiful. It made bile rise in the back of her throat. But she could feel some of the tension in his body give way. It was working.

"Shh, girl, it's okay. I know you're sorry. I'm going to show you how to make it up to me. I know what you need." He pressed his hips into her, letting her feel his erection. "And I can't wait."

She closed her eyes, willing herself not to lose it completely or vomit behind his hand. Her entire body trembled from the effort of trying to appear calm.

"I'm going to move my hand now," he said against her ear. "You know we're just playing now. You don't have to be scared. You don't need to scream. We're just going to have a fun night for real this time. I'm going to give you what you want."

She nodded her promise. But the second he moved his hand away from her mouth, she screamed like she was on fire.

"Shit!" His hand instantly clamped back down, but it'd been enough. Within a few seconds, her neighbor's door flew open and Josh came charging out in his boxers, blond hair wild. Carlos was right behind him, mostly dressed and carrying a baseball bat.

"What the fuck?" Josh's eyes went wide as he took in the scene.

Cora yelled behind the guy's hand.

"Oh, hell no." Carlos charged forward, rage in his eyes and the bat looming in his hand. "You better get your fucking hands off her, asshole."

Her captor dragged her back a step. "Whoa, man, chill out. It's not what it looks like." The voice behind her had changed completely—from deep and menacing to dude-bro speak. "We're just playing a game. She's in on it. Tell him, Lenore."

The hand moved away from her mouth and words burst out of her in a rush. "Get the hell off me, you crazy fuck!"

"Lenore?" The guy's voice turned confused.

"Her name's not Lenore," Josh said, stepping up behind Carlos and looking ready to throw down. "And if you don't get your hands off her, my boyfriend's going to show you how good his batting average is."

"Damn straight," Carlos said. "Your big-ass head will be an easy target."

"Jesus. Calm the hell down." The man released Cora at that and she nearly fell on her face as she bolted away from him in those god-forsaken heels. She ran to the spot behind Carlos and then spun to face BigMan. The guy *was* a big dude. Beefy and barrel-chested and thick around the middle. But his face was young—a college-boy face. And he seemed . . . bewildered. He lifted his palms to them. "Look, bro. I think this is just a big misunderstanding. I wasn't here to cause trouble. She wanted this. She's got a safe word."

"Call the cops, Josh," Carlos barked.

But Cora reached out and put a hand on Josh's arm. "Wait."

Josh gave her a what-the-fuck look. "Hon, we have to—"

Cora didn't have time to explain about how complicated it could get with her mom the police captain knowing or one of her mom's officers interviewing some guy Cora had met in a kinky video game. "Just . . ."

"Wait, *you're* not Lenore."

The blurted statement from BigMan drew all of their attention.

The guy stepped closer, his eyes evaluating her face, her hair, her body in the light coming from Josh and Carlos's open doorway. "And if you are, you're a goddamned liar."

Carlos waved the bat. "Back off, man."

The guy halted his step but shook his head. "Jesus Christ, I've got the wrong girl. You're . . ." His gaze traced over her again and he winced. "Yeah, there's no way you're her."

The words were like a bucket of ice water. She didn't want anything to do with this nutjob, but the dismissiveness of his words cut deep. She could hear his opinion as loud as a bullhorn: *How could someone like her possibly have anything to do with the sexy, beautiful Lenore?*

Cora straightened her spine, gathering every ounce of will she had to look righteous and unaffected. "I don't know who the hell you are or who you're looking for, but if you're not off my porch in the next thirty seconds, I'm—"

But it was too late. The sirens blared from down the street. Another neighbor must've called.

BigMan jumped the railing and bolted.

A few hours later, Cora had been interviewed by two cops she knew, which meant her mother would find out—yay—and she'd drank too much of Josh's gourmet coffee, which had left her jittery. She hadn't given the police the full story. She'd stuck with the lie that she had no idea who the guy was and that it was apparently some case of mistaken identity.

Carlos had given her a raised brow. He'd probably grill her on another day, but she wasn't going to admit to anything more than that on record. And she appreciated that after the cops left, he and Josh had hung around with her for a while to make sure she was okay and hadn't pushed for more information.

But now she was alone and should probably go to bed, but there was no way she could sleep. Instead she wrapped herself up in her grandmother's afghan and sat in front of the dual computer monitors in her makeshift office space in her bedroom. She pulled up the Hayven game. She'd missed the window of time to chat with Dmitry by many hours, but that wasn't why she was signing in now. Hell, she may never chat with anyone in the game again after what had happened tonight. If someone like BigMan could get her information, she wasn't safe from anyone. She hadn't gathered a lot from BigMan in the few times they'd chatted, but she'd figured out quickly that he wasn't the brightest bulb on the Christmas tree. How the hell had someone like him gotten her personal information?

Time to find out.

She opened up the log-in box and used her password manager to enter the long, complicated string of numbers and characters. Then, she clicked the checkbox for stealth mode. She didn't need anyone knowing Lenore was online right now. The game queued up. Her inbox was stuffed with unread messages. Dmitry had sent her an invitation to play privately but, of course, she'd been too busy being attacked to answer. She minimized the mailbox to get into the main part of the game. The interior of the house she'd built for herself in Hayven came into view, a cute little cottage in the woods. The game was first-person style, so she was looking out from the perspective of Lenore, who was currently lying in bed.

But Cora wasn't there to be Lenore right now. She was on a mission. She opened chat mode and went into her list of people she'd interacted with before. Their screen names were there along with an icon letting her know who was actively online and who wasn't. BigMan wasn't online. Neither was Dmitry.

She clicked BigMan's name to open up his profile. It was relatively vague but had more than hers did. He listed his profession as *athletic trainer* and his age as thirty. Yeah, okay. No way was that guy a day over twenty-two. She scanned down. Located in north Texas. No pets. Favorite sports team—Dallas U Coyotes. There were multiple exclamation points behind the team name.

"Bingo." The word slipped passed her lips as she opened up another log-in page for Hayven on her second monitor. She typed in BigMan232 and then for the password tried *Coyotes*.

Guys were notorious for choosing their favorite sports team as a password. She'd seen it way too many times at the police station. But that one didn't work, so she tried a list of variations: *coyotes*, *DallasCoyotes*, *DallasU*, *GoCoyotes*, *GoBigOrange*. The system didn't seem to have a limit on how many times someone could try a password—a shitty lack of a security—but it served her purposes right now. She typed a few more and started to wonder if she was going down the wrong track when she remembered a T-shirt she'd seen Carlos wearing one day. *Fear the Coyote*. She typed that in and the screen changed, bringing her into the castle BigMan had fashioned for himself. Of course the dude had built himself a castle.

"Gotcha, motherfucker."

It was a bizarre feeling to see through his "eyes" in the game, but she didn't linger. Even though it was virtual, it felt creepy being in his head. She clicked into his account settings. There it was. William Bentley Barrett, twenty-one, Fort Worth address. Everything was there for the taking. If she really wanted to work at it, she could probably grab his credit card number, but she had no interest in that.

She needed to get some idea of how this guy had gotten to her. Maybe he played dumb online and really had some mad tech skills. She closed out Lenore's page on the other screen and opened up Facebook. She searched for William's name, found him easily enough, and opened his page. He hadn't bothered to set up any privacy settings and he used the same password for that account— flag number one that he wasn't some closet computer genius.

She clicked around to the About section and his timeline. He worked as the front-desk attendant at a local gym. Was a student at Dallas U. Used to play on the football team but got sidelined by an injury. He'd liked a few sports-related pages and local dance clubs. His Instagram feed looked to be nothing but photos of big plates of food and muscle-flexing selfies. He'd chatted with a few girls from his college, but all of it seemed pretty lighthearted. Nothing stood out.

She frowned and tapped her fingers on her desk. Weird. She closed out the page and went back to his Hayven profile. She clicked on his inbox. It wasn't nearly as full as hers. A few requests to play. A few update emails from the game. But then a subject line caught her eye. *Tired of being teased?*

She opened the email and sucked in a breath.

Special alert. Lenore Lux wants to take this to the next level and is local to your area! She's ready to play for real. Click the attachment for her information so you can set up some fun.

The words didn't make sense to her at first. It was just too god-damned unbelievable, but then angry heat flooded her. With a shaking hand, she opened the attachment and there it was—a screenshot of the information she'd entered when she'd joined the site. Her name was listed as C. L. Benning, the name she used on her credit card. And her address was there plain as day. Luckily, because it was a screenshot, her credit card just showed up as dots in a jpeg, but what the fuck did it matter when someone was literally advertising her home address?

Her eyes skimmed to the bottom. Below all the information was a short list.

Safeword: Watermelon

Wrong.

Likes: Toys, Edge Play, Anal, Bondage, Rape Play

Scene request: I would love to be taken captive by surprise.

Her stomach dropped and her skin went cold.

That wasn't her list or her request. She'd never filled out that portion. She wouldn't have. Someone had doctored this and sent it out.

Christ.

BigMan had acted like a psycho, but he'd thought she'd been the one to initiate. He'd thought she'd made a goddamned request. Whoever had done this could've gotten her *raped*.

The back of her throat burned and she was trembling again. What if this note went out to other men? And what if she wasn't the only one affected? Who the hell would do something so sick?

She scrolled up to see where the email had come from, but it was the admin address from within Hayven, the same one that announcements and updates came from—which was also the same address she was supposed to use to contact customer service to make a complaint.

Fuck. If she sent in a complaint, it'd go straight to whoever had hacked the damn thing in the first place. But someone needed to know what was going on. God only knew how many people had been doxxed and put at risk.

She hit Print on the email for evidence and then signed out of William's account. She opened up the main site for Hayven and went to their Contact page, knowing she'd probably be led through some winding trail of customer service via some faraway country, but she was surprised to find the site was owned and operated by a company with a Dallas address—Restless Games, Inc.

She'd never heard of them, which was strange since they were local, but maybe it was a start-up. Knowing that the servers that held her private virtual world were housed that close by gave her a dart of anxiety, but if the company was in town that at least gave her hope that she'd actually be able to talk to someone who could get this fixed quickly.

Because this shit needed to get fixed. Now. The fact that a company that was responsible for such intensely private personal information hadn't caught this yet pissed her off. The email had been sent to William days ago. How could the company not realize their system had been compromised?

She scrolled down. There was an eight-hundred number and the address. She jotted down both. It was just past four A.M. so she wouldn't get an answer now, but at least she had a plan of attack.

Attack.

She rubbed the chill bumps from her arms.

Time to check the locks one more time.

FOUR

Thirty more reps. I can do thirty more.

Hayes Fox dropped into a one-arm push-up and breathed through the burn in his body. *One. Two.* Sweat dripped onto the mat he'd laid out in the garage. The temperature outside was already climbing into the eighties even though it was barely six in the morning. But the heat didn't bother him. He'd grown accustomed to uncomfortable conditions a long time ago and relished the level of intensity it added to his workout. If he was thinking about the heat and the exhaustion in his body, he wasn't thinking about other shit.

Seven. Eight.

He always defaulted to old-school rock for workouts, so Guns N' Roses's "You Could Be Mine" blasted from a nearby radio, thumping hard along with his heartbeat.

Nine. Ten.

The music turned down.

He didn't look up. *Eleven. Twelve.*

Expensive black shoes came into view. "Good morning, Rocky. Are we going to run steps next or maybe drink some raw eggs?"

Hayes kept going. Up. Down. "You wouldn't be able to keep up, Muroya."

A drop of his sweat splashed onto Ren's shoe. Ren moved out

of the way and then swiped the drop with his finger. "You'd be surprised what I can keep up with."

His best friend's tone was smug, but there was a current of something underneath that made Hayes falter in his count. *Fuck.* He dropped down onto his forearms and knees, breathing hard. He didn't need this right now. After a long night of no sleep and a racing brain, he wanted to get lost in a mindless workout. "Did you need something?"

"I need lots of things," Ren said cryptically. "What are your plans today?"

Hayes looked up to find Ren leaning against the wall, already dressed for work in a bright blue T-shirt, gray sport coat, and dark jeans. His inky black hair was styled just haphazardly enough to look like he hadn't styled it at all. He sipped his coffee and gave Hayes an expectant look.

Hayes rolled onto his back, sat up, and grabbed a towel from a nearby weight bench to wipe the sweat off his face. "My plan is to finish this workout and then spend the rest of the day putting together financial documents for our newest investor. I got your email. Good work last night."

Ren didn't acknowledge the praise. Instead, his gaze moved over Hayes's shirtless form—brief, but enough that Hayes didn't miss it. His friend was sizing him up. Hayes knew how different he looked now. He'd always kept in shape. But three years locked behind bars had left him with nothing to do but think and push his body to the limits. He'd become a machine. No one fucked with you when you looked like he did. But his best friend didn't seem to know what to make of this version of him.

Hayes didn't ask his opinion. He'd promised himself when he got out that he'd keep the boundaries with Ren clear. They were best friends and business partners. Their days of partying, sharing women, and blurring lines in their relationship were done. Hayes couldn't be that guy anymore.

"Good. Then you can put together those documents at the office," Ren said with a nod.

"What?" Hayes blinked, Ren's words dragging the conversation back into focus. "I don't need the office for that stuff."

He eyed him. "Don't care. You told me six months, Fox." He pulled his phone from his pocket and held it up. "I marked it on my calendar. Today's the day, my friend. The CFO returns."

"You marked it on your calendar? Of course you fucking did." Hayes rolled to his feet. He didn't need to be having this conversation with Ren looming over him. "I'm not prepared for that today. All the stuff I'm working on is here. None of my old suits are going to fit. I have errands to run."

Ren pushed off the wall and walked toward him. "Don't give me that shit. We own the company. You can wear whatever you want. And you can have someone at the office run the errands."

A cold feeling crept through his chest, frost encasing his lungs. The office. Returning to work. Being in charge of the business again. "Ren, I—"

"Stop." Ren clamped a hand on Hayes's sweaty shoulder and squeezed. "It's time, Fox. Wyatt and Jace Austin invested in *us*, not me. And last night I got Grant Waters on board because I assured him you were going to be back at the helm with me this week. We're finally gathering some steam again. This is the time to return, hit the ground running, show the people who believe in us that this is a strong company."

"You don't need me for that," he repeated. "It's easier for everyone if I stay behind the scenes."

"Fuck that noise," he groused. "Look, I get it. It's going to be hard coming back after all that happened. But it's our company and there's no reason for you to hide. You didn't do anything wrong."

Hayes scoffed and shrugged from beneath Ren's touch. "You think the people who work for us believe that? The cops certainly don't buy it."

"If any of our employees don't, they can fuck off and go work somewhere else," Ren said, the words sharp and his jaw going tight. "I don't care what anyone else thinks. I care that your office has been empty for too damn long. The place needs you back. Shit, *I* need you back. I didn't sign up to do this on my own, man. I've kept things going, but you know we've always been better as a team. Balls are getting dropped. I only have so many hands and mine were meant to draw, not balance P&Ls or woo investors. I'm so far out of my wheelhouse, I'm going to need a GPS to get back."

The last words tumbled between them, a rare admission from Ren that he needed any help with anything, and that hit Hayes square. All those years ago when they'd started their original company, now renamed FoxRen Media, they'd gone into partnership not just because they were best friends but because business-wise, they complemented each other.

Ren was the creative one—an artistic genius and idea man— but scattered in his thoughts and methods. Impulsive. When they'd met as teens, Hayes had been the one to help temper that, to slow him down and show him how to focus his ideas. To find ways for Ren to channel all that talented energy into something useful so he could get away from the hell he'd been living in at the time. And on the flip side, Ren had kept Hayes from playing it too safe in business, had helped him take risks, think outside the box. He'd also been the one to make sure Hayes didn't work himself to death and had some fun in between.

But Hayes had left Ren on his own with the company for three and a half years. Longer really, since Hayes had pretty much checked out after he'd been charged. Since getting out of prison, he'd taken back the basic financial duties, but he hadn't been involved in the day-to-day operations. He'd put that all on Ren's plate and left it there. He'd thought staying out of it would be for the best. He didn't want to deal with the rumors and discomfort of employees. He didn't want his past tainting the newly renamed company or Ren by default. Ren already had enough in his own past to deal with.

But now, standing here and looking at his best friend, he realized that he'd been acting like a damn coward. No, he couldn't go back to how things used to be. That Hayes was dead. But that didn't mean he got a pass to leave Ren on his own to handle all the work of running the company. That didn't mean he got to hide.

Hayes released a breath and wrapped the towel around the back of his neck, pulling it taut. "Can I at least finish my workout first?"

Ren's mouth curved into a victorious smile. "Of course. But you know, if you just got laid, you wouldn't need to do Thor's workout every morning to shake off all that frustration. See how relaxed I am this morning? You should've come to that party with me last night. Lots of fun to be had."

Hayes grunted, but the comment dug into him like a burr. Ren thought Hayes's self-imposed abstinence was ridiculous. Maybe it was. His body certainly protested on a regular basis. He'd found ways to work around the need, accepting that nothing would ever be a substitute for the real thing. But anytime he thought about going there again with anyone for real, everything inside him locked up.

Things weren't as simple as Ren was making them sound. Hayes didn't have vanilla sex. It'd never done anything for him. Dominance and kink were inextricably twined with his desire. But that lifestyle was the one thing he could never allow himself again. Going to the party with Ren would've been the worst kind of torture. Seeing all his old friends from The Ranch, being reminded of the life he'd once had, knowing he could never have it again. It was too much to face.

Ren sighed when Hayes turned away. "You know, Grant asked about you last night. He said your membership is still yours if you want it. And there are submissives he trusts implicitly who—"

"No." The word was a bark—loud and hollow in the cavernous garage. He didn't even want to hear the words. His fists curled.

Ren was silent for a long moment. "And my offer still stands. I wasn't so wasted that I don't remember what I said."

Hayes's teeth clamped together. He didn't need to be reminded of that either. He thought about it every goddamned time he looked at Ren lately. A few months ago, on one particularly rough night after getting out, he and Ren had gotten shit-faced drunk. And Ren had put it out there. *If you can't trust anyone in your bed, fuck me. Close your eyes and pretend I'm a submissive. Hold me down, hurt me, whatever you need to do. You know I can handle it. I've handled worse than you.*

The offer had knocked Hayes right onto his ass. They'd never gone there despite Ren being openly bi and Hayes having experimented a time or two with guys when he was in college. He and Ren had shared submissives. Dominated them as a team. But he and Ren had always kept a clear line between them. When they'd met, Ren had been seventeen and so fucked up by the guy he'd been with that he'd expected everyone to use him, to treat his body like a commodity. Ren had made offers, but Hayes had sworn then that he'd never touch him, never take advantage, and he'd kept that promise.

He'd done it to protect Ren. But now he was keeping that line there to protect himself.

This friendship was his anchor right now. Unlike most of the other people who had called themselves friends, Ren had stood by him when he'd gone to prison, not just believing him unequivocally but fighting to get him out. He couldn't screw that up and break that long-standing promise for the simple relief of slaking his lust and curiosity. Plus, he knew Ren was only offering because he was worried about Hayes. After what he'd been through as a teen, Ren exclusively topped and had never given up control to anyone again. He wouldn't willingly offer himself to Hayes for any other reason than pity.

And Hayes would become a monk before he'd become a pity fuck for anyone.

"I'm fine."

Ren didn't respond immediately but Hayes could sense when he moved toward the door. "I'm leaving in an hour. You can follow me there."

The music dialed up again, the thrashing cymbals matching the noise in Hayes's head.

He didn't look back. He dropped back to the ground, switched arms.

One. Two. Three.

Ren stood in the doorway that led from the garage to the kitchen for way too long, watching Hayes do those punishing pushups. The guy looked like a beast—strong, angry, dangerous. The music clung to him like a demon, pushing his movements in time to the relentless beat. Muscles flexed. Sweat rolled over his skin. Ren couldn't look away.

From this angle, it was like watching a stranger. A beautiful, possessed stranger. Ren had, of course, noticed that Hayes was getting ripped in prison. Every time he visited, the guy seemed to have gotten harder both physically and emotionally. It'd been survival. Hayes was smart, and when facing down a twenty-year sentence, he'd done everything he could to ensure he was that scary motherfucker who other inmates would steer clear of. But Ren hated that Hayes still had to endure these torture sessions just to get through a day.

His body looked sick, sure. Ren would be lying if he said he didn't enjoy the view. Hayes thought that the offer Ren had made was some sacrificial bullshit, but really, it was selfish. Ren had accepted long ago that despite them both being dominants and Hayes being predominantly straight, his friend would always hit his sexual radar. It'd been there from the start, and it was an imprint he couldn't erase.

And really, Ren hadn't expected Hayes to take him up on his offer. Hayes had made a promise to him when they'd first met all those years ago, and he didn't break promises. Part of that comforted Ren. But the other part frustrated the hell out of him. He saw how Hayes looked at him when he didn't think Ren was watching. The way his gaze slid over his body. Hayes wasn't indifferent to him. But he couldn't see Ren without seeing the past. And that's what pissed Ren off.

He wasn't some fragile, messed-up kid anymore. And yeah, he hadn't been willing to let anyone have the control since that horrible year. The thought of putting himself in that position made him go cold inside. But with Hayes . . . with Hayes those thoughts had a different temperature, especially as he stood here and watched his friend shirtless and dripping with sweat. In his gut, he knew he could go there with him.

But none of that mattered. It was a no go. Hayes was committed to this new life of deprivation and isolation.

Ren had thought that when they'd finally gotten his conviction overturned that Hayes would be able to walk out of that prison and get his life back. The business that they'd built together would get out of the slump it'd gone into after the story broke about Hayes. Things would return to some kind of normal. But the man who'd gone in was not the man who had come out.

That conviction had taken a successful, proud guy who'd been able to command a room with just a look and turned him into this—a guy who didn't sleep, who worked out to the point of obsession, and who closed himself off to the world. To Ren.

And he had no idea how to help.

But at least today, he'd gotten a yes from him. Hayes would keep his word and come into the office. Ren had stooped low and used guilt to get him there, but it'd worked. Now he just needed to figure out how to *keep* him there.

Ren gave Hayes one last lingering look. The man was a sight. Up. Down. Up. Down. Grunting like he was fucking. One hand behind his back. A man on an endless mission.

Ren's cock began to take notice. He shook his head, adjusting the front of his jeans, and turned to go back into the house. He didn't need to travel down that mental road again. It was one filled with roadblocks and dead ends. Instead, he needed to stay focused on getting Hayes back to work. The key today would be to ease him in. Not too much thrown at him on day one.

But when they arrived at the office later that morning, that plan got shot straight to hell with a booster rocket.

FIVE

Ren knew something was wrong when he and Hayes stepped through the frosted-glass doors of FoxRen Media and Malik, one of the app designers, was behind the main desk in the lobby instead of Anita, their receptionist. Malik's dark hair was sticking up on one side like he'd grabbed it and yanked, the phones were ringing, and no one else was in sight.

He glanced up when Ren and Hayes walked in, looking like some possessed cartoon version of himself. "Oh, thank *God*."

"What's going on?" Ren asked, frowning.

Malik's gaze darted to Hayes then back to Ren. "Anita called in sick and Collin is still out for vacation. The phones have been ringing nonstop because a server went down, which Chelsea is working on, but I should be helping her with that. And then some woman came in first thing this morning demanding to talk to you and refusing to discuss whatever she's here for with anyone else." Malik gave him a pleading look. "Can I just send everyone to voice mail?"

Ren groaned. "Send them there for now and then look in the directory. We've worked with a temp service before. Call them and see if they can get us a receptionist for the day. After that, go help with the server. That's priority number one."

Malik nodded. "Right. Got it."

"And what happened to the woman who wanted to talk to me?" Ren hiked his messenger bag higher on his shoulder.

Malik jabbed his thumb toward the door that led to the executive offices. "I didn't know what to do with her and she was . . . persistent, so I just told her to sit outside your office and wait."

Ren rubbed his forehead. "Of course."

Because letting a stranger without an appointment into the office was an excellent idea. But Ren kept the comment to himself. The fact that the kid had attempted to handle front office operations when that was clearly out of his comfort zone deserved some credit.

Malik punched a few buttons on the phone. "How do I get this to roll over to voice mail? Goddamn, does it ever stop ringing?"

"Just leave it. I've got it." Ren leaned over the desk and hit the button that would put it in overnight mode. "By the way, Malik, this is our CFO and co-owner, Hayes Fox. Say hi and then get to the server."

Hayes, who'd been silently watching the meltdown, lifted a hand in a stoic greeting.

Malik paused at that, his eyes going owlish. If Ren were drawing him, he'd have put a little thought box with expletive symbols above Malik's head. "Oh, um, hi, Mr. Fox. Nice to meet you."

"Hayes is fine," he said, voice gruff.

Malik nodded but didn't look like he'd be calling Hayes by his first name anytime soon. He made some vague motion with his hand. "Uh, I'm going to go and help Chelsea."

"Yes. Do that." Ren watched the guy hurry back through the door and then turned to Hayes with a smirk. "So, welcome back."

Hayes lifted his brows and crossed his arms over his chest, stretching the white Henley tighter across his shoulders. "Is it always on fire like this?"

Ren shrugged. "Nah, only about fifty percent of the time. I had to cut the staff down in the last year to try to save some money. It works for the most part but gets insane when anyone's out."

Hayes frowned.

But Ren didn't want to get into how the business had declined after Hayes had gone to prison or how Ren had spent a big chunk of their profits on the lawyers and investigators who'd gotten Hayes's conviction overturned. They had both seen the numbers. If Ren hadn't renamed the company and introduced Hayven to the market two years ago, the company would've gone under.

It'd been the right move even though he'd had to go behind Hayes's back to do it. When Ren had told Hayes about his idea for the game, Hayes had told Ren to scrub it. *Think how it will look*, he'd said. But Ren had gone against his wishes, named the game after Hayes, and had set up a separate company front that tied the game only to Ren to make it harder for the media to make the connection. Then he'd brought it to market like a big, blazing *fuck you* to all those people who thought Hayes was guilty.

It had saved the company from closing up shop, but they still had a ways to go to get robust again. He needed to get Hayes involved in the daily operation so that Ren could spend more time on game enhancements and developments instead of being the firefighter all the time.

"Come on." Ren opened the door and they headed to the left, where the executive offices were located. He didn't want to go through the trouble of introducing Hayes to everyone yet. The place was in crisis mode, and Hayes wouldn't be ready for that song and dance anyway. He put a hand on Hayes's shoulder when they got to his old office. "Why don't you get settled in, get things back how you want them, and I'll go see what random-persistent-woman-off-the-street wants?"

Hayes eyeballed his closed office door like it was going to explode and then looked back to Ren. "Tell that kid not to send strangers back here anymore. What if it's some ex of yours or something? She could be burning your office down in revenge as we speak."

Ren laughed. "She could just add it to the rest of the fires. But yeah, I'll let him know."

Hayes blew out a breath and grabbed the door handle. "How bad is it going to be in here?"

"Do the words 'additional storage area' mean anything to you?"

"Fuck."

Ren glanced down the hallway. "I'll stop by in a while and help you haul some of that shit out of there."

Hayes shook his head and went into the room. Despite the curse that followed once Hayes saw the state of his office, something buoyed in Ren's chest. Hayes was back.

Well, physically at least.

Ren left him to it and headed around the corner to his own office. Sitting in the chair outside his door was a woman who had her head down as she typed furiously on her phone and bounced her jean-clad knee. Not an ex. He didn't really have those anyway. He never stuck with anyone long enough to get to the labels portion of coupledom. But something about her seemed familiar.

He set his bag down on his assistant Collin's desk, strode over, patience low, and looked down. "Can I help you?"

The woman startled, so involved in whatever she'd been doing that she hadn't noticed him approach. But when she lifted her head, the sight jolted his system like an electric shock, and the night before came crashing back.

No fucking way.

Hallway girl? She was wearing glasses today and less makeup, but there was no doubt it was her. Dark wavy hair that looked like she'd taken a dip in the ocean and let it dry in the breeze, the ghost of childhood freckles across her nose, and big hazel eyes he'd never forget.

His mind couldn't process the two things, the spheres collid-ing. The woman from the party at his job. *She'd sought him out?* He hadn't even told her his name. And last night she hadn't been able to get away from him fast enough.

But the way she was staring at him told a different story. Her eyes had gone wide and her bottom lip hung open like it'd forgot-ten how to close. She hadn't been looking for him. She was as surprised as he was. "Uh . . . I was waiting for Mr. Muroya."

Her knuckles went white around her phone and she tipped for-ward in the seat like she wanted to run, the heels of her Chuck Taylors lifting off the ground. She'd already figured out that he was the guy she'd come to see, and she wanted to bail.

Too bad he was standing in her way.

He smiled, slow and pleased. "Is that right?"

Last night, he'd been more than a little intrigued by the woman who had so boldly watched him with Naomi. He'd been doing a friend a favor, playing a part in a scene, which should've been fun, especially when they were doing it at a professional party instead of at The Ranch. But beyond the obvious pleasure of a blow job, he hadn't been able to get into the right headspace for the scene. A problem he'd been having way too often lately.

Then, he'd looked up and found this woman watching, and everything about the scene had flipped. Energy had surged through him, his body had come alive, and his dominant instincts had rushed forward. Being watched was a kink of his, but this had been something altogether different. The way she'd been looking at him . . . There'd been fear there, that knee-jerk reaction to being caught, but there'd been something else, too. Something that had made him want to call her over, to give her the very thing her eyes were asking him for. Then she'd run off. And when he'd approached her in the light of the party, she'd been bordering on hostile. The way she'd acted had made him think he'd read her all wrong. So when the blonde had rushed up to save her, he'd figured hot mystery woman had a girlfriend, that he'd been barking up the wrong tree.

Now she was here. And the color that appeared in her cheeks after her gaze quickly skimmed down his body told him a different story. *Right tree.*

The morning had just gotten infinitely more interesting. "Guess you're in luck. I'm Ren Muroya."

Her eyes closed, her worst fear obviously confirmed. "Of course you are."

He couldn't help but grin wider at her fuck-my-life expression. "So, Cora, Lady of the Dark Hallway, what exactly can I help you with?"

Fuck. My. Life.

Cora didn't know what she'd done in a previous existence, but apparently it'd been evil because the universe was screwing with her. She'd spent all morning tracking down the head of Restless Games, first calling a number that never picked up, then going to an address that turned out to be just a mailbox, and finally having to go through more computer detective work than she was in the mood for to find the parent company and where it was located. After that, she'd had to wait an hour in this office. Now, she'd finally found who she was looking for and it was this guy.

Blow-job guy.

Or as the world knew him—Ren Muroya, CEO and co-owner of FoxRen Media and, apparently, Restless Games.

She cleared her throat, trying her damnedest to erase last night from her mind and focus on the business at hand. This was serious. She didn't have time to care that he looked even better in jeans than he had in his suit, and she wasn't going to pay attention to that smug, I-have-the-upper-hand way he had about him. She refused to let her introvert gene take over just because he was hot.

She channeled professional Cora. The one who used to work in an all-male IT department and knew how to stand her ground. "I'm here because you have a big problem with your game Hayven."

Muroya's eyebrows shot up. "You're here about Hayven?"

Ha. There. She'd finally surprised him instead of the other way around. "Yes. I know you own it."

He crossed his arms, the amused expression in his eyes dimming. "I'm not sure where you're getting your information, but—"

She held up her palm and stood. Though really, that didn't give her much more to work with since he had to be at least six feet tall and easily towered over her. "Let's not waste time, Mr. Muroya. I could go into how I weeded out that information, but we'd end up at the same conclusion and I'd rather get to the point."

His jaw was hard now, his dark eyes flinty. "Are you a reporter?"

"What?" She blinked, thrown off by the question and the dose of disgust in his voice. "No. I'm . . ."

She didn't finish the sentence, and he stared at her expectantly.

God. She didn't want to say it. Not to him. Not to anyone.

"You're what?" he demanded.

If internal organs could cringe, hers did. "I'm a member."

The tightness in his jaw went slack at that. "Of *Hayven*?"

She adjusted her glasses and used that as a reason to look away and toward the hall. She'd never told anyone about the game. No one knew that secret shame, the things she did in that world, the fantasies she played out. How she pretended to be someone else entirely. How she had cyber/phone sex with a stranger. Heat burned up her neck. "Could we do this in your office? I'd rather not discuss everything out here."

He seemed to snap out of his stupor at that. "Oh. Of course. Right this way."

He turned and his fingertips landed gently on her upper arm to guide her. The move was polite, not at all aggressive, but he may as well have had electrodes taped to his fingers for the current it sent radiating through her. She had to breathe through the reaction.

Must. Focus.

He led her into a spacious corner office, complete with wrap-around windows and what looked to be authentic mid-century-modern furniture. His desk was in the center—simple and clean—with only a laptop. But against the left wall was an impressive workstation with three oversized monitors and a number of gadgets. That area wasn't so Zen. There were sticky notes everywhere and pads of paper stacked haphazardly. On the wall were pinned sheets of papers—drawings. She wanted to step closer and examine them, but she wasn't here for a tour.

He ushered her into the chair across from his desk and then took a seat on the other side. His gaze met hers, expression focused but impossible to read. "So, let's start over. You're not a reporter."

"No."

"You're a member who has somehow figured out that I'm the one in charge, and you've had some problem with the game."

"Yes."

He leaned forward on his forearms, the little move somehow creating an intimate just-between-me-and-you vibe. "Okay, well, I'm always happy to help a customer. But to be honest, if you're looking for tech support, I'm not your guy. My skills lie elsewhere."

He didn't say the last part in any particular way, but her brain twisted the words and dumped a big sprinkle of sexual innuendo on them. She'd seen some of those skills last night. She'd seen the way those hands he had folded on the desk gripped a woman's hair in passion. She'd heard how his voice sounded when he commanded a woman to take his cock.

Cora gripped the arm of the chair hard, trying to get ahold of the spiraling thoughts, and took a steadying breath. *Just the facts,*

Cora. Focus on that. "This isn't a little tech support issue, Mr. Muroya. You've had a major security breach, and all of your members are at risk until you fix it."

The frown was instant, the casual posture gone. "What?"

She straightened in her chair, professional mode kicking in. "I'm not sure what you have in the way of an IT Security department here, but they're sleeping on the job. The admin address has been hacked, and someone is sending emails out to your members with personal information of other members."

His entire demeanor shifted. His forehead creased, jaw flexing, and anger flashed in his gaze. "You're sure of this."

Not a question, but she answered it anyway. "Yes."

"How?"

She unzipped her bag and pulled out the email. She'd taken a permanent marker to the places where the name Lenore was mentioned, but she'd left the rest untouched. She set it on his desk. "This was sent from the main email address to someone I'd blocked in the game. My personal information was included and then whoever sent it got creative with the rest. Rape fantasy being a theme."

Ren picked up the sheet, his eyes scanning it, his expression darkening as he went. "You've got to be kidding me."

"No. And the man they sent the email to was local and took it literally. When I got home from the party last night, he was waiting for me outside my house."

Ren's head snapped up.

Cora swallowed, some of the anxiety from last night trying to bubble up again. "He grabbed me, thinking I was up for some kind of force fantasy, but my neighbors heard the scuffle and intervened. He ran off when the cops showed up."

Ren expression went lax, horrified. "Christ. He— Are you okay?"

She wet her lips. "I'm all right. I got lucky. But I don't want to think about what would've happened if someone hadn't heard. The safe word he was given wasn't mine. I wouldn't have had a way to stop him."

Ren closed his eyes briefly, like he was honestly pained at the thought.

She didn't give him a chance to respond. She wasn't here for sympathy or to talk about her terrifying night. She wanted things fixed. "Until this breach is closed, you're putting everyone in jeopardy. Not just for what happened to me, but exposure in general. People enter their information into your game, thinking their private details will remain that way. I have no idea how many people received emails like this about me. I didn't sleep last night because I couldn't stop thinking about who else could show up."

Ren shook his head and ran a hand through his hair. "God, Cora, I'm so sorry. This is— Obviously, we'll do whatever we need to do to get this fixed. I can't imagine how frightening all that must've been. If you need a place to stay temporarily to feel safe, we can set you up in a hotel or pay for an alarm system for your place or something."

"I appreciate that, but I'm not coming here for a handout. I just want you to close the holes, to let members know there's been a breach, and to warn them that if they receive an email like this, it's a fake."

"Of course. I can't believe someone would do this." His fist curled against the desk. "What could possibly be their endgame? Can they steal the credit card numbers?"

Cora blew out a breath. "Depends on how good they are. I don't know how hard it was to break into your system. He could've gotten into the email by some simple phishing. One of your employees might've clicked on a bad link or went to a dummy log-in page and revealed the password. But if someone just wanted to grab card numbers, they had no reason to go through the trouble of sending out emails like this. Whoever did this wanted to screw with people. I don't know if it was targeted at me in particular or if it's more widespread. But whoever it was did their homework. They knew enough to make it realistic."

"What do you mean?"

She frowned. "The subject of the email said, *Tired of being teased?* Whoever it was knew that this guy was interested in my character and that I turned him down. So this person either scanned chat transcripts or is already a player in the game."

Or was watching her chats with Dmitry. *You like the idea of being captured?* She rubbed chill bumps from her arms.

Ren considered her. "If it's another player, it could be personal."

"Sure. It could be as simple as I pissed someone off and he decided to go after me. That'd be easier to pinpoint. But if it's more than just me . . ." She lifted her hands, palms up. "Then it could be anyone. Someone being a sick asshole. Someone who has an issue with Hayven or the content. One of your competitors. A bored teenager."

He looked down at the email and a line appeared between his brows again. "And this was the email the hacker sent to the guy about you?"

"Yes."

He peered up. "And how did you get that? Did the guy give it to you?"

Cora pressed her lips together. She had to be careful. What she'd done last night hadn't quite been legal. But Ren, guy who gets blow jobs from other people's girlfriends at parties, probably wasn't going to call the ethics police on her. She adjusted her purse in her lap. "I'm an IT security specialist and am certified in white-hat hacking. I needed to know how he got my information."

His eyebrow arched. "So you broke into his account."

She shrugged. "Let's just say he was uncreative with his password choices."

The corner of Ren's mouth twitched, a flicker of amusement lightening the serious expression. "I see."

She crossed her arms. "Good thing since obviously your security department is playing Candy Crush or scrolling through Facebook instead of checking the system."

The thundercloud expression returned. "We had to contract that work out when the guy we had in that position moved away a few months ago. Believe me, that contract will be terminated as soon as we're done here. This is beyond unacceptable."

Cora didn't like to hear about anyone losing a gig, but she was glad Ren was taking this seriously. "You need to hire someone to hack into the system, find the holes, and close them up. And beef up the security in the game all around. Find someone who can think like a criminal. You're handling outrageously private information and will lose every last one of your members if they think they're not protected. Not to mention put yourself at risk for lawsuits."

"Right. Of course." Ren leaned back in his chair, squeezed his temples.

She could tell it was sinking in, the utter catastrophe this could be for his customers and company. It sucked. For everyone involved. And she appreciated that he wasn't giving her some corporate speak, playing the political, what-can-I-say-so-you-don't-sue-me game. In fact, he'd said enough to take blame that she'd have grounds for a lawsuit herself. But that wasn't why she was here. This hacker was nasty and dangerous. People needed to be protected.

"You may be able to stop it before it goes widespread," she said, trying to throw out a seed of hope. "You don't know what you're dealing with yet. But the clock is ticking. He's gone unchecked for a few days at least."

Ren looked up, his eyes meeting hers. "Any recommendations on who to hire? Someone who could start immediately."

Her mouth opened then shut again. She'd almost said the obvious—her. But did she really want to put that out there? If he actually was interested in hiring her, she'd be working with this man. This man who'd put a woman on her knees, shoved his dick in her mouth, and let Cora watch. This man who already knew too many of her secrets, who knew she was in the game. She didn't like people knowing those private things about her. She'd learned growing up that secrets were the most dangerous weapons. If you trusted someone with them it was like handing them a loaded gun and telling them exactly where best to aim. She shifted in her chair. "I may know a few people."

He tilted his head, like a big, dangerous cat watching prey cross the Serengeti. "Isn't that what you do?"

"I—"

"Are you working for someone else right now?"

She cleared her throat. "I own my own business. I do contract work."

"So you don't think you're good enough to tackle this breach, then?"

Her teeth clicked together at that, the casual comment digging under her skin. "I'm one of the best at what I do, Mr. Muroya. Maybe I'm worried you can't afford me."

There. That last part was a lie, but at least it sounded like a good excuse. And it could be half-believable considering the party he'd seen her at last night.

He flipped the printed email over, grabbed a pen, and then scrawled something on the back. He slid it her way. "Will that hourly rate suffice?"

Cora stared down at the number. Blinked. Forced her jaw not to unhinge.

Fuuuck.

Okay, so it was almost three times what she was charging clients right now. Depending on how long the job was, it could mean actual security for a little while. And no ramen. But was it worth it?

The awkwardness scale was going to be off the charts. She'd seen him in a private moment. But beyond that, she'd revealed a glimpse of herself. There'd been a long few seconds between him looking at her in that hallway and her leaving. He'd stripped away a few layers and had continued to tug at them when he'd sat down at her table.

He'd seen more than she wanted anyone to see. In the safety of her own home, she could be Lenore. But, if he discovered it was her, she'd be seen as that strange girl who was so pitiful she'd had to build a character who looked nothing like her just to get laid in a video game. The thought made her want to fold in on herself. She liked those two spheres of her life not touching. No Venn diagram interaction.

But how the hell was she supposed to walk away from that kind of money? This had to be better than living week to week or having to take some gig at an overnight call center. And it'd look solid on her résumé. Plus, she was good at her job. If she really wanted this fixed, the best way to ensure that was to do it herself.

But even knowing all that, something made her hesitate. A warning bell. She'd been looking for clients for months.

This all felt too easy.

She pushed the paper his way again and sat back in her chair. "Why are you offering this to me? You don't know me. You don't even know my last name. I could be terrible at my job."

He gave her a humorless smile. "Benning."

"What?"

"Your last name. I checked the guest list last night after you left."

"Oh." She didn't know how to feel about that. He'd probably checked it to make sure she wasn't going to report him for a lewd act.

"And for the record, I make quick decisions but not haphazard ones. I'm making you the offer for a number of reasons."

She gave him a skeptical look.

"Don't believe me? Fine. Here's what I know about you so far." He lifted a finger to count off. "You easily broke into this guy's account and figured out what was going on. You found me and tied me to Restless Games even though I know exactly how many layers you had to go through to get that information, so I know you've got skills." He nodded toward his door. "You're obviously determined since you got your way back here today and waited. You're going to be more motivated than most to fix this because you're personally involved in it. And you're already part of the game, so I don't have to worry about your delicate sensibilities being offended by our kinky little universe."

The air sagged out of Cora.

"And I know that what I just offered to pay you has got you interested at least on that level."

She looked up.

His lips twitched up at the corner. "Don't play poker, Cora. Your nostrils flared when you saw the number and your whole body went tense."

"I—"

"So," he said, not giving her a chance to protest, "what's holding you back must be because of the incident last night. So let's just get that out on the table and clear it. Now that I know you're kinky, I can stop worrying I freaked you out last night with that little cuckolding scene. It happened. You watched. I didn't mind. It doesn't have to be big deal. Just pretend we ran into each other in a club and follow the standard discretion rules. And—"

"I never said I was kinky," she blurted.

He paused, head tilted. "You're a member of Hayven and *not*?"

She cleared her throat. "I just like interesting games. I mostly observe."

Lie. Total fucking lie. Ever since she'd met Dmitry, she'd done nothing but participate. But she'd rather he think she was some wallflower voyeur than reveal who she was in the game.

He considered her for a long moment, but then nodded. "Fair enough. Either way, there's no need for what happened last night to affect work. Work is work. Personal is personal. I know how to divide the two. I assume you do as well."

Something about the way he said it gave her pause, but he'd switched to business mode and that soothed her nerves some. "Of course."

"Excellent. Bottom line is my game has a major problem, and you're telling me you have the skills to fix it and can start quickly. Because of the sensitive information you'll have access to, I'll need a background check. That's the only time constraint. But assuming that will come through over the weekend and all come back fine, I'm offering to contract you for your services for that hourly rate, starting Monday if you're available. Are you interested?"

Cora wet her lips, overwhelmed by the turn this conversation had taken. She'd walked in with a complaint and now there was a job offer sitting in her lap. She could pretend to think it over, put up some kind of effort. But her mama didn't raise no fool, and Cora would be the biggest of them all to turn down a gig that paid this well. She took a breath and put her hand out. "I guess we have a deal, Mr. Muroya."

His hand closed around hers, firm, warm. "Ren."

"Excuse me?"

"Call me Ren." He gave her a half smile. "I only require that kind of formality in very specific situations and work isn't one of them."

She coughed, choking on her own spit. *Sir.* The word from last night whispered through her head.

He laughed, releasing her hand and standing. "Sorry. You're too easy to shock, Cora Benning. We're going to have to work on that if you're going to be hanging around here."

She shook her head and stood. She couldn't tell him that she normally wasn't so easy to shock, that it wasn't the words, it was *him*. The man short-circuited her brain.

He stepped around his desk and plucked a business card from the holder on the front of his desk. "I'm going to call Shari from HR. She'll meet you up front and get everything she needs from you. Unless you hear from me, plan to be here Monday morning to start. In the meantime, I'll get an alert email sent out and I'll have the game taken offline until we get this fixed. If you have any questions before then, call me."

She took the offered card and pulled out one of her own to hand to him. Grace would've been proud. She'd finally handed out a business card. "Thanks. Here's mine."

He tucked the card in the inside pocket of his sport coat. "And my offer for the hotel stands. I don't want you feeling unsafe."

She tried not to notice how close he was now and that he smelled like some combination of minty shampoo and expensive coffee. "That's okay. I live in a duplex and the two guys next door are already on alert. Plus, I'm not going to be caught with my Taser at the bottom of my purse again."

Ren's expression turned grim. "I hate that our game is part of this. I know you don't know me, but this isn't the kind of thing I take lightly. One of the main reasons I developed Hayven was to provide a safe place for people to explore that private side of themselves without having to deal with the risks involved in trying to find real-life kink partners. That's why I require my gamemasters to be relentless when policing harassers or trolls. I never wanted anyone to feel anything but protected. It truly is supposed to be a haven. That's always been my goal."

Cora blew out a breath. She knew that much to be true. She'd seen issues crop up in the game and promptly knocked down. One guy who constantly made disgusting comments to women in the game was struck by lightning and burnt to a crisp, never to be seen again. Another who always interrupted other people's play was swept away by a velociraptor. That one had made her laugh. "I've seen your gamemasters get pretty creative with deactivating accounts."

The corner of Ren's mouth kicked up. "They're two very sadistic, very creative women with sick senses of humor. The job fits them perfectly."

She slid his card in the front pocket of her purse. "I appreciate that you recognize how serious this is. I promise I'll do everything I can to get it fixed and get your system better protected. There's nothing more dangerous than information in the wrong hands."

"Agreed." He put his hand on her lower back. "Come on. I'll walk you out and get you set up with Shari."

The touch was just as electric as the first, but this time it seemed even more intimate—those long fingers gently pressed against the dip in her spine. She imagined that hand sliding farther down, gripping her flesh like he'd gripped that woman's hair. *No.*

A shuddery breath went through her, but she fought hard not to show any reaction otherwise. She reminded herself that she would be working with this man, that he had shown no interest in her anyway, and that she was only reacting like this because he was unfairly good-looking and she had too much pent-up sexual energy. He was cheesecake and she was the girl on a diet. This would pass.

Ren led her out of his office and toward the hallway. His hand remained parked on her back as they turned the corner and he chatted with her about the company. But before they could make it to the lobby, a door opened on the left ahead of them and a massive roadblock filled the space.

A man with Greek-god arms stepped into the hallway. His face was hidden by the stack of boxes he was carrying, but there was no missing the size of the guy when he turned his back to them and started down the hallway.

Oh my. Cora couldn't help but take in the view. As tall as Ren, if not taller, with Atlas shoulders and an ass that did things to the worn pair of jeans that were bordering on obscene. He bent over to set down the boxes at the end of the hallway, and she had to bite her lip to keep from groaning aloud.

Ren made a sound under his breath.

She quickly turned her head. "What?"

He gave a smug smile as they continued walking. "Nothing."

Shit. Had she made some sort of noise? She hoped to hell she hadn't.

"Hey, Fox," Ren called out when they got within a few steps of the man.

"Yeah?" The guy straightened the boxes so that they wouldn't tip over and turned their way, his gaze landing first on Ren and then sliding to Cora.

The front view was even better than the back. Green eyes, gold-brown hair that would probably be curly if grown out, and a stubbled jaw that should've made him look harsh but only fired up her long-standing Indiana Jones fantasies. He looked like he should be chasing bad guys through the jungle instead of in some tech office.

Cora smoothed a hair away from her face and tried for a polite smile, but she wasn't sure the expression made it all the way there. And he didn't return any warmth if it did. If anything he looked wary.

Ren nodded toward her. "I wanted to introduce you to Cora Benning. I've just hired her to fix some security issues in one of the games. She'll start Monday."

Fox frowned. "Security issues?"

"Yeah. I'll go over it with you in a few minutes. I'm just walking Cora out to take care of details with HR."

Fox put his hand out. "Hayes Fox."

His voice was a rumble, that growing thunder right before a storm reached you. She took the offered hand, and the minute his fingers wrapped around hers in a firm hold, all intelligent thought emptied from her brain.

Ren clapped Hayes on the shoulder. "Hayes is the co-owner and our CFO. He's been working remotely as of late, but he's moving back into his office today. So you'll be seeing him around."

Hayes was unapologetically holding her gaze, evaluating her, *reading* her. She didn't know if she was passing whatever test he was giving her, but she couldn't seem to look away. Or act like a normal human being. *Use your words, Cora.* She swallowed past the knot in her throat and pushed down the ridiculous reaction. "Nice to meet you."

His eyes narrowed for a second, like he'd noticed some chink in her armor, and she shifted uncomfortably in her Converse, but then he released her hand. "Well, I've got to get the rest of this stuff out of the office. I'll leave you to it."

He stepped past them without waiting for a response. She couldn't help but turn to watch him go. When he was out of sight, she let out a nervous laugh. "Well, that went great."

Ren gave a dismissive shrug. "Nah, don't worry. That was Fox's version of a warm welcome. You're good. Come on."

Cora followed him down the hallway, but when she peered back one last time, she saw Hayes leaning against his doorjamb— watching them with a deep frown.

That same odd, crackling awareness moved over her. *Danger.* She turned forward and rubbed the goose bumps from her arms.

Maybe she should've stuck with helping out at Marv's Auto Parts.

SIX

Hayes stood in the doorway of Ren's office, two cups of fresh coffee in his hands. The windows were dark at this hour, and Ren had his back to him as he sat in front of his triumvirate of monitors. His hand gripped the back of his head and his legs were splayed out in front of him like he'd just run a marathon and collapsed in the chair.

"That bad?" Hayes walked over and set the coffee on the corner of Ren's messy desk. Ren had briefed him this morning on the security breach, but then had told him not to worry about it, that he'd handle things. Hayes hated that Ren still felt like he had to kid-glove him with work stuff. So he'd insisted on taking on the logistical tasks while Ren dug into the game to see what he could find.

Ren had relented and Hayes had introduced himself to the team, even though that'd been the last thing he'd wanted to do today. Everyone had seemed professional and welcoming enough. Ren had obviously prepped them that they should be expecting him to return soon, but he'd caught a few watchful glances. He was sure there were whispers after he'd left the room, but there was nothing he could do about that. It was a new part of his existence that he was going to have to get used to. Released or not, he was a former convict. People would always wonder if he'd really done that horrible crime and had simply had enough money to get away with it.

But Ren was right. He couldn't hide forever. There was a company to run. So he'd gotten the awkward introductions out of the way, and then had delegated what needed to be done for the day. He'd gotten them to take Hayven offline. Then he'd set up a refund for this month's members to compensate for the downtime. He'd drafted a notice to go out to everyone to be on the lookout for fake emails. Despite the fact that they were in crisis mode, being busy had actually felt good. He liked having a mission, an objective.

But now it was bordering on eleven at night. Everyone else had gone home for the weekend and Ren had barely left his office. The guy could go into obsessive hyperfocus mode with stuff like this. He'd forget to eat and sleep if no one reminded him to take a break.

Ren ran a hand over his face and rocked forward in his chair to grab the coffee. "I don't know. I can't find anything obviously wrong, but I can feel the bastard's dirty fingerprints all over *my* game. And I know systems get attacked every day, but this feels like more than that. Be a troll, a troublemaker, a thief—fine, whatever. But this shit could get someone seriously hurt. Cora could've been raped."

"It definitely feels personal," Hayes said, stepping to the side and eyeing the row of Ren's drawings. Though members could personalize their characters, Ren had designed the components and liked to see how people put them together. A version of Master Dmitry was pinned up there, but Ren had left him shirtless and had inked in elaborate tattoos of snaking, thorny vines over his chest. Dmitry was trying to grab at them but they were part of his skin, leaving him in beautifully rendered anguish as he tore at himself. Hayes looked away, afraid Ren would notice his lingering attention on the art. "This attack took time to orchestrate. Whoever it was had to know enough about the game—who was talking to whom, who lived where—to even set it up."

"Exactly," Ren said, tone grim. "It has intent."

Hayes turned away from the wall of drawings and watched the steam curl off his coffee. "Did Cora say anything about possible enemies? A crazy ex or something?"

Ren's chair squeaked as he stretched. "I didn't have time to ask, but we can pick her brain on Monday. I was hoping to figure out if she was the only one affected or if it's more widespread. That would answer some questions and give us a place to start."

Hayes looked up. "If it's more widespread, we're fucked. No one's going to play a game like Hayven if they think their information isn't protected."

Ren groaned. "I don't even want to consider that possibility. We finally get solid investors backing us and our most profitable product could go up in flames." He pinched the bridge of his nose. "I'll wait until Monday before I panic. Hopefully, Cora will be able to find the clues and trails I don't know how to see and we can stop this before it goes any further. I was hoping I could do something to help tonight, but this is above my pay grade."

Hayes perched on the edge of the credenza. "You know for a fact that she's skilled enough for this job?"

Ren lowered his hand from his face and gave him a what-the-fuck look. "Of course. Why else would I hire her?"

Hayes sniffed. "Don't forget how well I know you. You feel guilty because she was attacked. Plus, I saw how close to her you were standing."

"Dude, I feel like absolute shit that she was attacked. It could've been so . . . I can't even think about it." A haunted look flashed through his eyes. "But that's not why I hired her. I went with my gut. And based on what I found on the résumé she sent me, I was spot on. She went to a good school and has worked for two top-tier companies. The only ding was that she apparently quit her last job with Braecom without notice. But there's a story there. She's not the flighty type."

"Oh, so you already know her type, huh?"

Ren shrugged. "I'm good at reading people. I know flighty. *I'm* flighty. She's definitely not. She's the type that probably has some itemized life plan written down with little checkboxes next to each task. Something went down at the last job to make her leave."

"And the reason you were standing so close?" Hayes pressed.

The corner of his mouth twitched—Ren's mischief mode. "I was doing that for the same reason you were giving her the shakedown."

Hayes grabbed his coffee and sipped. "There was no shakedown. I barely said a word to her."

"Bullshit. She caught your attention just like she caught mine. There's something about her that's just . . . I don't know. Interesting. Like she's got good secrets."

He wasn't going to honor that with a reaction, but Ren was right. Something about Cora *had* made him want to keep looking, to extend the conversation. He didn't quite understand the reaction. She was far from his usual type. When it came to women, he was typically attracted to ones with more in-your-face sex appeal, ones who embraced that ultra-feminine look. But Cora had been rocking some female Clark Kent vibe with her dark-rimmed glasses, skinny jeans, and a vintage Mystery Machine T-shirt that hugged her body just enough to reveal her barely-there curves. That tomboy look worked on her. Plus, a woman with a mind sharp enough to do high-level computer security and who hadn't retreated when he'd held her gaze? That was all too intriguing. Which meant he needed to steer clear. "I don't see it."

Ren snorted. "Oh, come on. You eye-fucked her in that way you used to do before we put a submissive through a scene. I'm surprised you didn't ask her for a safe word and make her call you *sir*."

Hayes winced.

"And she stared right back—all bold and shit." Ren's smile was far too amused. "I almost got a semi just watching the two of you. She'd be a challenge. A quiet one with all those hard-to-crack layers? *Hot.*"

"Ren." His tone held warning.

He held up a hand. "Don't get your feathers fluffed, Fox. I'm just calling it like I see it. And it was nice to see you give that look, to know that you're still capable. It's been a long time."

Hayes rubbed his brow and closed his eyes, a headache brewing. "It was just a look. And even if it was what you're saying, she's going to be an employee. And she's young."

"She's twenty-six. And we're contracting her services. I'm not her boss. And neither are you."

Hayes's head lifted at that. "Uh-uh. Don't go looking for loopholes, Muroya. The woman just got attacked because of *our* game. She's going to be working with us. Plus, you don't know anything about her. She probably already has a boyfriend or a girlfriend. She—"

"Watched me get a blow job from Naomi last night at the party and liked it."

"*What?*"

Ren looked all too pleased at Hayes's shock. He rocked back in his chair. "I did a scene last night. Chris Jenkins has a cuckolding kink and asked for my help. We were going to try it at The Ranch, but when we ran into each other at the party, I figured, why not? So Naomi and I snuck off into a hallway. I thought we were alone, but then I looked up and there was this woman in the dark, watching us."

"You've got to be shitting me. Cora?"

"Yep. Apparently, she'd been in the hallway already when we arrived. And, man, it was intense. She looked so . . . entranced. I could tell she wanted to stay. But I spooked her and she bailed. I found her at the party afterward, thinking maybe she was new to

The Ranch since there were a lot of members at the party. But she was freaked out, and obviously shocked by what she'd seen. We didn't even exchange names." He shrugged. "I thought it was done. Then, boom, here she was today. She had no idea she was coming to see me. You should've seen her face when she realized who I was. I almost felt bad for her. Until she checked me out. Then I just felt other things. So, obviously, it's fate."

Hayes ran a hand over the back of his head. "Fate is bullshit."

Was it fate that had locked him in a cage for three years? Fuck fate.

And he didn't want to think about blow jobs in dark hallways, of watching or being watched, of the woman he was going to be working with being interested in that kind of thing. He didn't need to know these details. He wanted to think of Cora as a sexless entity. A bot who would be working on their computers. Just like he was trying to think of Ren as a sexless best friend.

"You said she was freaked out by what she saw. So she's not kinky?" Hayes's words came out like a prayer.

Ren set his coffee aside and tilted back in his chair, making the springs groan again. "She says no. She wouldn't tell me who she is in the game. She said she just likes video games and is an observer in Hayven."

"There are lots of those. That's half our subscriber base." Hayes should know. He used to be one of those lurkers up until a few months ago when he'd met Lenore. But, of course, Ren didn't know any of that. Ren didn't know he played at all.

"Yeah. But I know what I saw last night, and I see how she reacts to me—how she reacted to you. Maybe she does just observe, but she's lying to herself if she thinks she's unaffected. She's wound up tighter than a ball of rubber bands and dying of curiosity. A voyeur at the very least. I saw it all over her face last night. She's freaked out by the urge, but it's there. You know what that does to me, Hayes."

Hayes groaned. "Stop."

Ren had always had a fetish for the newbies. He liked teaching and opening up people's world, that process of discovery. He'd prepare them for the lifestyle and then let them go so they could find a long-term relationship. That's how Ren's brain operated—new, new, new. He always wanted a new challenge, a new rush. But no one who would expect him to stick around.

He sipped his drink. "What does it matter to you anyway? You're doing your thing. I'm doing mine. If something happens between me and Cora, that doesn't have to affect you."

Hayes's jaw clenched.

Ren's eyes narrowed, gaze shrewd. "Unless you want it to."

"No." The word was like a thunderclap. Final. Definite. A lie.

He had no idea why the thought of Ren and Cora hooking up bothered the hell out of him. He didn't know Cora, and he was used to Ren's escapades. And it wasn't like Hayes was going to make some move on her. Even if the way she looked at him today had made his instincts prickle with awareness. For a brief moment in the hallway, he'd had a flash of Ren stepping behind her, whispering commands in her ear, telling her exactly what to do and what the two of them were going to do to her.

Hayes had gotten used to missing sex. But he hadn't been prepared for the deep ache for *more* that had hit him, that thrill of playing on the edge, that connection of sharing a woman with his best friend, that satisfaction of being in charge and making sure everyone found their version of bliss. His body had physically hurt with the rush of need and the grief that had been hot on its heels. He'd never have that again. Instead, Ren would pursue Cora, and Hayes would continue exactly as he was now. The thought was damn depressing.

"You know," Ren said, voice deceivingly casual, "when she first saw you in the hallway this afternoon, she made this little breathy sound. I don't even think she realized she did it, but it was obvious what she thought of the view. Not that I blame her. I mean, you're not as hot as me, but you're pretty close."

Hayes's head lifted at that, sending Ren a warning look.

Ren grinned. "Okay, *maybe* equally as hot. But the point is, she isn't repulsed by us. Always a good start."

Hayes shook his head. "There is no start."

"Come on, Fox. I know you're in monk mode, but a little harmless flirting never hurt anyone. This could be good for you. I think you're going to like Cora. And I have a feeling she'd like *us*."

"I don't need to like her. I just need her to get this breach fixed."

Ren tipped his head back and groaned. "Yeah, yeah. All work and no play. The Hayes who could crack a smile is gone. He will not try to make a friend at work. He will not enjoy the company of a smart, interesting woman just for the hell of it. He will not take up his very hot best friend on his very generous sexual offers. Broody dude will brood in his office all day long and be broody. I get it."

Hayes stared at him, the words said lightly but landing heavy. Every word was the truth. He didn't like the picture it painted. At all. He could remember a time when he and Ren had joked around, when they gave each other a hard time on a daily basis and made each other laugh. When being at work was like play—an adventure with his best friend by his side. They made video games, for God's sake, not nuclear bombs. Everything felt so life and death lately. How Ren had even tolerated being around Hayes since he'd gotten out was a freaking wonder. Hayes released a breath and scraped a hand through his hair. "Goddamn, I am a miserable fuck to be around, aren't I?"

Ren lifted his head, surprise on his face.

"And broody, Ren? Who uses that word? I'm not a eighteenth-century English lord."

Ren's lips curved. "You could totally pull that shit off, though. Lord of the manor? You'd be all over that. Wearing cravats. Bossing people around. The mansion would have to be named something super dark and creepy. Raven House or Blackwood Manor."

"And Lord Hayes never comes out of his room," Hayes said.

"And the drawing room is haunted."

"And there's a room in the east wing that always remains locked," Hayes added.

"Because that's where the bodies of the former servants are kept. They all killed themselves because the lord was so damn broody that they could bear it no longer."

"Ha. It'd be funny if it wasn't so close to the truth." He rubbed a hand over the back of his neck, feeling ten kinds of exhausted. "I'm sorry, man. I get so trapped in my own head sometimes that I don't realize how shitty it must be to be around me."

Ren sat forward, bracing his arms on his thighs. "I'm not looking for an apology. You know I'd put up with your broody ass for as long as it takes. You have the right to be angry and depressed and paranoid. You come by that stuff honestly. You've been through hell."

Hayes looked down.

"And believe me, I remember how it is to feel like you're drowning under the weight of all that heavy stuff. When you first met me, I felt like I was at the bottom of the ocean with bricks strapped to my feet. I didn't think I'd ever surface again. Hell, I didn't know if I wanted to. But this bossy white kid from across the street forced me to go to school every morning and talk to that nosy social worker. He made me draw my comics. He kicked my ass and forced me to go through the motions. And eventually, my brain caught up. I started seeing the other side, laughing again, having fun. *Living*."

Hayes's chest tightened. He could remember the day he'd first heard Ren really laugh. The kid had been so beat down, so quiet, for so long. But one day after school, Ren had brought Hayes to his aunt's restaurant to introduce him to sushi. Hayes had talked a big game that he could handle spicy food, so Ren had bet him twenty bucks that he couldn't take a big dollop of wasabi without spitting it out. Hayes had boldly popped it in his mouth and swallowed. It'd taken about five seconds before he was coughing, ten before he was crying, and fifteen before he was beseeching God for help and cursing the entire nation of Japan.

But then Ren had burst out with this full-throttle laugh that had filled the restaurant and had taken Hayes completely off guard. He'd never heard the kid sound so openly joyful. And suddenly the house of pain that the wasabi had brought on was worth every second. He'd finally gotten to meet the real Ren, had gotten a glimpse of the sarcastic, playfully sadistic smartass he'd eventually become. He'd surfaced in the ocean.

"Yeah, you *were* a broody motherfucker, weren't you?" Hayes said, trying to lighten the mood.

"I was worse. I wasn't broody, I was *emo* before emo existed. And you didn't let me get away with it." Ren stood and stepped closer. He thumped Hayes on the knee, making him look up. "So, that's all I'm trying to do for you. You annoyed the hell out of me back then. Now I'm returning the favor. I'm not going to sit by and let you lock yourself up in the manor, Lord Hayes. I'm going to push you. I'm going to point out when a pretty woman gives you a look. And I'm going to make inappropriate sexual offers. And you are going to appreciate it, dammit."

Hayes laughed at that, the sound hoarse and foreign in his throat. "I don't deserve a friend like you."

"That's the thing," Ren said, putting his hands on Hayes's shoulders. "You absolutely do. You're not just a good guy. You're the best guy I know, Fox."

Hayes's jaw flexed.

"All I'm asking is that you try," Ren said, voice softening. "*Let* me push you. Trust that I've got your best interests in mind. I've got your back, just like you had mine."

Hayes's heart was beating fast, his palms sweaty against his thighs. The thought of trusting anyone, even Ren, was so goddamned hard. But he heard what Ren was saying. Just one foot in front of the other—go through the motions. Stop running in place. "This sounds like a negotiation conversation at The Ranch."

Ren smirked. "Oh, hell no. You would be the worst goddamned sub in the history of subs. My arm would go out before I could beat you into submission."

Hayes grinned. "No doubt."

"So?" Ren asked, dropping his hands from Hayes's shoulders and folding his arms, the gauntlet laid down.

Hayes released a breath and pushed himself off the credenza. "Fine. I'll *try* to let you push. I'll come to work next week. I'll be less brooding lord and more the guy who used to work here. But the Cora thing is a no go for me. No women. No kink. That's all I can give you right now."

Ren nodded, relief at the edges of his expression. "I'll take that. For now."

Ren held out his hand like it was an official negotiation.

Hayes took it and squeezed but instead of releasing it, he tugged Ren closer. He touched his forehead to Ren's, their hands clasped tightly between them. "For what it's worth, you're the best guy I know, too. And turning down your offer was and still is the hardest thing I've done since getting out. I won't use you, Ren. Doesn't mean I'm not tempted." He swallowed hard, letting the truth slip free. "I've *always* been tempted."

Ren closed his eyes, breathed. "Fox . . ."

In that moment, Hayes wanted to cross that line, to do something about the attraction that had simmered unspoken between them for all these years. It'd been so goddamned long since he'd touched someone, been touched. He'd just have to angle his head, brush his mouth against Ren's. He didn't have much experience with men, but this wasn't just any guy. This was *Ren*. He had no doubt it'd be like a match struck if they ever let the smallest thing happen.

Then disaster would follow. Ren had friends. And Ren had lovers. The two didn't cross. Something happening between them would light a match and then it'd burn everything the hell down.

Hayes released Ren's hand and stepped back. "I'll see you at home."

Ren's Adam's apple bobbed. "Yeah. See ya."

Their gazes held for a second too long. Hayes turned and strode out the door before he did something he'd regret in the morning.

He'd agreed to let Ren push.

He hadn't agreed to jump off a cliff.

SEVEN

"What are you doing here so early, Junior?"

Cora glanced up to find Detective Andre Medina standing in the doorway of the computer room with a smile. She hated when people called her *Junior*, but somehow Medina pulled it off. Probably because he was so damn charming. He could tell you that you were under arrest and you'd happily hold out your wrists for his cuffs.

His hands were tucked in his pockets and his tie was loosened like he'd had a long night. He and his partner were working a horrid double-murder case, and the two of them were under all kinds of pressure from her mother and the media to get it solved quickly.

Cora pointed at the laptop in front of her. "I offered to dig through the Candor case since no one else was having any luck. I have another job to go to at eight, so I thought I'd sneak this in before then."

Andre frowned. "Is that the case with that teacher from the middle school?"

She leaned back in her chair and grimaced. "Yeah. Good news is I found some damning stuff. Bad news . . ."

"Is that the allegations are true."

She blew out a breath, already drained even though her day

had barely started. This was the hardest part of working at the station. She loved unraveling a mystery and liked that she could help, but she hated some of the stuff she had to see. The dark side of human nature was an ugly place. A teacher posing as a teen on Facebook and coaxing naked photos from his students was pretty fucking ugly. "Exactly."

Andre stepped inside and braced his hands on the back of the chair in front of her desk, looking more tired than she'd ever seen him. "Well, I hope the job you're going to next is less grim than this."

"The jury's still out on that."

"Another precinct?"

"No, it's at FoxRen Media. They have a pretty heinous hacker to deal with, though."

Andre's eyebrows went up. "FoxRen? I know those guys, the owners. Jace and my brother-in-law are investors in the company."

"Oh." *Fuck*. What was wrong with her? She should've never mentioned the name or that they had a problem. Andre's husband had invested in them? *Great*. Confidentiality fail. "Well, I'm sure I'll get their systems fixed in no time. Nothing to worry about long-term. Please don't say anything to anyone. I shouldn't have said—"

He held up a hand. "It's fine. Jace knows those guys well enough to trust them to tell him if something is seriously wrong. But . . ."

He glanced back toward the open door.

Cora frowned. "But what?"

Andre turned back to her, a crease in his brow. "Have you met Muroya and Fox yet?"

She sat up straighter, not liking the sudden wary tone. "Yes. Ren is the one who hired me and I briefly met Hayes."

"And what'd you think of them?"

Hot. Intimidating. "Ren seems like a handful but friendly. Sharp. Hayes seemed . . . quiet."

"Yeah. That's a good assessment." Andre stepped around the chair and sat, leaning forward and lowering his voice. "But do you know anything about them? The history?"

"I—" She pressed her lips together. "Not really. I mean, I know the company's been around for a few years, but I just got hired. I haven't had time to do any research."

Andre rubbed a hand over his stubbled jaw, looking like he was debating on telling her whatever it was.

"What is it, Medina? You're freaking me out."

Andre grimaced. "All right. Listen, Junior. I like your mom and respect the hell out of her, but I know she's crazy protective over you and can be a little over the top with that. You should've heard the talk she gave all the guys *and girls* before you started helping out here. So you're going to have to trust me when I tell you not to let your mom know that you're working at FoxRen."

Cora's brow scrunched. "What? Why?"

"Let's just say she wouldn't willingly let you within fifty feet of Hayes Fox."

Her stomach clenched. "What's wrong with Hayes?"

The lines around Andre's mouth deepened as he peered back at the door again and then looked at her. "Fox just got out of prison a few months ago."

"*What?*"

"Yeah. The original case went through here. It was before I got to this precinct, but your mom oversaw the investigation."

Her mind was reeling, remembering the intensity of Hayes, the way he'd looked at her, the way her body had responded. The edge of danger that had tripped her alarm bells. She swallowed past the dryness in her throat. "What was he in for? White-collar crime or something?"

Andre's jaw flexed. "Aggravated rape."

Her stomach plummeted and her skin went cold. "Shit."

"I know. But listen. I know the guy, knew him before he went in, and he didn't do what they said he did. He wouldn't have. The conviction was overturned. That's why he's out."

But she could barely hear him. "Rape."

"Hey," Andre said, trying to catch her eye. "Listen to me. You know I wouldn't give you the thumbs-up to go work for the guy if I thought there was even a glimmer of a chance he was guilty. But I promise you, your mother will absolutely not feel the same way. She helped put him behind bars. When he got out, she went on a rant about how he bought his way out of his conviction. So she will flip her shit if she knows you're anywhere near him."

Cora lifted up her glasses and rubbed the spot between her eyes, a headache hatching. "How do you *know*, Medina? What if he's a good liar? You see it all the time with sociopaths. They can trick their best friend, their wife, you name it. I don't want to be working with a rapist. No money is worth that."

Andre sat back in his chair. "It's absolutely your call. I'm just telling you that I one hundred percent know that he didn't do what he was accused of. That's all I can give you. The rest is his personal business."

She opened her eyes and put her glasses back in place, the news pressing down on her like sacks of grain. On one hand, she trusted Andre's word. The guy wouldn't tell her this unless he really believed it. He was as protective of women as they come. But she'd also grown up with a cop mother. People could be world-class liars. People who you'd never ever suspect were bad could do horrible things. The only people who could truly know if Hayes was guilty were Hayes and the woman he'd been with. And Andre wasn't one of those two. But innocent people had also gone to jail for crimes they didn't commit.

She felt sick to her stomach. She'd spent so much of her life avoiding danger, being on the lookout, learning how to be safe. That part of her said to bail, to not take the risk. Better safe than dead. That was the motto her mother had taught her. She could find another job. But at the same time, she was so damn tired of being on guard all the time, of looking for malicious intent whether she had reason to or not. She'd done everything she was supposed to and still somehow got attacked on her porch. Safety was never a one hundred percent guarantee no matter what you did. She wanted to be smart, but she didn't want to live a paranoid life. Hayes had made her nervous, but he hadn't *scared* her. She'd been drawn to him, not repelled.

If she was supposed to trust her gut, her gut wasn't saying *run*. She didn't want to run.

But she would have to be on full alert. She wasn't going to walk away from this job based on unproven information. She could handle herself and would make sure she was always in a safe situation—co-workers around, not working late, not being alone with him. And if Hayes showed any bad sign or made her uncomfortable in any way, she was out of there. But for now, she was going to trust her gut and Andre's word.

"Thanks for letting me know," she said finally. "There's no need to tell my mother anything at this point anyway. It's just a job."

Andre nodded and rubbed a hand over the back of his dark hair. "Okay, well, I'm going to get my paperwork out of the way and then go home. I think I forgot to sleep yesterday."

She shook her head. "You should ask one of the officers to drive you home."

He stood and stretched. "Nah. I have a toddler who thinks two A.M is an awesome time for chats. I'm used to existing on no sleep. But if I hit the point of no return, I'll call Evan or Jace to come pick me up. That's why I married them both. I always have a designated driver."

Cora smiled. "Good thinking."

"Right? I'm a genius." Andre gave her a mock salute and headed out. "Later, Junior."

"See ya." Cora watched him go, shaking her head.

Andre had a unique relationship—a husband *and* a wife—and all three parented their little girl, Lucy. When Andre had "come out" with that information at work, it had caused quite the gossip wave. *How does that work? Does that mean Medina's sleeping with the guy, too? Whose kid is it?* Everyone seemed to have a question or an opinion on the matter. *That will never last. You don't get to have cake and eat it, too. That child is going to be so confused.* But Cora had kept her thoughts to herself, all the while thinking, *He gets two people who love him so much they want to be with him forever. How amazing must* that *feel?*

Cora rolled her neck and resisted Googling Hayes on her phone. It was probably best she didn't know details right now. She just needed to get to FoxRen today, lock herself in an office, and tear apart their system until she found what she needed to take down the motherfucker who'd gotten her attacked.

Cora spun in her chair and closed the laptop she'd been working on. She didn't notice she wasn't alone anymore until the faint scent of her mother's perfume hit her. Her mother had worn the same scent since Cora was a kid. *Just because I'm a cop doesn't mean I can't smell good.* The jasmine-and-vanilla combo was comforting to Cora in a lot of ways. When she was young, it meant her mom was home from work and safe. Janet Benning had won for another night. But right now, Cora assumed it wasn't a harbinger of good news.

"So when were you going to tell me?" The words hit her in the back like tiny, sharp needles.

Cora closed her eyes, took a breath, and swiveled her chair around. "Hi, Mom."

Her mom wasn't in uniform today, but managed to look official anyway in her simple white blouse and pressed gray pants, her badge on her hip. Her dark bottle-red hair was pulled back into a stylish knot. She only had a touch of makeup on but somehow looked at least ten years younger than her fifty-two years. Effortlessly pretty as always. The frown lines on her face gave some of that effect away, though. "Coraline."

She groaned. No matter what, her mom always made her feel twelve years old again. "It wasn't a big deal. The guy ran off. I didn't get hurt."

"Do you know what it does to me to hear something like this from one of my officers instead of my own daughter? This happened last *Thursday* and you didn't bother to tell me? You could've been hurt or raped or worse. What were you doing out that late? And why didn't you have your Taser ready?"

"So we're blaming the victim now?"

"Don't pull that BS with me. You know that's not what I'm saying." The words were biting, but her brown eyes were swamped with worry.

That took the wind out of Cora's sails. "Look, I'm sorry. I went to a business mixer with Grace. It was outside of the city and wasn't over until late. I was tired and got careless. I wasn't paying attention like I should've been. Believe me, it won't happen again. And I didn't tell you because I didn't want you to worry."

Janet sank into the chair across from her and shook her head. "I told you that neighborhood wasn't the best. You can't plunk a hip coffee shop and an organic burger joint in the middle of a notoriously high-crime neighborhood and magically make it more safe."

"It's a *transitional* neighborhood. And it's not that bad. My neighbors are nice and look out for each other. And the hookers and drug pushers are at least four blocks away."

Her mom pinched the bridge of her nose, a sign she was hitting her smartass tolerance for the morning. "I don't know why you don't just move back home with me and Greg until you can afford something better. You know we don't need that whole house to ourselves and we're barely there anyway."

Cora pressed her lips together to keep the *Oh, hell no* from slipping out. This was an old argument. She loved her mother more than anyone else on this planet. And Greg, her mom's boyfriend of the last six years, was great. But Cora had done her time at home. She'd already lived that legacy. Being exposed to what her mom had would've made anyone paranoid and overprotective. Cora understood, but she wouldn't enter that brand of captivity again no matter how well-intentioned. "I'm twenty-six, Mom. I have a life plan to not become a cliché. And living in my mother's basement is the biggest of them all. I'm good."

"We don't have a basement."

"It's proverbial."

Her mother huffed a breath, her impatience obvious. "I'm worried about you, honey. Did you get a good look at the guy? Was it anyone you've seen before?"

"I've never seen him before."

"Are you sure? Could it be someone you investigated here? I hold your name out of things but it keeps me up at night wondering what might happen if someone finds out you're helping put them behind bars. Maybe it's time that you stop—"

Cora put up her hand, cutting her off. "I got a good look. He was a stranger. College-aged. I'd recognize him if it was a case I'd worked on. What I do here has nothing to do with what happened."

As much as her mom appreciated Cora's help on cases, she'd always been reluctant to let Cora continue with it. It'd started with an internship years ago—which was really a way for her mother to keep a close eye on her while she'd been in college. It was supposed to be temporary. But Cora hadn't wanted to walk away once she'd graduated. Where else could she work and feel like she was really making an impact? Where there were clear results? So she'd applied for a more permanent position that would have let her provide services to multiple precincts. Her application had been denied. Her mom had blamed it on the city not wanting nepotism, but Cora had known who'd made sure it didn't happen.

Janet pressed her lips together. "Do you think he'll come back?"

"No. He thought I was someone else. He thought I wanted to play some kind of game."

"What the hell kind of game would that be?"

She shrugged. "Who knows? Kinky sex games?"

Her mother blanched. In her jaded cop mind, kinky meant demented. She'd seen sadistic killers, and had no room to parse out sexual sadism from the sociopathic kind. They'd had that conversation after a popular movie, and Cora had given up trying to argue that there was a difference. "That doesn't make me feel any better, Coraline."

"I've already contacted the landlord to ask if he would put in an alarm system, and I got an extra dead bolt installed on both the front and back door yesterday." She lifted her purse from the desk. "And I'm carrying my Taser in my hand wherever I go. Plus, I'm not going to be working from home for a while anyway. I landed a contract with a tech company and will be in an office filled with people."

The tense lines in Janet's expression softened a bit at that. "Oh. Well, that's good at least. I hate knowing you're working at home all day. That's—"

"—the most popular time for burglaries. I know. I don't answer the door and one of the guys next door works from home often anyway. I'm careful. This was just a freak thing."

"Freak things get people killed."

"Mom." Cora's patience was waning. She needed more coffee for this.

Her mom's hands went up and she stood. "Fine. I'll stop. For now. But I want you texting me when you get home each night. Just let me know you're there and safe so I can sleep. And I'm sending an officer to dust for fingerprints on your porch. We might have this guy in the system already."

"Fine." Cora stood and arched her back, her joints popping

from sitting too long. She grabbed the laptop and handed it to her mother. "I've sent you a file with the evidence I found on here."

"Pay dirt?"

"Go throw a book at the bastard. And maybe cut off his balls for good measure."

She gave her a grim look. "I was hoping this one wasn't true."

"Yeah, me, too." She stepped around the desk and hiked her purse and laptop bag onto her shoulder. "I won't be coming in for a little while if this job goes the way I expect, but if something urgent bubbles up, let me know."

Her mom smiled at that. "Thanks. And I probably don't say it enough, but I do appreciate what you do here. I know the pay is crap."

"I don't mind helping. Family legacy to get the bad guys, right?"

Janet smirked. "I said all my life I wouldn't let you become a cop, but somehow you're here anyway. You find interesting ways to rebel, Coraline."

"At least I didn't do it by trying to date one of those handsome men in uniform out there." She tapped her chin. "Though, there's still time. Officer Cole is looking pretty hot with that beard he's rocking now. Is he single?"

Her mother gave her a droll look. "I take it back. Stick with this course of action. I don't want to have to murder one of my guys."

Cora grinned and leaned over to give her mom a kiss on the cheek. "Later, Captain."

EIGHT

Cora stretched her neck from side to side and then lifted her glasses to rub her eyes, her sleepless weekend catching up with her. Ren had set her up in a nice, though sterile, office and had given her complete access to their systems. She'd been working for hours and had already found two holes where she'd been able to break in and view secure information. There were simple patches to fix those, so she'd taken care of that, but she had no idea if that was how the hacker had gotten in. He or she had covered their tracks well. So for the last two hours she'd been painstakingly recovering email files and the activity log so they could get some idea of how widespread this was, but she was coming up empty on most fronts.

So much for walking in day one and knocking it out of the park.

A light knock sounded behind her. She slid her glasses back into place and spun her chair around. Hayes Fox's broad shoulders filled the doorway, his presence taking up all the space in the room though he hadn't even stepped inside yet. Her breath stalled. Today he was wearing dark jeans and this heather-gray T-shirt that hugged his body, displaying the sheer impact of how well built he was. A body that wouldn't yield if punched.

A body built in a prison yard.

She tried to look unaffected, not at all intimidated or like she knew too much. She'd managed to avoid seeing him today, but she'd known that would only be a temporary reprieve. The man owned the company. She was going to have to deal with him.

She cleared her throat. "Hi, Mr. Fox."

"Hayes," he said in that rumbly voice.

"Right." She managed a polite smile. "Sorry, that will take some getting used to. At my last job, my boss was all about the formality."

Hayes stepped inside, looking like he'd rather be anywhere else, and set a white box on her desk. "I'm not your boss. But no one calls me Mr. Fox anyway. It sounds like I'm a neighbor of Winnie-the-Pooh."

She blinked, the words absolutely not lining up with his deadpan delivery or what she'd expected him to say. She couldn't help the nervous laugh that escaped. "Right. Down the road from Piglet."

"Exactly."

She waited to see some kind of smile from him, some hint that he wasn't as scary as he seemed. But he wasn't going to give her anything. He was just going to stand there like he was waiting out some obligatory time period before it was acceptable to leave. Somehow that made her feel better. He wasn't trying to charm her. He wasn't trying to win her over. He wasn't putting on a front. If anything, it seemed like *she* was making *him* uncomfortable.

Which only made her want to pick him apart and figure him out. If she was going to be working with him, she needed to know, needed to get that gut read on him.

She eyed the box and then him. "So are you going to make me ask the question?"

His brows arched. "The question?"

She pointed at the package he'd deposited on her desk. "I can try to channel my Brad Pitt impression, but I warn you, it's not very good."

He stared at her for a long second and then his lips twitched, a dimple peeking through for the briefest of seconds. Not a smile but a preview that one could exist. "Ah. What's in the box?"

Lord. Just that hint of amusement had transformed his face from stern intimidation to unbearably handsome, almost boyish. If the guy ever fully smiled, any ovaries in a three-mile radius would probably explode.

"Yes. What's in the box? *What's in the box?*" The second time she said it with the desperate tone from the movie, knowing she sounded ridiculous, but wanting to see what reaction she got out of him.

He rewarded her with a half-tilt of his lips. "That wasn't bad. But I'm happy to report it's not a human head. Ren sent me over to tell you that we actually let people take lunch breaks and that you should eat. You can go out or you can have what's in the box—a chicken-salad sandwich, fruit, and a cookie from the restaurant across the street. We order in for everybody on Mondays."

"Oh." Until the mention of food, she hadn't thought about it, but now her stomach rumbled in protest. "Thanks. I guess I hadn't realized how long I'd been at this."

"You and Ren will get along well. He gets so involved in stuff he forgets to eat, too. He paced the house all weekend, trying to figure this out."

Her brows lifted. "You live together?"

Something flickered in his expression and he glanced away. "It's not like . . . Yeah, we do."

She winced inwardly. Obviously she'd pushed some button. She had no idea if it was because he was embarrassed to be staying at someone's house or if there was more to his and Ren's relationship than business. Now *there* was a visual . . .

Focus, rude, nosy girl. "Sorry, that's none of my business. Curiosity overrides my mouth sometimes."

"It's fine. It's not classified information or anything. We've shared a place since college." He peered at her screen but still didn't sit down. "So, any luck?"

Business talk. Okay, she could do that with him. That was a better plan than "shipping" her two new employers in her head or thinking too hard about the fact that this man was an ex-con. She turned toward the computer and tucked her leg beneath her. "Not much, but I can show you what I've gotten so far."

"Okay." Hayes stepped around the desk and perched on the edge of it to look at her screen. The scent of him drifted her way—fresh laundry and something earthy, like he'd rolled around in the grass.

She ignored that distraction and clicked open a few windows. "So, do you speak computer geek?"

"A little, but dumb it down for me. I'm only an MBA."

She smirked. The man didn't smile but there was a dry sense of humor hiding in there. Problem was she didn't know what else was hiding in there.

That thought had her spine straightening, the ease that had slipped in quickly evaporating. She told him what she'd found, explaining it in layman's language and showing him a bit of the process she went through. He asked good questions and seemed to listen carefully to her answers. He didn't speak computers but he was smart as hell. Analytical.

He crossed his arms and eyeballed the screen. "So what's that part you've highlighted?"

"That's when I think the system was first hacked. All the other admin access times were during working hours. This one is after one in the morning and the sign-in times in the days following are mostly night hours. So if that's the case, it means our guy got in the system about two weeks ago."

"Damn. That's a long time to have a free pass."

"Eons. And whoever it is, he or she knows enough to cover their steps pretty well. I can't see if other emails were sent. We'll have to rely on reports from users to figure that piece out. But I can see whose profiles were opened by the admin in that time period."

"So this wasn't just directed at you?"

"I don't know. It doesn't seem so, unless the person was trying to dig through files to find me. That would mean they were after me personally and didn't know who my character was in the game. But I'm guessing this is more big picture than someone just coming after me. I can't think of anyone who'd be pissed enough at me to do what they did."

"Have you had any conflicts with anyone recently that stick out? A co-worker, maybe?"

She shook her head. "No. People I worked with would've had no way of knowing I'm a member even if someone did want to mess with me. I haven't shared that with anyone."

"A former boyfriend or girlfriend, maybe?"

She didn't blink at the question. She'd gotten used to people wondering if she was a lesbian. Her clothes, her tomboy ways, and her lack of any long-term boyfriends tended to bring up the question—even from her mother. She'd wondered herself for a brief time in high school, considering that maybe that was why she'd always felt different from her female friends, but that hadn't been her answer. She wasn't gay. And she didn't want to be male. And boys had inevitably been the subject of her attraction. She'd just never felt comfortable being über girly. And when she'd tried to force the issue to fit in—subjecting herself to the dreaded make-over by a well-meaning friend—she'd felt like an imposter.

So now her friends probably assumed she was making some feminist statement that she wouldn't conform to gender expectations. But really, she just wore the things and acted the way that made her feel comfortable in her own skin. It was disastrous to her dating life but necessary for her own mental health. The only time she let herself step out of that was when she was Lenore.

She adjusted her glasses. "No. The last guy I dated had the skills for this kind of thing, but our relationship wasn't that intense and he didn't know I played the game. Plus, he wouldn't put out this much effort on my behalf. He didn't put out much effort in general."

In her periphery, Hayes turned toward her, and she could feel his curiosity. She grimaced. "Annnnd . . . that's TMI, sorry."

He made a little sound, almost like a laugh trapped in the back of his throat. "It's fine. But are you sure you can rule him out? What if he somehow figured out you were playing Hayven? Finding out your girlfriend is spending her time playing a kinky game with strangers instead of you could make a guy jealous or make him feel like he's inadequate. A guy with a twisted temper could think—*hey, if she wants some guy to treat her like that, I'll show her. I'll send some asshole over to grab her.*"

She sighed. "Kevin could be a jerk but not that brand of jerk. He didn't have feelings for me and wasn't possessive. I was just a convenient friend to hook up with. And even at his worse, he wouldn't do something to put me in danger. At the end of the day, he was a decent guy."

Hayes's gaze on her was unnerving—like he was absolutely, one hundred percent listening to every word. The fact that it seemed so strange made her realize how often people, men in particular, only listened with half an ear. "Okay, so a lazy shithead who doesn't know how to treat a woman but not an evil guy. We'll scratch him off the list."

The words were said with a touch of annoyance, like he was offended on her behalf that Kevin had acted like a dick. She had a flash of the much-bigger Hayes grabbing Kevin by the shirt and telling him to not treat a girl like a drive-thru restaurant where he could pick up a quick fix when it was convenient. She ignored the little zip of pleasure that image gave her. "Right."

"What about in Hayven? Have you had any conflicts within the game? Any scenes gone wrong? Members who gave off a bad vibe?"

Talking openly about herself playing the game was completely out of her comfort zone, but he was being so matter-of-fact that it helped tamp down some of the embarrassment. "No, nothing I can think of."

He considered her. "Look, I know it's personal, so I'm not asking for details, but it's important to look at all possibilities. Ren said that you're mostly an observer in the game, but have you actively played with anyone?"

Her fingers curled into her thigh as she tried to temper her reaction, but she could already feel her face getting flushed. "Uh . . . I don't . . ."

He leaned back, his hands loosely gripping the desk. "Okay, don't answer that yet. How about I tell you what my guess is first? I know this is a weird first-day-of-work conversation. Believe me. But this company owns and runs a kinky game. It's safe for you to assume that the people who developed that game came from that lifestyle."

Her throat was dry. "You and Ren."

He nodded, expression businesslike. "Yes. So nothing you say is going to shock or scandalize me. But I get that it's personal. So here's what I think, Cora. I think that you're in the game because you're more than a little curious. My guess is that you've participated—as a submissive."

She straightened at that. "Why would you assume that? Because I'm a woman?"

Those green eyes met hers again. "Because you got something out of a relationship where a guy used you for his own needs without giving you much in return. That's not what submission is. A real dominant would care more about your needs than his own. He would have to earn that surrender from you."

Goose bumps prickled on her skin. She knew about that version of dominance. She'd never experienced it in person, but Dmitry treated her that way.

"But the fact that you had that type of relationship shows me that there's some part of you that gets satisfaction from pleasing others and being . . ."

"Used," she said softly, the realization punching her in the gut. "God, that makes me sound pathetic."

His expression turned empathetic. "No, not at all. There's nothing wrong with that impulse. Submission is a beautiful, brave thing. But when it's undefined and directed at the wrong type of person, you can get taken advantage of. A dominant can get taken advantage of, too."

"A dominant?" She tilted her head at that. "How?"

His mouth flattened. "Doesn't matter. But the fact that you sought out Hayven shows me that you know more about yourself than you think, and I don't want you to feel embarrassed about it. Our game is supposed to be a safe place for those of us who feel left of center when it comes to sex and relationships. And you shouldn't be ashamed of that."

She rubbed the spot between her eyes. No use in hiding now. He'd pinned her to the board like a butterfly. "Okay, yes, I play as a sub in the game. It's been—an experiment. But I haven't had any major conflicts. The guy who attacked me was really the only one who badgered me. The rest of the guys have been respectful. And I play privately, so I'm not one to stir up drama or make a spectacle."

The muscles in his arms flexed as he rocked forward a little bit, a wrinkle in his brow. "Any serious relationship in the game?"

She wet her lips. *Yes.* But she didn't want to put that in the spotlight. This wasn't Dmitry's doing. "No."

He nodded and his shoulders relaxed a bit. "Okay, well let's not toss that out as a possibility yet, but what are your other theories?"

She reached out and touched the track pad to wake up her screen, happy to get out from under his scrutiny of her sex life—or lack thereof. Plus, the talking had gotten her a little too warm in the wrong places. She'd never openly discussed her attraction to kink with anyone except Dmitry. Admitting it out loud and knowing with crystal-clear awareness that the ridiculously good-looking man a few feet from her was a dominant was a little too much for her lizard brain. That primal part of her wanted to ignore the fact that this guy could be dangerous, that he'd just gotten out of prison, that she was working with him. All it wanted to see was that he was beautiful and probably knew exactly how to press her filthiest buttons.

She cleared her throat, trying to reel her thoughts back in. *He's an ex-con, woman. He might've raped someone. Check yourself.* "Honestly, I get the feeling it's bigger than some quibble between players. I'm trying to figure out if there's a pattern." She peered his way. "How familiar are you with the current players in the game?" Another thought struck her. "Wait, do you play?"

Lines appeared around his mouth. "I don't. But I'm familiar with the popular players and some of the dynamics. Ren and I both do a lot of oversight in the game. But obviously, I can't know everyone."

He knew the popular players, which meant he probably knew Lenore. Cora sent up a prayer that he didn't pursue who her character was in the game. It was one thing for him to know she played. It was another to have him know exactly how and with whom. She'd also be mortified for him to know how much she'd altered her appearance.

"Well, here's the list of profiles that were opened by the hacker. There doesn't seem to be an obvious pattern beyond the fact that these are consistent players, the ones who log in more than once a week. There are men and women, dominants and submissives. Some are local, some aren't." She swallowed as her eyes skimmed over Lenore's and Dmitry's names. Both of their accounts had been accessed. "It's going to take a while to figure out how these people are connected to each other—or if they're connected at all. Does anything jump out to you?"

He pushed up from the desk and moved closer to her screen.

But when he bent to look, he reached out to brace a hand on her chair and his palm landed against her arm instead. She jolted at the contact and her chair rolled backward, the wheels loud against the wood floors.

The reaction was completely outside of normal and his frown let her know that he'd noticed. "You okay?"

She gave a nervous laugh. "Yeah, sorry. Too much coffee this morning. I'm jumpy."

His eyes met hers, that evaluating look again, and he frowned. "You're scared of me."

Her lips parted to protest but she clamped them back, not knowing what to say.

He nodded. "Right. So you know."

"I— Yes. Sorry."

He rose to his full height, his posture going stiff and formal. "It's fine, Cora. It's not hard information to come by, and it's not a secret. I didn't mean to make you uncomfortable. You . . ." His gaze flicked away. "You made me forget for a second how women must feel around me these days. I'm sorry. I should've never crowded you."

"You didn't. I mean—" She let out a frustrated breath. "I wasn't uncomfortable. It's just . . ."

I don't know what to think. This man scrambled all of her signals. She got a flavor of danger from him, but it felt . . . sexual. Not violent. She'd been around enough criminals at the police station to recognize that niggling feeling that something wasn't right with someone, that intent to harm in their eyes. That's not what this felt like. But he'd gone to jail for rape. And was a dominant. The violence and sex intertwined there. And she didn't know how to pick them apart to determine if this man was a true threat or not.

He stepped around her desk. "You don't have to explain. You can email me the list and talk about what you find with Ren. I can get my information through him."

His tone was businesslike but there was no missing the resignation in his voice, the acceptance. He expected people to be scared of him.

Something about that made the question tumble out of her. "*Should* I be scared of you? Did you do it?"

He'd been striding for the door and he stilled. He didn't look back. "You're just going to ask me outright if I'm guilty?"

She cringed. "Well, I've never been known for my tact."

Plus, she knew her mother used that method with suspects. Be so blunt that they don't have time to mask their reaction or response.

He turned, arms crossed, expression tired. "Does it really matter what I say?"

She sat up straighter. "It does."

"I didn't do it."

He said it so matter-of-factly, so without a change of expression that she almost questioned whether she'd heard the words or not. "Okay."

"See? That doesn't change your mind at all, does it?"

"I—" She frowned, paused. "I don't know."

He gave a quick nod, like he'd expected nothing less. "I appreciate the honesty. I'll leave you to it, Cora. Copy me in on updates."

She should let him leave. She could avoid him now without effort because he'd be avoiding her, but she couldn't help thinking about what Andre had said, couldn't help sensing this . . . vulnerability in Hayes. What if the guy really had been wrongly convicted? What would that do to a person? Going to prison and knowing you're innocent . . .

"Hayes, wait."

NINE

The words hit Hayes in the back, Cora's hesitation clear. He closed his eyes and turned his head to look at her. Seeing her was still like a punch to the ribs. He'd forgotten himself for a few minutes. Talking with her, hearing about her life, her relationships . . . seeing all those subtle signs that screamed that she craved more than the previous men in her life had given her. Catching her sneaking glances at him a few times, looking at him as something other than a spectacle. It'd made him feel human again. Like a man. A little like the dominant he used to be.

Then he'd accidentally touched her and she'd nearly launched herself across the room. Seeing that fear in her eyes had been a knife in the side. Reality ripping through the fabric of that daydream where a woman could see him as more than a criminal.

He couldn't bear to stand here and take that look much longer.

"What is it?" he asked, his voice sounding like it'd scraped its way out of his throat with claws.

Her shoulders rose and fell with a breath, those hazel eyes unflinching behind her glasses. "For what it's worth, I don't *not* believe you. I *want* to believe you."

He stared at her, the statement shocking the hell right out of him. "You want to believe me?"

She flattened her palms on the desk, her short fingernails going pink against pale skin. "Look, I'm not going to lie. A big part of me is saying stay away from you. When women accuse men of rape, the statistics are overwhelmingly in favor of the woman being the truthful one."

He turned around fully and gave a nod. "Of course."

She tilted her head, consternation there. "But I also know convictions don't get overturned easily. So if they let you out, there must have been compelling evidence to do so."

He tucked his hands in his pockets, unsure where she was going with this. "There was."

"And it's none of my business and you don't have to tell me what that was but—"

"The woman who accused me retracted her original statement and admitted that someone had paid her to frame me." The words landed bluntly, but he couldn't muster up any emotion over it anymore.

Cora's eyes went wide. "Frame you? I— How? *Why?*"

He cleared his throat, that familiar chill going through him anytime he thought about everything that went down that night. "It's a long story. I don't mind telling you. Most of it can probably be found online—well, the media's twisted version of it anyway. But it's not exactly appropriate work conversation."

She frowned. "I just told you about my shitty past relationship and you labeled me a submissive. I think we've jumped that shark."

His brows rose. Cora had this layer of shyness at times, almost an innocence about her, but then there was also this outspoken side, this refusal to play games or mince words. She'd be a woman who would keep a guy on his toes.

She glanced at the open doorway, and it was obvious she was calculating her risk. *He* knew he'd never hurt her, but she couldn't trust that. So he imagined she was going through a checklist. There were people down the hall. They were at the office. She had a phone. "Shut the door. I'm willing to listen if you're willing to share it."

Hayes closed the door with a quiet click and walked back to the chair in front of her desk. He sat down and rubbed his palms on his jeans, unsure now that he'd made the offer whether or not he really wanted to do this. He didn't tell strangers his story. He didn't share. But for some unknown reason, he had this need to be honest with Cora. She wanted to believe him. And God, he needed to be believed by someone who wasn't related to him or bound by lifelong friendship. But telling this story was like cutting his chest open and letting her stare inside at all the ugly guts of his life.

"You don't have to if you don't want," she said gently.

He took a breath and looked up. There was no judgment on her face, just this open expression. *I'm listening.* And in that moment he realized that she truly was giving him an opening. This wasn't—*ooh, tell me your tawdry, scandalous story.* She wanted to know the truth. She was withholding her decision on his guilt. For now.

It was up to him to give her the information so she could make an informed decision. Honesty. That's all he could give her. "I'm guessing you've figured out that I'm a dominant."

He saw a flash of something in her eyes. Fear? Curiosity? He couldn't tell. But she answered with a stoic "Yes."

He gave a little nod. "Well, back then I was very active in the local scene. It was a big part of my life and most of my weekends were spent at a resort I belonged to. Most of my play was done there because I knew the members were vetted and the rules were clear. But I also did demonstrations for a local group."

When her brows went up he explained.

"Workshops. Negotiation skills. Rope techniques. Creative ways to edge someone."

"Edge?" She shook her head as if admonishing herself. "Sorry. I'll shut up. I have a bad habit of letting my curiosity override my filter. I'm sure that's not relevant to the story."

He shifted in his chair. "Edging is bringing someone to the brink of orgasm over and over but not letting them come for an extended period of time. It . . . can make things pretty powerful. Intense. Every touch feels like torture and pleasure all at once."

"Oh. Gotcha." Two blotches of pink rode high on her pale cheeks and her gaze dipped to his left hand where he gripped the chair.

The shift in her demeanor threw him for a second. What was she thinking? He flexed his fingers and she crossed her legs.

The simple move was like a shot of heroin in his veins. *She's thinking about my hands.* Perhaps how he'd edge someone. Maybe imagining how he could pet and pinch and penetrate with nothing but a few skilled fingers. Was she thinking about him doing that to her? The possibility was almost too much to consider. He was projecting, seeing stuff that wasn't there. He couldn't let himself go down that line of thought. *Off-limits.*

She lifted her gaze to his and held it for a beat too long. Just enough for him to see that blink of attraction there. She didn't know if she could trust him, but on some basic, physical level, she found him appealing.

Fuck. He didn't need to know that. Didn't need that kind of temptation waved in front of him.

"So something happened at the club?" she asked, her voice coming out slightly strangled.

He forced himself to focus. He would tell her his story. By the time he was finished, anything she thought she was feeling would probably burn into a bright blaze of *Get the fuck out of my office and stay away.*

"Yes." He looked toward the window, anywhere but the pretty, pink-cheeked Cora, and reeled himself in. "A request came to me through that group. A woman was looking for an experienced dominant to do a stranger role-play, one with an element of force . . . and pain. She told the leader she'd seen me speak and wanted to know if I'd be willing."

Cora's chair squeaked but she didn't say anything.

"I'd seen those types of things go badly before. Submissives trusting people they shouldn't. Guys who weren't trained dominants taking advantage of that kind of trust. So when the head of the group asked me, I said I would do it. He knew I'd done a noncon scene a time or two before."

He expected Cora to recoil at that. Even within the community, saying a role-play that simulated nonconsensual sex turned your crank was often looked at warily. But he wasn't going to feed Cora a line of bullshit. He dared a glance at her.

Cora's fingers were threaded in her lap and she visibly swallowed. "Rape fantasy."

He nodded. "Essentially. I wasn't down for anything overly violent. Delivering pain isn't my thing, but force and physical restraint were going to be major components. And the mindfu—" He caught the word before it slipped out, edited. "The mind warp of it all."

That was what had always held the appeal for him the few times he'd acted out that dark of a scene. That feeling of holding all the power, of putting his sub in the mindset of total helplessness. It could be freeing as hell for both sides. That total acceptance of normally unacceptable desires all within the safe confines of a scene. Not that he'd ever experience that again. Even if he wasn't on sexual lockdown, he could never go there again. Couldn't leave himself that vulnerable to anyone or enjoy that kind of scene anymore.

He cleared his throat. "As I'm sure you can imagine, it's not the type of scene to take lightly or mess around with. There's a lot of pre-work. I had her sign a contract with all the limits and safe words, everything spelled out. Multiple parachute cords for both of us to pull if things didn't feel right or go the way we wanted. All the things we were supposed to do. But we never met face-to-face. Because—"

"That would've ruined the stranger element," she said quietly.

"Yeah." He ran a hand over the back of his head. "So, I went forward with the scene, assuming both of us were on the same page. I met her at a bar and took her back to a hotel like planned. We got along fine. She seemed comfortable. She was supposed to resist me once we got to the room. I was supposed to get mean and not back off unless she gave me the signal or said one of her safe words. She never did. We went through with the scene. I provided aftercare and then I left. I thought everything had gone as planned. But a few hours after I left the hotel, the cops showed up at my door. She'd claimed I'd raped her and denied that there'd been any previous discussion or planning."

Cora's lips parted. "But the contract . . ."

"She said she'd never signed one. Said I was just a guy she'd met at the bar. And when I provided a copy of the contract, it wasn't her real name on the document. I had no way to prove she'd been the one to sign it. I had never met her. I had no idea if she was the woman at all." His stomach twisted, the memory of that always bringing back that sick feeling. "For a little while, I wondered if I had actually raped someone. Picked up the wrong woman and enacted some role-play she hadn't known was going on."

"Jesus."

He peered up, that old torment rolling through him. "That was the worst part. Prison I could handle, but thinking I'd hurt an innocent woman? I didn't know how I could live with that."

"Had anyone else met her before?"

"Yeah, the head of the group. He'd gone over the contract with her, recognized her as the woman who'd made the request, but he hadn't watched her sign it. The prosecution tore him apart on the stand. Made it look like he was just covering for a friend. And who wants to believe the head of some BDSM group anyway? Kink isn't understood or respected out in the vanilla world, especially around these parts. So the prosecution brought up all the 'sinister' things about kink to scare the jury—sadism, age play, humiliation. After that, I didn't have much defense in the case. They demolished my character, exposed my personal life, made my lifestyle look as dangerous as possible. There was never a doubt I'd go to prison."

She shook her head, what looked to be real empathy there. "So how'd it get overturned?"

He smirked and looked down at his hands. "Ren and his hard head. I'd still be there if he hadn't continued to hire investigators and lawyers. The guy wasn't going to give up on me even when there were times I didn't have any fight left." He rubbed the center of his palm, remembering how dark his thoughts had gotten at some points, how he'd started coming up with ideas of how he could end things in prison. The only thing that had stopped him was knowing how much it would hurt Ren. "Eventually, one of the PIs dug up that Holly, the woman, had been an escort in the past and that shortly after I went to prison, she went from living in a one-bedroom place on the bad side of town to a big house in an exclusive suburb in Florida. She'd had some type of windfall that no one could trace. We kept uncovering stones and that's what broke the case."

He could still remember that visit with the lawyer. *We've got something.* Hayes hadn't let himself believe the words at the time. His future had looked like a black hole and he'd been afraid to let any light shine through, to even grasp onto a thread of hope.

"It was almost two years before we had enough. But when Holly realized she could get arrested for lying on the stand and false reports, she came forward and admitted that she'd been paid by someone to set me up. She said she'd been threatened and was terrified not to go through with it. That she'd feared for her life."

"Paid by whom?"

Hayes clasped the back of his neck. "That's the million-dollar question. She gave a description of the guy who approached her, but it was so generic that we've got nothing to go on. And most likely, the person who approached her isn't *the* guy but just a guy who knows the guy or whatever. This wasn't some amateur job. And if she knows who it really is, she's not telling."

"Or is afraid to tell."

"Yeah." He lowered his head. He still felt that stab of guilt over Holly. Even if she had set him up, she'd probably been desperate for money. So desperate that she'd let herself go through that rough scene with him to get it. Taken his bruises, taken his body into hers. He felt sick thinking about it.

Cora peered at him, expression unreadable. "This is what you meant by the dominant is as vulnerable as the submissive."

"Yeah. I was too stupid to realize just how much back then. It was all in fun, an adventure. I never considered how much power the other person has in that kind of he-said-she-said situation."

She frowned. He could see her brain was working, taking all the pieces and putting them together, trying to make sense of them. He just had no idea where those pieces would land. He knew it was a far-fetched–sounding story. He wasn't sure he would believe it if it hadn't happened to him. He wouldn't blame her if she didn't buy a word of it.

"You have any idea who would want to hurt you that badly? You have to have some theories."

He tipped his head back and stared at the ceiling, rubbing his brow. "Prison gave me nothing but a cage, bad food, and time to think, so of course I have theories. But none have led anywhere."

"I'd like to hear them anyway."

He lowered his head to look at her and blew out a breath. "The company was booming back then. We'd taken out competitors. We had partnered with another tech company and had developed some new virtual reality technology that had big promise for the adult market. The big names in the industry were courting us, wanting to get their hands on that and a few of our other products."

"You had things other people wanted," she said, all business.

"We did. But we were also cocky and young. Way too arrogant. Flaunted our success. I'm sure we made more than a few enemies that way." God knows he had. The power and money had gone straight to their heads.

"We."

His gaze flicked up at that. "Ren and I."

She put her chin in her hand, gaze shrewd. "But they only went after you."

He shrugged. "If you knew us, you'd know that to come after me is to go after him and vice versa. We've been by each other's side since we were seventeen. We shared everything. The business, a house . . . women. All of it."

Her eyebrow twitched up at that.

He wet his lips, feeling way too exposed. "So it could've been a case of a competitor trying to cut off the head of the snake, take out the company via me. Or it could've been a matter of someone wanting to knock us down a peg. Or a scorned lover seeking revenge. I'm not sure we'll ever really know." He sighed. "All I know is that whoever it was wanted to destroy me. And succeeded."

She frowned at that. "No, he didn't. At least not permanently. You're out. You're here."

He scoffed, unable to hide the bitterness. "Yeah, I'm here where I can't even talk to a female co-worker without her worrying I'm going to attack her."

"I'm not—"

He held up his hand. "You don't have to defend yourself on that. You're smart. You assessed the risk and are protecting yourself. From the outside looking in, I'm red-level threat. I'm an ex-con who was charged with rape and has deviant sexual proclivities. I can't change any of that. All I can tell you is that I'd never hurt a woman."

"Unless she gave you permission to." The words were quiet but packed a punch.

His eyes met hers, something tense there. "Yeah. And not even then anymore. I'm . . . not part of the scene anymore."

Her lips parted, surprise there. "At all?"

"Not worth the risk. How would I know who to trust?" He said the words plainly but even he could hear the hitch in his voice, the sharpness.

"Right," she said with a nod. "Of course."

Hayes scrubbed a hand over his face, feeling drained and raw. Now she knew. Now she'd dismiss him like everyone else had. "I'm sorry if that was too much or TMI, as you'd say. I don't normally talk about any of this, but I just . . . I wanted you to have all the information. You don't have to believe—"

"I believe you."

His gaze snapped upward, shock echoing through him like a sonic boom. "What?"

She leaned back in her chair, expression unflinching and resolute. "I said I believe you."

All the air seemed to sag out of him, wonder replacing it. "Just like that?"

"Just like that. Thank you for being honest with me. I know that couldn't have been easy to share with a stranger. But I'm going with my gut. And I believe you."

Christ. She said it like it wasn't a big deal. Like people took him for his word all the time. He didn't even know what to do with that.

But before he could react, she braced her elbows on her desk, lines bracketing her full mouth. "But now we've got a bigger issue to tackle."

He couldn't process what she was talking about. His brain was still whirling. She believed him. This woman who'd just met him had listened to his story and accepted it. She had no idea what kind of gift that was. How long it'd been since anyone besides his mother or Ren had accepted his truth without question. He wanted to kiss her. He wanted to . . . No. He couldn't do any of that.

What he needed to do was listen to her. She was trying to tell him something. "What issue?"

"The person who came after you wanted to destroy you or the company. They tried to pin rape on you. What if . . ." Worry hovered in her eyes. "Hayes, I was almost raped because of your game. What if whoever set you up is coming after you again? What if they're behind this hack?"

Every ounce of warmth from the moment before drained out of him in one sinking rush, his body going cold as ice.

What if it's starting again?

TEN

Ren stood at his office window on Friday night, hands in his pockets, staring out at the dark parking lot. Hayes had left an hour ago with a hollow good-bye. That had been the routine all week. He'd shown up to the office every day, busting his ass and keeping his promise to not hole up in the house, but Hayes couldn't hide the darkness that had taken ahold of him again. And Ren couldn't blame him this time. He hoped to God that Cora's theory wasn't right, that whatever was going on with the system was a random thing, not something to do with Hayes. But none of them could shake off that possibility. It was keeping both him and Hayes up at night.

They all kept searching for answers, something to reassure them. Tonight Ren had combed through all the information he'd gathered this week. He'd interviewed each of the staff to see if anyone had seen anything suspicious come down the line or if they had any theories about who would want to hack their systems. Everyone seemed genuinely shocked that there'd been a breach. Raven and Thea, Hayven's gamemasters, had been pissed that a woman was targeted and had compiled a list of all the people they'd banned from the game just in case someone was holding a grudge.

It was a good theory, and one he'd explore, but the list of potential suspects was expanding exponentially and it was making his head hurt. Cora had reminded him earlier this week that regardless of *who* it was, they still could protect Hayes and the company. They just needed to make sure the hacker was locked out for good and that the system was safeguarded from future attacks. But he had an uneasy feeling that this was bigger than what they'd found so far. Nothing had come up yet. No one else had reported weird emails. But . . . Cora had almost gotten raped. If that had happened, it would've eventually come back on FoxRen and Hayes. It all felt a little too familiar.

He tapped his head against the glass.

A knock sounded behind him. He lifted his head and turned. Cora stood in the open doorway, bag over her shoulder and hair pulled up in a messy ponytail. "I'm going to head out. I've made some progress tonight on getting the email system ironclad, but I'm starting to see double."

Ren checked his watch. Almost eight. "Wow. I thought you'd already left. You trying to get Employee of the Year in week one?"

She leaned against the doorjamb, looking both exhausted and adorably mussed in her dark skinny jeans and wrinkled white men's dress shirt. "Maybe. Is there a prize involved with that?"

"Totally. An annual subscription to the Fruit of the Month Club."

"Sweet! I'm all over that. I've always wanted monthly fruit."

He laughed. "Seriously, though, no one's expecting you to work this late."

She shrugged. "I know. But I realize how much is at stake. It's not my neck on the line, but I feel like I'm holding a ticking time bomb and I'm the only one who can disarm it. You don't go home at five when you're the bomb squad."

He blew out a breath. "I hate that this has put so much pressure on you, but I can't tell you how much it means to both of us that you're going above and beyond. You're a superhero."

"Shh. Don't blow my cover." She gave a mock look of exasperation and hitched her bag higher on her shoulder. "And I really don't mind. Beyond wanting to help, puzzles drive me crazy until I figure them out. Any members report emails yet?"

He tucked his hands back in his pockets. "No. We sent out a second alert, but I'm sure not everyone has checked their email yet. People tend to sign up for our game with their non-primary email."

She nodded. "Well, at least it's still looking like I was the only one who got doxxed. We may have caught him at the start of whatever he was planning and minimized the damage."

"Please let that be the case," he muttered.

"I know. Fingers crossed. But in the meantime, I've closed up the holes and added a few more layers of security. We're back online for the weekend as of an hour ago. The email system is still offline, but members will be able to play again and messaging is back up. You and Hayes will also get a personal alert anytime the admin password is changed or if it's accessed during non-work hours. I'm hoping we can get all components back online before next week."

"That's good news, at least. Thanks."

"That's what you pay me the big bucks for." She gave him a brief smile. "Well, I'm going to get out of here. Have a good weekend."

He glanced back out the window and then to her. "Hey, I need to head out, too. Why don't I walk you down? It's late. I'd feel better if you didn't do that alone."

She shifted from one foot to the other. "Ugh, I hate that I have to worry about that. But yeah, thanks."

He grabbed his laptop and slipped it into his bag. "I hate it, too. But honestly, I could use the company. I've been locked in this office all day racking my brain, trying to figure this shit out, and I feel like I'm chasing my tail. I may have to install padded walls if I don't get out of here soon."

She lifted her brow. "Maybe you're hallucinating and I'm not an actual person."

He smiled. "No, then you'd be wearing a Princess Leia outfit. All of my hallucinations involve that."

She sniffed and touched her hair where her Leia buns would be. "No way. I am *so* a Han Solo."

He laughed, happy for a little levity after such a shitty few days. "You're right. What was I thinking? You have hot space cowboy written all over you."

Her lips lifted at the corner. Like she didn't quite believe him. He'd noticed that was her go-to when he attempted any type of flirting. Dismissal. Like she thought he was fucking with her. But he couldn't tell if that meant she wasn't interested or if she just assumed he flirted with everyone.

Okay, so he *was* a notorious flirt, but with her, he actually meant it. He liked that he made her a little nervous, but that she wasn't afraid to stand her ground and spar with him. She'd been a bit of a wreck when she'd first come to the office but that hadn't prevented her from negotiating terms with him about the job. And she'd been a beast this week under a monumental amount of stress. Not to mention she'd learned about Hayes's background and had tackled it head-on, asking Hayes up front what the deal was instead of whispering behind his back to get the story from others. It was the same combo that had intrigued him at the party. Bold and tough but with this underlying core of vulnerability. It captivated the hell out of him.

He suspected Cora had a lot of tightly locked doors that were dying to be opened.

He grabbed his car keys from his drawer, headed toward the door, and flipped off the lights. "Ready, Han?"

"Yep, let's blow this joint."

He grinned and lifted a brow. "Interesting choice of words considering our first meeting."

"Joint?" she asked hopefully.

"Not the one."

She made a let's-go motion with her finger. "Aaaand . . . we're walking."

He chuckled and fell into step beside her. "Come on. It's been a shit week. We're off the clock and I, for one, would like to talk about anything else but this hacker."

"So you choose *this* topic?"

"We may as well joke about it at this point. And really, you said *blow*. How could I resist? I'd lose my smartass card if I passed that one up."

She kept her face forward as they strolled down the empty hallway. "I'm making a mental note to refrain from using the word in any of our conversations going forward since apparently you're thirteen."

The words were so formal, so devoid of any hint of humor that a laugh tumbled out of him. "Fine. Shall we *go down* in the elevator, then?"

She sent him a narrow-eyed look that was all faded freckles and wrinkled nose. "I take it back—you're twelve."

"Probably. But I find it interesting that our unconventional first introduction is still making you blush. I wonder why that is, Benning."

She stiffened a bit at that. "I am *not* blushing."

He reached out and tapped her cheek. "You totally are."

"Ugh, maybe it's because I'm a nice, professional person. And it's natural to feel awkward about seeing someone you work with in a compromising position."

"Believe me, I wasn't compromised," he said wryly.

Her lips clamped together at that, the pink in her cheeks darkening.

"And I get the feeling you're not that nice. Nice girls don't become hackers. Nice girls don't join games like Hayven." They passed the abandoned front desk and he punched the button for the elevator. "Where's the fun in *nice*?"

She cocked her head. "No offense, but you don't know anything about me."

He turned to her and gave a little nod of acquiescence. "Fair enough. Let's fix that, then. We should grab dinner."

Her eyebrows went up, genuine surprise on her face. "You want to go to dinner?"

"Why not? Have you eaten yet?"

"I had a bag of Cheetos from the vending machine."

"Very nutritious. That doesn't count. Come on. There's a great Mexican place down the block. Good tacos and cheap beer. Five-minute walk. Let's do something besides work."

The way she was looking at him said she was trying to figure him out. What was his angle? This woman obviously didn't go into anything without analyzing. But he forced his expression into a neutral one. Truth was, yes, he needed a break from all this, and he needed to eat. But he'd be lying if he said his intentions were entirely based in practicality. It'd been a long damn time since a woman had intrigued him like this. Cora said she liked puzzles. Well, he did too.

And he was ready to unravel Ms. Benning.

⸻

Cora had no idea what she was doing. She'd had every intention of going home tonight and collapsing into bed. Of locking herself in her place behind the dead bolts and reconnecting with Dmitry before bedtime now that the messaging system was back up. But somehow on a random Friday night, she found herself sitting in a loud, divey, Mexican restaurant with her second beer in her hand and a ridiculously gorgeous CEO across from her.

Ren had ordered them a street-taco sampler, so they were working their way through that, but he'd been asking her questions along the way and offering anecdotes of his own. She couldn't figure him out. Sometimes he was flirty and funny, other times serious and focused on work. And she knew of his intimidating dominant side—which she was most definitely *not* thinking about because that would be *very* unprofessional. But since they'd arrived at the restaurant, he'd been nothing but friendly and gregarious. Relaxed. Hell, maybe he wanted her as his bro.

Ugh.

He talked a lot and jumped from topic to topic—a little manic—but that was kind of a relief for her. She liked when someone else drove the conversation and she could sit back and listen. It allowed her to catch her breath and get her bearings with new people.

"So you've been drawing since you were little?" she asked in between bites of food. He'd been telling her about how he got into designing games and how he'd drawn all the set pieces and the looks of the characters in Hayven.

He took a sip of his beer. "Mmm-hmm. Much to my family's horror. My mom's a medical researcher, Dad's a dentist, and my twin brother has a PhD in robotics. The artistic ADHD kid was so not in their wheelhouse. They had no idea what to do with me. And I had no idea how to deal with them."

She frowned. "That must've been tough."

The easy smile that had been on his face sagged a little and his gaze drifted to some spot behind her. "Yeah, well, what are the teen years without a little drama, right?"

"True enough," she said, though she sensed she'd somehow hit a nerve.

"So"—he turned back to her and grabbed another taco—"tell me about your first big hack. I know you couldn't have started as a white hat. You had to play first. Test things out."

The question caught her off guard and she set down her food. Her first big hack? Her stomach turned. "Discussing illegal activity with my new client would not be very smart. And I'm very smart."

He grinned. "Come on. I won't tell. We're after hours. And believe me, when I was younger, I did my fair share of things that I could be arrested for. You tell me one of yours. I'll tell you one of mine."

The waiter stopped by and asked if they needed anything else. Cora told him they'd take the check. Maybe she could distract Ren from this line of questioning. "Wow, it's getting late."

Ren's mouth tilted up, lips that were made for mischief. "Oh, no you don't. Now I really need to hear this story. Come on, did you break into the government or something?"

She sighed and set down her beer. "I wish it were something as cool as that. But no, it was just petty revenge. There was a guy in college who I hooked up with at a party after too much cheap liquor and a lot of bad decision making. The next morning without my knowledge, he took an unflattering picture of me and made a meme that went viral on campus."

Ren grimaced. "Classy guy."

"Yeah."

"And you made him pay for that, I hope?"

"I'd been messing around with minor hacks for a while, was part of a little underground club and stuff. Nothing major. But when that happened, I was so . . ." Mortified. Embarrassed. "Pissed. I broke into the guy's social media accounts and posted some updates on his behalf."

Ren leaned forward onto his elbows, eyes lit with interest. "Okay, now I need to know what these updates were."

She shook her head. "Uh-uh. I've said enough."

To prove her point, she shoved a tortilla chip in her mouth and chewed, pointing to her mouth. *See, no more talking.*

"Come on," he goaded. "Don't leave me hanging. Was it that he likes to pick his nose or he secretly loves Justin Bieber?"

She coughed, almost choking on her chip, and she could feel the mild buzz of the beer messing with her resistance. He looked so eager to know, so openly entertained. That type of attention was its own kind of buzz. She lifted a shoulder and swallowed her bite of food. "It was nothing, really. But I'm sure his friends and family were fascinated by all his deep admissions about how he humps his childhood Care Bear to get off and then cries about it. I may have also posted a photo of said Care Bear—who really was looking a little abused."

A loud laugh escaped Ren, one that rang through the restaurant. "Amazing. Mental note: Don't piss you off."

She lifted her almost empty beer and pointed the neck at him. "Wise advice. A woman scorned is dangerous. Scorn a woman with hacking skills and that's your ass."

"No kidding." He grabbed the check from the waiter and tucked his credit card inside. The guy was back in a minute and they finished up the last of their drinks. "Ready to get out of here?"

No. Yes. Maybe. "Sure."

Ren stood and pulled out her chair. When she got up, his hand easily rested on her lower back again to lead her out. So much of this had felt like a date, but she had to keep reminding herself that a) he'd said nothing of the sort, b) he seemed to be friendly to everyone, and c) he was not like this with the women he slept with. He was a dominant. She'd seen that side. This was nice-guy Ren. She'd misread the last guy she was with. She certainly wasn't going to read more into this one than she should.

They stepped outside and turned down the street that would lead them back to the parking lot outside of FoxRen.

For a while they were quiet, and Ren's hand slipped away from her as they walked along the row of darkened storefronts. Just two co-workers sharing the sidewalk. "So what was the meme? He must've really did you wrong to get Care-Beared."

She flinched at that. "Not important."

They reached the spot where her car was parked and he turned to her, concern in his eyes. "That bad?"

She looked away and her jaw flexed. "It was called *Beer Goggles: You think you went home with this but woke up to this.* I was, of course, the After picture."

"Ouch."

She shrugged, suddenly wishing they had ended the night fifteen minutes ago. "Yeah, well. Boys suck."

"Not all of us. Some of us get sucked."

Her head snapped up at that and without thinking, she shoved him in the shoulder. "Oh my God, you're . . . I don't even know what you are."

His smile was sly. "I'm completely inappropriate and incorrigible, or so I've been told. But it got that sad look off your face, so mission accomplished."

She met his eyes at that, the words pinging through her, and shook her head. "I can't believe I told you. Remind me not to drink around you. Next I'll be telling you about my first period."

"Sure, let's talk about that," he teased. "Was it like the movie *Carrie?*"

She groaned. "I resign."

"I don't accept this resignation." The night breeze ruffled his hair, but his eyes didn't leave hers. "And you realize it was bullshit, right?"

"What? The movie?"

"What that guy said. The meme."

She looked down and then made a show of digging her keys out of her purse. "I've got to get home."

"Hold up." He stepped closer to her. "Seriously?"

She crossed her arms and looked up. "What?"

"You believed him?" He stared at her, awareness dawning. "Shit. You *still* do."

"He was an asshole. I don't even think about that anymore."

She was lying. There were some things you couldn't forget. They were burned onto your psyche. She held her elbows tight, her defenses rising. The last thing she'd wanted to do was ruin this nice night with Ren by dumping all her insecurities into a big stinking pile between them. That guy in college had been a jerk. But he'd also been the first to let her know exactly where she stood in the desirability food chain. That fact had only been confirmed since. She wasn't the woe-is-me type, but she also wasn't one who could ignore hard evidence.

"Ren, I'm tired and I drank when I shouldn't have. Let's not get into our deep, dark teen traumas, all right? All of that happened a long time ago. And I think that whole thing was more about him impressing the pretty cheerleader he'd chosen for the Before side of the meme than insulting me."

"The pretty cheerleader." Lines appeared around his mouth. "I see. So you're the opposite of that, right?"

"Thanks for dinner." She turned to unlock her car.

"You have no clue, do you?" His voice hit her in the back.

She stilled.

"Turn around, Cora." The command was quiet but thrummed with authority.

She closed her eyes and took a breath. She needed to get into her car and go home. But she couldn't resist the pull, the tug of that voice. She slowly spun around.

Ren was two steps from her, affable expression gone. The hard set of his jaw and the fire in his eyes had replaced it. She recognized this man. She'd last seen him in a dark hallway. Her heartbeat ticked up a notch.

"Hear me, Benning." His gaze held hers. "You're a smart, sexy woman. I saw it the night we met and I see it even more now. Any guy with any sense would thank the goddamned universe if he woke up and had you in his bed. So fuck that dude. Anyone who would say that about someone is an insecure douchebag anyway. Don't for a second let what he said hit your radar and don't you dare take it as truth."

All the air whooshed out of her lungs.

"And don't look so shocked. You're beautiful. And interesting. And different. Own that."

"I—" She pressed her lips together. Her head was reeling, but she couldn't help the knee-jerk reaction, the instant disbelief. *Beautiful.* That wasn't a word to describe people who looked like her. That was a word reserved for supermodels and people like Grace. She shifted backward, bumping into her car. "Please don't do that."

He brows dipped. "Don't what?"

"Try to make me feel better. Give me a boost or whatever. Because, seriously, I don't need your pity."

He laughed. This sharp bark of a thing that echoed through the empty parking lot. "Pity? Are you kidding?"

Her teeth clamped together, anger rising. "You—"

But he moved so fast it made the rest snag in her throat. Both of his hands landed on the car behind her, caging her in and bringing his face close to hers. "Ready for completely and wholeheartedly inappropriate?"

He wasn't touching her anywhere but he may as well have pressed his entire body against her for the way her blood went hot. She couldn't speak. Couldn't move. All she could see were those dark eyes and she inhaled the scent of him, spicy food and man.

"I reeled myself in tonight. I asked you to dinner for selfish reasons. But once we were there and got to talking, I had a crisis of conscience. You're working with me. You've been through hell this week. You didn't need me complicating that. I forced myself to play by the rules. I made myself be good." He leaned close to her ear, his breath coasting along her neck. "But don't think for one second that I didn't want to talk you into my bed tonight, that I didn't want to show you that side of myself you saw in the hallway, and that I haven't been thinking exactly how good it would feel to have you beneath me."

All ability to breathe ceased inside her, her body going still as stone and melty as lava.

"So you can accuse me of a lot of things, Cora. Crossing lines.

Being selfish. Acting inappropriately. Because I'm doing all of those things right now. But one thing you can't accuse me of is pity." He pushed off the car, freeing her from the invisible hold, and took a step back. "I'll see you on Monday. And if you decide not to show up anymore because of this, I'll make sure you're paid through the next two weeks."

He turned and strode toward his car, leaving her standing there trembling and breathing hard and . . . way too turned on.

She wet her lips, a surge of bravery welling in her. "You never told me your breaking-the-law story."

The words rang through the distance between them, and she thought he might keep walking, but he stopped and turned around. "We'll need to schedule a seven-course meal to get through all of that."

"That long of a list, huh?"

His mouth kicked up at the corner. All bad boy and charm. "Yep, you game?"

She swallowed past the dryness in her throat, knowing what he was asking was about way more than a dinner. She was so damn far off the reservation. "I might be . . ."

His gaze heated, slid over her with open appreciation. "It's a date, then. Good night, hallway girl."

She sank back against her car, watching him go. *Good night, blow job guy.*

ELEVEN

Cora rolled over in bed, too restless to sleep. After getting home from her dinner with Ren, she couldn't stop replaying every moment, vacillating between analyzing the night to death and then getting warm all over again every time she thought of him bracing her against her car. She almost couldn't believe those things had actually happened. The way he'd looked at her when he leaned in, the things he'd said. *God.*

She'd never had a man be so blatantly sexual with her. Or made her feel so wanted—like he was truly fighting to hold himself back. That kind of focused attention was like a drug.

Guys usually stumbled into a hookup with her. Men didn't ask her on romantic dates. They didn't flirt with her in bars. It almost always started as a casual friendship that turned R-rated because it was convenient. She could earn a degree in Friends with Benefits. She'd long ago accepted that guys didn't think of her in that way until they knew her, and even then, it was contextual. *Yeah, we've had a few beers and watched a few TV shows and wow, it's late and hey, we might as well since we're both horny and have nothing else to do.*

But Ren hadn't played any of those games or made any of those excuses. He'd just put it out there. *I think you're hot. I'd like to have sweaty, kinky sex with you. You game?*

And she'd basically said yes.

She pressed her face into her pillow and groaned. *Shit.*

What the hell had she gotten herself into? She'd already decided that she wasn't meant for real-life kink that night at the party. But when Ren had looked at her with all that open *want* it'd been too potent of a rush.

I want you in my bed. I want you beneath me.

Those hadn't been his exact words but that'd been the meaning. For the first time in her life, she'd felt not only desirable but powerfully sexual. Not because she looked like Lenore. Not because she'd put on some phony act to impress a guy. But by being who she was. Without planning to, she'd shown Ren the version of herself that was most authentic, peeling back the curtains and showing the tender spots. And she'd seen it in his eyes. Ren Muroya had wanted the tomboy geek girl in the combat boots. It hadn't been an act. That attraction had rolled off him like a heat wave, making the air between them ripple with awareness.

And in that moment, she'd felt that gut-level ache to give in to it, to give him the control, to see where all that charged desire led them. She'd wanted to stick a white flag in the ground and surrender.

She could see it then in her head. Her saying yes. Ren pushing her into the backseat of her car, pinning her down, telling her exactly what he was going to do to her and how much she was going to like it.

Guh. She shifted onto her back in bed, her body restless and way too warm all of a sudden. What would have happened if she'd invited him home tonight? Would he be here now, putting her on her knees or bending her over the bed? Would he tie her up? Spank her? How would it feel to have that beautiful body of his draped over her, his cock sliding into her?

Her sex clenched at the thought and she groaned. It'd been almost two weeks since she'd touched herself. She usually reserved that for nights with Dmitry, but the game had been down. And right now, there was only one man in her head and he was flesh and blood, not a cartoon character, not an imaginary ideal.

Ren, with his dark eyes and wicked smile. Ren, whose hands were talented enough to create entire universes from his imagination. Ren, who'd let her watch him command another woman.

The last thought should've rankled, but it only dialed her temperature up more. Watching him take control had been one of the hottest experiences of her life. That taste of the forbidden shared among them all. What would that be like for real? To have all players in on the game?

Without reaching for it, the thought of Hayes slipped into her head. He'd said he and Ren had shared women once upon a time. When he'd admitted that, her libido had given her a hard kick, one completely inappropriate for the conversation at the time, but potent nonetheless.

Ren and Hayes were intimidating and sexy on their own, but together? *Jesus.* Could a woman even survive that? And how did it work? Did they pass the woman back and forth? Take her at the same time? Mouths and hands everywhere? Or did the guys touch and stroke each other, too?

Oh, fuck. Her brain tried to implode at that erotic thought and her sex turned into a pounding fist between her legs. Demanding. Insistent.

Cora gave up the fight and let her hand slide down her body, pressing where she was now throbbing and wet. She traced her fingers over the thin fabric of her panties, closing her eyes, and imagining Ren's hands there, Hayes's mouth. Or maybe both of their mouths, tongues tasting her and each other. What would it feel like to give over to them so completely? To get lost in all that desire?

Sensation curled through her as the fantasy played out in her head like a movie. She was back at work. But instead of her going to Ren's office like she had tonight, Ren and Hayes have come to hers.

She's at her desk, working, stressed. She doesn't hear them come in. She doesn't realize that she isn't alone anymore until hands slide onto her shoulders.

She jolts but doesn't move. She can smell Ren's scent, knows it's him.

He squeezes her shoulders. "Going for Employee of the Year in your first week, Benning?"

Her heart picks up speed at the simple touch, the sound of that smooth voice against her ears. "Is there a prize for that?"

"Yes, but you're going to need to do a lot more than this to earn it," says Hayes. "We don't give out rewards easily. You may have to work all night."

She swallows, closes her eyes, nerves and anticipation in her belly. "I think maybe I should go home."

"I didn't ask you what you think." Ren spins her around in her chair and pulls her to a stand. His eyes have that dark sparkle. The look from the party. And Hayes is right behind him, standing there like a stoic bodyguard, an immovable force. "You've stayed late. There's no one else here and there's still work to be done. Maybe if you do a good job, we'll let you leave."

"You can't make me stay here." The words come out in a rush, but in her gut, she feels that flurry of excitement, the appeal of the danger. She's at the mercy of these two men.

Ren smiles. "Of course we can. We're the only ones with the key to get out. And I don't feel so inclined to give you that key yet."

She closes her eyes. "What do you want for it?"

"I can think of a few things. I'm sure Hayes can, too."

"Oh, I've got quite a list," Hayes says.

"I want to leave."

Ren's hand slides down her hip and then finds the button on her jeans. He slowly drags down the zipper and steps behind her. "No you don't. Maybe we should let Hayes get a little peek of how bad of a liar you are."

Her eyes meet Hayes's stare. There's fire burning there. The desperate need of a man who doesn't let himself off leash anymore.

Then Ren's tugging her jeans over her hips. The cool air hits her hot skin as her panties are exposed to them both. Her legs are trapped together at the knees and Ren's fingers are tracing down, down, down until he finds her heat. Her obvious arousal gives her away. The blatant wetness staining the cotton fabric. She wants this. They both know it. Ren shoves her underwear aside and plunges two long fingers inside her.

She cries out from the shock and the pleasure of it.

Hayes's stare hasn't left her body and now he reaches down and adjusts the erection growing behind the fly of his jeans. He steps forward and crouches down to tug off her jeans. The panties are yanked away with them.

Now she's bared and spread, Ren's tan fingers disappearing into her cunt as Hayes kneels in front of the two of them, his gaze riveted on the slick state of her.

"I need to taste her," Hayes says in that gruff voice he has. "Spread her open for me."

Ren guides her back at that and sits on her desk, dragging her onto his lap and hooking her ankles with his. He spreads his legs, forcing hers to open like a book—a very X-rated book. The hard state of Ren's cock is pressing into her backside and she can't help but rub her ass against it. She needs some relief. She needs something.

But she doesn't have to wait long because Hayes moves forward and braces his hands on her thighs. Ren's fingers stroke her labia, displaying her for Hayes. "Look how fucking sexy she is." He spreads her obvious arousal over her flesh. "You're so needy for this, aren't you? Such a dirty girl. Taste her, Fox."

Hayes leans forward and drags the hot flat of his tongue over her sex, catching Ren's fingers along with them. She watches the scene from above, all three of them connected, and her body floods with heat.

Cora bit her lip and moaned in the quiet of her bedroom. The fantasy was spinning into vivid pictures without help and her body was rocketing too fast toward orgasm. She backed off, wanting to drag it out a little more, and reached blindly into the drawer of her bedside table. When she got a hold of the dildo she'd purchased at Dmitry's suggestion, she kicked off her panties, and brought the toy between her legs. She needed the pressure. Needed to be filled. Needed an ounce of what it might feel like to have these two men sharing her. She pushed the smooth silicon inside her slick entrance and closed her eyes, letting herself fall back into the fantasy.

"Yes, that's good, baby," Ren says against her ear. "You're going to be a very good girl for us. And then, you're not going to want to leave. You'll be begging to stay. Because you know exactly how long you've wanted this and how badly we've wanted you." Ren's hands slide up, palming her breasts and thumbing her nipples. "I can't wait to watch you ride his cock while you suck mine. Or maybe I'll suck his first and make you watch."

Her head tips back against Ren's shoulder as Hayes's tongue works magic against her clit. His thick, roughened fingers slide into her as he eats at her with singular focus. And soon Ren is groaning along with her. He adjusts beneath her and opens up the fly of his pants. He's got no underwear beneath and she feels the hot, silky skin of his cock brush along the crack of her ass. The streak of pre-come along her flesh.

Hayes stops licking her, his fingers still curled inside her. She's so close, but he's not going to give it to her yet. He gets to his feet, making Cora lift her head. He takes her face in his big palms, her scent all over him, and kisses her. Hot, wet kisses that taste like sex and need and desire all at once. She gets lost in the kiss, the feel of Ren's cock sliding against her, and then Hayes is pulling away.

His gaze goes over her shoulder to Ren. "Fuck her, Muroya. And give me her mouth."

And without consulting her, they're draping her over the desk, belly down. She's so close to orgasm, she can barely breathe. But when Ren steps behind her and grabs her hips, all she can do is beg. She needs him.

But before Ren grants her that privilege, Hayes steps in front of her, jeans unzipped and cock in hand. Like the rest of him, it's big and beautiful. He cups her chin and steps to the edge of the desk. "Suck me."

And as her lips close over the glossy head of his cock, Ren pushes into her, hot and long and deep. Fucking her across the desk like she's the most wanton woman in the world.

And she's loving it.

Cora gasped loudly, her fingers working her clit and her other hand working the dildo. The cool air from her ceiling fan washed over her overheated skin as she imagined Ren and Hayes taking her in the most undignified way possible, making her spread out for them on the desk, using her, making her take both their cocks. Her mouth full of Hayes. Ren deep inside her, his fingers teasing her ass as if marking where he'll take her next. She rocked her hips as any shred of shame slipped away from her.

The sound of her panted breaths filled the air as orgasm rumbled toward her fast. It usually took her longer to get there. But right now with Ren and Hayes in her head and her fantasy reel set on porn mode, her body careened toward climax.

Her fingers tugged her clit and her back arched.

Come for me, Cora. Show me how badly you needed us to fuck you, how much you crave this.

In her mind, Ren was holding her down, his cock pumping into her hard, and Hayes's hand was tight in her hair. She cried out, the sound bouncing off the walls of her room, and the men's names slipped past her lips like a chanting prayer. *Hayes. Ren. Hayes. Ren.*

For a few seconds, she rode that bliss, got lost in it, and then she was sagging into the mattress, gasping, and covered in a sheen of sweat.

She blinked open her eyes, the darkness and silence surrounding her, the buzz wearing off quickly as it always did. She'd long ago gotten over the shame of masturbation. But there was always a tang of embarrassment over just where her fantasies went sometimes. She wondered if other women had romantic ones, if they imagined flower petals and soft music and lovemaking. Even in her early days of sexual fantasies, hers had never had that flavor. Those imagined scenarios had always drifted into the dirtier zone, getting more filthy as her sexual vocabulary expanded. Kevin had told her she thought like a dude. Maybe she did. Whatever that meant.

She shook off the thought. At the very least, maybe she could sleep now. She got up, made a quick trip to the bathroom, and then collapsed back into bed, pulling the covers over her chilled skin.

She was just starting to doze when her phone dinged.

TWELVE

Cora blinked awake, groaning and cursing at herself for forgetting to turn the ringer off. She reached over to her bedside table and grabbed her phone.

Dmitry: Guess it didn't work out tonight. Hope you had a good week.

The simple words sent a wash of guilt through her. *Shit.* She'd messaged Dmitry when the game had gone back online that she'd chat with him tonight. She'd been looking forward to it. Had missed him. She'd completely forgotten.

Because she'd been with another guy. And fantasizing about men who weren't Dmitry.

Ugh. That sounded awful when she thought about it that way.

Lenore: So sorry. Something came up last-minute.

Dmitry: It's okay. Life happens. Ferreting out a mafia boss or just another infiltration of a drug cartel?

Cora smiled, but the layer of guilt still lingered.

Lenore: I'm posing as a woman of the night, trying to get the mafia boss to invite me into his secret lair.

Dmitry: Well, damn. I didn't plan on killing anyone this week. I'll add him to my list. No one gets to touch you without my permission.

Cora stared at the words. He'd said things like that to her before, and she'd taken it as joking. Part of the game. But was it, really? They'd both told each other they weren't currently dating anyone. And though they'd never put any labels on things, this had always felt oddly exclusive. But tonight she'd gone out with another man, had gotten off to fantasies of him and his best friend, had agreed to more. Suddenly, that felt like a betrayal.

Ren had made her heart pound tonight and her body stir. It was impossible not to be affected by him. The guy was ridiculously good-looking and charming, and somehow he made her feel comfortable around him. Comfortable and . . . sexy. Desirable. But Dmitry made her feel that way, too. And she had a deeper bond with him. One based on more than simple physical attraction.

They'd never seen each other face-to-face, but they'd talked for hours, had forged a friendship—a *relationship*. He'd become a big part of her life these last few months. But what did that really mean?

He wasn't real. Not really. He could be anyone. He could be putting on a show. She was doing that in her own way with how Lenore looked. She needed to remind herself of that. She wasn't supposed to put her life on hold for something that was a game with a stranger. That's not what this was supposed to be. So why did she feel so goddamned shitty for forgetting about him tonight?

Dmitry: Still there, L?

She scooted up her pillows, trying to shake off the thoughts and the guilt.

Lenore: Yes. Sorry. I've got a lot on my mind tonight, I guess.

Dmitry: Want to share with the class?

Her thumbs hovered over her phone screen, considering. She should probably keep this light, playful, stick to what they were good at. But she couldn't help herself. Game or not. Real or not. She couldn't lie. She and Dmitry had agreed not to share identifying details. But they'd also agreed to be nothing but honest on everything else.

Lenore: It's been a long week. I guess I'm starting to wonder what this is.

There was a long pause.

Dmitry: This, meaning us?

Us. It sounded right in so many ways. They were an *us*. But it was an illusion, a relationship hack. A cheat. She wet her lips, nerves trying to overtake her.

Lenore: Yes. I know we've been playing a game.

Dmitry: But it feels like more than that.

She blew out a breath. So he saw it, too.

Lenore: Yes. I know that was never part of the plan.

Dmitry: It wasn't. Doesn't mean it's not true. I've missed you like crazy this week. I realize that's not normal with this kind of thing.

The words touched her. She'd missed him, too. She'd wanted to talk to him about the attack. She'd wanted to share with him about her new project at FoxRen. She'd ached for that kind of late-night, download-your-day chat. That kind of talk you had with your lover. But of course, she couldn't have done those things without revealing too much. And he couldn't have told her about his day. Not really. And therein laid the problem. He'd become the man who knew her most personal secrets but nothing about her life. They were lovers and friends and absolute strangers. And she had no idea what to do with that. She had feelings for a stranger. Dangerously real feelings.

And she'd agreed to go on a date with Ren.

She breathed through the squeezing sensation in her chest.

Lenore: I've missed you too.

Dmitry: I wish voice chat was working. I feel like there's more you want to say. It's okay, L. Tell me what's going on.

Her throat felt tight.

Lenore: This is starting to affect real-life things and I'm not sure what to do with that.

Dmitry: Like?

Cora chewed her lip, contemplating, and then typed.

Lenore: I met a guy. Nothing's happened yet but it feels like something could.

Dmitry: And you want it to.

Lenore: . . .

Dmitry: Honesty, L.

She exhaled, the truth heavy in her gut.

Lenore: Yes.

Dmitry: Is he dominant?

Lenore: Yes.

Nothing appeared on the screen for a good long while, her response glaring there in black and white. But finally words popped up.

Dmitry: Is he a decent guy?

Lenore: I think so.

Dmitry: That's good, L. You deserve more than what I'm able to give you over the phone and in the game.

The response surprised her. And even though it was just print on a screen, she sensed a sadness to them. A resignation.

Lenore: But part of me feels like it'd be betraying you. That sounds a little crazy, I know. I guess I'm not good at drawing clear lines between virtual and real life.

Dmitry: If it helps, I'm so jealous of this guy I want to punch something. I'm pacing my house right now to avoid damaging a wall. I feel possessive. But it's not fair for me to put any restrictions on you.

A warm feeling crept through her chest at that. It helped to know that he felt jealous. She wasn't the only one who'd let the virtual bleed into real life. There were real emotions involved on both sides.

Lenore: We're a pair, aren't we?

Dmitry: A mess.

She let her fingers rest lightly against her phone. They'd had so many of these late-night conversations. Many had been sexual, but many others had been like this. Personal. Honest. This was what made it harder to find the boundary lines. If it were just sex, she'd be able to drop it. But somehow along the way, they'd developed more.

But she didn't know where they went from here. They were both getting in deeper than planned and things were getting complicated. She wasn't good at juggling. She could rationalize having a virtual-only sex life when she didn't want to make time for dating and had no real-life prospects. But she didn't know how she could justify shutting out real-life attraction when it fell in her lap in order to be loyal to someone she'd never get to meet. Or someone who she could meet and find they had no chemistry or that he was married or twenty years older than she was.

They were at a crossroads and the only way she could figure they could navigate it was brutal honesty. So she typed the question she'd been afraid to ask all along.

Lenore: Why do you do this?

Dmitry: Talk to you?

Lenore: No. Hayven. You seem experienced and knowledgeable and you're funny and sexy on the phone. What's keeping you from having a relationship in person?

Dmitry: Do you really want to go there, L? Do you want to have to answer the same question?

She frowned. They'd set up parameters early on. No real-life stuff. No identifying information. This is just a game. But she was tired of not knowing.

Lenore: I'll answer it. I'm here because my dating life sucked. And I think I could be kinky but am terrified to try it, to risk getting involved with someone who could hurt me or take advantage of the situation or shame me for my desires. It's hard to tell the bad guys from the good ones.

Dmitry: So you wanted to be safe.

Lenore: Yes. And I wanted to feel sexy. I'm . . .

She took a deep breath, trying to force herself to finish the words.

Lenore: just an average woman. I'm no supermodel. I don't turn heads. And I'm no Lenore.

She closed her eyes. There. She'd finally said it. He would know. She was a fraud.

Her phone dinged.

Dmitry: Have you lied to me? In any of the conversations we've had. In any of the things we've done.

Lenore: No.

Dmitry: Then you're just as much Lenore as you are the person the world knows. There's nothing average about you. I see you, L. Even if I have no idea what you really look like. I see you and that's all that matters to me.

The words brought unexpected tears to her eyes. The screen blurred and she had to blink to clear her vision. *God.*

Lenore: And you? Who have you shown me?

Dmitry: Me. This is the only place where I can let my guard down. You're the only person who sees this. I've never lied to you. But my life is complicated and there's no room for this part of me in it.

The words seemed so final, so . . . sad.

Lenore: Why?

Dmitry: That's one of those things I can't answer. And it's the reason that I can't tell you not to go out with this guy. You deserve to be taken on dates and touched and cared for. You deserve more than this.

Lenore: And you don't?

There was another long pause.

Dmitry: I know we're not playing tonight, but I'm going to give you a command. You ready?

Cora didn't feel ready at all. A cold feeling was creeping through her. But what else could she say?

Lenore: Okay.

Dmitry: You're going to be careful and smart. But you're going to tell this guy yes. And you're not going to think about me. Or feel guilty. Don't waste that emotion on me. You're going to go and live your life in the real world. You're ready for that. You are kinky. Embrace that. And when you find a deserving guy, your submission will be a gift and he'll be the luckiest bastard around.

Her throat tightened and she started to type, her thumbs moving quickly over the screen, but his next response came up before she could finish.

Dmitry: You'll never have any idea what you've given me these last few months. There aren't words. But I can't and won't let this keep you from living your life. Or even distract you from it.

She shook her head but her fingers were frozen against her phone.

Dmitry: I'm releasing you, L.

The simple words were like a linebacker hitting her chest, knocking the air from her. She didn't know what to say or how to react. He was releasing her. He was letting her go. All the months of talking to him almost every night, of having this secret relationship, this respite. And he was ending it.

She forced her fingers to move.

Lenore: This is because I'm not a supermodel, right?

She'd meant it to be snarky, her defenses trying to rally in the face of this unexpected blow. But he was silent for a long time and she started to wonder if that was the truth. Maybe he was trying to find a graceful way to bail now that he knew she was just an average girl. Maybe he was trying to feed her some bullshit to make himself look self-sacrificing. She was working herself up into a righteous anger by the time his response came.

Dmitry: No. This is because you deserve more than this. And because I don't get to fall for a girl like you.

Her whole body stilled.

Lenore: Don't walk away like this. We don't have to stop talking.

Dmitry: No, we really do. Take care of yourself, L. And don't settle. You're worthy of devotion. I wish I could be there to give you mine.

Tears slipped down her face and she started to respond but a message came up instead.

Dmitry has signed out.

The notification on the screen popped up so innocently. Four simple words. And that was that. The end. Have a nice life.

Good-bye.

I don't get to fall for a girl like you.

He'd typed the words, but she could have just as easily reversed them.

Because part of her had already fallen for him. And now he was gone.

With numb fingers, she tossed her phone aside and sank back into her pillows, feeling hollowed out and lost. She'd gone online to protect herself, to save herself the trouble of relationships, and all she'd done was set herself up for another fall.

A real one this time.

She'd just gotten her heart broken by a guy she'd never even laid eyes on.

THIRTEEN

Ren padded into the kitchen barefoot, half asleep, and in search of cold water. The light over the stove was on, the faint glow casting the rest of the kitchen in shadows, and the clock on the microwave informed the darkness that it was almost three. Ren yawned and grabbed a cup from the cabinet.

But the clink of ice cubes against glass had him jumping. He spun around, blinking and trying to get his vision to adjust. "What the hell, Fox?"

Hayes was sitting on a stool by the island, a highball glass in his hand and a bottle of whiskey next to him. "Morning."

Ren frowned. "It's the middle of the night. What are you doing?"

Hayes grabbed the neck of the whiskey bottle and gave it a little shake. "Drinkin'."

Ren set his cup aside. This wouldn't be good. Hayes wasn't a big drinker, but when he reached for a bottle, he usually went all the way. Luckily, it looked like most of the amber liquid was still in the bottle. He'd caught him early. "I can see that. Any particular reason?"

"Do I need to pick just one?" Hayes set down the bottle and stared at his glass, a distant look on his face.

"Okay, so existential drinking. Got it."

Hayes laced his fingers around the glass, not looking up for a long time and seemingly lost in his own thoughts. Ren watched him, not knowing what to say and wondering if he should just leave him to it. Sometimes a man needed to drink alone.

"You ever get that feeling like you can't win no matter what?" Hayes said finally. "Like, no matter how careful you are, your fate is already written in stone somewhere? It's like that movie we watched when we were in college, that one with the kids avoiding the plane crash but then they all start dying in other ways?"

"*Final Destination.*"

"Yeah."

Ren scrubbed a hand over his face, trying to clear the cobwebs and process this conversation. "Sure. I mean, I guess everyone feels stuck like that at some point. I felt that way when I was with Gordon. Like no matter what I did, all roads would lead back to him. Inescapable destiny."

Hayes frowned. "That disgusting piece of shit wasn't your destiny."

"No. Thank God. But that doesn't mean I didn't feel that way at the time." He eyed Hayes, trying to gauge whether he was in the mood to talk or looking for an argument. He decided to risk it. "And for what it's worth, what you're going through now isn't yours either. We're going to figure this out."

Hayes exhaled loudly. "You don't know that. We may never figure it out. I may have whoever this is lurking over me until he gets what he wants." His fingers tightened around his glass. "I've shut down my goddamned life since I got out of prison to protect myself. I've created my own cage. And still someone's figured out a way to get to me. What the hell could I have possibly done to piss off someone this bad?"

"Nothing," Ren said flatly. "*Nothing* you might've done justifies what's been done to you. Unless you've killed someone I don't know about."

Hayes sent him a grim look. "Don't joke. I came close once. You remember that first night you slept at my place when we were kids?"

Ren didn't know where Hayes was going with this but he had a feeling it would require alcohol. He walked over to the island and grabbed the bottle. He poured a shot into his empty water glass and took a sip. The liquid burned down his throat. "Sure. Christmas Eve that year I came back."

"Your parents were having that party."

Ren groaned. "Yeah a big family thing. My personal nightmare. All these people wanted to talk to me, welcome me home. But I couldn't even fake normal. I couldn't see how I'd ever fit in to that again, so I hid in my room. Then Gordon called."

Hayes grimaced. "That psychopath had radar for knowing when you were vulnerable."

"Yeah. He said all the right things that night. Apologies. Promises. And even knowing that half of it was lies, that felt more normal than what I was having to deal with at my house." Ren took another swallow of the whiskey, remembering that cajoling voice in his ear. *You don't have to pretend with me, baby. You can be who you're supposed to be. Mine. I'll take care of you. Come home with me.* "My mind was still twisted up with him. I remember thinking, *At least with him I know what to do.* Just listen and obey and fuck how and who he told me to. I didn't have to worry about more than that."

Hayes looked up at that, his gaze haunted. "I was outside sneaking a cigarette and saw you jumping out your window with a backpack." He shook his head. "I knew exactly what you were doing. God, I was so fucking pissed at you."

Ren smiled at the memory. So this was his almost-killed-someone story? Ren believed him. He could still see a lanky seventeen-year-old Hayes coming out of the shadows, smoke curling around him. They'd developed a tentative friendship at that point. He'd told Hayes about Gordon one night when they'd gotten drunk on cheap rum. About how he'd fallen for this older, rich guy and had run away with him, thinking he was going on some kinky adventure where he didn't have to worry about disappointing his parents or failing in school. But a few months into running away, he'd realized Gordon had pulled a bait and switch. Ren had found himself trapped in a fucked-up, abusive relationship masking as BDSM. Gordon had groomed him, made him the perfect slave, made Ren love him, mindfucked him to the nth degree. Then he'd started lending Ren out and charging men for the privilege. All to prove just how completely he'd owned Ren. It'd been a year before a cop had recognized Ren on the street from a flyer and picked him up as a runaway.

And even after getting returned home, Ren still hadn't labeled Gordon as the enemy in his mind. But Hayes certainly hadn't had a problem telling Ren what a psycho the guy was. So when Hayes had caught Ren sneaking out, he'd known where Ren was going. And he wasn't going to let it happen.

Hayes had shoved Ren against the wall, tossed Ren's cell phone in the bushes, and asked him what the hell he thought he was doing. Ren shook his head. "You told me if I was so desperate for someone to tell me what to do, you could do that. Then you informed me that I'd be sleeping in your bed that night."

Hayes mouth curled at the corner, a hint of pride there. "And you listened. I was always meant to be a dom."

"Yeah, well, I thought this hot guy was coming on to me. A scandalous, angry fuck with the neighbor suddenly sounded like a good alternative plan to going back to my demented ex. I didn't figure out until you got me over there that you really meant for me to just go to sleep. Fucking tease."

Hayes sniffed. "I didn't realize how what I'd said had come across until you got to my house and asked if I had condoms."

"You should've seen your face," Ren said with a smirk. "So scandalized. And so annoyingly straight."

"Not that straight. The first hour I laid there next to you, I couldn't get the thought out of my head. I spent the first part of that night freaking out that I was hard as a rock over a dude."

Ren leaned onto his forearms, this new revelation sending a curling warmth through him. "Yeah? Damn. I wish I would've known. I so would've handled that for you. I could have taken your bi-virginity."

Hayes met his eyes. "That would've been a more fun use of our time. I stayed up all night instead because I was scared you'd bolt. I could see you still had Gordon's shackles on you even though you'd left him. I knew if you saw him again, you'd go back."

Ren frowned and traced the rim of his glass with the tip of his finger. "Inescapable destiny."

"More than you realize," Hayes said quietly. "He came for you that night."

Ren's attention snapped upward. "*What?*"

"I never told you because I didn't want you to be tempted. I was still awake and saw someone pull up on the side of your house. Real polished-looking dude in an Audi. Wearing a tie at one in the goddamned morning."

Ren stared at him, stunned. "He came to *my family's house?*"

Hayes dipped his head. "I saw him out there, staring at your window, probably checking for an alarm system to see if he could get in or lure you out with some bullshit sweet talk. And I looked at you sleeping in my bed and, I don't know, I had this protective surge and all this rage welled up. I'd watched my dad manipulate my mom for so many years when I was growing up, watched how easily she'd get drawn back in when he showed the smallest of kindnesses after being such a dick to her. I just . . . I reacted. I found my dad's gun and stalked across the street like a goddamned lunatic."

Ren couldn't even form words. He grabbed a stool and collapsed onto it.

"He never saw me coming." Hayes looked toward the hallway, eyes unfocused. "I put the gun to his head, told him if he ever came within ten miles of you again, I would kill him. And that if he didn't get back in his fancy car and leave for good, I was calling in his license plate number and reporting his pedophile ass."

"Jesus, Hayes. You could've gotten yourself killed. Gordon was . . . What the fuck were you thinking?" Ren scraped a hand through his hair, old fear grabbing him. Fear of what could've been.

He'd seen Gordon beat the shit out of those who didn't fall in line. And the man had always carried a weapon. "What did he do?"

Hayes turned to look at him. "He was a smug son of a bitch. Called me 'kid' and told me you'd never be free of him. That every time you gave yourself to me, you'd be thinking of him, performing the tricks he taught you how to do. That he'd taken the good parts of you and left just a pretty fuck toy behind."

Ren's insides twisted. That kick of insecurity, that seed of doubt Gordon had continuously sowed, was like a phantom limb. The belief was no longer there, but the memory lingered—*you're nothing without me*. He gripped the edge of the counter and shotgunned the rest of his drink. "Why didn't you ever tell me any of this?"

Hayes looked down at his hands, his fingers white against the glass. "Because back then, I was afraid you'd believe it. I knew it wasn't true. I saw how special you were, how talented. I always saw that. I knew you'd come out of it and be successful. But I also knew I'd never use you like that scum had. I'd never put you in that situation no matter how badly I wanted to touch you sometimes."

Ren pinched the bridge of his nose, all the information almost too much to take in.

"That's why I've always kept that line between us," Hayes said. "Not because I couldn't imagine being with you that way. Not because we were in business together. But because I didn't want to be another person to use you. And if I'd taken you up on the offer you made a few weeks ago, I would've been using you."

"It's not using if I offered," he said, but didn't look up.

"Yes, it is. You offered because you're a good friend. Because you're a fixer. You were trying to fix *me*." He sighed. "The selfish part of me wanted to say yes. But I've got enough fucking regrets already. I didn't want to add more, especially at your expense. So I tried to find other ways to get by." The ice cubes in Hayes's glass clinked. "I started playing in Hayven."

Ren lifted his head at that. Hayes's expression was tense, like it'd taken a piece of him to admit that. Like he was ashamed. He needn't be. "I already know about Lenore."

Hayes's attention flicked upward. "Wait, *what*?"

Ren shrugged and poured himself more whiskey, though he didn't drink it yet. "I overheard you talking to her one night when you didn't realize I was home yet. I didn't meant to eavesdrop, but the name Lenore is pretty unique. So when I signed into the game the next time and saw that she only played with Dmitry, I put two and two together. Plus, I remembered that your mom's family was Russian. Dmitry made sense." Ren frowned. "You could've told me, you know. It's not like I'm going to judge you for playing."

Hayes shook his head and scraped a hand through his hair. "I didn't want you to know because it's fucking embarrassing. The big bad dominant relegated to virtual sex and his own hand. It's pathetic."

Ren leaned forward on his elbows. "You think the players in our game are pathetic? That Lenore is?"

"You know that's not what I mean," he groused.

"You used it for exactly the purpose we created it. As a safe place. Before I knew you were playing, I figured you were just relying on porn."

"Maybe I should've gone that route instead," Hayes said grimly and took another pull of his drink.

"Why?"

"Because this isn't existential drinking. It's breakup drinking."

Ren lifted his eyebrows. "Come again?"

Hayes scoffed. "Leave it to me to fuck up even the simplest things. Lenore was supposed to be a means to an end, a distraction. Something to make sure I didn't get weak and do something stupid—like take you up on your offer. I wasn't supposed to get to know her or *like* her. I picked her because her avatar was so over the top—like she was there to be shallow and make it all about sex. But somehow, in the sea of people in Hayven, I managed to choose this sexy, fascinating woman. And I got attached. Can you believe that shit? I don't get attached to subs. You know how I am."

Ren took a sip of his drink. "I'm guessing she bailed?"

"No. I did," he said with a heavy breath. "I wasn't the only one to get attached. I had to end things tonight because she was starting to let it affect her outside relationships. I've strung along a woman who should've never been wasting time on me and I hurt her tonight. And I know I've been hurting you, too." He looked up. "It feels like no matter what I do, I'm screwing things up or hurting people because I'm having to live scared. And I'm tired of it. I'm fucking angry, man. My life's been stolen away. And I have no idea how to find my way back. And that . . . is pissing me the hell off."

Ren took a breath, something like relief stirring in his chest. This is what he wanted to see. Angry Hayes. Hayes who wasn't going to take shit lying down. The Hayes who'd risked his own safety to make sure Ren didn't get into Gordon's car that Christmas Eve night. The man who'd saved him and challenged him to be more.

Ren met Hayes's stare. "Maybe it's time you stop looking for a way back and look for a way forward."

Hayes's jaw flexed. "And how am I supposed to do that?"

"You said it yourself. You've been living scared. Stop."

"Right. Sure. It's that simple," Hayes said, sarcasm dripping from his words.

"It can be." Ren pushed the stool back and stood, something settling inside him and an utter calm coming over him. "You said you wanted me. You said you were tempted. If that's the truth, then come to bed, Fox. Take what you wanted back then. What we both wanted. Stop being scared that we're not strong enough to handle it."

A tortured look flashed through Hayes's eyes. "Ren . . ."

He put his hand out. "I can't be your Lenore. But I know how to submit. And I promise I'm a whole lot better than a whiskey hangover."

FOURTEEN

Hayes stared at Ren's outstretched palm, the ache in his chest making him feel like he was going to crack open. "I said I don't want to use you."

Ren stepped closer, took the glass out of Hayes's hands, and drained the contents. Hayes couldn't help but watch his throat work, couldn't stop his gaze from sliding down Ren's bare chest, the tattooed skin, the beautiful lean body he was almost as familiar with as his own.

When Ren plunked the glass back on the counter, there was a calmness there in his eyes. "Use me, huh?"

Hayes swallowed. Nodded.

Ren's lips lifted at the corner. "I hate to break it to you, but I'm not some dude you picked up at a bar. I'm not one of those guys you experimented with in college. This isn't a hookup, Fox. We've been in a relationship since we were seventeen." Ren leaned forward. "You wouldn't be using me. You'd be consummating what's already there."

"What's already there," Hayes repeated.

Ren cocked his head, a wry look on his face. "You think I would've put up with your broody ass for so long if I didn't already love you?"

Hayes blinked, the words like a cymbal crash in his head.

"I mean, goddamn. I've had to deal with you for all these years, pine and write you letters while you were in prison, accept your questionable taste in music, share women with you and *not* touch you, too. And I've gotten absolutely no fringe benefits from all these selfless acts. Not even a hand job every now and then. You suck as a boyfriend. Just so you know."

Hayes stared at him, the words hitting him like a cattle prod. "You *love me*?"

Ren crossed his arms over his chest, brashness there but also a hint of vulnerability. "What? You don't love me back, asshole?"

"Well, yeah, but . . ." The words hung in the silence. They'd slipped out easily, without effort or angst. Hayes had never told anyone except his family that he loved them, but he felt the simple truth of the statement like it was part of his DNA.

"But?" Ren lifted a brow.

He shook his head, the mild buzz from the alcohol doing nothing to soften the impact of this revelation, and scrunched his brows. "But nothing, I guess."

Ren grinned. "Excellent. So you love me."

"I . . . Yes." *Yes.* "I love you."

Something flickered in Ren's eyes, relief maybe, but it was gone as quickly as it appeared. He leaned forward and braced his hand on the counter, a smug look of challenge replacing the tender one. "Good. Now, what are you going to do about it?"

Hayes stared at him, and it was like a curtain parting, a new world revealing itself. They *loved* each other. Had for a long time. He could have this. Without guilt. He could touch Ren. They both wanted this.

That knowledge felt like chains falling away from his limbs, that dragging pull of weight lifting from his chest.

He rose from the stool, a jolt of something powerful and freeing moving through his veins, and reached out to grab the waistband of Ren's pajama bottoms. Ren's fists clenched, like he was fighting hard to keep himself still, fighting not to take over. Hayes dragged him closer, the warmth of his skin radiating against Hayes's knuckles. "I'm going to take you to bed."

Desire darkened Ren's gaze. "You sure you remember how to do this, Master Hayes?"

The sound of the old name rang through Hayes, rousing long-dormant things. It'd been a hell of a long time since anyone had called him that, and Ren's roughened voice saying it was like a physical stroke to Hayes's cock. But he wasn't going to require that formality from Ren. The last thing he wanted to do tonight was trigger bad memories for him. "You don't have to submit. I just want you."

Ren swallowed hard and held the eye contact. "Maybe I need it as much as you do. Maybe you're not the only one who's been living a little scared."

Hayes inhaled through his nose, trying to bank the need fighting to overtake him. Four years. It'd been four years since he'd had anyone in his bed, since he'd touched or been touched. Four years since anyone but Lenore had kneeled for him. And over a decade since he'd first wanted Ren that way. His voice was strained when it came out. "What's your safe word?"

Ren's gaze flicked away. "I never had one."

The admission twisted Hayes's gut. That fucking sociopath hadn't given Ren any kind of reprieve. A sixteen-year-old kid trapped with someone with no mercy, no heart. "Well, you'll always have one with me. Pick one."

"Black."

"Good." His hand was still gripping Ren's waistband and he let his fingers slip below the elastic. It didn't take long for him to reach what he was looking for. He brushed his knuckles over the damp head of Ren's cock, earning a hissed breath from Ren and an answering punch of desire in his own gut. Hayes groaned. It took everything he had to reel in the impulse to yank Ren's pants off right there, turn him around and bend him over the counter. The primal ache to just fuck and fuck until they were both raw and

spent was like a beast snarling at the gates. The years of deprivation pressed at his will, those years in a cage urging him to act like
a starved animal. But he wouldn't rush this. He wouldn't fuck this
up. "Take me to bed, Muroya. We've both waited long enough and
I don't want to do it on the kitchen floor. At least not this time."

Ren smiled this smile of dirty intent and grabbed him by the
shirt. "Let's go, Master Hayes."

They were quiet as they made their way down the hallway, but
Hayes was sure his pounding heart could be heard down the block.
Ren had asked if he still remembered how to do this. He sure as
hell hoped so.

Ren bumped open the door to Hayes's bedroom with his elbow.
Stacks of books lined the side of the bed and a big-screen TV dominated the other wall. Other than that, Hayes hadn't put out any
personal things. All his stuff was still in boxes in storage. It was
like he'd re-created an upgraded version of his prison cell. Bland.
Empty. Temporary.

Depressing as shit.

"Not my room," Hayes said.

Ren didn't question. He just backed up and went farther down
the hallway until they reached his room. Unlike Hayes's bedroom,
Ren's looked lived-in, comfortable. Modern pen-and-ink artwork
on dark blue walls, a king-sized bed with mussed white sheets,
clothes thrown over a leather bench by the window, and no televi-
sion to distract. Ren had always believed that bedrooms were for
sleeping and fucking, not electronics.

Hayes wasn't coming here to sleep. Ren stepped inside ahead of
him, and Hayes shut the door with a push of his foot. He eyed the
armoire on the far side of the room. It'd been a while, but he
doubted things had changed. Ren had always kept a good supply
of toys tucked away in that cabinet.

But Hayes didn't need any toys tonight. Ren would be more

than enough. Too much probably. It would take everything Hayes had to maintain his control.

"Turn around. Let me look at you."

Ren faced him, thumbs hooked in the waistband of his pants, a cocky stance. Some things never changed. The guy had always known he looked good. Not that Hayes could argue the point. Finely honed muscles beneath beautifully tattooed skin and deep brown eyes that made filthy promises he knew Ren could keep. Ren had always turned heads and wasn't ashamed to use that to his advantage. Hayes smirked. "Your dom is showing."

Ren sniffed, all challenge and smugness. "Guess you'll have to fix that for me, sir."

Sir. The formal address made Hayes's cock flex against the zipper of his jeans. Hayes took slow steps toward him, closing the distance between them and holding his gaze. He stopped in front of him. Ren's erection was prominent against the soft fabric of his black pajama bottoms. Hayes's fingers flexed, wanting to feel that heat against his palm, but he resisted. *Patience.*

"Show me you're not too drunk to be making this decision."

Ren smiled, stood steadily on one foot, and started reciting the alphabet backward.

Hayes cut him off before he reached *A.* "Undress me."

Ren wet his lips, the subtle shift in his demeanor revealing he wasn't as calm and collected as he wanted to appear. He stepped closer and went for the buttons on Hayes's shirt. He focused on the job. One button. Two. Three. But the simple feeling of Ren's fingers brushing against Hayes's chest was enough to send goose bumps over his skin and more blood to his cock. The fabric came open and Ren's eyes raked over him, open hunger there. He pushed the shirt off and onto the floor.

"I like the way you look at me. What are you thinking? No editing," Hayes said, voice gruff.

"That your body is fucking amazing. That I'm glad I finally get to touch you." His mouth twitched into a chagrined smile. "That I wouldn't mind seeing you tied up for me so I could explore."

The response didn't surprise him. Ren had been trained to be Gordon's slave, but he'd been a dominant for far longer. The guy was a natural in that role. And though Hayes had never had an inclination to submit, the image didn't turn him off like he would've expected. Trust was a funny thing. "What would you do to me if you had me bound?"

Ren lifted his gaze, his hands gripping Hayes's belt. "I'd take my time with you. Edge you. I haven't forgotten how you are in scenes. You get off on holding back and denying yourself, focusing all your energy on the sub. And right now, knowing how long it's been, I'd be able to torture you really good. I bet I could get you to come with barely a touch." The backs of his fingertips teased against Hayes's hip bones. "I'd strip you naked, tie you up, and then I'd describe all the things I've imagined doing to you."

Hayes's throat was dry, but he didn't want Ren to stop talking. "Like what?"

Ren slowly pulled the leather belt through the buckle. "I'd tell you in detail how I would suck your cock. How I'd put my tongue everywhere and fuck you with my fingers while I did it. Then I'd describe how it would feel to be deep inside me. How tight and hot that'd feel around your dick. How hard I like to be fucked."

Hayes groaned.

Ren dragged the belt out of the loops. "Or I'd tell you about those times when I'd sleep over at your place and stroke myself and fuck my fingers while you slept next to me. How I'd come all over myself and have to clean up without waking you."

"Fuck." The words were like gasoline on a bonfire. Ren dropped the belt to the floor and Hayes grabbed Ren's wrists. He drew them behind Ren's back, holding them there. "You're a dirty bastard. You got off while I was sleeping?"

"You're a deep sleeper."

"Tell me what you'd think about when you did it."

Heat flashed in Ren's eyes as their erections brushed against each other. Hayes's grip tightened.

Ren didn't look away—bold as ever. "You. Holding me down, taking whatever you wanted, shoving your cock in my mouth, my ass, using me. Fantasies of you always had a flavor of force."

Hayes frowned. "I would've never forced you."

"I know. That's why I could go there in my head. You were the opposite of everything I'd been exposed to before that point. With you, I knew I could get the thrill of that game without the threat. I'd always been attracted to the game. That's what got me in trouble in the first place."

The admission was almost too much for Hayes to take in. A force fantasy was what had gotten him thrown in jail. The thought of ever doing that again scared the hell out of him. And in general, his dominance had always been on the more pleasure-focused side rather than the edgier one. But he couldn't deny that there was a piece of him that craved that darkness sometimes. And the thought of playing that game with Ren was all kinds of tempting.

He released Ren's wrists. "Finish what you were doing."

Ren inhaled and nodded, like he was dragging himself back from that fantasy reel as well. He went to work unfastening Hayes's jeans. "You did this for me that first night. You probably don't remember."

"Oh, I remember." The words rumbled from Hayes as the memory played in his head as fresh as ever. "You were wearing jeans that were two sizes too big for you and black briefs. You got hard. I got awkward."

Ren smiled but didn't look up as he unhooked the button on Hayes's jeans and dragged down the zipper. "I was hoping you'd take it as an invitation."

"I wasn't ready for you." Hayes planted his hands on Ren's shoulders. "But I'm RSVPing now. Get on your knees, Muroya."

Ren stilled at that, his gaze jumping upward.

Hayes pushed. "I said *knees.*"

Ren lowered down, and for the first time, Hayes saw a flicker of that vulnerability, a snap of nerves, reminding Hayes that this was the first time Ren had submitted or bottomed for a guy since Gordon.

Hayes took a steadying breath. "You have a safe word."

"I'm well aware."

Hayes took that for what it was. Ren would use a safe word if he needed it. "Touch me. Show me you know how to handle cock."

Ren's expression lit with a hint of that trademark wryness and he dipped his hand in the open fly of Hayes's jeans. Hayes had skipped underwear today, so there was no barrier when Ren wrapped a hot hand around him and stroked.

Hayes groaned and he tipped his head back. "Goddamn."

The physical sensation of being stroked by someone other than himself was mind-blowing in its own right, but knowing it was Ren stoked the embers to a blaze. It'd been too long. Too fucking long since someone else's hands had been on him. So many lonely nights in prison. So many long nights since. There was no helping it, no time for analyzing. He had planned to simply put Ren on his knees for a test, to make sure he was okay with this, not to be selfish. But primal instincts took over. The hand and hot breath on his dick were too much.

"I need your mouth, Ren." His voice sounded choked to his own ears, a throat knotted with warring factions. His fingers dug into the hard muscle of Ren's shoulder.

"Yes, sir." The soft hush of fabric sounded as Ren tugged Hayes's jeans down and off. Not hurried. Not frantic. Methodical. Tortuous. Hayes's stomach dipped in anticipation. But nothing topped the soft sound of pleasure from Ren when he dragged his fingers through the trail of hair that led down Hayes's abdomen and then took Hayes's cock in his hands. That under-the-breath curse. A simple whispered word that meant everything.

That was all Hayes needed to hear. There was no masking that reaction, what it meant. Ren wanted this as much as he did.

This was right.

Ren stroked him with long, confident fingers, slow and sensual, spreading the fluid at the tip over the head and teasing the underside with his thumb, mapping him, learning the terrain. Hayes's fingertips bit into the flesh of Ren's shoulder, and he tried not to think of why Ren would be so good at this, about how he'd been trained to please. The soft light of the lamp surrounded them, cocooning this forbidden exchange in a cloak of silence, a dream world, and it allowed his dominant side to shimmer fully to the surface. "I didn't tell you to play. Give me your mouth."

Ren continued to tease. To stroke and cup him. A challenge. *Make me.*

Force me.

It sparked something in Hayes, flint against steel. Acting on nothing but pure gut, he reached out and gripped the back of Ren's head. He hadn't fooled around with a guy since college. So this was a different sensation, the short, silky strands against his fingers instead of long locks, but not an unwelcome one.

Ren grunted at the grip but didn't fight him as Hayes guided him forward. The second Ren's lips closed over the head of Hayes's cock and slid down its length, fireworks went off behind Hayes's eyelids. "Oh, *fuck*."

It'd been years. *Eons.* He'd thought a blow job was a thing a man could never forget, but he had. He'd forgotten the intense bliss of that hot, wet suction, that sensation of every molecule in his body being attuned to one very specific place. He tipped his head back and held on to Ren like a life raft, rocking forward and forcing himself to make it last, to go slow, to not ram his friend right through the wall with the force of his need.

Ren groaned around Hayes's shaft like he was relishing every single suck, like he could do this forever, and then he shifted forward, taking Hayes to the back of his throat and holding him there.

A chain of filthy words slipped out of Hayes in one uninterrupted rush, and Ren only took him deeper. Both Hayes's hands clamped around Ren's head. "Christ, Muroya. You trying to kill me?"

Ren eased back a bit, his tongue dragging along the underside of Hayes's shaft at a painfully slow pace.

The sudden change made Hayes's eyes flutter open. He had to see, had to look. He glanced down, finding Ren staring up at him, the warm glow from the lamp lighting half his face. Hard angles and hot desire. It was a bizarre sight, his best friend with his mouth wrapped around his cock. But it was the heavy lust in his eyes, a flavor of which Hayes hadn't seen before in Ren, that tugged something inside him. They'd shared women. He'd seen Ren in many compromising and intimate moments, but this was different. It wasn't submissive exactly. There was still that I-dare-you gleam in Ren's gaze, but there was satisfaction, too. He was getting off on knowing he was responsible for Hayes's pleasure.

He gripped his hair tighter. "I didn't tell you to stop."

Ren's eyes narrowed as he held the gaze and took Hayes deep again, working his throat and blowing Hayes's mind to bits with every sweep of his tongue. Then he cupped Hayes's sac in a warm palm and slid a teasing fingertip farther back.

More cursing fell from Hayes's lips and he gritted his teeth to hold back the orgasm.

Staring at each other was almost too intense. It was like they were at war. Who was going to win? But somehow it made it hotter. More electric. This was a side of Ren he'd never seen. The great dominant on his knees and enjoying it.

He licked his lips. "You like doing this, Muroya? Does sucking my cock make you hard?"

Ren's gaze lit with wicked satisfaction.

Hayes tipped his head up. "Show me."

Ren pulled off with a wet popping sound and leaned back. Hayes looked down, finding an impressive outline in Ren's pants. The sight made his blood run hot. He'd seen his friend with a hard-on and naked more times than he could count. But this was different. This was for him. Ren was getting off on submitting. Hayes's voice was hoarse when he spoke again. "Take it out and jerk yourself while you suck me. But don't you dare come."

Ren's throat worked, but after a brief second, his hand went to his pants. He dipped his fingers inside the fly and pulled out his long, curved erection. It was a cock the women they'd been with had always said hit them in just the right place. Now Hayes found himself wondering if it did the same in men.

"Give me your hand," Hayes said, the words coming without thought now. Ren lifted it and Hayes spit in his palm. "That's all you get. Fuck yourself and don't come unless I tell you to."

Ren's cock flexed against his belly and fluid glistened at the tip— a ringing endorsement that this was working for him, giving Hayes an extra boost of confidence that he hadn't taken this too far. Yet.

Ren wrapped his hand around himself and stroked. Hayes was fixated by the tight grip, on the way the slick head darkened when Ren moved his hand toward it, but soon the view was blocked when Ren leaned forward and licked Hayes from scrotum to tip, making him moan and forget everything else he'd been thinking.

Hayes couldn't watch anymore after that. He was too lost. Too far gone. He let his head fall back and went along for the ride.

Ren sucked and licked and massaged, edging Hayes, knowing exactly how to bring him to the brink and then back off. And all the while the wet sound of Ren's hand on his own dick played background music. The guy was taking his fucking time. Walking that fine line between pleasurable and unbearable for them both. And Hayes should've wrested back the control. The sub didn't get to tease him, but it felt too fucking good and he wanted to savor this.

But soon, both of them were too close to wait any longer. The sound of Ren's fist became faster, more frantic, and the motions of his mouth matched pace. Hayes couldn't stop the grunts he was making, and before long, he was shoving his cock down Ren's throat, out of control and desperate.

He didn't want to come this way. He didn't want this to end this quickly. Sensation rocketed through him like a locomotive. "Can't. Gonna."

He gave Ren the chance to pull off, assumed he would, but Ren only doubled his efforts, taking him deep and pressing a fingertip against Hayes's hole. Stars burst behind Hayes's eyelids, leaving streaks of light, and the force of his release barreled through him. A shout scraped over his throat as he came, long and loud, and shot everything he had down Ren's throat.

Ren groaned along with him and hummed through his own orgasm, finally pulling off and coming all over his hand and the pristine wood floors.

Messy. Out of bounds. And so fucking hot, Hayes's cock jerked in aftershock.

Hayes's head bowed and his heart thumped like it was going to pop out of his chest. Sweat rolled down his back. But despite the orgasm, his body didn't settle. He still felt this pounding need. Too many years of denial were built up. His cock was still half-hard.

He reached out and grabbed Ren's bicep, helping him to his feet. "You came without permission."

Ren smiled, lips slick from sucking Hayes's cock. "Guess you should do something about that."

Hayes couldn't help it. He laughed. Goddamn, how had he not realized he loved the arrogant son of a bitch? He grabbed Ren by the neck, tugged him forward, and kissed him.

Ren stiffened for a moment, like he hadn't seen that coming, but then he gripped Hayes's waist and pressed his mouth and body to his, giving in to the kiss. Skin to skin. Lips and tongues colliding.

Hayes sank into the connection, the taste of his come mixing with the lingering flavor of whiskey and Ren. His hand tightened on Ren's neck as he deepened the kiss and soon his cock was hard and bumping up against Ren's. *Yes.* Apparently, he wasn't the only one up for a round two. They ground their hips against each other and hands explored until they were both fully hard again.

Hayes had forgotten how erotic it was to simply kiss and be touched, to have no barriers, to play. He'd rarely done that with subs. The scenes had always been more structured. He walked Ren backward until he hit the bed. They tumbled onto the mattress together, making out like teenagers and grunting and groaning like they were going to explode. Ren was as aggressive as he was, taking and touching and shifting their positions. But when Hayes pinned him down and locked his arms against the bed, he didn't miss the catch of breath in Ren's throat.

Hayes broke away from the kiss. "Supplies?"

Ren's pupils were so big his eyes had gone black, blitzed on lust. "Drawer on the right."

Hayes reached over and rummaged around, grabbing what he needed. He tossed the lube and condom on the bed and braced himself over Ren. "Want to know a secret?"

Ren's Adam's apple bobbed. "What's that?"

Hayes leaned down next to Ren's ear. "I knew what you did in my bed. I used to pretend to sleep so I could listen to how hot you sounded when you came. I'd jerk off every morning remembering it."

Ren hissed out a breath.

"Now let's see if all that fantasizing was worth it."

He climbed off Ren and flipped him onto his stomach. Part of him wanted to fuck him face-to-face but that's not what Ren had fantasized about. He'd wanted dominant, aggressive Hayes. He'd wanted to be used. And Hayes would happily give him that.

Hayes yanked Ren's pants the rest of the way off and then shoved Ren's thighs forward, spreading him. The sight was one that had Hayes's cock painfully hard again. The strong, sleek body of his best friend glazed in sweat and open for him. Hayes loved women and their bodies, that softness and all those curves. He loved to worship at that altar. But there was also something unbearably arousing about a powerful man like Ren surrendering to him, especially knowing Ren didn't afford anyone else this privilege.

Mine.

He poured lube into his palm and took Ren's cock in his hand, stroking it and making it glossy and slick, taking his time and getting Ren rock hard again. He ran his thumb over the slit and teased.

Ren's fingers curled into the sheets. "Fuck, yes."

"You think you can handle me, Muroya? I know it's been a long time." Hayes slicked lube over Ren's opening, massaging and teasing and enjoying the sounds the moves earned from Ren. He pushed the tip of his thumb inside.

"*Christ.* If you don't fuck me right now, I really may tie you down and beat you," Ren said, his hands now tight fists. "You're not going to hurt me. I still use toys sometimes. Please. Fuck."

"Maybe I'll just tease you all night. Play. I mean, I've already come. I've got time."

"Oh, fuck you. You've made me wait for a goddamned decade. You aren't that much of a sadist." Ren rocked back, taking more of Hayes's thumb.

The sight of part of him disappearing into Ren's body and the feel of Ren's muscles tugging was all it took. His cock flexed against his belly and need roared through him. He pulled back and grabbed the condom, fumbling for a bit. Out of practice.

But once he had it rolled on, everything else came as natural as breathing. He grabbed Ren's hips, positioned him just how he wanted him, and slid home.

FIFTEEN

Ren's eyes nearly rolled back in his head when Hayes's thick cock breached him. The sound that burst from Ren's throat probably sounded like pain, but it was one hundred percent goddamned pleasure. He reached down and grabbed his own cock, squeezing and stroking to intensify the high.

He hadn't bottomed for a guy since Gordon. Part of him had wondered if that side of his desire had been stolen after what he'd been through. He'd been with men since then and never had the urge. But with Hayes it'd always been there. Only in the fantasies where his best friend starred did that craving surface. And now the man was inside him.

"Tell me you're okay," Hayes said from behind him, breathless as he eased in and seated deep. "Please God, tell me you're okay, because *fuck* . . ."

Ren smiled into the sheets. He loved hearing Hayes so undone. How many times had he imagined this those nights when he was a teen? The straight, bossy neighbor boy breaking all the unwritten rules between them and taking him rough. "I'm so okay. You don't have to be gentle. Fuck me like I know you want to, like a man who's been celibate for four years. I can handle you, Fox."

Hayes's grip tightened on Ren's hips. "You have no idea the things I want to do to you. Don't tempt me."

Ren looked back over his shoulder, the sight of Hayes's sweaty and flushed muscles flexing as he slowly thrust into Ren was possibly the hottest thing he'd ever seen. "Do it. Don't fucking insult me. I won't break."

Hayes's gaze met his, ferocity there. Wildness. Danger. *There he is.* That was the man who'd come out of prison. Angry. Hungry. Dominant.

But he was holding himself back. Chains still on him.

Ren shifted back, taking Hayes all the way and tightening his muscles. Daring him.

It was too much. It was all over Hayes's face. The chains snapped.

Hayes made a sound close to a roar and dragged Ren almost all the way off and then yanked him back onto his cock with a harsh grip, the sound of skin smacking skin and Hayes's animalistic sound of pleasure filling the room. And that was all it took. Before long, they were gasping and fucking hard and rough. Ren would have bruises. He would be sore. He didn't care. They both needed this.

Ren couldn't keep his head up or watch any longer. He buried his face in the pillow and jerked his cock with his hand, his muscles starting to quake with warning. Hayes angled himself inside Ren just right, rubbing over the perfect spot with each deep stroke. Ren's body lit on fire. "Fuck, fuck."

"That's the idea," Hayes said, thrusting hard, making the headboard tap the wall. "You feel so goddamned good. So hot and tight. Perfect."

Sweat rolled down Ren's face and he lost a grip on his thoughts. All that was left were the sounds, the skin, the thick cock impaling him, and his slick hand jerking himself with so much vigor it almost hurt.

Hayes draped over Ren's back and grabbed his hair, gripping tight and pressing Ren's cheek into the mattress. "That's it. Take what I give you. You're not in charge right now. You're mine. You're fucking *mine.*"

That was all it took. The command in his voice, the impersonal way he pushed his face into the bed, like he was just a tool for his pleasure, pushed all those buttons Ren wasn't sure he had anymore. "Can't . . . Fox."

"Go for it, sub. Mess up your sheets and show me how much you like having my big cock shoved in your ass."

"Shit, *shit*." Ren had thought he'd last longer considering he'd come already, but there was no stopping it. His cock pulsed in his grip and he shot all over the sheets and his stomach, crying out and begging for harder and faster from Hayes.

Hayes obliged, his pace a punishing speed and his big body crushing Ren into the bed. Then he buried deep, his hand tightening in Ren's hair, and his body stiffening. The shout that came out of him bounced off the walls like thunder and Hayes came in long, powerful thrusts.

By the time Hayes had emptied himself into the condom, Ren was panting like he'd run a marathon and swam a few miles. He blinked his eyes open, feeling dizzy. "Jesus."

Hayes slid out carefully, tossed the condom in a trashcan by the bed, and then collapsed onto his back next to Ren. He stared up at the ceiling, his chest still rising and falling with rapid breaths. "Holy shit."

Ren tucked his arm under his head and used what little energy he had left to roll onto his side. His body protested the movement but that used-up ache was its own reward. "I know, right? I'm a fantastic lay."

Hayes turned his head to look at him and then broke out into a loud, belly-deep laugh. One that shook the bed. "You're such a shit."

Ren couldn't keep the grin off his face. How long had it been since he'd heard that laugh? God, he'd forgotten what it sounded like.

Without thinking too hard about it, he leaned forward and kissed Hayes. Part of him was worried the guy would backtrack now that the immediate lust had been satisfied, but Hayes didn't flinch or pull away.

He kissed Ren back and then smiled. "Hold that thought. I'll be right back."

Hayes climbed out of bed and walked away in all his naked glory. Muscles flexing, body still glistening with exertion. Ren watched him disappear into the bathroom and groaned. Damn. He'd better not wake up and this all be some wet dream. Because this felt too good to be real.

The shower came on and soon steam billowed out the crack in the door. More time passed than should've. He sighed, wondering if Hayes was in there having a silent freak-out.

But after another minute, Hayes poked his head into the bedroom. "Water's warm. Shower's big."

Something tight in Ren's chest eased. He rolled out of bed. "Awesome. We're going to have to crash in your room tonight, by the way. The sheets are trashed."

"I can't help it if you have no self-control."

Ren snorted. "Uh-huh. Let me shove my dick up your ass, fuck you just right, and see how long you last."

Hayes's mouth tilted into an enigmatic smirk. "You never know. Maybe one day that can be arranged."

Ren's eyebrows shot up. He'd never known Hayes to bottom for anyone, but the possibility made Ren's mouth water. Ren stepped into the steamy bathroom and pulled open the shower door. "Don't tease me, Fox. I have a long memory."

Hayes stepped in behind him and wrapped his arm around him from behind, the hot spray of water dousing them. "And a long something else."

They didn't get out the shower until the water had gone cold.

———

Right before dawn they collapsed into Hayes's bed, exhausted and spent. Hayes closed his eyes and yawned. "So we could've been doing this all along, huh?"

"Yep."

"And the Complete Dumbass Award goes to . . ."

Ren pulled the blanket to his waist and tried to adjust to the unfamiliar pillows. "You're not a dumbass. You just overthink things. Always have."

"And you leap and hope for a net."

"That hasn't always been the best thing either." Ren dropped back onto the pillow, giving up on finding the right position, and lay on his back. "I wish we could've figured this out a long time ago, though. Would've saved us a lot of grief. Plus, just think how much more fun all those threesomes would've been if you hadn't been so afraid we'd bump ugly parts."

Hayes frowned in his periphery.

Ren didn't miss it. "What?"

"Nothing."

Ren turned onto his side to face Hayes. "No way. That look has no place here tonight. What's up?"

Hayes opened his eyes, staring at the ceiling. "I don't know. I just got this image of you at The Ranch having that kind of threesome with other people. It wasn't . . . a pleasant thought."

Ren studied Hayes's face. Was that *jealousy*? He wasn't sure he'd ever seen that on Hayes. The sight both warmed and worried him. "If it makes you feel better, I haven't done a threesome without you."

Hayes turned his head to look at him, surprise there. "But that was the kink you liked best."

Ren shrugged a shoulder. "I liked it best because I got to share a woman with my best friend. It wasn't the same without you. Since everything happened, I've only been with subs solo."

Hayes considered him and Ren could almost hear the gears in his head grinding. "This complicates shit doesn't it?"

"Meaning?"

"Your other relationships."

Ren's stomach dipped. He hadn't thought that far. Always leaping. *Fuck*. Part of him wanted to tell Hayes he would commit one hundred percent to him if that's what he wanted. He loved Hayes unequivocally. But another part of him knew what that would entail, sent anxiety creeping through him.

Hayes reached out and tapped Ren's forehead where lines had apparently gathered. "Relax, Muroya. I know you're dyed-in-the-wool poly. I'm not going to ask you to give up women. Plus, I wouldn't ask you to sacrifice the dominant side of yourself. Believe me, I know how fucking depressing that is."

Ren blew out a breath. "But?"

He gave him a chagrined smile. "The thought makes me jealous as hell."

The words curled through Ren, wrapped around some part of him that he didn't know existed. Hayes would be *jealous*. That felt . . . kind of nice. He'd never had a lover be jealous. Gordon had been possessive but not jealous. He'd gotten off on lending Ren out. But Hayes's feelings did make things trickier.

Ren tried to imagine the roles reversed. What if he knew Hayes was dominating women when Ren wasn't around?

A sharp kick of *oh, hell no* went through him. He frowned, the feeling foreign and altogether uncomfortable. He'd never gotten jealous before, even when he'd already accepted that he loved Hayes. Sharing women with Hayes had always been a rush. And watching Hayes fuck someone else had been Ren's own voyeuristic fantasy come true. But thinking of Hayes doing that without him there? It didn't sit well.

But . . .

Ren propped his head on his hand, knowing he needed to tread carefully. "There could be an easy solution to that."

Hayes sniffed. "I've learned there aren't easy solutions to much of anything, especially when it's your solution and you have that look on your face."

Ren gave him a sly smile. "You may not want to hear it, but there's an obvious option. I don't fuck someone else unless you're there."

Hayes's jaw flexed. "You know I can't—"

"You said you wouldn't risk *sleeping with* a woman. You don't have to. There's lots you can do just being there. You could be in charge of the scene, take the lead. You know how to dominate some-one without ever laying a finger on them. Plus, I know how much you like to watch. And if you need to touch or be touched, I'm there."

Hayes's expression was hard, tense. But he didn't say anything.

"It could work, Fox. Think about it." Ren's blood was pumping despite his utter exhaustion, the idea growing into a big whirl-ing swarm of hope inside him. The two of them together again, *really* together, and then bringing in a third. In Ren's world, that's what utopia looked like.

Hayes let out a breath and let his head sag back onto the pillow. "I don't know. I think I'd still have a hard time trusting some stranger."

Ren mimicked his position and stared at the turning ceiling fan. The quiet of the room crept in. Just the sound of their breath-ing, the hum of the air conditioning, and the *tick tick tick* of the clock in the hallway.

"I asked Cora out," Ren said finally.

Hayes's breathing stalled.

"Well, actually, it'd be more accurate to say I propositioned her. I told her I wanted her beneath me and to show her my dominant side."

Hayes made a choking sound. "You what?"

"Yeah, in hindsight, that may have been a little forward." Ren smiled in the darkness.

"Ren, you can't just—"

"She said yes."

Hayes sat up at that, shifted to face Ren again. "Hold up. She said *yes?*"

"Yep. Surprised me a little, too, to be honest." Ren looked up at Hayes. "But it's there, man. I believe her when she says she hasn't done kink in real life. But that doesn't mean she doesn't want to. She vibrates with this undercurrent of sexuality. I'd lay big money that she's got all kinds of deliciously twisted fantasies in her head. But for whatever reason, she doesn't think she's worthy or capable of them."

"Why the hell not?"

"From what I gathered, she's been the victim of insecure assholes who don't know how to see what's there. Men who don't know how to deal with her not fitting into some easily defined category. She's a straight woman who dresses androgynously and has no desire to change that. Maybe genderqueer, though I have no idea if that's how she thinks of herself." He shrugged. "She's different. You know what the world thinks of different. And beyond that, she's crazy smart and straightforward and doesn't play games, which can intimidate people." He sighed. "She thought I was fucking with her when I flirted with her. Like I was going to make fun of her or something."

Hayes made a face that said he'd like to introduce those assholes to his fist. "Idiots. All those differences are what make her so goddamned interesting. And sexy. That day I told her my story, she wasn't afraid to take me to task or ask questions about the lifestyle stuff. When I talked about edging, she couldn't keep her eyes off my hands. I could almost hear her thoughts and had to fight not to get hard. And every time she describes all those intricate hacking terms to me, I get this image of making her do that in a scene. Having her recite high-level computer shit while we drive her crazy and try to break her concentration."

Ren lips twitched at that. "*We,* huh?"

"I mean—"

"You mean exactly what you said. I could talk to her, you know," he said, keeping his tone even. "See what her thoughts are on . . . things. On you."

Hayes grimaced. "Don't even bother."

"You just admitted you're attracted to her."

"She's not going to want me encroaching on her thing with you. She's new to all this stuff. You're enough to handle."

Ha. That wasn't a no.

"Now you're making assumptions about her without asking her opinion," Ren said, pushing up on his elbows. "I have a feeling she'd be insulted. You may be surprised. She likes you, and who knows what kinky thoughts are floating around her brain? You've already told her we used to share. It's not like it'd come out of left field. I was thinking of inviting her to The Ranch. You could come along, no expectations."

Hayes's expression turned closed, the blinds shutting. "Enough, Ren."

Ren had opened his mouth to say more but then clamped it shut. He'd pushed enough tonight. He didn't want to risk chasing Hayes back into a corner. Tonight had been a big step. That was enough.

So instead of playing debate, he pulled Hayes down next to him. "Enough talk. Let's get some sleep. It's been a long week."

Hayes seemed relieved to let the conversation die and settled into the spot next to Ren, his heavy presence both new and familiar at the same time. They'd slept together like this countless nights. But back then they were boys who couldn't touch. Boys who were scared. Tonight they were men who refused to be afraid.

And Ren sure as hell wasn't going to take that miracle for granted. They'd figure out the rest later. He threw his arm over Hayes and fell fast asleep.

SIXTEEN

thursday

Cora had her earbuds tucked in her ears, music blaring, as she stared at the list of names she'd made. She was trying like hell to concentrate, but it wasn't working. She'd promised herself that this week would be dedicated to work. She wouldn't ruminate about what had happened with Dmitry last Friday night. She had a job to do and she had the potential date with Ren. She didn't need to focus on a virtual breakup. But her internal lectures weren't proving effective today. She *missed* Dmitry. And she was restless, trying to figure out why she was so torn up about losing him when she had a guy like Ren offering to make her fantasies come true.

But the more she'd thought about it, the mystery hadn't been that hard to solve. With Ren, it would be a hot hookup. She was attracted to him, intrigued by him, and liked him as a person. But she wasn't a fool. Ren wasn't looking to date someone seriously. He was a successful CEO, a dominant, and by all appearances, a player. She didn't mind since he was upfront about it. But he wasn't going to fill that spot Dmitry had in her life. And Ren had proven that this week. Though he'd been playful and flirty with her since their dinner last Friday, he hadn't set up another date. Everybody was busy. If they decided to go out again, it would happen when it happened. Their connection was the definition of casual.

Nothing had been casual about what she'd developed with Dmitry. She'd gotten attached, not just to the sex, but to the conversation, the connection they seemed to have despite the fact that they'd never met. They got each other. And now he was gone.

And she'd given him up for a hookup with Ren, something that might not even happen.

How had she ended up here again? *Ugh.* She barely resisted tapping her head against her keyboard. She'd thought the virtual world would insulate her from this. But no, if anything, this hurt worse than any of the others. She'd let Dmitry in. She'd let herself care for him. Maybe even loved him a little . . .

No. You couldn't love someone you'd never met. It was infatuation with a fantasy. Plain and simple. At least that's what she kept telling herself. And round and round her thoughts went.

Argh. She shoved her chair back and tugged her earbuds out. She needed a change of scenery. She was supposed to be meeting up with the guys in half an hour to go over what she'd worked on this week, but right now she had a tangle of information and nothing was lining up. Maybe a little caffeine would help.

She headed out of her office in search of the drink machine. They had to have one here. She'd been drinking coffee from the break room for the last two weeks, but right now she was craving something fizzy. She passed by Malik's office and stuck her head in. "Hey, is there a Coke machine on this floor?"

Malik looked up from his screen, eyes a little dazed like she'd broken him from deep concentration. "Uh, there's one by the men's bathroom but it steals your money half the time. Try the one down at the end of the executive hall. It's usually got more stock in it because it's a longer walk."

"Thanks."

She backtracked and took the turn toward the hall that led to Hayes's and Ren's offices. That part of FoxRen was much quieter, the clicking of keyboards and ringing of phones dimming in the distance. Hayes's door was closed tight when she passed and Collin, Ren's assistant, looked to be out to lunch. She eyed the door at the far end of the hall that led to the stairs and heard the telltale hum of a vending machine. *You have arrived at your destination.* She pulled a wrinkled dollar out of her pocket and headed that way.

But right as she was passing Ren's office, she heard a strange noise—a gasping, pained sound. She halted her step and looked at Ren's door, wondering if she'd imagined it. But the noise came again. Almost a choking sound. *What the hell?* Instinct kicked in and she reached for the door, pushing it open a crack to check on him. She was about to call out and ask if everything was okay, but she froze solid when she got a view of what was inside the office.

Ren was there, but he was far from hurt. He was backed up against his desk with Hayes's big hand wrapped around his neck. And they were . . . kissing.

And touching.

Cora couldn't move and couldn't look away. The two men were clinging to each other, soft groans and gripping hands. And she had no idea how to feel. The rush of warmth through her body said one thing, but her brain was screaming another. The guy who'd said he wanted her in his bed was with someone else. And by the looks of it, their relationship was far more than casual.

Ren's hand slid between their bodies and gripped Hayes's erection. Hayes hissed out a breath and clamped his hand over Ren's, rubbing along with him.

It was sexy as fuck—the raw, primal need between them. Heat gathered between Cora's thighs despite the snap of shock and jealousy. She'd never seen the stoic Hayes look quite so undone and had never seen Ren look more intense. And she absolutely should not be watching this private moment. She reached for the door handle, intending to slip out and shut it, but the movement caught Ren's eye. His attention jerked her way and his eyes went wide. "Cora."

"What?" Hayes's head turned, his gaze colliding with hers. "Shit."

"I— Sorry. I was—" She made some lame motion with her hand that was meant to be code for *I was getting a drink*.

Hayes took a big step backward and turned away from Cora.

"I'm going to . . . Yeah." She moved to grab the door handle again.

Ren pushed himself off the desk, not even bothering to conceal the obvious state of his erection. "Cora, wait."

But she was already turning and cruising back the way she came, her body tense and her thoughts too scattered to concentrate on any one. All she knew was she needed to get back to the safety of her office. Pretend this hadn't happened.

A hand landed on her shoulder. "Hey, hold up. Please."

She halted her step, more out of habit than anything else, but her entire body was trembling. She kept her eyes forward and fought to find her voice, her defenses. "We've got to stop meeting like this."

He sniffed and the grip on her shoulder eased. "You think?"

"I didn't mean to interrupt. I— Just let me go back to my desk. Please."

"Hey," he said gently and stepped in front of her, his eyes searching hers. "Just take a breath and slow down. We should talk about this."

Her brows shot up. "Oh, no, we shouldn't. We should label this *none of my fucking business* and *par for the course*."

He frowned. "Par for the course?"

She hadn't meant to let that part slip out. "Yeah, par. Of course this happened. Of course you've got something that intense going with someone else."

"It's not—"

She put her arms out at her sides, the frustration boiling up and over. "Whatever. It's fine. I just— Just tell me one thing, all right? Why in the hell did we have that night at the taco place? Why would you tell me all those things and make it sound like maybe we'd do that again, like maybe we'd do more than that when you already have *that* with someone?"

Ren's shoulders sagged and he ran a hand through his hair. "We had that night because I like you. I still do. And that night . . . I didn't have this. Hayes and I, it's complicated. But I can promise you what you just saw is new. We've been together a long time but not in that way."

She smirked, defensiveness rising to push past the hurt, the disappointment. She'd lost *Dmitry* over this guy. She'd thought . . . Well, she shouldn't have thought. She should've known better. "Well, yay for you two. Nothing like a date with me to make a guy realize how much he wants someone else."

She turned to go and he grabbed her hand. "Cora, don't. Please."

Her teeth clamped together. She wouldn't cry. Wouldn't let him see how this burned. This wasn't about him. He didn't owe her anything. It was just another inevitable outcome.

"I was going to talk to you about all of this. I needed time to process things. Like I said, it's complicated."

"Well, I saved you the trouble."

His frown deepened. "No, you didn't." He stepped closer. "Look at me. Come on, Benning."

She forced her gaze upward. So many guys called her Benning. But somehow when he said it, it didn't sound like bro speak. It sounded like an endearment. That made her want to cry more.

"This doesn't change the things I said to you that night. I still mean them. You said this was none of your business. But that doesn't have to be true. This could be your business."

She stared at him like he'd grown a second head. "Your relationship with someone else could be my business. What the hell, Ren?"

"You know what I'm saying," he said carefully. He stroked his thumb over her knuckles. "How long did you watch?"

Her gaze slid away and her fist balled against her thigh. "Ren—"

"Were you turned off by it? Seeing us like that?"

"That is *so* not the point."

She caught a quirk of his lips in her periphery. "Oh, I disagree. In fact, that's the point I'd like to focus on most. I've been honest about being kinky. And you already knew Hayes and I used to share women. Yet, you said yes that night anyway."

"I said yes *to you*," she said, her voice coming out too sharp. "Not to being you and your boyfriend's temporary blow-up doll."

Though, hadn't that been exactly what she'd fantasized about that night in the dark privacy of her bedroom? Being used and passed between the two of them. But the reality hadn't included the two guys being so obviously into each other. She didn't want to be a third wheel. She spent too much of her life already looking from the outside in.

"Hey," he said, his voice gentle. "I would never disrespect you like that. And I know you said yes to me. That was all I was suggesting at the time, honestly. The Hayes thing was unexpected."

"Congratulations." The bitterness in her voice probably wasn't fair, but so be it.

Ren sighed and his hands went to her shoulders. "Look, I know this feels like a bait and switch, and I'm sorry for that. That's my fault. But can you trust me for a second?"

She met his eyes, defiance rumbling through her bones.

"I don't want you to walk because you're scared or angry. If you want to leave and tell me to go to hell, do that after you hear what I have to say. I like you . . . a lot. Every word I said that night was true. And I know I'm unconventional. Most people would and *do* bolt when they find out how I am, who I am. But I feel like maybe you know that feeling, too. Like maybe you can find something you've been looking for if you put the fear aside for a minute." His palms were warm against her shoulders. "Come back to the office with me. Just for a few minutes."

She stared, not wanting to give in, but the truth of his words and the nakedness of his expression were doing more to her than they should. He was handsome and rich and talented. He could probably check off all those boxes on most people's wish lists for the perfect guy. But she could hear what he was saying. It was all smoke and mirrors, not the real him. The real Ren was like her. Different. Other. On the outside. He understood. *Maybe you can find something you've been looking for . . .*

After a few more seconds of tense silence, she gave a little nod. "Okay."

He let out a breath and moved alongside her, pressing his palm to the base of her spine. "Thank you."

When they walked back into the office, Hayes was sitting in a chair by Ren's three-monitored workstation, elbows on this thighs and hands clasped behind his neck. He looked up when she and Ren entered the room. His eyebrows rose and he stood. "I'll leave you two—"

"Sit," Ren said, his tone brooking no argument.

Hayes sent him a look but lowered back into the chair.

Ren perched on the edge of his desk and guided Cora in front of him so that she was facing Hayes. Her position between the two of them, even with Hayes at a distance, was far too close to her fantasy from that night to convince her body not to react.

"Cora," Ren said, his voice like the calm surface of a lake. "I know you've had some shitty experiences with guys in your life. You've been mistreated and used and unappreciated. I get how this looks, how this might appear to you. But I swear to you on my life, I would never treat you that way. And I would never lead you on or play with your emotions like that."

She closed her eyes, the personal words far too revealing. She didn't want them to see her like that. The truth was too mortifying.

"And I'm not a liar or a cheat. I'm telling you with one hundred percent honesty that when you said yes to me that night, I felt like a lucky son of a bitch. The thought of exploring kink with you, of showing you submission, makes me hot all over just thinking about it. And I can absolutely still do that. Hayes has given me his blessing."

Her eyes popped open at that, catching Hayes's watchful gaze. He gave a slight nod.

"But I'm also going to be honest and say that in a perfect world, I'd want you both in my bed. Together. Sharing. Watching. Touching."

Some expression flickered over Hayes's face—something hot and dangerous, but he quickly smoothed it. She shuddered and had no doubt Ren had felt it in his light grip on her shoulders.

"But you're afraid of the unknown and letting your guard down, and Hayes is afraid of another woman betraying him."

"Betraying?" she blurted. "I would never—"

"I know that," Ren said. "But he doesn't. If he did, I have no doubt that he would've been pursuing you from day one. Tell me I'm wrong, Hayes."

Hayes's jaw ticked. "I'm not going to lie to her."

Cora's lips parted.

"And right now," Ren said, his voice a low song against her ear, "he's probably desperately wishing that I would touch you, that I would show him what I want to do to you. He'd probably want to tell me exactly how to tease you, how to make you beg, how to make you come."

She sucked in a breath and her skin flushed, fever hot.

His fingertip traced the curve of her neck. "And I'm guessing you might not mind that so much. I'm guessing you're already a little turned on from watching us kiss. That you're as much of a voyeur as we are. That you're dirtier than you'd ever admit out loud."

She swallowed hard and it was impossible to miss the erection becoming visible in Hayes's jeans. This was doing it for him. And God help her, it was sending her thoughts off the rails, too. Her heart was pounding and the spot between her thighs throbbing.

Ren slid off the desk and pressed his front to her back. She gasped at the feel of his erection against her backside. "He won't touch you, Cora. And if you say the word right now, I won't either. I know this is a big leap and not for everyone. You can walk out and we'll all pretend we never had this conversation. I'll leave you alone. Continue our professional relationship. But if you stay, you can have this. No video games needed. No one to judge you or criticize. You can always say stop if it goes too far, but aren't you tired of wondering what it might be like to let go for real? To try some things instead of just wondering about them? To submit . . ."

She pressed her lips together, trying for the life of her to access her logical side. They were offering her fantasy—right here, right now. Sex. Kink. Two ridiculously beautiful men. "We're at work."

"With a door that locks and an assistant who knows not to disturb me when my door's shut." His hands slid down to her hips. "All I'm asking for is your honesty. I would never push this on anyone, but I'm trusting my gut here. Tell me you aren't attracted to us, Cora. Or that you hate the idea of being watched or shared." He pressed his nose to her hair. "Tell me that if I pulled your zipper down and slid my hand inside your jeans I wouldn't find you wet."

Embarrassment burned a path up her neck to her cheeks. It was like he'd stripped her already, looked in her head, and plucked out her thoughts. Her fists flexed and her blood pumped to all her most sensitive places. "You know I can't tell you that."

Hayes let out a breath and a whispered *fuck*.

Ren's hand slid to her belly, holding her to him, exhaling as well. "Thank you."

She licked her dry lips, riveted by the look on Hayes's face.

"See," Ren said with a smile in his voice. "Look what we're doing to him. He's imagining you slick and turned on, picturing my fingers sliding inside you while he watches. I bet if we're really good, he'll have to take his cock out and stroke himself."

A hard shiver went through Cora. "Christ."

Ren pressed a kiss to the curve of her shoulder. "The door is locked. You're safe with us. But you say *red* and we stop, no questions asked. Understand?"

Oh, God, this was really happening. She wasn't in her room.

This wasn't some fantasy reel. Or a scene in Hayven. She was about to let Ren touch her while his lover watched. This was insane. They were at work. It was the middle of the day. But somehow her brain couldn't snuff out the need rushing through her like wildfire. It was burning down every argument—a funeral pyre of logical thought. "I understand."

Ren's body relaxed behind her, like he'd half expected her to bolt. But then he lifted his head away from her shoulder. "You with us, Fox? Safe word applies to you, too. We all have to want to be here."

There was a challenge there. Something in Ren's voice had gone hard. That's when she realized that Hayes and Ren hadn't done this kind of thing since Hayes had been out. He didn't trust women. She was a threat. She wasn't the only one jumping hurdles by being here. Hayes was facing down miles of them.

Hayes looked up, torment there. Torment and something else. *Hunger.* "I'm not going anywhere unless she wants me to."

His gaze flicked to Cora, and she found herself shaking her head. "Stay."

Those green eyes of his lit with something she hadn't seen from him before. Something fierce and intensely, deceivingly calm. The dominant.

Ren shifted behind her and nerves rushed to the surface, making her go stiff.

"Shh," Ren said against her ear, soothing hands running up her sides. "I've got you. Just relax. There are no expectations and you don't have to put on a show. Just let me make you feel good."

He turned her in his arms and captured her gaze. Demanding she hold it without saying a word. Suddenly there was no Hayes in her vision or the intimidating thought of a threesome, just the beautiful man who'd told her the other night how much he wanted her in his bed. The man who'd fueled her fantasies since the day she'd met him.

His hands cupped her face. "This is what I wanted to do that night."

And with that, his head dipped down and he kissed her. Soft. Tender. Almost sweet. A first-date kiss.

But that little how-do-you-do slowly morphed from gentle to something altogether more heated when their lips parted. His kiss cajoled, promised things. *This is how I'll take my time with you. I'm not going to skip steps. I'm going to savor you.* Then his tongue touched hers and electricity sparked through her like live wires had been cut. His taste, his singular focus, everything about it lit her up. Stroke by stroke he dialed up the intensity. A slow, wicked burn.

When his hips pressed against hers, letting her feel how turned on he was, she moaned into the connection and wrapped her arms around his neck. It'd been a long time since she'd made out with anyone, but she couldn't remember it ever being like this, like she wanted to drown in it and never come up for air. Like he could make her lose her shit with just his mouth.

Ren's hands slid to her neck, gripping and holding her just where he wanted her, and she couldn't help but remember that just a few moments ago, it was Hayes's tongue in his mouth, his cock in his hand. *Fuck.* The image was too much and she arched into him, rubbing his erection against the spot she needed it most. Ren groaned and pulled her knee up, rocking her against him. Soon, she was breathless and burning up and so turned on that she was cursing the heavens that she hated skirts so much. One would be so convenient right now. She needed more, his touch, skin against skin.

Ren broke away from the kiss, panting and little wild-eyed himself. "Tell me how long it's been, Cora."

"Huh?" He expected her to answer questions in this moment? To access words? When her brain was all *guhhhhh . . .*

"Since you've come?"

The question snapped her to attention. "Uh."

"Tell me."

Her ears burned. "Last Friday."

A pleased smirk touched his lips and he gathered her against him, those colorfully tattooed arms wrapping around her. "After our dinner."

"Yes." Her palms were trapped between them, pressed against his chest. She loved the feel of the hard muscles beneath her fingertips, wanted to tear his shirt off Hulk-style. "Probably while you were in bed with your hot boyfriend."

Hayes made a sound that sounded suspiciously like a laugh.

"So were you thinking about me when you did it?" Ren asked, touching his forehead to hers, his tone playful.

She rubbed her lips together, finding a glimmer of bravery. "I'm more creative than that. I was thinking about you both."

Ren's grin spread wide, a predatory edge to it. "I knew you liked him. I love when I'm right. So what were we doing to you in this sordid fantasy?"

"How do you know it was sordid . . ."

He lifted a brow.

"Fine. It was sordid. And *private*."

"Mmm, private is so overrated. Especially when it's guaranteed neither of us are going to judge you. It's only going to make us hotter." He kissed down her neck, making her thoughts splinter again, and then he turned her in his arms to face Hayes again. Ren's hands trailed up her rib cage and cupped her breasts through her T-shirt, sending sensations straight downward. "Be bold, Benning. Tell him what you imagined us doing to you. Own it."

Cora could barely lift her gaze without wanting to hide her face.

Hayes was watching her with his full, stoic attention, his presence somehow calming in the storm of arousal. He gave a nod. "Go ahead."

She swallowed past her constricted throat. "I'll tell you, if y'all tell me what you two did that night."

"Ah, look at you. You can't hide that voyeur streak. I love it," Ren said against her ear. "Deal."

He said it so easily. Like he'd have no trouble detailing what he'd done with this man. And Lord, did she want to hear. But there was a price. She took a deep breath, gathering her courage. "I imagined that you two wouldn't let me leave work until I took care of you . . . both of you."

A pleased sound rumbled through Ren. "Nice. And what did we make you do?"

"Ren . . ."

"No shame, Cora. I promise. Nothing you can say will out-dirty us. Believe me."

She wasn't sure about that. Her real-world experience wasn't extensive but her filthy mind was a shameless slut. "You bent me over the desk and fucked me while I went down on Hayes."

Hayes groaned and closed his eyes, agony moving across his features. As subtle as could be, his hand shifted up his thigh and he pressed a hand over his erection, squeezing it.

The sight made her toes curl in her Doc Martens. Seeing such a hard-to-crack man struggling to keep himself in check because of her was a heady rush. It made her feel sexy. Invincible.

"Fuck, yes," Ren said after pressing a kiss to her shoulder. "I knew you had a dirty mind."

Cora closed her eyes. "Your turn."

Ren's thumbs grazed over her nipples, slowly, back and forth, making her clit pulse like there was a wire attached between the two zones. "That night, I submitted to Hayes. He made me suck his cock and then he held me down and fucked me like a man who's been celibate for four years. Made me come all over my nice clean sheets."

The words were like gasoline on an already burning blaze, the visuals behind her eyelids overwhelming her. Hayes's big broad body over Ren's, wrists captured in his hands, hips pumping hard. She didn't know why the thought of them together excited her so much, but goddamn, it did.

"She likes that, Fox," Ren said. "You should feel how fast her heart is beating, how hot her skin is."

"Show me," Hayes said, his voice full of gravel. "Take her shirt off and touch her."

Cora tensed but only for a second because Ren's warm hands cupping her breasts drained her of cogent thought.

"Lift your arms, gorgeous."

She probably should've thought about it more. She was about to expose herself to these men. At the office. And there was no hiding under these lights. But she was too far gone.

All she wanted to do was obey.

SEVENTEEN

"Good girl." Ren grabbed the hem of her T-shirt and tugged it over her head, leaving her in her plain cotton Calvin Klein bralette. Her nipples were hard points beneath the fabric and her chest flushed pink. He stepped in front of her and ran the back of his hand over the swell of her breast. "Perfect."

"I would've bought something prettier if I'd known you'd be seeing it," she said, a little breathless.

His brows dipped and he leveled a gaze at her. "Don't you dare. Not on my behalf, at least. Wear what you like. In fact, I can't think of anything hotter than you standing here in your white cotton and those combat boots."

The words surprised her, dragged her out of her erotic haze for a second. "You have a tomboy fetish, Muroya?"

Ren smirked. "I suspect it's just a Cora fetish." He drew a circle over her areola, sending goose bumps along her skin. "What turns me on is seeing *you*—the woman you are when no one's watching. No act. No pretending to be something you're not comfortable being. That's what I want. Plus, this cotton is mighty thin. I can see all the shades and secrets of you in this. Bonus."

She braced her hands on the desk behind her as he went for the button on her jeans. The look he was giving her, the hungry way he was gazing at her body made this seductive impulse bubble to the surface, one she'd never had before. She wanted to tease him, to be playful. She wiggled her hips slowly, letting the denim work down her hips, revealing the top band of her underwear.

Ren groaned and tugged her pants the rest of the way down. When she ventured a peek over his shoulder, she found Hayes watching, his hand still over that thick erection. She could see the intensity in his expression. He wanted to do more than watch, but she had a feeling there'd be no convincing him to join in. She had to trust them with her body. That was a lot. But the trust he'd have to put in her to take it further would be monumental. Too much. He didn't know her. She could lie about him just as easily as the other woman had. And God only knew what he'd think if he found out who her mom was. But in that moment, seeing the want on his face, she wished she could take that burden off him. Convince him that it was okay. To let go for a minute.

Ren had her step out of her boots and then stripped off her jeans and bra. He was crouched down in front of her and lined up with the perfect view of the damp state of her underwear. He slid his hands up the outside of her thighs and then leaned forward, pressing his mouth and nose to the cotton of her briefs and inhaling. The touch made her groan in both relief and frustration, his nose and lips nuzzling the spot desperate for attention.

"Lie back on the desk, Cora. I need to taste you."

Some nonsense word slipped past her lips, but there was no stopping herself from obeying. If that meant Ren was going to put his mouth on her, she'd do a goddamned backbend if that was what he asked of her. She scooted fully onto the desk and braced herself on her elbows, unwilling to give up the view of Ren and Hayes.

Ren shrugged off his jacket and tossed it to the side. Then he kneeled in front of her and dragged her underwear down her hips. In three hot seconds, she was bared and exposed to him in the most vulnerable of ways. Up close and personal, under full lights.

She had a flash of self-consciousness, but it didn't last long because Ren pressed his hands to the back of her thighs and opened her to him fully. The rapt look on his face was enough to chase away any doubts. That couldn't be faked.

"You're so fucking sexy, Benning," he groaned and ran a finger over her slit, the slick heat of her arousal beyond obvious. "Look how ready you are. I'm losing my mind thinking about you touching yourself that night, thinking about us. I wish I would've known how wound up you were. I would've never left you that way."

He kissed her inner thigh and ran his tongue along the crease where leg met hip, making her moan and arch. Her eyes fell shut but then the light shifted against her lids, making her open them again.

Hayes had walked over and stood a few feet away, gazing down at her face. Not her body, not her spread thighs or Ren's tongue along her skin but her face. "Tell him how you did it. How do you like getting yourself off?"

She swallowed hard at the rumble of Hayes's voice, a powerful command wrapped in his brand of quietness. Shyness tried to overtake her, but she couldn't look away from him, couldn't ignore the need in his eyes. This was costing him something, too. He was putting aside armor just like she was, trusting her to see that private side of him, the side that craved her submission.

She found her voice. "I used my fingers, but it wasn't enough so I grabbed a toy."

Hayes's jaw flexed, the only indication the words had gotten to him. He reached out and palmed the back of Ren's head. "Taste her, Ren. And use your fingers."

Ren grunted beneath the touch but his eyes flashed with heat. "Best directive I've gotten at work all day."

Ren caught her gaze, hot promise there, and then lowered himself between her thighs to take a long, languid lick.

Her heels dug into his back as her body instinctively reacted, her head tipping back and sensation racing up her spine. "Fuck."

It'd been so long since she'd had anything but her own hand. And there was no toy that could mimic the hot, wet feel of a skilled tongue. Ren went to work before she could catch her breath, licking and sucking and kissing every tender part of her, his stubble scraping her inner thighs and making everything acutely aware and sensitive. She rocked into the touch and tried to hold back the moans that wanted to slip out. They were in a locked office, not a soundproof room. But it was a fight with every sweep of his tongue.

And when he tucked two fingers inside her, curling them just right, she almost levitated off the desk. Her head tapped against the wood.

But she didn't want to miss a minute of the show, so she forced her head up, bracing herself on her elbows, and watched Ren's dark head move between her thighs, Hayes's hand still in Ren's hair as if puppeteering the whole thing. The view was mesmerizing, like watching an erotic movie made just for her. And it was almost as if she was floating above it all, seeing herself spread along the desk and watching these men overtake her, but the pleasure rippling through her was far from distant.

Her head lolled to the right, the sensation too overwhelming, and her attention landed on the erection in Hayes's jeans. The zipper looked to be screaming for mercy. She wanted to touch, to reach out and drag him closer, to taste. But that was off-limits. "Can I . . . make a request?"

The words came out choppy, her breaths too quick.

"Of course," Hayes said, a hint of a dimple showing. "Doesn't mean you'll get your way, but you can always ask."

She let her gaze dip then looked back to him. "You asked me how I get off. I want to see how you do."

His eyebrow arched and Ren lifted his head for a second, his mouth slick and his eyelids heavy. "I knew I liked you, Benning. She wants to watch you, Hayes. Give the lady a peek."

Hayes's lips pressed together and his Adam's apple bobbed,

like he was having a vicious debate behind the cool mask, but he gave a little shake of his head. "Not today. I'm getting enough pleasure just watching the two of you."

Cora frowned, could feel the restraint in his words, but she wasn't going to push. This was about stretching her boundaries but not crossing his. "Something to look forward to another day, then."

He gave her a humorless half smile at that, but didn't confirm or deny. Instead, he reached out and pushed hair away from her forehead, a gentle brush of a touch that sent a shimmer of heat over her. "Make her come, Ren. Give her what she needs. I want to see her let go."

Ren didn't say another word, and the heat of his tongue landed on her like a shock after its absence. Hot against cool. But it didn't take long for her race to orgasm to kick back in. He pumped his fingers inside her and didn't hold back with his mouth, feasting on her like she was the finest meal he'd ever had. Her arousal and his tongue making everything slippery and noisy and lewd and hot as fuck.

And before long, her toes were curling against him and her breaths were coming hard and fast. She forgot to be quiet. "Oh, God."

"Let us have it," Hayes said. "Let it all go and take what you need."

Ren's tongue lashed at her and then he sucked her clit between his lips. The pressure and sensation exploded all into one and her head tipped back, a loud cry bursting from her. It was too noisy, too much for discretion. She rocked against him, and grabbed for him. Her hands landed over Hayes's on Ren's head. Their fingers linked and together they guided him against her, letting her wring every ounce of pleasure from his mouth.

When she couldn't bear anymore and felt turned inside out, she collapsed onto the desk and let her hand fall away. All that was left were the sounds of her breaths sawing out of her.

Ren gently guided her legs back down and pressed a kiss to her hip. "Beautiful. Thank you."

It was a period at the end of a sentence. Not acceptable.

She reached for him. He was going to go the route of *this was just for you*, but screw that. She didn't know what would happen when they walked out of this room. She didn't know how reality would filter this scene once the erotic fog cleared, and she didn't want to walk away without having this man, without seeing what he was like when all the self-control went away.

She grabbed hold of his T-shirt, dragged him down, and kissed him. Her taste was still on his lips and that had her libido kicking into second gear. Ren resisted for a second but when she hooked her leg around his hips and pressed against him, he groaned and melted into the connection.

They kissed full and deep, desperate, and her own need ramped up again.

He broke away, breathless. "Benning, I'm trying to be good. But you're not helping."

"Good." She shifted up and reached for his belt. "You have a condom?"

He made a pained sound. "Hayes, get my wallet out of the drawer in my desk, outside pocket."

Hayes moved swiftly into action and handed Ren the foil packet. Ren's stare burned into her. "Tell me you want this, Cora. Tell me this isn't too far."

She unzipped his fly and slipped her hand over his erection, the soft silk of his boxers hot against her palm. "I want you, Ren. Have since the party. And I want Hayes to watch."

"Fuck. Yeah, I'm not that noble." He yanked his pants down and rolled on the condom.

Cora watched the latex roll over that beautiful curved erection, her tongue pressing to the roof of her mouth, and then she turned to see Hayes. The man was focused on the same thing—Ren's adept fingers sheathing himself. So fucking hot.

Before she could process it all—the sight of Ren between her thighs, her spread naked across a desk, and Hayes watching—Ren gripped her under the knees and the head of his cock pushed into her. They both moaned and her short nails dug into his shoulders at the full feeling of having him inside her. God, yes. She'd definitely forgotten how good this could feel. The heat of a man, the need rolling off him.

Unlike the kiss they'd first shared, Ren didn't ease into things. She'd pushed him past the point of patience. This was his control fraying at the edges. She loved it. He pumped into her with long, deep strokes, the angle just right and his tattooed arms flexing beside her.

"Is this what you want?" he asked, voice full of grit and his eyes full of challenge. "Hard and fast?"

"God, yes."

His pants weren't even off, just hanging loose on his hips, and his T-shirt was still on. It was dirty, urgent fucking, and she wasn't sure she'd ever felt anything better. There was nothing nice or relaxed or friendly about it. He grabbed her knee and hooked a leg around his hip, angling deeper, the head of his cock teasing at her entrance in a way that felt altogether new. Vaginal sex had always been pleasant but not intense. But right now, she could feel the shape of his cock, the head, the smoothness right at her entrance every time he fucked into her, lighting up nerves she didn't know she had. And before long, she felt another orgasm knocking at the door.

Sweat beaded his brow and that messy hair was falling in his face. Ren Muroya, undone. She wished she had a photo of him just like this. She'd never need porn again. But when he tucked his hand between them and found her clit, there were no more thoughts of photos or anything else. Light exploded behind her eyes and she cried out, the climax rolling over her.

Ren wasn't far behind and his thrusts became harder, more urgent until he was gasping and cursing, pushing her across the desk with the force of it all. Her head slipped off the edge, but before it tilted all the way back, two big palms clasped it, cradled it. *Hayes.*

The thought was enough to send her into hyperspace. She let her thoughts go and just enjoyed the ride, fell into the bliss. Ren deep inside her, her head in Hayes's hands, and both men watching her fall apart beneath them.

She would be ruined. How would she ever top this?

But she wouldn't worry about it now.

This was living in the moment. She'd hold on to it as long as she could.

And not until Ren was sliding out and covering her with his jacket did she open her eyes. Hayes was gazing down at her, still cradling her head, some unreadable expression on his face. She figured she should say something, but before she could, he bent down and pressed a gentle kiss to her forehead. Inhaling deeply, like he was trying to breathe her in.

For some reason, it made her want to cry. But she held the urge and let the guys silently help her off the desk. Every part of her felt oversensitive, electric, and exposed. She didn't know what to say. Or if there *was* anything to say.

She tucked her arms into Ren's jacket, accepted her discarded clothes from Hayes, and slipped into the small bathroom attached to Ren's office to put herself back together. She braced her hands on the sink and stared at her reflection as she regained her breath. She didn't recognize the flush-cheeked woman in the oval mirror. Who was that girl with the wild hair and slick lips and dazed look? Who was that woman who'd just jumped off a cliff without thinking of the consequences?

This had been insane. And kind of amazing. The girl in the mirror smiled. She reached out and touched the reflection, spreading her hand like she was touching the person staring back at her. She didn't know this girl yet.

Or maybe she'd known her all along but had been too scared to look.

What would that girl do? She wouldn't think about what this

meant or what happened next or wonder if anything would happen again. She would hold this moment and enjoy it for what it was. *Own it.*

With that decided, Cora quickly cleaned up and got dressed. She stepped back into the office and found only Ren waiting for her.

Ren walked over to her, took her hands in his, and gave her a soft kiss. "How goes it, Benning?"

"It goes."

His lips curved. "Freaking out?"

"Not yet."

"Good. No need to. That was . . . a great way to spend a lunch hour."

She laughed and glanced at the closed office door. "Where's Hayes?"

Ren's smile dipped. "He said he needed some air. More likely, he needed to walk off a raging case of blue balls."

"Is he okay? I feel bad that—"

Ren laced his fingers with hers. "Hayes has to approach this in his own way. I know he loved every minute of what just happened, but it's got to be torture not to participate."

"I would've let him. I asked him to."

Ren sighed. "I know. But you have to understand how badly he was burned. That mistrust is his only defense. I think he'll get past it. But it's going to take time."

"I don't blame him. But it's unfair that he has to be so careful. He didn't do anything."

"I know. But if you decide you want to do this with us, take things further, he's going to have to be able to trust you without question before he fully lets go."

She slipped her arms around Ren's waist and pressed the top of her head to his chest. "Until then, you'll take good care of him?"

He kissed the top of her head. "In all ways. That's what I do. That's what he's done for me."

She looked up at him, the words telling her everything. "You love him."

A statement, not a question.

Ren smiled, resigned. "Impossible not to."

The words should've worried her. She was potentially entering into a tryst with two men who were in love. The risk of her getting hurt was high. But it was also a comfort knowing that these guys were so deeply bonded. It didn't leave any gray area. She knew where she stood. She didn't have to fall into her old trap of pinning false hope on relationships. In the end, it would be those two. Not her and Ren. If she was going to do this, she needed to be okay with that. Accept the ending before the start.

"I better get back to work. I've still got a hacker to catch."

Ren rubbed her arms. "Tell me you enjoyed this and want to do it again. Preferably soon. Preferably with me."

She smiled. "Is that a command or a request?"

He tilted his head, mischief in his gaze. "A desperate plea?"

"Who am I to deny a desperate plea?"

His grin went wide and he kissed her again. "Back to work, Benning. I've got meetings this afternoon. But we'll talk soon."

EIGHTEEN

When Cora got back to her office, she collapsed into her chair, trying to regain the focus that Ren and Hayes had blown to bits. How was she supposed to work while her body was still humming in the afterglow and her brain was short-circuiting? What was she supposed to be doing again? Oh, right. *Find a hacker.* Yes. That was it. She rolled her shoulders and woke her screen. Back to work.

It took her a few more minutes to cool down fully and get back into the mind-set of the hunt. But the amount of work in front of her helped her not overanalyze what had just happened with the guys. That was a problem for future Cora to pick apart. This was what present Cora needed to be focused on.

She scanned the screen. All the profiles that were accessed by the perp were there on her list. She tapped a few keys and then leaned over to snag pages from the printer. She'd compiled a separate document to see who had history with whom, who had chatted, and who had privately played. It had taken all week to gather everything. She'd pretty much holed herself up in the office and hadn't interacted with anyone during work hours. She worked best when she put blinders on and shut everything out except the mission. But even before the detour to Ren's office, the information was getting tangled up in her head, too many scattered pieces.

She set her chin in her hand and let her attention run over the documents, wishing it was like a movie and all these lines and connections would just appear in front of her in midair and make some kind of sense. But all she could see was lists and more lists and spreadsheets.

"Ugh. Enough staring." She once had a professor tell her that when numbers don't make sense, draw a picture. He'd meant charts, but she had a better idea for this. She grabbed her laptop from her bag and opened up a free-form text editor that let her draw concept maps. She needed to see these connections as more than just names on a page. She laid out her papers and started typing in the names, putting little ovals around the submissives, squares around the doms, and color-coding for gender. Then once she had everyone in there, she started to draw the lines between the people. A single line if they'd chatted in the last six months, a double line if they'd played, a squiggly line if they were exclusively paired.

She got lost in the project and regained her hyperfocus. Lines started to fill the page, ovals joining others, connections becoming more obvious. And the more she added, the more a pattern started to emerge. A very obvious one.

She frowned, checked her work. At the center of the tangled web of lines and shapes were three names, three dominants. And one was very, very familiar. A pit settled in her stomach. Well, *shit*.

———

Hayes leaned back in his office chair and massaged his temples. He'd finished most of what he'd planned to do this afternoon, but his head was starting to throb. Probably because all the blood in his brain had been rerouted to his dick for an hour after he'd left Ren's office. Sharing a bed with Ren this week had been earth-shifting enough, but seeing him with Cora today had poked the old Hayes with a cattle prod, making him want to fight to the surface. It'd taken everything he had to turn Cora down when she'd asked him to join in. But the risk was too high. Despite what he'd witnessed this afternoon, Cora was still a stranger to him.

A sexy, smart, drive-him-to-distraction stranger.

"Knock, knock."

The sound startled him and he lowered his hand from his eyes, his gaze shifting to the doorway. Cora was leaning in with a tentative smile. She'd put her hair in two braids and had thrown on a gray army-style jacket over her blue Smurfs T-shirt. It shouldn't have been alluring in any way, but he couldn't help the way his baser side perked up at the sight of her. He'd like to undo those braids. Or maybe have Ren hold them while he guided her mouth onto Hayes's cock.

He groaned inwardly. *She's coming here about work. Put the dirty thoughts away.* He needed to show her that what had happened didn't change how he'd treat her at work. "Hey."

"Am I interrupting?"

He sat forward in his seat, the chair squeaking under his weight. "I could use the interruption. What's up?"

She stepped inside, a notepad and file folder clutched to her chest, and a hesitant look on her face. "Okay, so I'm not going to lie. This feels a little awkward."

He gave her a brief smile. "Just let it roll over you. It will pass. I promise I have the ability to be professional and to separate what happened from work. Two different worlds."

She chewed her lip, considering him. "Okay. I can compartmentalize if you can. Plus, I need to run some stuff by you if you have time. Ren's out at a meeting and I think you may be able to help."

She let out a breath and he could tell she'd probably practiced this little speech, which was kind of endearing.

"Of course." He indicated the chair in front of him for her to sit. "Tell me what you've got."

Cora strode across the room and settled in the chair, a little wrinkle in her brow and a tense set to her shoulders. Unlike earlier when she'd been vibrating with energy, she suddenly seemed worn-out and . . . disturbed.

"You found something bad."

She sighed and set the notepad down. It was filled with small, round handwriting that seemed to be no-nonsense and pretty all at the same time, just like her. "Yes and no. I've confirmed that no other emails went out except the one to me and the guy who jumped me. That's the good news."

"Okay. But?"

"But like I showed you when we first talked, a list of other profiles were accessed. I thought they'd just been read, but this week, I found others were altered. Ren got on chats with a few people and verified that there were changed safe words and new information that the customers didn't put in. Like mine. All of them having that flavor of putting someone in a position to get hurt. All women. So it seems like our guy was planning on more of this and either got interrupted or is waiting for some reason."

Hayes frowned. The idea of an enemy lying in wait was not a comforting one. "That's concerning."

"Exactly. So I started looking through site activity histories, trying to match people up, see if there were any connections that stood out. Who talked to whom. Who played with each other. If anyone was blocked or had some sort of falling-out. I mapped it out and three names kept popping up. Almost every person's account that was accessed had interacted on some level with one of three particular players—three male dominants."

"Okay, that's a promising lead."

"Right. But I couldn't get much from their Hayven profiles. So I pulled the credit card pages of those three to get real names and addresses. I was trying to avoid that because it feels a little sticky privacy-wise, but I was out of other options. I needed real info to Google them to see if I could find any red flags."

Hayes leaned back in his chair and rubbed a hand over his jaw. "And you found something."

She put her fingers on top of the notepad, her expression grim. "Yeah. Two of the men seem to check out. I was able to find them on Facebook and LinkedIn, cross-reference their info. All seemed pretty standard. Neither are in tech jobs or had anything that stood out. But the third—the credit card info was dummy info. Some business that doesn't exist—at least not online. And I couldn't find any name connected to the account. I think that could be our guy."

Hayes's stomach dipped, dread curling through him. "What's his Hayven name?"

She sighed, her face drawn. "Dmitry."

Hayes kept his expression as placid as possible. "Just because you can't verify who he is doesn't mean he's the hacker. Maybe he's just extra cautious about protecting his identity."

She nodded. "Maybe, but it seems suspicious. Someone smart enough to have that level of security is a flag in and of itself."

Hayes rubbed his brow bone, the information sinking in and twisting around in his head. He obviously knew *he* wasn't the hacker, but the fact that those on the list were tied to him in some way pretty much confirmed their deepest fear. "Fuck."

Cora cleared her throat, ignoring his outburst. "And, just so you know, I could probably get more information on this guy if we need it. More than what I could find in the system. But it may mean venturing into some ethically gray areas. That's really what I needed to run by you."

Hayes looked up at that, wary. "What do you mean?"

She shifted in her chair, looking altogether uncomfortable. "I, well, I know Dmitry in the game. We . . . chatted regularly, developed a friendship, which just freaks me out now, thinking about it. He seemed like a good guy, but maybe this was all some part of his mind game. I was chatting with him the night of the attack. He would've known I was heading home."

Hayes stared at her, only hearing half of what she'd said. "Wait, you've talked to Dmitry *regularly*?"

"Yes. I know I said I mainly observed in the game, but I was lying to protect my privacy. I guess that's kind of a moot point now after what happened this afternoon. But the only reason I'm bringing it up is that I could try to draw him out since he trusts me a little. We broke things off recently, but I may be able to get him to talk to me. Poke around."

Alarm bells were going off in Hayes's head, adrenaline like a dam break in his blood. She'd talked to Dmitry. He'd only talked to one woman regularly. One who'd dominated his mind for months. One who he'd had to let go. One who . . .

Was sitting right in front of him.

Worlds collided in his head in a fiery crash. *Wham!* Fantasy smashing into reality. The manufactured images of Lenore mixing in with the woman sitting across from him. *I'm just an average girl.* Memories of so many nights of talking, teasing, playing. He'd made this woman come. He'd made her laugh. He'd opened himself up to her in a way he hadn't to any woman in years. He'd been grieving the loss of her.

This woman.

Cora.

Cora was *Lenore*.

She frowned. "I mean, I obviously don't want to put the company at any legal risk. I just . . . If we can find out who this is, we may be able to press charges or at least know *why* . . ."

His thoughts were like a tornado in his head and he had to curl his hands to keep them from trembling. "Dmitry isn't the guy."

She blinked behind her glasses, probably put off by the tone and harshness of the words. "What?"

"I know who Dmitry is. He's not the guy."

"You—" Her lips opened, closed. "You know Dmitry?"

"I do." He stared down at his blotter, unable to look her way.

He was afraid his poker face would falter. God, how had he not considered Cora could be Lenore? Lenore had been smart like Cora. She'd not shown up online the night of the attack. And then that last night they'd talked . . . *I met a guy. A dom.* She'd met *Ren.* It all seemed so obvious now.

But everything about her was so different from what she portrayed as Lenore. He knew that people altered their appearances in the game, but Hayes had been expecting a tall, outgoing blonde. Not the quirky techie who wore shirts with eighties' cartoon characters on them. Cora had her own look, her own style, and sex appeal in spades. And she didn't apologize for that. Why had she changed so much about herself in the game?

But Ren's words came back to him—about how Cora had been hurt, overlooked, passed over because she was different. The realization made his chest ache. Cora had created Lenore to be the woman she thought people wanted, who she thought she was supposed to be.

Cora shifted in her chair. "Is the guy someone who might want to mess with the company?"

"No." Hayes peered up, finding her tense and worried. "Cora, I'm Dmitry."

She stared at him, her expression going lax. "What?"

The shock in that one uttered word was absolute. Stark.

He wanted to reassure her, to explain, but he was reeling himself. She was Lenore. This was the woman he'd started to fall for. The thought was like a slow-burning wick inside him, one that had a bomb on the end.

She pressed the heels of her hands to her eyes. "You're Dmitry."

"Cora—"

"Give me a second here." She didn't lower her hands. "Did you know? Please tell me you didn't know. Tell me that I haven't been some joke since I started."

"Of course I didn't know. I wouldn't have— I would've never put that together. You—"

"Aren't blond and stacked and built like a brick shithouse?" she bit out. "Yeah, I'm aware."

He frowned. "That's not what I was going to say."

She shook her head, lowered her hands, and stared at her lap. "God, I thought I'd been through some mortifying moments in my life, but the universe keeps upping the ante. I can't even look at you right now. The things we talked about, did . . . *Shit*."

"Yeah, you probably shouldn't look. If I see your face, your international espionage career will be ruined."

The words seemed to catch her off guard, and she made some sound in the back of her throat, like a laugh with a rope tied around it. He wanted to reach out, touch her, pull her into his lap and curl his body around her, more so than any moment in the office earlier. This was a fucking revelation, a blinding light. Two hours ago, she'd been Cora, the smart, sexy woman Ren was pursuing. A stranger. But now she was Lenore. A woman he'd trusted, one who'd snuck past the guard. In so many ways, that woman felt like *his*. His submissive. His girl.

But he wasn't stupid enough to think she felt the same way. This changed everything. He wasn't Dmitry. This wasn't Hayven. This was no fantasy.

"I know I'm not who you wanted me to be," he said in a low voice. "The big bad dominant spy turns out to be an ex-con who's just trying to put one foot in front of the other each day without fucking everything up. That's not very sexy. I'm sorry."

She finally lifted her gaze to his, her eyes flickering with too many things to pick out one. "*That's* what you think? That's what you think I'm freaking out about?"

"I—"

"You know you're more than that, right? Where you've been the last few years isn't who you are."

His jaw flexed. "It's a big part."

"A small part. You know what I see? I see a guy who started a successful company and made it through a really tragic thing. A guy who didn't want to make me feel uncomfortable when I started here. The guy who when my head was about to tilt off the desk earlier cradled it so I wouldn't get hurt." She held his gaze. "You're the guy who Ren looks at like you hold his world in your palm."

He swallowed.

Her attention traveled over him, openly taking him in. "And you're not all that different from the game. No blue hair, but you're still big and intimidating. Ridiculously good-looking." She rubbed her lips together, a rare bout of shyness surfacing. "Unlike me, who lied and went all Kate Upton when I'm more Tina Fey."

"You didn't lie," he said simply.

Her lips kicked up at the corner. "Of course I did. I look nothing like—"

He sniffed. "You think I gave a shit about what your cartoon character looked like?"

"You—"

He gave in to the urge and reached out to her, gently touching a fingertip to her forehead. "This, Cora. This is who L was to me. Your words. Your wit. The way you"—he cleared his throat again and sat back in his chair—"the way you trusted me, submitted to me."

A pink tinge stained her cheeks, her almost invisible freckles standing out in relief.

"And even though I couldn't pinpoint it, when we first met in person, I felt something. Like this jolt of awareness. Maybe it was recognition. Some gut part of me recognizing that part of you. I couldn't figure out why I couldn't get Cora the hacker out of my head."

She smirked at that. "Not your usual type."

"No," he said simply.

She stiffened, his brutal honesty obviously catching her off guard.

"You're not. Not in the obvious ways. You're the kind of woman I prefer to be friends with."

She winced and looked down, hiding her expression and grasping her elbows. "Right."

He frowned, realizing how she'd taken it, and stood to step around his desk. He sat on the edge of it and bumped his knee against hers. "Look at me."

After a breath, she lifted her head, her defenses clear in the set of her jaw.

"I mean that I only slept with people who were no risk. They were there to do some kink and go on with their day. Ironic, considering how that worked out for me. But I didn't want to start up something with someone who I could actually get attached to, who I wanted to spend time with outside of the sex. I mean, fuck, look how long I avoided crossing that line with Ren."

Her brows dipped.

"I cared about him too much. And someone like you . . ." He peered toward the window, remembering those long conversations with Lenore, how comfortable they'd become, how much he'd looked forward to the chats with her, not just the sex talk. "Someone who could make me laugh and help me forget all this shit I've been going through, someone who challenged me and turned me on at the same time? Someone who wasn't afraid to match me toe-to-toe on kink?" He looked back to her, forcing himself to meet her eyes and be naked with the truth. "That's like world-class danger for a guy who doesn't want to fall in love. Lenore was a risk, but she was behind a screen. You, on the other hand, are a full-on terror threat."

Her lips parted, those hazel eyes of hers tracking over his face with something akin to wonder. "I—I don't even know what to say to that."

"Say it was real," he said softly.

"That what was?"

"Our conversations. The things we shared. The things we did together. The feelings you said you felt."

She wet her lips and bravely met his eyes. "It was real." Her throat worked as she swallowed. "It still is. I've been miserable all week missing you."

Every ounce of air he'd been holding whooshed out of him.

Without letting himself think too hard about it, without giving the anxiety time to take hold, he reached out and took her hand, pulling her to her feet. He guided her between his knees, cupped her face, and kissed her, letting everything he'd felt for Lenore over all those months pour into it. She was here. She was real.

He was so *tired*. Tired of hiding. Tired of keeping so many emotions tucked away. Tired of being scared. Tired of fighting his instincts.

He'd let himself go with Ren and now the woman who had become such an important part of his days was here before him, in the flesh, her heart beating hard beneath his fingertips, her mouth against his. He wasn't going to let this moment slip by and he wasn't going to be scared.

So he held her face in his palms and kissed her like he meant it, and he didn't let go for a long damn time.

NINETEEN

"I think we should go out." Ren plopped into the arm-chair across from Hayes and took a sip of his beer.

Hayes looked up from his spot on the couch where he was going through Cora's notes yet again. A rollicking Friday night. "What?"

"Out. The three of us. Take a break from all this stuff and have some fun. Well, fun outside the office. Apparently, I missed a hot make-out session yesterday afternoon."

Hayes set down the highlighter he'd been using on the notes and rubbed his brow, trying to process Ren's request. "You want the three of us to go out? Like on a date?"

Ren shrugged. "Why not?"

"Uh, maybe because you don't date. And we've never taken a woman we're sleeping with out unless it was to The Ranch."

Ren tilted his head in a come-on-now way. "Are you actually going to sit there and pretend Cora is just another sub we're doing scenes with? Like you're not secretly over there doodling hearts around her name and trying to figure out a way to get me out of the picture now that you know she's Lenore?"

Hayes snorted. "Get you out of the picture? Wow, is the great

Ren Muroya *insecure*? Someone call the media to document this. The world is ending."

"Fuck you, Fox," Ren said, his tone offhanded but the line of questioning ridiculously transparent. "I'm just saying, you've typically gravitated more toward women. And she's—"

Hayes sat up, reached over and grabbed Ren's shirt, and kissed him like he liked to fuck him, rough and deep and without coming up for air. When he was done, he shoved Ren back into the armchair and sank back onto the couch, adjusting the front of his jeans where his cock was perking up for the party. "You're not my consolation prize, dickhead. As some wise Japanese dude pointed out recently, I'm in love with you. And apparently, I'm stuck with that affliction. I fear it's lifelong. So be worried. You're not getting rid of me."

Ren eyed him and took another pull of his beer, but his shoulders visibly relaxed and the corners of his eyes creased—a hidden smile. "Only you could manage to call me a dickhead in some grand romantic speech."

Hayes reached for his own beer. "What can I say? I have a way with words."

"And for what it's worth, I like that you're into Cora, that she's your Lenore. I don't know her the way you do yet, but I want to. I don't remember things ever clicking quite like they did in the office yesterday, even with you not touching her yet. It felt . . . natural. Easy." He stared down at his bottle, a wrinkle in his brow. "I just . . . well, I guess I've never had anything at stake when we've shared a woman in the past. Now it feels . . . bigger. Complicated." He let his head fall back against the chair, closed his eyes, and sighed. "This love thing is kind of a pain in the ass."

Hayes laughed and lifted his bottle. "Ain't that the fucking truth."

Ren's eyes blinked open but his gaze remained on the ceiling. "So we should go out. People who are trying to have some kind of relationship go on dates. Plus, we haven't had a chance to just hang out with Cora and have a good time. Now that you can feel comfortable with her, what's stopping us?"

Hayes frowned. "I do feel comfortable with her. But that doesn't mean I feel comfortable going out in public. Can't we just invite her over?"

"Yes, because that's not an asshole move. Let's follow up a quickie at the office where we sent her back to work with an offer of *Hey there, we really don't feel like doing the date thing. Want to come over and we'll order pizza? Maybe tie you up and fuck afterward?*"

Hayes sniffed. "Yeah, okay. I see your point."

"Come on. You can go over all those notes on Monday. Cora's locked up the system. The guy who's after you can't get to you that way anymore, so we don't have to spend every waking moment on the hunt. And you shouldn't have to be scared to go in public. Aren't you stir-crazy? Work. Home. Work. Home."

Hayes grunted.

"Plus, look what we've got at our fingertips. A gorgeous woman who's dying to try more kink and who for some unknown reason is into us both. And we have each other. I feel like I've opened all these awesome Christmas gifts, but then no one's letting me take them out of the box so I can play with them."

Hayes's lips twitched into a smile at that. "You've taken me out of the box plenty this week."

Ren flipped him off.

"Christmas presents, huh? Are you going to pout now? Maybe throw a fit."

"You know I could. I was a nightmare of a child," Ren said. "I still have it in me."

Hayes sighed. "You know I'd love to take you both out, but it's . . . hard. Being out. If people recognize me—"

"Then let them look. So the fuck what. We've got nothing to hide."

Hayes ran a hand over the back of his neck, but he couldn't seem to say no to Ren. And the thought of all three of them just going out for a night of fun did hold a hell of a lot of appeal. They'd done all of this ass-backward. Cora deserved better than that. "Fine. But something low-key, all right? Dinner, a movie, something like that."

"Absolutely. Low-key. I'm going to go and give her a call." He hopped up from the couch and ten minutes later returned with another beer for Hayes.

"She shot you down?" Hayes asked.

"Tonight's a no-go, but we're all set for tomorrow night. She has plans with her friends but said that we could go along with her."

Hayes's mouth flattened. He hadn't signed up for friends or actual socializing. "Out with her friends. Where?"

Ren settled into the chair and propped his feet on the coffee table. "No big deal. Just karaoke night at that gay club that opened a few weeks ago."

"*Karaoke?*" Utter horror filled Hayes. "I said low-key. You better be kidding, Muroya."

Ren's smile went big. "Guess you'll find out."

Fuck. He wasn't kidding.

Cora fussed with the neckline of her shirt before opening the door for Ren. She felt ten kinds of self-conscious in the outfit. But when Ren had asked her to go out on a date with him and Hayes, she didn't want to show up in the same old thing. She'd tried a dress Grace had loaned her, but she'd felt like she was in drag. Plus, Ren had told her he liked her style. It wasn't like he'd expect her to show up glammed out. So she'd settled on a pair of black cigarette pants, a silver tank top, and a pair of heels she'd tucked in the back of her closet. Hopefully, she wouldn't break her neck.

When she swung open the door, she found Ren standing there and looking like he'd stepped off the pages of a men's magazine.

Dark jeans, thick-soled black boots, and a deep blue button-up shirt rolled up at the sleeves and open at the collar. His gaze traveled slowly over her. "Well, damn. Maybe we should stay in."

She smirked. "That bad?"

He grabbed her by the waist and dragged her to him, pressing a quick peck to her lips. "That good. You look great. Though, you sure you want to torture yourself with those shoes?"

She smiled. "I figured I should try to look like a girl sometimes."

"Screw that noise. Just do you. Who says there's a certain way to look like a girl anyway?"

"The world."

"Fuck the world. The world also says I shouldn't be going out on a date with two people. The world has issues."

"Mmm, agreed. Speaking of which, where's Hayes?"

"Meeting us there. He said he had some errands to run first, but I'm guessing he just wants a getaway vehicle in case gay karaoke is a little too much for him."

She laughed. "Gay karaoke is too much for anyone. I think that's the point. I'm not entirely sure how I got roped into it. Maybe I was drunk when I agreed."

"Whose idea was it?"

"My best friend, Grace, and my neighbors. I think this is their attempt at making sure I don't become a workaholic. They have no idea what I've been doing at work."

"Or who."

"Exactly. I tried to protest but there's no stopping Grace when she gets an idea in her head. I'm a little surprised you two volunteered to come along, though."

"To karaoke? Oh, I'm all over that." He gave her a sly grin. "I'm Japanese. I was born for karaoke."

She tilted her head and cocked a brow. "Oh, really?"

"Okay, so maybe I've never actually *sang* karaoke, but I know I'd be amazing at it. I'm pretty amazing at everything, you know.

You think they'll have Taylor Swift songs? I like that one about Starbucks lovers."

She snorted. "I'm glad you're looking forward to it, because I'm definitely not singing."

"Oh, yes you are, Benning. I obnoxiously invited us along on your friends' night out for the sole purpose of hearing you sing."

She crossed her arms. "Good luck with that."

"There's nothing a little alcohol can't fix. Plus, I'm infinitely charming and persuasive. Your stubbornness has no chance against my awe-inspiring powers."

He gave an evil laugh and she rolled her eyes, but the truth was she couldn't help but be charmed. He did have that superpower. He put her at ease and guided her to places she'd never thought she'd go with a joke and a smile. Her friends were going to love him.

Some of the nerves that had been hopping in her belly calmed down. The thought of bringing Ren and Hayes to meet her friends had seemed risky when Ren had suggested it. So much about her life lately was separated into neat categories—her "real" life in one sphere, Ren, Hayes, Dmitry, and Lenore in this other place. Bringing the two together was scary. Her friends could reveal all kinds of things about her if the alcohol was flowing. They had enough dirt on her to be the equivalent of the mom showing naked baby pictures.

And Ren and Hayes held even deeper secrets, things her friends would never suspect about her. But at the same time, she didn't want to have to lie or hide anymore. It hadn't just been her months as Lenore. Sometimes it felt like she'd spent her life putting on a show, changing costumes, rotating masks, never knowing the right script. She was tired.

She needed to trust that her friends loved her, that Ren and Hayes liked her as is. She just wanted to be Cora—whoever the fuck that was. And this would be a good, though slightly terrifying, step in that direction.

Plus, the thought of going out for a night of fun without all the work stuff and angst hanging over them was damn appealing.

"I think charming people don't point out that they're charming." She put her hand on his shoulder to steady herself and kicked off the dreaded heels and then grabbed a pair of black lace-up boots she'd left by the door. She slipped them on and tied them.

Ren smiled.

"And if I'm forced to sing, you're going to have to be up there with me." She stepped onto the porch and hooked a finger in his belt loop. "Plus, I'm thinking I'd be an idiot not to bring the hot Japanese guy to my epic karaoke battle. The competitors will be so intimidated."

Ren flashed a grin, looped his arms around her waist, and planted a quick kiss on her lips. "Right? We're going to kill it."

"Truth. Something could die if I attempt to sing. That's for sure."

He laughed at that, the sound echoing down the empty street, and then released her so she could lock up. Ren grabbed her hand when she was done and led her down the front steps and to his car like a proper date. A twinge of giddiness moved through her at that. She couldn't remember the last time a guy had taken her out. Kevin had been all about hanging out. Not going out. And he certainly hadn't treated anything they'd done like a date.

When Ren released her hand to open the car door for her, Cora reared up and gasped. The street was dark and the bushes in her driveway had blocked it, but parked at the curb was a gleaming Corvette Z06. Moonlight gleamed off its shiny hood. If there were such things as car angels, they'd be singing.

Ren cocked his head. "You all right?"

She nodded quickly, breaking herself from her frozen state. "Yep."

But really, she was still staring. The machine was something to behold—metallic red and obnoxiously sexy in the way only American muscle cars could be. She wanted to roll herself on it like a girl in an eighties rock video. But she tried to be cool about it. She did *not* want to look like one of those women impressed by a hot car. She managed to contain herself until she and Ren climbed inside and he turned on the engine. The sound of it was like a lion's roar, deep and full and ready to eat up the road.

Cora sucked in a breath and touched the dash. "Good God."

Ren looked over and chuckled. "Right? I think the same thing every time I turn her on."

Turn her on. Well, the car wasn't the only one getting that treatment.

"Is now the right time to admit I have a total car fetish?" She petted the dash again.

"It is *always* the right time to confess your fetishes. I'd love an itemized list in fact. With pictures." He gave her an I-dare-ya grin. "But I wouldn't have guessed car fetish for you."

"Yeah, looking at the piece of junk I own, you probably wouldn't. But man, if I had the money to blow, this is exactly the type I'd buy. Fast and obnoxious and fuck-the-speed-limit red."

"Now you're turning *me* on." He pulled out onto her street. "Where'd you pick up a thing for cars?"

She ran her fingers over the seat. "My dad taught me a lot about them, and he's let me take spins in some of the cars he's refurbished over the years. He's the chief mechanic for Bax Renway."

"The stock-car driver?" Ren leaned back and glanced over, looking impressed. "That's awesome."

"Yeah. It's fun. I get great seats when the races roll through Texas."

Ren tapped his fingers along the steering wheel like there was music only he could hear. "Was it hard to have a dad who traveled all the time?"

"Not really. He's my biological dad but never lived with me or anything. He and my mom were just good friends and were never in a romantic relationship. When she decided she wanted a baby and hadn't found the right guy yet, he volunteered to be the donor and to be a part of my life if I wanted him to be."

"Wow."

"Yeah. He's a good guy. We don't see each other much since he's always on the road, but we try to get together a few times a year. He would approve of this car."

Ren laughed. "But would he approve of me?"

She cocked an eyebrow. "That is to be determined. My guess is with this car, he would suspect you're *that guy*."

He gave her the side eye. "That guy? I'm thinking this is an accusation."

She leaned back against the buttery leather of the seat. "Yes. The guy who knows he's gorgeous and has money and can get a girl—or boy—in bed with a spin in his hot car and a smile."

Ren laughed. "Is that what you think of me, Benning?"

She shrugged. "I don't think you'd need the car."

He peered over and his mouth kicked up at the corner. "Maybe I'm just overcompensating with the car. This could be smoke and mirrors."

She rolled her eyes. "Right. For what?"

"My deviant, kinky, polyamorous ways."

"Uh-huh," she said, not hiding the sarcasm. "Such a burden."

He looked back to the road, some of the humor slipping from his expression. "Believe me, most people aren't that open-minded or interested. Maybe for a night, an adventure to prove to themselves they're a little wild. And that's fine. It's fun. But really, I'm just a prop in those games. I'm not the guy someone wants to date, not when they realize those things are a part of me, not a sideshow or temporary diversion."

The quietly spoken words caught her off guard. She'd never thought it about it from that angle. She imagined lovers fell into the laps of men like Ren and Hayes without much effort from the guys. They were handsome and successful, funny. But that wasn't all they were. Long-term, they came with a lot of fine print, a lot of complications that didn't fit into the neat package society called relationships or romance or marriage.

Then another thought hit her and she frowned. "You think that's what I'm doing, isn't it? Making you two my wild adventure to prove something to myself?"

God, *was she*? That didn't feel like the truth, but if not that, then what was this?

Ren glanced over at her, his expression softening. "I wasn't saying that. And if that's the case, it's absolutely okay. This is supposed to be light and fun. And I know you don't see us as props."

"Of course I don't," she said, appalled by the idea.

He smiled. "Sorry, I don't even know why I got all serious on you. I guess I'm just realizing that I haven't been on an actual date in a long time. This is foreign territory for me."

She let out a breath. "That makes two of us. I'm not the most dateable person either."

He sniffed derisively and focused on the road again. "Benning, don't fool yourself. You're supremely dateable."

She blinked, the words lingering between them, and then cleared her throat, searching for something to get them into safer territory. "So why'd you pick this car?"

Ren shrugged. "After discovering the Batmobile when I was a kid, I've always had a hard-on for fast cars. I had four speeding tickets and one fender bender under my belt within the first six months of getting my permit."

"Your parents must've loved that."

"They took away my permit and threatened to send me to military school."

The engine roared as Ren picked up speed on the interstate. The streetlights flashed over the dark red hood in a steady, hypnotic pattern. "I'm guessing they didn't make good on that threat."

Ren blew out of breath. "No. I didn't give them time. I ran away right before I turned sixteen. Didn't come home for a year."

She turned to him at that. "Wow. Because of the car thing?"

He lifted a shoulder but the move was tense. "Because of a lot of things. My parents are good people, but I'm from a family of over-achievers and was definitely not up to par. I preferred art, got in trouble a lot, had issues focusing in school. Plus I had all these mixed-up feelings about my sexuality and no one to talk to about it. It made me reckless and too brave for my own good. So when I met a guy and he decided to move to Vegas, I took off with him."

She shook her head at that, trying to imagine how bad things had to be to leave home at fifteen. "Sounds like your high school years were way more adventurous than mine. My big act of rebellion was messing with the school computers and rigging them to play my favorite Broadway songs when they booted up."

Ren's expression changed in the reflection of the streetlights. "Believe me, running away was the stupidest thing I ever did. I should've gotten over myself and listened to my parents."

She sensed there was more to the story. His normally devil-may-care attitude had dropped away. "What happened with the guy?"

Ren's smile was grim. "Let's just say I found out the hard way that he was not a good man."

She frowned. "I'm sorry."

"Yeah. But it is what it is. And if I hadn't made that colossal mistake, I may have never met Hayes."

"How'd that happen?"

"He lived across the street from my parents. When I got picked up by the cops and carted home, I was all screwed up. Hayes caught me doing stupid shit and almost going back to Gordon—the guy. He set me straight. Pretty much decided I was going to listen to him and that was that. Bossy bastard."

She laughed. "Hard to imagine the Hayes I know doing that. But . . ."

"But what?"

"I know him as Dmitry. I could totally see *him* doing that."

Ren smiled. "I still can't believe you two were talking all that time. I'm glad you were, though, and that it was *you*. He finally knows there's a woman he can trust. I can't tell you how huge that is."

She nodded and looked out at the night. "Is that why I'm here? Why we're doing this?"

"Huh?"

"The three of us. You already said you don't normally date. And you two are together now. Hayes reached out to Lenore because he was lonely, but that was before you two reconnected. Y'all don't really need me involved." She shrugged. "You suspect I'm here for adventure. But why do *you* want me here? Am I here to prove that Hayes is back to the guy you used to know? Am I like the beta test? The final systems check to make sure he's good to go?"

"Cora—"

"I mean, if that's the case, it's fine. Honestly. I'm going into this knowing you're together and in love. And you just said tonight is supposed to be light and fun. But I like to know where I stand so that I can keep that clear. Is this like a one-big-night thing and then we move on?"

"Is that what you really think?" A car honked behind them because the light had turned green and Ren hadn't moved. Ren cursed and punched the gas, then took the next turn, pulling onto the shoulder of a side road. He put the car in park and shifted to face her. "Cora?"

"Of course that's what I think. There aren't many alternatives to consider."

Ren looked more than a little annoyed. "There's a long list of other alternatives. How about, we like you? And beyond how much I like hanging out with you, you and Hayes have had this entire relationship online. I don't know what all went on, but I know that you were important to him. That he was torn the fuck up the night he broke things off with Lenore."

She looked down at her hands.

"We're such a fucking mess," Ren said on a laugh, "each of us trying to figure out the other's motives. Maybe we should consider that we're all in uncharted territory here and just figuring this out as we go along. That there is no master plan beyond the fact that we're seeing where this goes."

Cora's lips rolled inward, the fervor of Ren's speech getting to her. "So this is really like . . . a date to see how things go?"

He looked to the sky and laughed. "I love how you say that like you don't believe it. Yes. Of course it is. Have you met me? I'm the opposite of the guy with a master plan. Did you miss the part where I got pissed at my parents and took off with an abusive psycho without thinking past the next day?"

She swallowed hard. "He was abusive?"

Ren grimaced like he'd just realized he'd let that slip. He let out a sigh and looked past her shoulder toward the darkness for a long second then back to her, meeting her eyes. "Yeah, he played dominant but was really a sociopath in disguise. Enjoyed using teen boys like me and loaned them out for sadistic games with his friends."

Her chest squeezed at that. "Ren . . ."

He looked down, a rueful smile touching his lips. "Yeah, this is so not how I saw tonight's conversation going. It was supposed to be way sexier and didn't involve deep, dark confessions about my fucked-up teen years or my thoughts on dating."

She reached out and grabbed his hand. "Hey, I told you that I didn't need the car, but maybe I did need this."

He peered up, questions in his eyes.

"Realness," she said softly. "I'm not sure I could ever trust *that guy*. That guy is intimidating as hell. That's one reason why I keep questioning how I play into all this. That guy can be a little too smooth, too perfect. But maybe I can trust this one. The one who's still gorgeous and smart and has a hot car but who also isn't afraid to be straight-up honest with me and let me see the not-so-shiny parts. Thank you for that."

"I won't lie to you, Cora. I never have."

"I believe you."

He ran his thumb over the top of her knuckles. "And I won't use you. I can't tell you what's going to happen tomorrow or the next day. But I promise that whenever I'm with you, there's no side game going on, no secret subtext that you're not a part of. I'm just feeling my way through it like you are."

She smiled. "There has been a lot of feeling. And groping."

A half smile from Ren. "I'm hoping there's more to come."

"I will refrain from making a dirty comment with the word *come*."

"You are the pillar of strength." He lifted her hand to his mouth and kissed the top of it. Then he brought her hand to his chest and leaned forward. Their lips met in an unhurried way, sweet and exploring. Almost like they were meeting for the first time. His fingers teased at the nape of her neck and her eyes fell shut, her hand curling into his shirt. A soft sigh escaped her and Ren deepened the kiss, drawing her into the trance of simply kissing this man and giving herself over to the possibility of him.

He whispered her name in the breath between kisses and then went back to melting her into a puddle with his lips.

This. This felt right. So much more than sexual. Real. Honest. A connection to this beautiful man who'd lived through some of his own horror and had felt like an outsider, too, a man who she had more in common with than she would've ever considered.

And for the first time, she found herself entertaining the very real possibility that she could fall for him. Maybe a part of her already had.

After a few long minutes of kisses and soft touches, Ren leaned back, a tentative, almost wondrous expression on his face. He cupped her face and dragged a thumb over her cheek like he was seeing her for the first time. He gave a little headshake, as if to pull himself from some train of thought, and that trademark smile lit his face, chasing away the naked expression. "So now are you ready to sing really bad karaoke with me tonight?"

"I will never be ready for that."

He lowered his hand and shifted in his seat. "How about if we win the karaoke battle with your friends, I'll let you drive the car?"

She grinned and rubbed her hands together like a cartoon villain. "Will you let me take her to a deserted road and put this baby through her paces? I need to feel the full extent of all that power beneath me."

He put the car in gear. "Stop talking dirty to me, Benning. But yes, you, me, this car, and a deserted road will be all yours."

She laughed, tucking away the lingering buzz of the kiss and the feelings stirring in her for later analysis. Tonight was supposed to be about fun. She would try not to overthink it. "Deal. Let's go sing our asses off."

TWENTY

Cora and Ren arrived at the club about fifteen minutes late after their little detour. The place was already teeming with people but Grace, Carlos, and Josh had apparently gotten there on time and had snagged them a big round booth in the corner of the club—or at least that's what Grace had texted her along with, *Stop working and get your ass here.* She'd been tempted to text back, *Sorry, making out with hot guy. Give me a minute.*

But she was glad she hadn't because when Grace caught sight of her heading their way with Ren, her face would've made a perfect meme for OMFG. Cora wished she had a camera.

Ren pressed his hand to the base of her spine and leaned close to her ear to be heard over the really bad rendition of "Purple Rain" a guy was singing on stage. "Guess you didn't warn them you were bringing dates."

She grinned. "And ruin the chance to see that look on my best friend's face? Hell, no. She jumped my shit when I didn't try to get your number at the party."

Ren chuckled and put his arm fully around her waist, leaving no questions about his status as her date. "I like this best friend. You *should* have given me your number."

"I don't give my number to guys I catch getting blow jobs in hallways."

"Details."

Cora kept her smile in place as she walked over to the booth. Carlos and Josh looked up at the same time and both did their own version of Grace's surprised expression. Eyebrows crawling up foreheads, parted lips. God, everybody really had decided she was a sexless hermit. "Hey, guys."

"Hey, yourself," Grace said, openly giving Ren a once-over.

Cora tipped her head toward Ren. "This is Ren Muroya. I'm working on a project for his company." *And sleeping with him on my lunch hour.* "Ren, this is Grace."

Ren nodded and shook Grace's hand. "Yep, I remember you. Lady who saved Cora from my evil designs at the party."

Grace laughed. "That obvious?"

Cora snorted. "And these are Carlos and Josh, my neighbors."

"The ones who scared the psycho away." Ren reached across the table to shake their hands as well, his affable expression going more serious. "Next drink's on me for that."

"Don't worry about it," Josh said, trying to wave off the offer.

But Carlos bumped Josh in the shoulder. "What he means to say is, *Yes, thank you, we will always accept free liquor from kind strangers.*"

Josh draped his arm over the back of the booth behind Carlos and his lip curled into a smug smile. "Yes, that's how I got you to come home with me. Free liquor."

"Don't believe him," Carlos said between sips of his drink. "I wasn't that easy. It was expensive liquor. *Patrón.* I have standards."

Ren laughed. "Then Patrón shots for everyone."

"Woo-hoo," Grace chimed in and lifted her martini glass. "I'll toast to that. Plus, Cora will probably need three of them to get her up on that stage."

Cora groaned and whirled a finger in the air. "Just bring me the bottle."

Something buzzed in Ren's pocket and vibrated against Cora's hip. Ren tucked his hand between them and grabbed his phone, reading the screen. "That's Hayes. He's trying to find us." He gave her waist a quick squeeze. "Be right back."

"Sure."

Ren released her, stopped a few steps away to tell the waiter something, and then disappeared into the throng of people. When Cora turned to climb into the booth, she had three expectant faces greeting her. She scooted next to Josh and gave them all an innocent shoulder shrug, enjoying being on this side of the dynamic for a change. "What?"

"You know what," Josh said. "I thought we were here to get you out of the house and away from your lonely workaholic schedule and you walk in with *that guy*?"

Cora had to laugh. *That guy*.

"So you're working with the dude you escaped from at the party and are now on a date with him?" Grace said, stunned. "You said you didn't give him your card."

"Long story," Cora said, wishing she had a drink. She was trying to play it cool, but everything that happened with Ren in the car was still whirling around her head. And soon Hayes would be here, too. Hayes—her other date. And Ren's date.

God. She was in so far over her head she needed a damn oxygen tank.

"So where'd he go off to?" Carlos asked.

"His business partner is joining us for a drink." She looked toward the crowd and as if on cue, Ren and Hayes squeezed through. "There they are."

Cora was struck by the two of them walking so close. The crowd didn't allow for much else, but now that she knew what she knew, she couldn't help letting her mind notice all the little things.

Their obvious comfort with each other. The way Hayes cleared the path for the both of them with gentle nudges to the people in their way. These two powerful men loved each other. And they were inviting her in for a little while. She could be in their bed by the time the night was done.

Cora's skin went tingly at the thought. Anticipation. Nerves. A little bit of fear.

"Whoa," Grace said, breaking Cora from her thoughts. "Dibs on the big guy. He's . . . Yeah."

"Back off, Gracie," Cora snapped, the response automatic and rife with warning.

"I—" Grace's lips pursed, annoyance there. "What? Is he taken or something?"

Josh coughed and Cora glanced at him. He gave her an I-didn't-say-a-thing look, but curiosity gleamed in his eyes.

Cora smoothed a wrinkle from her pants, trying to get ahold of her reaction and look nonchalant. "Yes. He's taken."

Truth.

"Damn, that's all you had to say. Jeez." Grace sipped her drink, eyeballing Cora over the rim. "You need to get some alcohol in you, woman. You're tense."

Before the guys reached the table, the waiter stopped by and dropped off a bottle of Patrón and a line of shot glasses. "Would you like me to pour?"

Carlos got a wide grin at the sight of the bottle. "Line us up, brother."

The waiter got to work, pouring with expert precision and setting them up with the liquor. As soon as he strode off, Ren and Hayes sidled up to the table. Hayes looked about as comfortable as a guy with rocks in his shoes and ice cubes in his shorts. From the outside looking in, he had that look of a straight guy silently freaking out that he was in a gay club. But he wasn't straight and she knew that wasn't it at all.

She recognized that skittish yet stoic vibe. That was the same act she pulled when forced to socialize with strangers. Being around this many people freaked him out. His gaze slid to hers, something tense there, an SOS to a fellow introvert maybe. That snapped her into action. "Hayes, so glad you could make it. You can now bear witness to the utter destruction of whichever song I choose to sing for karaoke night."

He stared at her for a second, but then, as if he had heard the words through water, he gave his delayed response. A brief smile. "Well, I can't miss that."

Cora introduced him to everyone, using only his first name just in case anyone followed the news too closely. She scooted over, trying to make room for both of them, but only Ren could fit.

Grace slid over and patted the spot next to her. "Hayes, you can sit next to me. I don't bite."

"Well, that's just because Cora told her you were taken," Carlos supplied. "Otherwise, Grace *would* bite you."

Grace laughed and snapped her teeth at Carlos, but Hayes lifted his gaze to Cora's. A cocked eyebrow and a secret almost-smile. The invisible connection across the table sent a dart of electric awareness through her. He liked that she'd declared him off-limits.

The look didn't get lost on Ren. He pressed his hand over her knee and traced a little circle over her kneecap. It was a simple touch, nothing outwardly sexual, but it lit up things in Cora's body. They were all thinking the same thing. She could feel it. *What will the night bring? Will it be the three of us tumbling into bed in one hot, sweaty tangle? Will I submit to these two men and give up the control for real?*

Cora's heart tried to beat out of her throat and sweat gathered between her breasts. She grabbed a shot glass. "Time to drink!"

Ren laughed softly next to her, as if he'd read every damning thought in her head. But he didn't say a word. Just slid her a glass of water after she'd downed the shot and watched her sip.

Half an hour later, Cora was wondering if maybe the shots hadn't been the best plan of action. Her head was swimming after the third and her laugh had become too loud. She also found herself leaning into Ren, who took the cue and draped his arm around her. Man, he smelled good. He probably tasted better.

"Thanks," he said against her ear.

"Hmm?"

"You said I smelled good."

"Shit. Did I say that out loud?"

He huffed a laugh against her neck. "Yes. And you can taste whatever you want. But maybe ease up on the liquor before you do that. I'd hate to think you needed beer goggles for us."

She groaned, thinking of the meme. "Same goes for you. Though, I've heard I look better after alcohol."

"Hey." He put a finger under her chin and turned her face toward him. "I'm drinking club soda, gorgeous. And the view's fantastic."

He brushed his thumb over her lips and she shivered.

"But relax. I've got you. No need for nerves. It's just a night out with friends."

He was giving her that assurance. *You've made no promises. We've got no expectations. Be in the moment.*

She licked her lips, tasting the salt of his skin lingering there. "Okay."

Grace, who'd been chatting animatedly with Carlos and oblivious to Cora and Ren's private conversation, clapped her hands and snapped Cora out of her erotic haze. "Okay, it's time for me to make my debut. Everybody up. I need help picking a song. Plus, I might need background vocals."

Carlos grabbed Josh's shirt as Grace tugged at him. "Save me from the crazy blonde."

Josh laughed and handed him another shot. "Drink up, babe. If she needs a background singer, that's all you."

Carlos kicked back the shot and said a prayer in Spanish.

Hayes scooted out of the booth to let the three of them free and looked ready to bolt. But Grace patted his bicep. "You, too, big guy. You can sing bass."

The look on Hayes's face was so stricken that Cora burst into a laugh.

He narrowed his eyes at her as she got to her feet. "Traitor."

She pressed her fingers over her mouth so that the laugh wouldn't turn into a drunk-girl guffaw, and Ren wrapped his arms around her waist and set his chin on her shoulder. "Maybe a little Guns N' Roses, old man?"

Hayes flipped him off as Grace got ahead of them and waved them all toward the dance floor and stage. Hayes sniffed. "There is more chance of this place getting hit by a comet than me singing karaoke."

Ren laughed and grabbed Cora's and Hayes's hands. "Come on, this will be fun."

"I'm with Hayes. This is a bad idea."

But Ren was already pulling them into the press of bodies on the dance floor. The smell of sweat and lust suffused the air and mixed with the alcohol humming in her veins. They got jostled and lost hold of one another. Ren had to step in front of her. She put a hand on his shoulder to create a train and reached back for Hayes.

He glanced down at her hand in surprise.

But she didn't want to overthink it. Let her friends see what they see. She wiggled her fingers. "Come on. You're gonna get lost."

Hayes's big warm hand closed over hers, making her feel tiny in comparison. "Lead the way."

Having her hand on Ren's muscular shoulder and the other clasped in Hayes's hand helped them stay together but left her without much protection from the undulating bodies around her. The club played real music in between the karaoke performances and the patrons seemed to want to take advantage of the good music while they had it. Dancing people closed in around her. Hips bumping her, hands grazing. The physical effect wasn't unpleasant, especially mixing in with the good buzz she had going from the tequila. Her skin seemed hypersensitized, every nerve ending aware and hungry as limbs and fabric brushed over her.

She closed her eyes, letting the sway of the crowd take her for a second while still holding on to her two buoys. The song was hypnotic with a pounding beat, the grinding rhythm of sex and sin. But before long, she could feel the sea sweeping her up in the motion. Her hand slipped from Ren's shoulder and her other arm bent at an uncomfortable angle. Hayes released her, saving her from twisting it the wrong way.

She felt adrift but free all at once. Strangers danced against her, a mix of voices and music and fun. She put her hands above her head and let the music take her. *Thump. Thump. Thump.* The beat vibrated beneath her feet. But when someone bumped into her hard and she almost lost her balance, her eyes popped open.

Flashing lights were all she could see for a moment and then blurred faces as people moved around the dance floor. *Whoa.* Her head was spinning. She grabbed blindly, trying not to topple over. Too much tequila. Not enough air. But no one was standing still and it was like trying to grab bobbing boats.

She listed to the left a little too sharply, one of her shoes catching on a sticky spot on the floor, and she felt the fall coming with no way to stop it. But before she could sprawl onto her ass, Ren was there in front of her and Hayes behind. Hayes grabbed her waist and Ren pulled her against him. "Easy there, Benning."

"Shit." She braced her hands on his shoulders and the warm wall of Hayes closed in behind her. "Glad I didn't wear those heels. Sorry."

"No worries. We've got you. We won't let you fall." His face was only a few inches from her, his body pressed up along hers. The three of them moved without thought to the music, the two leading her effortlessly and keeping her on her feet.

"Better?" Hayes asked, voice close to her ear and sending a shiver down her neck.

Her feet were under her again. "Yeah. Much."

Ren grabbed her hand. "Let's go sing while you're still buzzing. Then it's soda for you for the rest of the night."

She pressed her face to his shoulder. "No singing. Hayes, tell him not to make me sing."

Hayes laughed behind her, the sound warm and rich against her ears.

"Oh, no you don't," Ren said. "No playing the big guy for sympathy. For anything else we do tonight, you can always say no. But this part is a foregone conclusion. Don't leave me with karaoke blue balls."

She snort-laughed. "You should go solo."

"Not happening. Don't make us put you over a shoulder and drag you up there."

The song ended and Hayes stepped back. She turned to look at him, giving her best puppy-dog look. "Please save me."

He smirked. "You're cute when you beg. Maybe we'll see more of that later."

Her lips parted, the suggestion receiving a resounding yes from her libido, but she tipped her chin up. "Low blow, Hayes."

Ren grabbed her hand. "Come on, time's a-wastin'."

She stumbled a bit in her boots.

"Hold up." He stopped their progress and for a brief, shining moment, she thought maybe he'd let her off the hook. But instead he bent down.

"What are you doing?"

He grabbed her ankle and laced up the boot that had come untied. "I need you in fighting shape. There will be dance moves in our performance of awesomeness. I don't want you falling into the audience."

"I—"

His palm slid under her knee and squeezed, sending a shiver up her leg. The simple move had her wanting to blow this joint now. But too soon, Ren stood again. "Let's go."

Reluctantly, she followed. Grace, Carlos, and Josh were huddled around the binder that listed all the songs by the time they reached the front. Hayes stepped to the side, his gaze on Ren and Cora, his expression amused. Traitor, indeed. Ren tapped Grace on the shoulder. "Mind if we jump you in line? Cora's dangerously close to losing her buzz."

Grace lifted her head and turned to Cora, a giddy look on her face. "No shit? You're actually going to sing? Yay!"

"I have not agreed to such—"

But Ren tugged her hand and dragged her toward the deejay. "Oh, you so have."

Cora sent her friends a helpless look, but they seemed to be enjoying her downfall. Cora glanced at the crowd, which had now turned to face the stage, ready to roast the next horrible act to go up. Her stomach flipped over. "Ren, I—"

But Ren was already whispering something to the deejay and then guiding her to the stage. The club wasn't huge but it was packed on a Saturday night, and every one of Cora's shy-girl genes had a simultaneous panic attack.

A few people hooted and hollered when they got on stage— including Josh and Grace. And a few whistles went up, no doubt for Ren, who looked like he belonged on a goddamned stage. Cora, on the other hand, wanted to run. The last time she'd been on a stage she'd been trying out for the school play in ninth grade. She'd had some surge of bravery, letting her love of theater override her nerves. But that had lasted about two-point-three seconds because she'd frozen and had forgotten every line.

Her throat went tight. "I can't do this. And what if you picked a song I don't know?"

"If you don't know this song, we're getting a divorce. The girl who rigged the high school computers for Broadway better show me what's she's got." Ren handed her a microphone and leaned over to peck her on the lips. "You've got this, Benning. Have fun.

No one gives a shit about how good we sing. They're probably hoping we're awful. They just want to be entertained."

"People are gonna throw drinks at us."

"Not a chance." He turned to the crowd, flashing them a winning smile, and then spoke into his microphone. "We're going to give this to you good, ladies and gentlemen, but I need a leather jacket and a boa if available."

Cora blinked. *What the hell?*

The request seemed random and ridiculous, but before a few seconds passed, someone had passed a leather jacket up to the stage from the crowd and a gorgeous drag queen in the front row had kindly donated a pink feather boa.

"Excellent," Ren said. He turned his back to the crowd and slid on the jacket in a reverse striptease, garnering catcalls.

She laughed. She couldn't help it. The guy was so freaking shameless. He waggled his eyebrows at her and then strode over to drape the boa around her neck, leaving her standing there in a shimmery shirt and pink feathers.

He lifted her hand and kissed the top. "Showtime."

The lights went down and Ren made a production of pretending to slick back the sides of his hair. The music started up and the first few notes were instantly recognizable. She closed her eyes and shook her head, unable to stop the goofy grin on her face.

Grease. Of course.

Ren popped the collar of his jacket, gave her a look dripping with sex appeal, and did his best John Travolta as he sang about chills multiplying and losing control.

Cora didn't even have to look at the screen scrolling the words. She'd sung this song an embarrassing amount of times in the safety of her own room. Not that she could've taken her eyes off Ren anyway. He was all in, committing to the role and clearly not afraid to go over the top with his performance. When her part cued up, the smile he sent her was one of pure, boyish delight.

And it was damn contagious. She grinned back, knowing it was about to be the do-or-die moment. She could muddle her way through the lyrics, let everyone see just how uncomfortable she was. Or she could channel that tequila buzz, focus on the sexy, ridiculous spectacle in front of her, and forget about the crowd.

She was going to murder Olivia Newton-John's part with a dull, rusty butcher knife, but she might as well do it to the fullest. People would assume she was drunk. She kind of was.

So with a confidence she channeled from some place outside herself, she put a hand to her hip, strutted across the stage, and sang to Ren that he better shape up. Because, dammit, she needed a man.

Or *men*, as the case may be.

Ren beamed and went nose to nose with her to sing his part and to back her up across the stage. When she got to the edge, he turned her in his arms and pressed her back against his chest. He was deliciously warm, his heart beating as fast as hers.

She knew the next line said the word *affection*, but she was starting to feel this now, feel the energy of their audience. She playfully ground her backside against his front and changed the line. "If you feel an *erection*, you're too shy to display . . ."

The crowd erupted and Ren laughed hard behind her.

She spun in his arms and planted a hand against his chest, giving him a mock seductive look, continuing to change the words. "Better change your direction. Point it that way."

He grinned wide, stole her boa, and then started singing the female portions. Ren sang about needing a man to keep him satisfied as she hijacked his leather jacket. He chased her across the stage and they continued to sing their switched parts.

By the time the song ended and they set their microphones down, the crowd was cheering and singing along. And Cora was blitzed on the high of it all. Ren wrapped his arms around her and picked her up off her feet to spin her around. The world blurred around her, sounds blending, and all she could see was Ren's face in front of her, that handsome face and laughing eyes. She couldn't stop herself. She hooked her legs around his waist, clasped his face in her hands, and kissed him.

It started out playful, a little more show for the performance, but it quickly went from fun to something altogether more heated. Ren's hands gripped her ass, presumably to keep her from falling, but the contact made her groan and soon their tongues were twining and she was kissing him like a starving thing.

The people in the club egged them on and finally the deejay spoke over the loudspeaker. "Now who's going to follow *that* performance?"

The stranger's voice broke Cora from her lusty haze and she pulled away from the kiss, panting. She stared down at Ren with wide eyes. "Shit."

"I second tha—" His gaze shifted over her shoulder, his words hanging unfinished, like he'd caught something shiny in his vision. The heated look from a moment earlier disappeared and his mouth sank into a frown. "Let's get off this stage."

"Is everything okay?" She glanced over her shoulder, but all she could see were the bright lights and the happy crowd.

Ren stared in the same direction for a moment longer then shook his head. "Yeah, it's fine. I thought I saw— Never mind. Time to give the spotlight to someone else."

She nodded. "Yeah. Sure."

She unhooked her legs and he set her on her feet. Her knees wobbled a little beneath her, the adrenaline and the alcohol a little too much for her system. They dropped off the boa and jacket with the deejay, and then Ren put a hand to her lower back to guide her toward the stairs that would get them off the stage. Her friends were there, clapping and offering praise.

Grace gave her a big hug and whispered in her ear, "Holy shit, girl. You better hit that and then tell me all about it."

Cora snorted and gave her a playful swat on the hip. "You're terrible."

She leaned back and fanned herself, glancing at Ren. "Whew, you guys are going to be a tough act to follow. Carlos, you gonna come up there and make out with me?"

"You wish," he said.

"God, do I." But she just grinned and jogged up on the stage to grab the microphone. "Who wants to hear some P!nk?"

The crowd seemed down for that and Grace started a rousing rendition of "Slut Like You."

Cora and Ren walked toward the edge of the crowd, both needing air and something to drink. Josh and Carlos could cheer Grace on. But when Cora and Ren broke through the thickest part of the spectators, Cora pulled up short. Leaning against the wall near the side of the stage was Hayes, expression darkly sexy and gaze solidly on them.

Something tightened in her belly. Hell, she'd just made out with this guy's boyfriend right in front of him. But he looked anything but offended. Instead, the head-to-toe perusal he gave the two of them could've set their clothes on fire.

Ren still seemed distracted, though, peering over his shoulder one more time before asking Hayes, "Is that water?"

Hayes lifted the unopened bottle in his hand and Ren took it from him. "Thanks." Ren took a long swig from it and then held it out to Cora. "Drink. You're flushed."

She almost told him her pink cheeks had nothing to do with lack of hydration, but she grabbed the bottle and drank. She caught Hayes watching her. When she was done, she handed the water back to him. "How bad were we?"

"I was highly entertained. Too many clothes on the both of you, though." His mouth kicked up at the corner, smug. That's when she saw the glimmer of it. Dmitry. The man with a wicked side and a sense of humor. That sent a little thrill through her. A thrill and nerves. She'd barely been able to handle that guy on the phone. "So, um . . ."

"We should dance," Ren declared.

Cora looked to him. "What?"

"Come on. Grace actually sounds pretty good, and they'll play something after she's done. We'll dance and then get out of here."

"I— Yeah, okay," Cora said.

"Have fun," Hayes said, voice even.

Ren glanced between the two of them and shook his head. "Oh, hell no. It's all of us or nothing. We're here to have fun. Let's go, Fox."

Hayes's mouth tightened. Almost like the words had jabbed him, but finally, he let out a breath. "Fine. One dance."

Ren led them to the dance floor as Grace's song ended and the deejay switched back to club music since no other suckers had volunteered yet to sing.

Ren put a hand to her hip and Hayes wrapped an arm around her waist from behind. The small sober, logical part of her said that she should maybe be worried that her friends would see her sandwiched between them, that they'd get ideas. Accurate ideas, but ideas nonetheless. But then she had to laugh at herself. As if her friends would ever entertain the idea that hermit Cora was going to bed with both of these guys. They'd believe she was an alien from the planet Zort before they believed that.

So she closed her eyes and found that place inside her that was getting easier and easier to access lately, that part that didn't worry so much about what other people thought, and she danced. She hadn't done it since college. And maybe not even then. Just dance without a care. Usually it took massive amounts of alcohol to even get her moving, but with Ren's and Hayes's hands on her as they danced and the scent of them surrounding her, she couldn't think about anything else but the sweet oblivion of this moment. The pure feeling of it.

One song turned into another and another, and the guys moved her between them, sometimes having her face Hayes, sometimes Ren. And they danced with each other, too. A few of the people around them joined in at times, the whole thing becoming one big, happy mass of humanity. It was freeing and amazing and so much fun, Cora found herself laughing for no reason at all. Soon she was slick with sweat and moving without thought, hands in the air and hips rocking.

When a song with a slower beat replaced a fast one, Hayes spun her around and gathered her to him. Ren closed in behind her, cocooning her from any interference.

She lifted her gaze, catching Hayes staring, creases around his eyes, a hint of amusement there. She probably looked like a beet. Her face felt burning hot. Her makeup was no doubt melting off.

His smile was slow.

"What?" she asked, swiping sweat off her brow. "I look like I've been dipped in a pond, don't I?"

He chuckled and warmth rained on her with that sound. His fingers stroked her tailbone. "No. You're beautiful when you let go like that. Eyes closed, face tipped up to the lights, uninhibited."

She wet her lips, tasting salt there. "Yeah?"

"Yeah." He brushed his mouth along her jaw and pressed a kiss below her ear, sending shivers racing over her skin. "We can bring you to that place without the alcohol, Cora. Beyond it. I want to see you let go. No phone lines or computer screens in the way."

She lost her breath for a second, and he pulled her fully against him. Dancing still, but making it impossible not to feel the hard length of him against her hip or the heat of Ren behind her. If a body could groan without sound, hers did, their obvious arousal like liquid fire through her veins. She didn't pull away, didn't want to. Instead, she let her baser instincts take over. She channeled Lenore and ground herself against them both.

Hayes's hand slid beneath her hair and cupped her neck. "I want you, Cora. We both do. Tonight."

God. The words were like a hypnotic spell mixing with the music and wrapping around her. And all she could manage to do was nod. *Yes. Yes, please. Yes, now.*

His thumb traced over the hollow of her throat. "Tell us to stop and we stop."

The feel of that big hand around her throat was erotic in a way she didn't want to analyze. She closed her eyes, let the music and the feel of having these two men against her invade her senses. She didn't say stop.

She tipped her head back, and Hayes kissed down her throat. Soft brushes of his lips, barely-there kisses, but it was like jolts of electricity straight down to the pulsing spot between her legs. And Ren matched the move with gentle presses of his lips against her shoulder. They held her hips, holding her in place, and letting her feel just how much they wanted her. She moaned at the feel of them pressing against her and making promises. Her clit ached, her heartbeat relocating below her waist, sensation trying to sweep her under.

Ren's breath was hot against her ear. "Time to take you home with us, Benning. I'm not sure I have enough restraint for another dance."

She swallowed past the dryness in her throat, every libidinous molecule in her body screaming *Yes!* but her logical side trying to hold on to a thread of sanity. She leaned back, meeting Hayes's eyes, needing to see his honest answer. "Are you sure this is what you want? Are you sure you're ready?"

Hayes pushed a sweaty lock of hair away from her face. "I'm sure. I trust you, Cora. I want you. But this is your call. There's no pressure here. Ever."

Ren kissed the top of her head as they swayed to the music, not really hearing it. "Yes. This is always your call. Any of us can throw the red flag at any time. You're safe with us."

The song ended and the swaying slowed.

"Next up we have Josh and Carlos singing 'Under Pressure'!" the emcee on stage announced.

Half the crowd cheered, half groaned. But Cora barely registered the words.

Her head was whirling now and it had nothing to do with the alcohol. But it wasn't fear. Maybe that should've been there. This was a risk. Her mother would've been appalled. But how many nights had she wondered what it would be like to really be under Dmitry's hand, to give him the control? And now the man was here with his best friend, someone she was feeling more and more for every day. When else would she have the chance to have this? To simply give in to the urge and give herself over to two men she cared about? They were trusting her. She wanted to trust back. "Let's get out of here."

Ren squeezed her shoulders and Hayes kissed her. "Let's go."

She found her way to Grace, watched Josh and Carlos perform, and then told everyone good-bye. But before she could head back to find the guys, Josh pulled her aside, his eyes searching her face. "You good, Cora?"

She smiled. "Meaning?"

"I mean, I saw you dancing. You're going home with two guys?"

Her face heated. "Uh, I—"

He lifted a hand. "Believe me, Lord knows I'm not judging. But this isn't like you. I just want to make sure you're okay. How much did you drink?"

His concern warmed her. She reached out and grabbed his hand to give it a squeeze. "I'm good. A little buzzed, but I danced most of it off. And . . . things have happened between the three of us already. I did that stone-cold sober. I'm just good at keeping secrets."

A big grin broke across his face. "Well, goddamn, look at you." He pulled her into a quick hug. "But text me in the morning to let me know you're okay. I've heard of Ren Muroya. If you're doing kink with someone new, it's never a bad idea to let a friend know where you are and do a check-in. Got me?"

She leaned back and lifted her eyebrows. "You've heard of Ren? Good things or bad things?"

He smirked. "So good that I'm jealous. And if it were bad, you know I'd warn you not to go. Now, go have fun, be safe, and use condoms. Lots of condoms."

She laughed. "Got it."

She gave him another quick hug and found her way back to the guys. Hayes had grabbed a to-go soda for her from the bar. He handed it over. "I thought you might want a little caffeine."

"We have plans. Many plans," Ren added with a grin.

She laughed and took a sip of Coke. "Don't think I can keep up?"

"We'll see," Hayes said. "Plus, we need to sober you up."

She smiled. "You've got nothing to worry about. No beer goggles."

She was a little buzzed, yeah. But alcohol had no part in this decision. She was under an entirely different influence.

The potent mix of two men who looked at her like she meant something to them.

And who were starting to mean something to her.

TWENTY-ONE

Hayes's fingers flexed against the steering wheel as he pulled into the driveway behind Ren and Cora. He'd had the whole drive to contemplate what was about to happen, twenty minutes to talk himself out of this, but all of his old arguments had no shot against the magnetic pull he'd felt seeing Ren and Cora get playful on stage.

For the first time in as long as he could remember, he'd had *fun*. Seeing his best friend and the woman he'd known as Lenore goof around on stage had sent this light, helium-filled sensation through his chest. Like all the weight he'd been carrying around for years had lifted for a few minutes. He'd laughed and grinned like an idiot. And then she and Ren had gotten swept up in the moment and kissed.

He'd seen them do much more than that in the office the other day, but something about the way they'd grabbed at each other, the all-encompassing desire, had set off all of Hayes's switches. He loved that they were so into each other. And he loved even more that they were into him. He wanted to capture all that desire in his hand and play with it, bring all three of them to places they may not have visited before.

So though he knew it was still a risk, was aware that nothing would ever be one hundred percent safe, he refused to let his past cling to him right now. Tonight, it was time to be himself, the Hayes who used to be able to walk into The Ranch with his head high and his confidence firm. To be the guy he'd let himself be in Hayven. Tonight, the outside world didn't exist. All that was important were the two people climbing out of the car in front of him.

Hayes got out of his SUV and locked up. Cora was laughing at something Ren had said, and Ren was carrying her drink and spinning his keys around his finger.

"What's so funny?" he asked.

Ren sent Hayes a smile. "Cora's got a hard-on for my car. I'm not sure what would get her off more tonight—going inside with us or tossing her the keys and letting her take this thing on the open road."

Cora bit her lip and twirled her hair, feigning indecision. "Hmm, decisions, decisions . . ."

She stole the keys from him.

Ren groaned and swept an arm out, grabbing Cora around the waist before she could escape. "No way. No car until you put out. Thems the rules."

When Cora started to playfully struggle, Ren handed the drink to Hayes and hiked Cora up over his shoulder. She let out a string of laughing curses. "Pig!"

"Oink, oink, baby," Ren said, heading up the walk and giving her ass a playful smack.

She lifted her head, sending Hayes a look. "You're going to let him treat me like this?"

Hayes brows lifted. "You realize he's the easy one of the two of us, right?"

Her gaze darkened at that, like the thought both scared her and made her desperately curious. "Oh."

He gave her a slow smile. *Well, hello, Lenore.* Lenore had been green, but she'd always been curious, wanting to dance along new edges each time. Brave and daring. And in that look Cora was giving him, he could see that she hadn't been faking that part online. She got off on a little thread of fear being worked in, on pushing herself past that.

When Ren stopped at the side door and set Cora on her feet to let them in the house, Hayes took Cora's chin in his hand. "Tell me you want to do this."

Her throat worked, her gaze suddenly going serious. "I want to do this."

"What's your safe word?"

"Red."

"Good. You can use yellow, too, if you need us to check in with you. Those will always work. And I remember your limits and preferences in Hayven, but this is real world. What do we need to be aware of?"

She rubbed her lips together. "I'm not sure. I don't know how I'll feel about things like pain and bondage even though we role-played some of that in the game. But I'm willing to try stuff and see how it goes. Just nothing extreme."

He brushed her hair away from her face, feeling the tremble beneath his touch. Cora was putting on a brave face. He had no doubt she wanted this tonight, but she was nervous as hell. He let his hand slide to the back of her neck. "This is going to be good, okay? You know me. The way I was in the game is the way I am. I'm not into heavy pain play. I'm not going to permanently mark you or demand anything crazy. All I ask is that you keep an open mind and give yourself over to this tonight, over to us. My goal is to make us all feel good and to give you a chance to see what it's like. That's it."

She nodded in his grip, some of the tension in her face softening. "Okay."

Ren stepped up behind her, his eyes meeting Hayes's over her shoulder before he wrapped his arms around Cora's waist. "You sure there are no other limits, gorgeous? We've got filthy minds. You've been warned."

She smirked at that, some of her trademark attitude rising to the surface. "That's not news. And I do have one request."

"What's that?" Ren asked.

"No blindfolds."

Hayes nodded. "No problem. Don't like feeling disoriented?"

Her mouth went into a fully wicked smile at that. "No, I just don't want to miss the view. In fact, if y'all just want to give me a few demonstrations and let me shamelessly objectify you, I'm totally good with that."

A laugh burst out of him and he shook his head. "Not this time." He backed her into the house, Ren stepping backward along with her, and Hayes kicked the door shut. "You've done enough watching from the sidelines." He bent down to kiss her. "Time to play, L."

The sound of the nickname he called her on the phone kicked the joking mood right out of her. In one second, they were being playful and teasing, in the next, she realized she was really doing this. Ren and Hayes, both dominating her, both touching her. A hard shiver worked its way through her body, making things hotter instead of chilling them.

Hayes set her soda on a table by the door. She realized she hadn't even had time to drink it. But caffeine was the last thing she needed. Because the way Hayes was looking at her had everything dialing up to eleven inside her. Humming. Buzzing. Vibrating with anticipation. There was no chance in hell she was going to get sleepy. She was a deer in the middle of an unfamiliar forest with two mountain lions stalking her. She wasn't going to blink, much less get sleepy.

Hayes locked the door behind him and didn't bother to turn on a light in the kitchen. Ren was behind her but not touching her any-more. She could feel the heat of his body near, hear the soft fall of his breaths. His awareness. Hayes reached out and brushed the back of his hand over her breast. Her nipples had already been straining against her bra but the simple heat from his touch made her arch and gasp. Everything seemed hypersensitive. Almost too sensitive. She inhaled a deep breath, trying to center herself, calm down.

Hayes dragged his hand back over her, making electricity curl down her belly and pulse between her thighs. She shifted in her boots.

"Look at you," he said, his voice low. "You're so keyed up you can barely stand still. You'll never make it for what we have planned."

She closed her eyes. "I'm trying. I promise. But I think I was halfway there already when we were dancing."

"Halfway there, huh?" Ren asked.

"Yes. Apparently, I'm way too easy."

Hayes smiled and stepped closer to her, his big hand spreading over her ribs. "Cora, you're far from easy. Deprived is more like it. But don't worry. We'll take care of you. This isn't going to be a one-course meal."

His hand slid down to cup her sex, the heel of his hand putting pressure right where she needed it. She groaned and Hayes closed his eyes like he was inhaling that sound.

Only then did she remember that this was the first time he'd touched a woman in years. This wasn't just going to be sex for him. This was going to be him finally taking off the last of the shackles. And God, did she want to see him freed.

How many times had she imagined standing before Dmitry like this? Him being real? Feeling his touch and seeing his face? All of those talks and late nights culminating with them being with each other without any barriers? It was almost too much to hold in her head at once.

Ren's fingers traced up the sides of her neck in an almost lazy massage as Hayes held her in his palm, making her ache and want to grind against his hand. Ren's lips brushed her ear. "I bet you're so wet from having two hard cocks rub all over you at the club that you've ruined your panties. I bet you're all slick and pink just thinking about the things we could do to you."

Cora's teeth pressed together, the words working through her and making her too hot for comfort. In her previous life, she would've been embarrassed, felt awkward by her level of arousal, but she couldn't seem to find those emotions right now. He wasn't wrong. She was ridiculously wet. If this went on much longer, the state of things would be visible through her pants. She tried to stay still, but she was squirming at the still presence of Hayes's hot palm against her. She needed relief. "Please."

"Mmm, please what?" Hayes asked, a predator scenting his prey. "I'm not sure I know what you're asking for. Better be specific."

Her eyes were squeezed shut. She couldn't look at them and feel this all at the same time. "Please touch me, stroke me."

"Stroke what?" Ren said. "Use your words, Cora."

The heel of Hayes's hand rocked ever so slightly, not nearly enough, and he knew it.

"Please," she begged. "My clit. Please rub my clit. I need— I'm dying here."

"Just rub it?" Hayes asked. "You've got low expectations, L. I think we can have more fun than that. What do you think, Ren?"

"I think you've waited a long time to taste your lovely Lenore," Ren said to Hayes. "And I can tell you, remembering how she tastes has already got me hard."

"Hmm, he makes a good case," Hayes said, that tortuous hand still moving too slowly to do anything but drive her out of her mind. "But I think I might need to taste you both."

Cora's eyes popped open at that.

Hayes had a dark, pleased smile. He moved his hand away, making her want to beg all over again, and pressed the same hand over the thick outline in his pants, giving himself a squeeze. "Both of you get undressed. I don't want anything on either of you."

Cora stiffened, old self-consciousness coming back, but after a beat, Ren seemed to sense her nerves and stepped in front of her. He gave her that heartbreaker smile of hers. "Want help?"

She swallowed hard and nodded.

Ren went to work, pulling her top off as she unbuttoned her pants. Before long she was down to her underwear and bra, boots kicked to the side. Ren unhooked her bra, letting it fall away, and then he let his gaze slowly glide over her. He traced a fingertip over her panties, making her shudder, and then he tugged them down and off, leaving her bare and exposed in the low light.

"Now me," he said softly.

Cora licked her lips and went for the buttons on his shirt. She could feel Hayes watching them and somehow that only made her burn hotter. She liked knowing that this was turning him on, that they were giving him a show. So she decided to give him a little more.

"Can I touch you?" she asked Ren.

Ren's eyes darkened. "Who am I to deny that kind of request?"

She glanced over at Hayes, who gave a little nod. Silent permission.

She took her time unbuttoning Ren's shirt and pushing it open and off his shoulders. He was so beautifully made that she enjoyed having a second to just indulge in the view. The colorful tattoos snaked down his arms and up over the front of his shoulders. There were intricate patterns and embedded pictures that one day she'd love to spend time cataloging. But for now she gave in to another impulse and leaned forward to run her tongue over one of his nipples. She bit gently.

Ren groaned and his muscles flexed. His long fingers tangled in her hair as she made her way down his chest and abdomen. When she got to the jut of his hipbone, she bit again. He hissed out a breath. "Fuck."

"Muroya likes a little pain," Hayes said, his voice heavy with arousal. "Look what you're doing to him."

Cora let her gaze travel downward, where Ren's erection was straining against his fly. On impulse, she lowered to her knees and ran her tongue along his cock through the material. Ren's grip tightened in her hair. "She's not the most obedient sub."

But there was no censure in the words, and he didn't stop her.

She unhooked the button, slowly took down the zipper, and then grabbed the band of his boxer briefs to draw them down. She exposed the head of his cock and trapped his shaft against his belly. The crown was glistening with fluid and her tongue pressed to the roof of her mouth. She wanted to lick along the head and capture every drop. The urge threw her off for a second—that utter need to taste him, not just to make him feel good, but for her own pleasure.

Her gaze jumped up, catching his stare. She knew the question was all over her face. His jaw tightened like it was taking all of his restraint to stay still. "Ask me first."

Her throat felt like it'd shrunk three sizes. Ask him for the privilege of sucking his cock? The idea should've rankled. If Kevin had pulled that shit, she would've rolled her eyes. But that was because, in truth, she hadn't ever been all that motivated to go down on any guy. She hadn't craved that experience like she did right now. She'd done it to be nice. She wasn't going to do this to be nice. "May I please taste you?"

"Taste what?" Hayes said, stepping beside Ren. "Remember, I've met Lenore. I know you're not shy. Not when it comes to this. So let's not pretend."

Cora straightened her spine. He was right. Why the hell was she trying to act demure or shy with them? In her fantasies, she didn't play that shrinking-violet game. "I want to taste his cock."

"Good." Hayes reached out and swiped his thumb over the head of Ren's erection, catching the fluid there. The move elicited a grunt from Ren and the rapt attention of Cora. Hayes lifted his glistening thumb and pressed it to Cora's lips. "Taste him, then."

She closed her eyes, a ripple of heat going through her. Just seeing Hayes so casually touch Ren pushed buttons inside her. He was showing her rather than telling her. *Nothing is off-limits. All of us can enjoy. All of us can touch. No one's here to say no or put up walls.*

She opened her eyes, lifted her gaze, and sucked Hayes's thumb into her mouth, the taste of Ren mixing with the salt of Hayes's skin. Pleasure flared in his eyes as she ran her tongue along the underside of his thumb and then sucked. Ren's fingers, still in her hair, pulled tight.

Hayes cleared his throat and pulled his thumb free. "Ren, take your pants off and get on the table before I lose my patience."

Cora smiled inwardly. She'd tempted Hayes. She could see it all over his face. He had a plan, but right in this moment, he'd wanted to grab her and shove his cock in her mouth, take his own pleasure before seeing to either of theirs. He was reeling himself in. For some reason, it was comforting knowing they were all on edge already. They were all weak tonight.

Hayes put out a hand and helped her to her feet. He ran a hand down her back. "Are you cold?"

She couldn't help the laugh that slipped out of her. "Are you kidding? I could heat a small village right now. Meat could be roasted over me."

He smiled and pulled her close, her naked body pressing against his clothed one. His palm cupped her ass and squeezed. "I'm into you, Cora Benning. Have I mentioned that yet?"

"You tell that to all naked girls in your kitchen?"

His expression turned wry. "Has nothing to do with the nudity, though that is greatly appreciated."

"Enormously appreciated," Ren added.

"No, you make me smile. Have been doing that for a long

time." His fingernails pressed into the flesh of her ass, making her toes curl, and then he gave her a swat. "Now I want to give you something to smile about."

Knowing it was probably out of the realm of the rules, but doing it anyway, she pushed up on her toes and pressed a kiss to his mouth. "You already have, Master Dmitry. I've been smiling over you for a long time."

Something flickered over his expression at that, something tender and real and potent. Her chest squeezed tight, but the look disappeared as quickly as it was there. He cleared his throat, that stoic mask slipping back into place.

It was time to play.

TWENTY-TWO

Cora's heart pounded hard against her ribs as Hayes led her over to the table. Ren was watching them, jeans open and hanging loose around his hips, the dark trail of hair tracking downward to the hard state of his cock. Hayes took Cora's hand and placed it in Ren's. A gift. Like she was something to be offered.

The move had the desired effect and she felt herself slipping into the role. *Theirs.* When she'd played with Dmitry, she'd learned over time to let her mind relax, to turn off the inner chatter and just focus on being. It wasn't unlike meditation in a lot of ways—a relief from her busy brain and nonstop analyzing. But this was that state notched up ten levels. And as Ren wrapped his fingers around hers, she could sense some new plane hovering right in her grasp. The nerves of this being in person and not virtual were trying to hold her back, but seeing the intent look on Ren's face and feeling Hayes's steady presence behind her helped.

Ren reached out and tucked a lock of her hair behind her ear. "Don't be scared, Cora. We'll take good care of you."

"I know." And she did. She didn't know why she felt so sure of that, but she felt it down to her bones. "I just have trouble getting out of my head sometimes."

His lips curved as he sat on the edge of the table and pulled her to him, bracing her between his spread knees. "I know you don't want to miss the view, but close your eyes for a minute. Just feel."

She did as she was told and then after a breath, hands and mouths were on her. Ren kissing her neck, Hayes's big hands wrapping around her from behind and palming her breasts, Ren's thighs locking her in place. *Unh.* She tipped her head back and it landed against Hayes's chest. He pressed a hand over her forehead, holding her against him and notching his erection against her backside. Another hand—Ren's—dipped between her legs, finding her slick and hot. He tucked two fingers inside her.

She let out a soft gasp, the sensations overwhelming—hands everywhere, heat branding her each place they touched, and Ren's slow, decadent invasion. She rocked against Ren's fingers and Hayes's erection, never opening her eyes.

"That's it, baby," Ren said softly. "You don't need to think about anything because there are no decisions left to make. You're ours right now. This soft skin. This sweet body. This wet cunt that's just begging to be filled up."

Hayes's hand slipped between the cheeks of her ass and teased her opening, circling it with his fingertip and awakening nerves there. "Other places that need filling."

Her stomach tightened and she let out a sigh that didn't sound anything like protest.

"Think about all the ways we can use you," Ren said. "All the ways we can make you feel good."

Her breath soughed out of her, her body rocking in an undulating rhythm she was barely conscious of. *Yes. This.* There were too many sensations, too much everything, to do much thinking. And she felt the welcome state of surrender pushing at the edges of her mind. Hadn't this been what she'd always secretly craved? The thing that had driven her to Hayven in the first place? Being with guys had always felt like so much work. She worked too much already. She didn't want to be in charge of sex, too. These men could give her that. All she had to do was let them.

So she did.

The fingers and kissing and touching blurred together and the muscles in her body began to soften, melt, until she realized she was mostly being held up by the two of them. Hayes grasped her around the waist and locked her against him. Ren's heat disappeared for a moment and there was the rustling of clothes.

Her eyes fluttered open and she lost her breath all over again. Ren had shoved his pants the rest of the way off and had lain back on the table, knees spread, cock in hand. He was giving himself slow strokes, his eyes on her. Her gaze watched those long fingers handle his cock with wanton familiarity. This was what he looked like when he touched himself in private. It felt unbearably intimate and erotic to watch. A fresh rush of heat moved straight downward and she went from aroused to on fire.

Hayes pressed something into her hand. "Get his condom on, L. I want to watch you fuck him."

She swallowed hard and tried to get her hands to work. She tore the condom wrapper open and stepped forward. Ren was still watching her, eyes hooded, hand slowly working the fluid beading at the tip over his shaft.

"One second," Hayes said.

She paused and Hayes moved from behind her to the side of the table. He lowered his head and licked the head of Ren's cock, his lips meeting Ren's fingers as Ren continued to stroke himself.

Fuck. Cora stood there mesmerized as Ren groaned and Hayes got Ren's erection glossy and flushed. Hayes lifted his head and met Cora's gaze. A question there. Maybe a test. Was she really aware of what these two guys being together meant?

She was. And she was so down for it. They were gorgeous together. Sexy and confident and . . . *Yes, please.*

"Now put it on," Hayes said with a smug little smile.

Ren hadn't stopped stroking himself and he reached out with his other hand to grab hers. He placed her hand over the one sliding over his cock, their fingers interweaving. For a moment, they jerked him together. Then Hayes's hand joined in and Ren's head fell back to the table. "Y'all keep that up, you're going to get a special surprise quicker than you expected."

Hayes gave one of those rumbly, under-the-breath laughs and moved his hand away. "Condom, Cora. The man's got no self-control."

"Oh, yes, right." Cora fumbled a bit but managed to roll on the condom, earning another grunt from Ren as her fingertips grazed his scrotum.

Ren reached for her again. "Come here, gorgeous."

She took the offered hand and climbed onto the table with him, thankful when it didn't break beneath their shared weight. He kissed the top of her hand and she started to position herself over him but he shook his head. "Turn around, baby."

She lifted her brows but soon Hayes's hand was on her, guiding her to face away from Ren. "I want to do more than watch."

He got her to straddle Ren's hips. Ren's legs were hanging off the edge of the table, bent at the knees, but she had enough room to get in position. Hayes held her hands, helping her keep balanced. "You guys are lucky I do yoga."

Hayes stepped closer to the edge of the table and reached out to stroke her clit. "We're lucky in more ways than I can list right now."

She bit her lip to keep in the moan. Everything inside her felt ready to detonate.

"You should see how hot the two of you look right now," he said, voice low and dark. "You so slick and hot. Him hard enough to pound nails. Can you hear how wet she is for you, Ren? Imagine how warm and tight she's going to be around your cock."

Ren shifted restlessly beneath her. "Stop teasing, Fox."

"Oh, but it's so much fun." Hayes took his fingers away from Cora and swiped the remnants of her arousal over Ren's sac.

"Fuck," Ren said. "Why did I agree to let you take lead again?"

Hayes massaged Ren's balls in his palm. "Because you love it. Because you know it's better when you work for it a little." His gaze met Cora's. "Lower yourself down on him. But only take the crown in."

Cora wanted to groan this time. "Just the tip?"

"Trust me," he said softly.

She trusted him, but Lord, she might die if they dragged this out too long. She could remember exactly how good Ren's cock had felt filling her. She wanted that feeling right this second. But she'd agreed to play this game, agreed to surrender. She wasn't going to back out on the deal.

She reached out to brace her hands on Hayes's shoulders and then she eased herself down. The moment Ren breached her, the breath she'd been holding whooshed out. The thick tip stretched her, making her aware of every detail of his flared head. *Oh, God.*

Hayes's eyes focused on the place where she and Ren joined, his breath quickening and a hungry expression crossing his face. He pressed a hand against her, his thumb stroking her clit and making her eyes want to roll back in her head. When he spoke again, his voice sounded more strained. "Move just a little, Cora. Just enough to feel him going in and out."

Her jaw tightened as she tried to channel every bit of her control. Hayes's thumb stroking her clit and the feel of Ren's cock at her entrance was like the sweetest, most brutal torture. She wanted to grab Hayes's hand and make him go faster and to plunge herself onto Ren with abandon, claim the orgasm that was right there out of her grasp. But she forced herself to follow the instruction.

With as much restraint as she could, she dipped her hips a bit, taking in Ren just enough to make it past the thickness of the head but then up again. She didn't see the point of the teasing but when she repeated the motion, things changed. Oh. *Oh*. The shallow thrusts alighted nerve endings she hadn't been aware of. She'd long accepted that sex meant a full feeling but not necessarily sensation inside. But this, this was different. The feeling of the crown of his cock teasing and stretching her entrance was foreign and new and *oh my God*.

Then when she thought things couldn't get more intense, Hayes shifted. She could tell what was coming the minute Hayes moved, but she didn't let herself believe it. Not until Hayes got to his knees and put his mouth right where they joined.

The feel of the heat of his tongue nearly sent her into orbit, and behind her, Ren let out a colorful monologue of cursing. Hayes acted like he didn't hear a word of it. He licked and sucked at Cora and bathed Ren's cock with his tongue, still not giving her leave to sink down and take Ren fully inside her.

All she could do was keep up the shallow thrusts and feel the blinding, amazing sensation of Hayes going down on her while another man fucked her. She tried to savor, to take in every blissful nuance moving through her, but it was like trying to contain an angry tiger with just her hands. Release banged at the doors of her self-control. "Shit. I can't—"

"Motherfucker." Ren was tapping his head against the table. At least that's what it sounded like. "Please, Hayes. Let us . . ."

Hayes hummed his opinion against her skin, making her nails dig into his shoulders.

She tried to count. She tried to write code in her head, anything to not go over yet. Her eyes fell shut as she breathed through her world trying to shatter behind her eyelids.

"No coming yet," Hayes said, lifting his head for a moment. "And, Cora?"

She tried to find her voice. "Yes?"

"You said you wanted to watch. So watch," he said, challenge in his tone.

She opened her eyes at that and looked down, her breaths coming in short bursts. Hayes spread her with his thumbs, giving her a view of everything he was seeing up close and then he held her eye contact as he dragged his tongue over her.

The sound that came out of her mouth was one she didn't recognize. The feel of it was enough, but seeing his head between her thighs, licking her as Ren fucked her was going to kill her. But then he ran two fingers along her folds, getting both good and wet, and slid them down, down, down. They disappeared between Ren's cheeks.

Hayes gave her a dark smile, his hand seeking, and then he ran his tongue along the place where Ren and Cora were joined as he pushed his fingers into Ren. It was the hottest, sexiest thing Cora had ever seen. And the second Hayes's fingers breached Ren, she could feel the answering jolt in Ren's body. Her sex clenched hard around him.

"Holy fucking shit. I'm never going to last like this, Fox. You're, she's—"

"Then fuck her," Hayes said finally. "Fuck her hard and make her come."

That was all it took. Ren grasped her hips from behind, dragged her down onto his cock, and buried deep. "Fuck, God, yes."

She let out a bone-deep groan that matched his. Everything felt alive, full, on fire in the best way. She might die. But she'd do it with a smile on her face.

Hayes went back to work, his mouth on her clit and his fingers working Ren, and everything went hazy behind her eyes. She couldn't watch anymore. She couldn't think. She was only a passenger now.

She grabbed Hayes's hair to find something to hold on to and let it all take her, Ren fucking into her with deep, desperate strokes, and Hayes using all he had to bring them both to oblivion. Before long, she was tipping her head back and crying out like a wild thing—gasping, lung-emptying noises—and light burst behind her eyelids. Everything that had once been neatly put together fell apart. Shattered. Done. Never to be put back together the same way again.

She was all sensation and body parts and feeling. And she loved every fucking second of it.

Ren followed her over the edge a moment later, pumping hard and making sexy gasping grunts as he came.

For a few long shining seconds, there was just the sound of their mingled breaths and her heart beating in her ears. Her thighs were quivering beneath her and her muscles were jumping with aftershocks. She was never going to be able to move again.

But before she could announce this—that she was permanently stuck in this position and they would all just have to deal with it—hands were grasping her under the arms and helping her off of Ren. Hayes sat her on the edge of the table and then swept her up into his arms. "Let's get you someplace more comfortable."

She let herself melt into his hold, not trusting herself to do much else. She kept her eyes closed most of the time as they moved through the house and eventually she was brought into a bedroom with a big bed and low lamplight. She blinked in the change of light as Hayes laid her on the bed. Art hung on every wall. Pen-and-ink drawings.

"Ren's room," she said offhandedly.

"Yeah. His is better suited for this. Bigger bed."

"The slut," she murmured.

"Hey, I heard that," Ren said with a smile, climbing onto the bed next to her. He bent down and pressed a kiss to her lips. "That was amazing, Cora. Thank you."

"Mmmpfh," she said, drunk on afterglow. She turned her head to find Hayes on the side of the bed, staring down at the both of them. His erection hadn't abated but he hadn't made any move to get undressed. She let herself openly stare. "Now what can we do for you, Master Hayes?"

His mouth lifted at the corner. "I'm patient. I'm giving you two a break."

That sounded like the worst idea ever.

Cora rolled onto her side and Ren's fingers drifted idly over her thigh. She smiled up at Hayes. "Breaks are overrated. Haven't you heard that I'm a workaholic?"

"Mmm," Ren said. "It's always been Hayes's weak spot as a dom. Too damn generous and not selfish enough. I've always had selfish nailed."

Hayes grunted. "Believe me, I wasn't suffering out there. You two are quite a show."

Ren's hand drifted down between Cora's legs and his fingertips gently grazed her still-sensitive lips. Her toes curled and Hayes's attention focused there.

"I bet Cora's got more than one measly orgasm in her," Ren said casually. "Spread your legs for him, gorgeous." Ren guided her top leg into a bend and up, opening her to Hayes and still play-ing with her, dumping desire right back into her blood. "She's wanted Dmitry for a long time. Don't you think it's time to give that to her? And time to end your drought? Have you forgotten how good it feels to have a woman's heat clamp down on your cock? All that slickness surrounding you?"

Hayes's green eyes had gone almost black, his attention focused on Cora's spread thighs and Ren's teasing fingers. Ren was putting her on display, talking about her like she wasn't there, but that only made it more illicit, hotter. *I've already had a piece of this. Come and get yours.*

Plus, it was probably wrong, but she was unbearably turned on by the fact that she would be the first woman Hayes had been with in years. She kind of liked the slightly wild way he was looking at her, like he didn't trust himself to play nice or be gentle.

Hayes's jaw visibly flexed. "Stop, Ren. I can't— I don't want to . . ."

"He's afraid he's going to hurt me," Cora said, catching Hayes's gaze and holding it. "He's too keyed up. He's worried he'll be too rough."

Hayes glanced away. "Just give me a few minutes."

Cora pushed herself into a sit. "I'm not scared of you, you know?"

"Maybe you should be," he said gruffly. "With you looking like that . . . all I want to do right now is hold you down and fuck you until I can't see straight."

"Then do it," she said, tucking her legs beneath her and tipping up her chin. "I can handle you."

And even if she'd probably have trouble admitting it out loud, one of her top fantasies was rough sex. Hayes knew that. It was Lenore's favorite.

Ren's hands slid onto her shoulders. "We've got you, Fox. Both of us. You know I won't let you hurt her. If you push too far, she's got a safe word and she's got me."

Hayes lifted his eyes to Ren, every part of him tense. "Ren—"

Ren's hands slid down Cora's arms and drew her hands behind her back. He locked her wrists together in his grip. "Look at our pretty captive. Take her, Hayes. It's time."

TWENTY-THREE

Every chain holding Hayes back seemed to snap at once. He prided himself on his self-control. After the show in the kitchen, his cock had been ready to explode, and he'd managed to reel himself in. But how was he supposed to resist this? A beautiful woman he cared about offering herself to him without restriction.

He knew too much. He knew what Cora's secret fantasies were. And that was tempting him beyond measure. Lenore had always come the hardest when he'd given her rough scenarios, being tied up or held down, being fucked hard and the orgasm being forced out of her.

Ren sat his chin on Cora's shoulder, her small breasts jutting out from his grip on her wrists, and he reached around to strum her clit. She moaned softly. He could see her trembling with need again. Ren smiled. "If you won't fuck her, I'll just do it again. Maybe slide deep into her ass this time. I love how she feels around my cock, love how she rides me. Have you ever been taken that way, baby?"

Cora groaned.

That was it. The breaking point. Hayes was a strong man. A controlled man. But he wasn't inhuman. He ripped at the button on his jeans and yanked down the zipper. They wanted to tease him? Wanted to goad him into hard and fast? Well, they were going to get it.

He pulled out his cock, giving it much-needed room after the torture of being pressed up against his pants all this time, and rolled on the condom he'd tucked in his pocket. Cora's gaze zeroed in on his cock, her breath catching. He liked that. Liked seeing the desire clear on her face. Made him feel a little better about what he was about to do.

"You didn't lie about that either in the game," she said breathlessly.

He stalked over to the bed and let himself slip fully into the role. "Tell me your safe word, Cora."

"Red," she whispered, her eyes going a little wide at his tone.

"Let her go," he said to Ren. "She's mine."

Ren released her wrists and Hayes gripped Cora's arm, flipping her onto her belly. She landed with a squeak of bedsprings and a gasp, all that pretty flesh flushed and glistening with the start of sweat. He grabbed her waist and dragged her to the edge of the bed, letting her feet touch the floor. "You use that word if you need it, you hear me?"

"Yes, sir."

"Swear to me."

Her back was rising and falling with quick breaths. "I swear."

"Good girl." He lifted his hand and did exactly what he'd wanted to do since he'd seen her beautiful ass slide out of those pants tonight. He spanked her with a satisfying *thwap*.

She yelped, caught by surprise, and her fingers curled into the comforter.

"Hold her down, Ren," Hayes said, squeezing the base of his cock at the rush of need, at the sight of his handprint on her skin. "Lenore used to get so wet over the thought of my hand turning her ass pink. Let's see how reality compares."

Ren clamped his hands over her wrists, his own gaze going hooded. Hayes swatted Cora again and she squirmed. But no safe word. And the squirming only drove him up higher. She was trying to rub her clit against the edge of the bed.

"Spread your legs. Show me what you think of this."

After a second, she obeyed and all that delicate slick flesh appeared in front of him. The human body was a beautiful thing. He loved things about both the male and female form. But there was something about seeing a woman in surrender, open and aroused, that was like goddamned art.

He spanked her again, watched her cunt clench, her body beg for touch. He traced a finger over her pucker. Cora groaned.

"Mmm, next time," he said, teasing her a little more. "Lenore said she played with a plug sometimes. How about you, Cora?"

Cora was breathing hard now. "I never lied to you."

Ren made a sound of approval. "You're so goddamned sexy. Christ."

"You've got him hard again," Hayes said, still teasing her hole. "I bet he's imagining how your ass would feel. Bet it'd be tight with my cock buried in your pussy at the same time."

"Oh, fuck," Cora whispered, rocking back into his touch.

He smiled. "Pace yourself, dirty girl. We've got all the time in the world to play. But maybe Ren can give you a little taste while I finish your spanking for goading me into this."

He gave Ren a look and didn't need to say anything. Ren stretched to pull open the bedside drawer and grabbed the bottle of lubricant. He had his fingers slicked up before Cora could properly catch her breath. His hand slid down her backside.

"What are you doing?" she asked, her muscles tensing.

"Shh," Ren said. "You're going to relax for us. And you're going to enjoy this."

Ren pressed a finger against that tight little rosette, and Hayes watched as Ren pushed into her. Cora's heels lifted off the floor and she moaned. The sight made Hayes want to bury himself right there, right now, but he breathed through the urge to rush.

As Ren slowly fucked her ass with his finger, Hayes grabbed a riding crop out of Ren's cabinet and then went to work, smacking her ass, her thighs, and delivering light taps to her pussy until Cora was panting and writhing on the bed.

"Spread your legs wider," Hayes said, voice filled with gravel.

After a second, she followed the instruction and he inhaled a deep, shuddering breath, taking in the hot, decadent smell of sex.

She was a beautiful mess laid out before him. Arousal slicked her inner thighs, her pussy was flushed and red, and her muscles were clenching around the second finger Ren had pushed into her like she was begging for more. She may not be sure if she liked pain play yet, but the girl was going crazy from the flogging. And he was going crazy for her.

Cora was perfect. Everything Lenore had been but in a better package—a smart, quirky, strong package. And sexy as fuck. He had worried he was falling for Lenore, a fantasy, but it turned out he was falling for someone very, very real. Falling hard.

The thought scared the shit out of him. He'd just come to terms with his feelings for Ren. He didn't know how to process this other separate attraction, this attachment. But right now, he wasn't going to worry about it. It'd been four years since he'd felt the pleasure of a woman, and months of fantasizing about Lenore. That ended tonight.

He tossed the crop aside and spanked Cora a few more times, needing to feel her flesh against his palm, wanting to see her juices slide down her thighs. But soon she was begging, not for him to stop, but for him.

Sir, Dmitry, Hayes. All those words came out her mouth. But the ones that stuck most were the last ones she said. "Please. I need you."

I need you. It was the plea she'd made on the phone so many times when she'd get too turned on to edit herself, but the one he'd never been able to satisfy. The one that had made him ache for her. The one that had made him feel the most helpless.

He wasn't helpless anymore. He could answer her.

He stepped forward, Ren automatically backing off, and he nudged her legs wider with his foot. Then he took her wrists in his hands, pinned her to the bed like he knew she craved, and sank inside her.

Cora cried out and her neck arched, but Hayes barely heard it because the reactions in his own body were too loud to be drowned out. Her heat surrounded him, already tightening like a fist, and the indescribable feeling of being sheathed fully inside her made his brain shut down. He was no longer thinking about everything that had led him to this moment. Or worrying about the risk. Or thinking about anything at all. All that was left was feeling and the utter need to fuck this woman and make both their worlds crack in two.

He let go of her hands, and Ren took over pinning her down as Hayes grabbed her hips and dragged her back onto his cock, lost in the sounds she was making and the sensations moving through him. "Yes, God. *Cora.*"

Cora responded in kind, her voice catching high in her throat with every gasp, every thrust of his hips, and soon he didn't trust his legs. He told Ren to release her and he helped her fully onto the bed before flipping her over. Her eyes were dazed when she blinked up at him, drunk on lust and full of desire. Perfect. "Still with me, L?"

He knew that wasn't her name, but somehow the endearment felt right in the moment. It was the name of his sub. When she was like this with him, she was L. And the way she smiled at the mention made something turn over in his chest. She reached up and dragged her fingertips over his stubble, almost in wonder. "I'm so very with you."

"Beautiful." He bent to kiss her and then he guided her legs over his shoulders, trapped her arms above her head, and thrust into her, sinking as deep as their bodies would allow.

"Touch her, Ren," he said between panted breaths. "Show her what it's like to have us both."

Ren didn't hesitate. He moved next to them and let his hands roam over her, caressing her breasts and pinching her nipples. She arched her back at that and her inner muscles gripped Hayes hard.

"She likes that," Hayes ground out.

Ren lowered his head and put his mouth where his hands had been, sucking and nipping her flesh until Cora was making noises he'd never heard her make before. Ren's hand reached down and grasped his own cock, jerking roughly.

The sight of Ren, the feel of Cora, and the sounds they were all making coalesced into one swirling cloud of sensation, and Hayes felt his control slipping. He'd had a lot of sex before everything went down. He'd done a lot of kink. But he knew enough to recognize when things were different, when things mattered.

There was nothing clinical or structured or neat about this. This was not a scene at The Ranch where they'd all walk away unscathed later. This was dangerous.

This was new.

But he couldn't find it in himself to be scared.

He reached between his and Cora's body, finding where she needed to be touched the most, and he pumped deep. He could sense her orgasm building in the squeeze of her body and the quickness of her breath, the dam about to burst.

"Come for me, L."

As if she'd been waiting for just those words, she cried out and he went over with her, taking everything she offered and riding her hard, leaving bruises on her and marks on him. Marks that couldn't be seen but wouldn't be erased. And when Ren bowed up, cried out, and came all over Cora's bared breasts, Hayes had no thoughts left in his head.

This was what bliss felt like.

This was what it felt like to be alive again.

And these two people had brought him there.

There were no words, so he didn't speak any. He slid out of Cora, disposed of the condom, and then they all collapsed into a messy heap on the bed, breathing hard and sweating and floating down from the high.

And then right when all got quiet, when awkwardness could've crept in, there was laughter.

He didn't know who started it—probably Cora—but once it started, they all caught the bug. So they lay there, exhausted and naked and covered in questionable fluids, laughing the laugh of the delirious.

Because they all knew. It was impossible not to feel it.

They'd just found something none of them had ever had.

And no one had any idea what to do with it.

TWENTY-FOUR

Cora lay in bed between Hayes and Ren, staring at the ceiling and trying to fall asleep. The guys had dozed off pretty quickly after they'd all taken a shower. Neither of them had tried to discuss or pick apart what had happened yet. She'd been happy for the reprieve. She wasn't ready to talk. She hadn't expected for things to go like they had—to *feel* so much afterward. She wasn't sure what to do with that.

She'd laughed like a crazy person when they were done because a big part of her had wanted to cry. Things were supposed to be good, exciting, sexy. They weren't supposed to blow her world apart and make her want things she wasn't going to get. Being with them had felt like the purest expression of her sexuality, of herself. Like for a little while, all the things that had always been off in her dating life had clicked into place. She'd never felt so free with anyone, so in her own skin, so cherished. *Loved*, even. Which was ridiculous. That's not what this was. Her brain chemicals were hijacking her brain and mixing up good sex with emotional stuff. But she needed time to sort herself out and get her armor back up before having any kind of conversation with these two. She couldn't let them see how deeply they'd affected her, how much she was starting to feel for them. Her poker face would be shit right now. They'd see right through her.

So she was thankful they hadn't pushed. She would feel better and more centered after a good night's sleep. She could tackle the hard stuff in the morning.

But even though she felt dog-tired, she couldn't fall asleep. She'd felt a little light-headed after sex and had chalked it up to not having eaten enough before going out. But now she felt downright nauseous. She had no idea if it was just worry stirring things up or if it was something else. She tried a few different positions, trying to get settled, but the sick feeling only got worse. *Ugh*. She needed something to settle her stomach.

With a sigh, she gingerly pushed herself upward and scooted down to the foot of the bed, working hard not to disturb the guys. Hayes rolled on his side when she brushed against him, jostling the bed, but his eyes didn't open. He reached out as if seeking her warmth and his hand landed on Ren's thigh instead. For a moment, she let herself just look at the two of them. In sleep, they went from hot and intimidating to boyishly adorable. Smooth expressions and messy hair. Soft snores. She could get used to that sight.

No. She couldn't let her mind go there.

Ren had said this could be more than one night, that tonight was to see where things went. But she had no idea what they were feeling, and more than one night didn't mean a relationship. It simply meant more sex. And she couldn't pretend that anything more than that wouldn't be enormously complicated.

With a frown, she got to her feet and hunted down something to wear. She found one of Ren's dress shirts draped over a chair and slipped it on. Her stomach rolled.

Blech. She needed crackers and something fizzy. Stat. She was making herself sick with all her swirling thoughts.

Working hard not to bump into anything in the dark, she made her way down the hallway and into the kitchen. The place looked like the aftermath of a drunken striptease. Her clothes were strewn on the floor, her panties hooked under the leg of a chair at the dining table. There were smudge marks all over the table from grappling hands and naked bodies. She wondered if the guys had a maid service. What was the charge to remove butt prints? That made her snort. The maid would be in for quite a scene.

Cora opened the stainless steel fridge in search of soda but all that was in there was bottled water, a few beers, and orange juice. Her stomach staged a protest at even the thought of orange juice and she pressed her fingers against her lips. *No bueno.*

She grabbed a bottle of water and shut the fridge. But when she turned around, she spotted the cup from the bar, sitting on a table by the side door. It would be watered down by now but may be enough to do the trick. She set down the bottled water and went for the drink. The insulated cup had kept some of the ice from melting and the fizz was just what she needed. She took off the top and drank a few big gulps.

The carbonation seemed to start its magic almost instantly, and after snagging a few saltines from their pantry and finishing the drink, she went back to bed. The guys were still fast asleep, Ren snoring lightly. She carefully climbed back between them and tucked herself under the covers. Hayes automatically threw his arm over her and snuggled against her.

She smiled, settling into the warm place between them, and closed her eyes, deciding that she would just enjoy the moment and leave the hard thoughts for tomorrow.

But a little while later, when she shifted slightly to adjust her position, something in her equilibrium flipped over and the bed felt like it tipped sideways beneath her. *Whoa.* Her eyes popped open, but a wave of dizziness hit her. She groaned, the room listing in her vision. Her fingers gripped the comforter.

Something was wrong. This was . . . Things didn't feel right. She closed her eyes, trying to breathe through the wave of vertigo, but that only made it worse. She reached out blindly for Ren, attempting to alert him, but her arm wouldn't cooperate. Everything felt slow, drunk. Out of her control.

Panic tried to rise in her, alarm bells sounding, but she wasn't able to hold on to the thought long enough to take action. Her lips parted, her voice trying to form a protest, but nothing came out.

She was just so dizzy and . . . sleepy.

Her eyes fell shut. The world went black.

And the guys never knew a thing.

TWENTY-FIVE

Boom. Boom. Boom. The thumping sound filled Hayes's dream. A cop was hitting the prison bars right next to his head, trying to wake him up. He had his hand over his ears and was yelling at them to quit. But the banging wouldn't stop. *Boom! Boom!*

Hayes's eyes popped open, and he blinked into the darkness, coming out of the dream with blurred awareness. For a second, he couldn't place where he was, but when one of Ren's drawings came into view in a shaft of moonlight from the window, his head cleared. Cora's warm body was tucked beneath his arm, their legs fused together with a sheen of sweat. But she was still asleep. The banging started up again, and Ren rolled over to face him, mumbling, "What the fuck?"

"The door. Someone's knocking on the door," Hayes said, peeling away from Cora and glancing at the bedside clock. Three thirty in the morning.

Ren eyes opened at that. "What? It's the middle of the night."

The knocking came again along with a muffled voice. Hayes sat up and got out of bed in search of his jeans. "I'll go see what's going on. Stay here with her."

Cora seemed deep in sleep, her body rising and falling with slow breaths, her hair damp with sweat.

Ren pushed up on his elbow. "Be careful. If anything looks suspicious, call the police. There was a break-in down the street a few weeks ago."

Hayes gave a nod, but unease was curling in his gut. Late-night phone calls were bad enough. Late-night knocks were worse. He tugged on his jeans and strode down the hallway. The heavy thudding knocks started up again as he made his way to the front door. He was just leaning down to peek through the peephole when the voice on the other side shouted, "Police, open up."

Police. That sense of dread he'd had over the knocking jumped straight to all-out fight-or-flight. Hayes had never wanted to hear those words again. They'd preceded his arrest all those years ago. But before he gave in to the panic, he reminded himself that in the normal world, police were coming to help or to check on something. Maybe there was a gas leak in the neighborhood or another break-in. Maybe someone had seen something outside the house. Hayes took a deep breath and opened the door.

The two cops on the other side seemed surprised to have the door finally open. The male half of the pair put a hand on his holster, like he expected Hayes to leap at him.

Hayes supposed he looked like a threat, standing there shirtless and wild-haired and taller than the two of them by half a foot. "Can I help you?"

"Are you Hayes Fox?" the female cop asked, her voice hard.

The words punched at Hayes. He tried to remain calm, tried not to jump to conclusions or panic. "I am. Is there a problem?"

"Do you have a young woman inside your home right now?" the male cop asked, trying to see past Hayes's shoulder.

Hayes's jaw tightened. He wanted to ask them what the hell business it was of theirs, but he'd learned in prison that mouthing off to cops got you nowhere good. "Can I ask what's going on? Why are you here?"

"Sir, we're going to have to ask you to step aside and let us come in to check to make sure everything's okay," the female cop said, flashing her badge at him.

"What?" A sick feeling was creeping through Hayes. "Everything's fine. Why wouldn't it be?"

"Sir, someone who recognized you from the papers called in a report that they saw you earlier tonight at Bar None and that you slipped something into a young lady's drink and then left with her. We need to come in and make sure that everything is okay."

Hayes's blood turned to ice.

"What's going on?" Ren said from somewhere behind him.

"Sir, stay where you are," the male cop said to Ren, his voice loud and hard, like he'd been practicing that particular tone by watching too many cop dramas on TV. "We need you both to move aside and let us come in."

Hayes knew there was nothing he could do to stop them. They didn't need a search warrant if they thought someone was in immediate danger. He backed away, everything going in slow motion in his head as he processed what they'd said.

Ren looked to him, eyes wide. "What the fuck is going on?"

"Someone said they saw me drug Cora at the bar," he said flatly.

"Is that her name?" the female cop said sharply. "Are you admitting you drugged her?"

"Of course he didn't drug her!" Ren said, his temper and fear rising to the surface. He stared at Hayes, his skin going ashen.

"I need you to calm down, sir. I didn't ask you the question," she said, holding up a hand to Ren and looking to Hayes.

"I didn't drug her," Hayes said, his hands starting to shake. "She's in the back bedroom, sleeping."

"Stay here with them, Crandall," the female cop said to her partner. "I'll go check on her."

Officer Crandall gave a quick nod, hand still hovering over his belt, keeping all of his tools of the trade within reach as he eyed

Hayes and Ren. "Gentlemen, I need you to take a seat on the couch, hands on your lap where I can see them."

Ren looked like he was going to protest, but Hayes gave him a quick shake of his head. Ren let out a breath and followed Hayes to the couch. Hayes sat there, his mind going into some shut-down mode. He hadn't drugged Cora. But deep in his bones, he knew that wouldn't matter. It was happening again.

He'd let his guard down, and he'd lost the chess match again.

"It's going to be okay," Ren said firmly. "We didn't do anything. Cora will tell them."

Hayes wanted to believe that was true. But he couldn't fight that feeling of inevitability. Just like that movie, he'd escaped his plane crash, but fate wasn't going to let him get away with it. This was part of some plan, some puppeteer running a long game. And he wasn't going to stop. He wasn't going to leave Hayes alone.

Hayes bowed his head and closed his eyes, letting that despair sink in.

But soon his own fate was forgotten when he heard the female cop's voice from the back of the house, calling Cora's name. Hayes head snapped upward, expecting Cora to come running out from the hallway, pissed as hell at the questions.

But Cora didn't come out of the hallway. And he didn't hear her voice.

"What's wrong?" Ren asked, his voice going tight and body tense.

But there was no answer. All they could hear was the cop calling for an ambulance on her radio.

That's when everything shifted. A new kind of fear filled Hayes. Not fear of what was going to happen to him. He already knew how that would go. But a to-his-marrow terror that something had happened to *her*. *Cora*. Cora, who had been curled in his arms only a few minutes before. Cora, who had belly-laughed on their bed after they'd all made love. Cora, who he'd told he'd keep safe tonight.

He jumped up from the couch, adrenaline and a single-minded need to see her filling him. "He asked you what's wrong?"

The cop went on alert. "Sir, I need you to sit down."

"No, tell us she's okay." He stepped forward. "Let me see her—"

But that was the last he got out. The sudden movement had snapped the cop into action. In one quick second, the Taser was off his belt and aimed. Pain like Hayes had never felt lit him up and he went to the ground like a felled tree, his knees landing hard and his body jerking.

He only vaguely registered the female cop still calling Cora's name. And Ren calling his. Then he was on the ground, unable to move, and cuffs were being put on him.

Cuffs went on Ren, too.

And after only a few months of freedom, Hayes was back in a cop car on his way to the station, where he was going to be charged with rape.

TWENTY-SIX

Boom. Boom. Boom. Cora winced. Someone was punching her in the head. That had to be what was happening because she couldn't open her eyes for the sharp pain pounding through her skull. She groaned, wishing that whoever it was would just knock her the fuck out.

Stop.

"Coraline? Can you hear me?"

Don't call me Coraline. No one got to call her that except her mother. But the words came out as a mumble.

A warm hand pressed over her arm and squeezed. "Sweetheart, can you try to open your eyes? Please. You're okay. It's going to be okay. I'm here."

Mom? The thought registered, cleared a little of the fog. What the hell was her mom doing here in her bed? Cora tried to lift her hand to her head, anything to stop the pounding, but her fingers got tangled in something.

"Easy, baby. They've got you hooked up to a few things."

Hooked up to a few things? Cora attempted to open her eyes, but the bright white light that broke through her vision was like an ice pick to her eye sockets. "Shit. Bright."

Her voice was sticky in her throat. Clogged.

There was a flicking sound and the lights went down. "Sorry. Is that better?"

Her mom's hand returned to Cora's arm. Cora cracked her eyelids open again, finding a softer, dimmer level of light. She blinked, trying to adjust and breathe through the pounding headache and the wave of nausea. God, what the hell had happened?

Worst. Hangover. Ever.

Her vision cleared, the woman leaning over her coming into view. Her mom, bare-faced and in street clothes, eyes red-rimmed. She gave a brief, tense smile. "There you are."

Cora blinked a few more times, trying to figure out where she was and why her mom was here. "What's going on?"

"You're okay," she said again, voice a little quivery. "You're at the hospital. But you're going to be all right."

That thought arrowed right through the hazy state in her brain. Her muscles stiffened. "Hospital?" She glanced around, now recognizing the bare, clinical walls, the machine she was attached to, the thin sheets against her skin. Panic started to creep in. "What happened?"

Janet sat on the edge of the bed and offered Cora a little paper cup of water.

Cora pushed herself up on the pillows and sipped, the ice water harsh against her dry throat but welcome.

Once Cora had taken another swallow, the lines around her mother's eyes deepened. "Do you remember anything, sweetheart? I know you're groggy, but try to think. It's Sunday. Do you remember anything about yesterday?"

Cora frowned, her brain trying to connect thoughts, make sense of the world in which she'd awakened. It was Sunday. What had she done yesterday? Her head was pounding too hard to concentrate. "I'm not sure. I think I cleaned house yesterday morning? Can't you just tell me? Did I crash my car or something?"

She was starting to get nervous. Janet Benning was nothing if not straightforward. Why was she questioning her instead of just telling her?

"I . . ." Her mom considered her and then let out a resigned sigh. "Do you remember going out to a club last night?"

"A club?" At that, pictures flashed in Cora's brain. Her friends at the table. Lines of tequila shots in front of them. Dancing. "Oh God, did I drink too much? Is that why I'm here?"

Something flickered through her mom's eyes—pain. "Coraline . . ."

That sent true fear rushing through Cora. Her mom was as tough as they came. The fact that she looked to be bracing for something sent Cora's stomach flipping over. "Mom, tell me what's going on. Now."

Janet took Cora's hand and pressed it between hers. For a second, her eyes went shiny like she was going to cry, but then she pulled it back and took a breath. "Honey, last night someone drugged your drink."

"*What?*"

"We have the two men in custody, baby." She pressed her lips together as if trying to maintain her composure and shook her head. "And I'm so sorry to be the one to tell you this, but we found you at their house. We're not sure what happened, but we're pretty sure they . . . took advantage of you."

Everything left in Cora's stomach threatened to come up. She'd been drugged. *Raped?*

The idea terrified her to her core, but as the words settled over her, worked their way through the fog in her brain, they didn't seem to make sense. For some reason, they didn't feel like truth. She could feel the aches in her body, but something was off.

Her mom was talking again but Cora had closed her eyes, trying to make sense of it, trying to grab on to memories. Parts of her day were coming back to her like torn pieces of photographs blowing in a breeze. She grasped for them.

She'd gotten up to clean the house. She'd had a lazy day, but she'd been excited. She'd danced around the house to music while vacuuming. What had she been so excited about?

She played through the scenes in her head, trying to fill in the blank spots. In her head, she could see herself cleaning, pulling out her clothes. Nice clothes.

Date clothes.

"I had a date," she blurted.

She opened her eyes and found her mom had been talking and tears were now officially in her eyes. Janet stopped whatever she'd been saying and blinked. "You remember?"

"Yes." She pressed a hand to her forehead, rubbed. She'd had a date. With Ren. And Hayes. *Two men.* Oh, shit. She looked at her mom. "Wait, are the men you arrested Ren and Hayes?"

Her mother's expression hardened. "They won't ever bother you again, baby. I swear to you—"

"Oh, God. No. They didn't." *Shit. Shit. Shit.* "They wouldn't—"

Her mom's eyes turned empathetic. "I'm sorry, honey. I know you were working with them. I'm sure you would've never suspected. But you don't know people. And Hayes Fox has a history—"

Oh, no. Oh, *fuck.* Cora sat up taller, trying to get the pounding in her head to subside enough so that she could make sense to her mother. "No, Mom. No. They wouldn't have done this. I—"

Ugh. How was she supposed to say what she needed to say to her mother?

"Cora, you're confused and probably in some sort of shock and the drugs—"

"No," she said more firmly, cutting her off. "I'm not in shock. I remember. I went home with Hayes and Fox. Of my own free will. I—I was out with both of them."

Her mom blinked like Cora had clapped in front of her face. Then her stunned expression smoothed into a firm one. "Cora-line, I don't know what you think you know, but you tested positive for a date rape drug. And the officers found a cup at the house from the bar that had traces of the drug."

Cora shook her head. That didn't make any sense. But her memory was in patches. She had a big black spot in it. She remembered getting to Hayes and Ren's place. She remembered kissing in the kitchen. They'd ended up in the bedroom. They'd had amazing sex. Some of the details were fuzzy but she remembered that much.

A drink from the bar?

Another thought occurred to her. "How did someone find me? Did the guys call for help?"

Janet was in full frown now. "No. A tip came in. Someone at the bar recognized Hayes Fox and said he saw him drop something into your drink. He texted a pic of Fox offering you the drink. Officers were sent to the house."

Cora's skin prickled. "Who sent in the pic?"

"Why does that matter?"

"It matters. Who was it? A bartender? Did they give a name?"

"It was anonymous."

"Of course it was." Cora's heart was pounding so hard against her ribs the machine next to her started to sound like it was going to short out.

Her mom's gaze jumped to the machine. "I need you to calm down, Coraline. I think the drugs are still mixing up your brain. You wouldn't go home with two men you hardly knew. I've taught you better. You're smarter than that. And I know it's scary to consider that—"

Cora clamped her hand over her mom's. "I need to talk to the guys."

"What? You most certainly will not. You're not going within a mile of those disgusting excuses—"

"No, Mom. *Listen.* Someone's setting them up. Like the last time when Hayes went to prison. I've been working with them because of a hacker. This is just the next step. They're doing it to him again."

Her mother stood at that, her hackles raised. "I promise you, Coraline. I don't know what line of bullshit those men fed you, but Hayes Fox is a criminal. He got off because he had a good lawyer and too much money. You should've seen the marks on the woman he raped. And you have some of those same marks on you."

Heat flooded Cora's cheeks. The night was coming back to her in bits and pieces but she could feel the tenderness of her backside, could see the faint bruises on her wrists, and had an idea how all that had happened. "Mom, please. I need you to trust me on this. You said I was smart. Act like you believe it. I swear to you these men are good men. They would've had no reason to drug me. I wanted to be there. I wanted the things that happened to happen. I don't know how the drug got in my drink, but I would bet my life on the fact that it wasn't put there by one of them."

Janet crossed her arms, her expression tired. "I'm going to call for the nurse. They need to check you out while you're awake. And you need more sleep."

Before Cora had a chance to respond, her mom stepped outside the door. A minute later she could hear the conversation drifting to her. Words like *confused* and *in denial* were clear enough. Cora pulled wires off her body, sending the machine into a fit.

The nurse rushed in. "Ma'am, I need you to—"

"I need to check out."

The nurse, a broad woman with a tight bun, looked unmoved. "We can't do that until the doctor comes by and gives the go-ahead. He'll be making rounds in the next two hours. I need you to just relax for now. We can get you something—"

"I want to check out."

"You can't—"

"Yes, I can. I can do that—what's it called? That AMA thing. Please get someone who can make that happen. I'm fine. I have a headache, but I wasn't raped. I'm not in denial. And I sure as hell don't need more sleep. I've slept enough."

The nurse's expression conveyed her frustration, and Janet looked ready to physically hold Cora back. But Cora knew enough to know that they couldn't hold her unless they thought she was a danger to herself or someone else. She could leave "Against Medical Advice" if she signed a form. Sometimes it was a benefit to have been a cop's kid and have heard all her mother's shop talk.

So after a tense few minutes of trying to negotiate, the nurse strode off to get the forms.

Cora's mother was red in the face by the end of the exchange. "You need to stay. This is ridiculous. The drugs are making you act irrational."

"I'm not being irrational." Cora found a bag her mom had apparently brought up to the hospital with fresh clothes. She tugged on the yoga pants and T-shirt. She could feel her mom watching her. Angry. But worried, too.

And that's when it registered that her mom truly believed this. She wasn't trying to be a pain in the ass. She thought Cora had been drugged and raped and was now going off the deep end. She didn't have access to all the information Cora had. So with a sigh, Cora walked over to her and put her hands on her shoulders.

"Mom, listen to me. You said it yourself. You've trained me to be smart about these things. To be cautious. Paranoid, even. I've been on the lookout for dangerous men all my life. Do you think I would've gone home with two guys who I didn't absolutely, one hundred percent trust? Do you think if I truly believed I'd been raped that I wouldn't be the first in line to throw the book at these guys?"

Janet shook her head. "Baby, you're young and naive. Men will take advantage of you. You can't know everything about people . . ."

"No, I can't." Cora put her arms at her sides. "And you can't either. But I can promise you, I know enough. And if you and the police aren't going to help figure out who really did this, who's really setting up Hayes, then I'm going to have to find out myself." She took a deep breath. She couldn't even think about Ren and

Hayes being behind bars right now. She couldn't let that image sink in. "You taught me that not everyone or everything is as it seems on the surface. And what you're doing right now is just looking at the surface, at the obvious thing. Why in God's name would Hayes put himself at risk so publicly again when he just got out of prison?"

She frowned. "Poor impulse control."

"Ha—if you knew him, you'd realize how far from the truth that is. And if they had this grand plan, why come out with me and my friends? Why create all those witnesses? I would've gone out with just them."

"Witnesses said that you were drunk. That helps their case to pin this on your behavior."

"But I wasn't drunk! Call my friends. Talk to Josh. I had a few drinks but was sober by the time I left. Josh checked in with me before I left to make sure I was good."

"You hadn't had the drink yet. It was in a takeaway cup."

She groaned. "Why would they drug me in public when they could've just slipped me something at their house? I was already going home with them. I wasn't going to their place to play checkers. I was already willing."

"To have sex with two strangers and to let them abuse you."

Cora closed her eyes. Part of her wanted to die discussing this with her mother. *Awkward* wasn't an adequate enough word to describe it. But she was tired of being ashamed, of hiding, of being the girl who wore all the masks. "Yes. I'm kinky, all right? I've dabbled in that lifestyle online for a while and wanted to try it for real with them. So yes, I wanted to be with both of them. And I wanted them to be a little rough. It was all with consent. I don't remember everything, but I remember that much without doubt. And it's okay that you don't approve or that you think I'm weird or being young and stupid, but I need you to believe me. I need you to trust my judgement on these two guys. They are not the criminals."

Her mother stepped back and lowered her head. "I'm sorry,

Coraline. I love you and I'd much rather know that you were just being wild and that no one had hurt you, but I can't in good conscience believe that these guys didn't do this to you. The evidence doesn't lie."

The words hurt more than Cora expected. Her mother would rather trust a stranger's word than hers. All her life she'd played by her mom's rules and it hadn't made a difference. But she held back the tears that threatened and nodded. "Innocent until proven guilty. Right. Sure."

She walked over to the cabinet, which thankfully held her purse and phone, and then walked out in search of the nurse so she could sign the papers.

She loved her mother more than anyone in the world. But right now, there were two men sitting in jail who needed her.

She wasn't going to let them down.

TWENTY-SEVEN

Ren paced the cell, unable to sleep or sit or do much of anything but walk and stress. They hadn't told him anything. He had no idea if Cora was okay, and Hayes had been taken to a different part of the station. The not knowing was going to kill him. If someone would just tell him that Cora was okay, he could at least breathe. Ren had called their lawyer, hoping that Jim could get him some information, but he'd had to leave a message.

A cop came down the hallway, a bored look on his face. "Muroya, you have a visitor."

"Thank Christ," Ren muttered, raking a hand through his hair. At least if he had a lawyer here, he had a chance at getting news or getting the hell out of this place.

"Turn your back to the door so I can cuff you."

Ren did as he was told and then the deputy let him out of the holding cell. He directed him to walk a little ahead of him and guided Ren down the hallway and into the main part of the station.

The cop cleared his throat before they got to the visitation room. "You're only going to have a few minutes. Don't do anything stupid."

"I'm only going to have a few minutes with my lawyer?" Ren asked. "The hell I am. It's my right to meet with counsel."

The cop smirked. "This isn't counsel. And I'm not losing my job over this. So be quick. Got me?"

"What?"

But Ren didn't have to ask again because when the cop swung open the door, Ren found Cora sitting at the table inside. She looked up, face drawn and pale, hair gathered in a haphazard ponytail, and a haunted look in her eyes.

"Benning." All the air whooshed out of him and he nearly dropped to his knees. "Thank you, God."

Ren wanted to rush to her, to hug her, to feel for himself that she was okay, but when he jerked his arms forward, the cuffs reminded him where he was. He took a breath, trying to calm himself.

"Go on." The cop let him step inside and then shut the door behind Ren.

Cora's gaze slid to his arms, registering the cuffs, and she winced. "Does he have to wear those?"

A voice from the corner of the room answered. "I'm trying to stick as close to protocol as I can, Junior. Plus, Muroya's put enough people in cuffs. He can handle wearing them for a few minutes."

Ren's gaze hopped to where the voice had come from. Andre Medina stood there in a suit, arms crossed, badge on his hip, and expression serious.

He gave Ren a little nod. "You have a few minutes. If her mother found out I let you two talk, she'd have my job."

"Her mother?" Ren asked.

"The police captain," Cora said grimly. "She's my mom."

Ren stared at her. "*Janet Benning* is your— The one who helped put Hayes away?"

"The very one, unfortunately."

"I— Why didn't you say something? Jesus. If Hayes knew . . ."

He would've freaked the fuck out. He would've assumed Cora was some kind of trap for him.

"I didn't know how to bring it up, and it's not time to focus on that now. If we don't get something done quickly, she's going to be the one putting you both away this time." She nodded at the chair across from her. "Please, Ren, we've only got a few minutes."

He slid into the chair awkwardly, the cuffs making everything more difficult. "First, tell me you're okay. They couldn't get you to wake up. They kept calling your name. I was so fucking terrified. I didn't know . . ."

Her businesslike expression faltered for a second and she reached out, flattening her hand between them even though Ren couldn't reach out to touch her, and met his gaze. "I'm okay. I feel like I've been hit in the head with a two-by-four, and I can't remember a big chunk of last night, but I'm all right. Rohypnol packs a punch."

His stomach clenched. "Cora, you have to know that we never would've put anything in your drink. I—"

She lifted her hand. "Please, don't even. Seriously. I remember enough to know that I wanted to be there with you two. I know neither of you would ever hurt me. But I *was* drugged. And there's a picture of Hayes handing me the drink. The cops have the cup with traces of the drug. Do you remember anything about the Coke he gave me?"

Ren looked down at the table, trying to remember how everything played out at the bar. "It's got to be the soda we left with. Hayes got it from the bar right before we were leaving."

She nodded. "I remember that much, too. But I don't remember how much I drank. I Googled the drug that was used on me. It's quick-acting. Half an hour and it starts taking effect. That would've been right in the middle of everything. Did you notice me getting drunk at any point after we left? I know I was sober when we headed to your house."

He frowned. "No, I don't think you drank much from what I remember. We talked in the car on the way home. You may have taken a sip or two but when I brought the drink inside for you, it was still pretty full. I remember having to hand it off to Hayes because I almost spilled it. But I don't know where it ended up after that. But you weren't acting funny or drunk. Once we were home, you were talking and present and steady on your feet. Well, until"—he glanced at Andre, who was studiously focusing on his phone—"until you were, you know, off your feet."

Cora's cheeks went pink. "You didn't hear that, Medina."

"*No hablo ingles,*" Medina said without looking up.

Cora sniffed. "And after that, nothing weird? I can remember some of what we did, but things get fuzzy halfway through."

Ren shook his head. "We showered and you were fine. We went to bed. That's the last I remember before the cops banged on the door."

She stared down at her hands, forehead wrinkled. "I had to have drank more afterward. Got up or something. That's the only thing that makes sense. But I guess that really doesn't matter at this point." She looked up, her jaw set. "What matters is that someone drugged my drink and someone called in a false tip. I have a feeling—"

"It's the same goddamned person."

"Exactly," she said, her fist curling against the table. "We dragged Hayes out, and the motherfucker jumped on the chance. He had to have followed us there and waited for an opportunity. Who the fuck carries roofies on them just in case the opportunity comes up?"

"You'd be surprised," Andre said without looking up.

"Either way, it's got to be our guy. My mom slipped up and told me the caller was a man. But she wouldn't tell me anything else. I doubt she knows much more than that." She rubbed her lips together. "There were so many people there last night, but do you remember seeing anyone you knew? Anything strange?"

Ren sagged forward in the seat, his head hurting. He played the night through his head. He'd been having so much fun that all he'd really focused on was Cora and Hayes. It'd been the perfect night—two people he cared about, dancing and laughing and singing . . .

He straightened.

"What?" Cora said, picking up on his shift in demeanor. "You saw something?"

Ren glanced up, his heartbeat speeding up. "After we sang on stage, I was looking out into the crowd and there were so many faces out in the audience. But for a second, I thought I saw a familiar face. It was in my periphery and I just caught a glimpse. When I looked again, the guy had disappeared into the crowd. I figured I'd imagined it."

Cora's hands pressed flat against the table and even Andre was looking their way now. "Who, Ren?"

Ren swallowed hard. "Gordon. For a second I thought I saw Gordon."

Her face went slack. "The guy you ran away with?"

"Yes, but I've thought I've seen him before. It used to happen all the time after I came back home. My psychologist at the time said it was post-traumatic stress. I was seeing his face in strangers. I thought it was the same thing last night. He didn't even have the same hair color. The lights on stage were in my eyes. I just dismissed it."

Cora's eyes had gone big. "He could be the one. It makes sense."

Ren frowned. "But it doesn't. All of this shit has been directed at Hayes. Hayes is the one who went to prison. If Gordon was still holding some crazy grudge over me leaving him all those years ago, he'd come after me. Hurt *me*. It's not like I'm hard to find. And it would've been so much easier to frame me. I'm way more reckless than Hayes has ever been."

Cora leaned forward on her elbows, her gaze burning into him. "Not necessarily. Think about it. There's something more devastating than being hurt. What hurts worse than that?"

A pit settled in his stomach, the realization rocking through him. The words whispered out of him. "Watching the person you love the most get hurt instead."

"Yes."

Ren couldn't even wrap his head around that, but as he said it, the truth resonated through him. He'd briefly considered Gordon when everything had started. His mind naturally went there. But he'd dismissed him just as quickly because Gordon hadn't even known Hayes. It wouldn't have made sense for him to target Hayes.

But now Ren knew more. Gordon hadn't just met Hayes. He'd been threatened by him all those years ago. Hayes had put a gun to his head. And Gordon would not be a man to take that lightly. His pride was everything to him. Respect required or pay the price. Ren had paid the price many times when he'd lived with Gordon. Maybe he was still paying it.

No, maybe Hayes had paid it on Ren's behalf.

The thought made him go cold inside. If Hayes had gone to prison all those years because of Ren's stupid mistakes when he was a kid . . . If he'd suffered because . . .

He didn't even know how to deal with that.

"Ren," Cora said, breaking him from his sinking thoughts. "We don't have much time. I need you to tell me everything you know about Gordon *right now.* Every detail that can help me track him down."

Ren's head snapped up at that. "Track him down? The hell you will. There's no way I'm letting you go anywhere near that guy, even virtually. You've already paid enough of a price for this. If it's him, he'd hurt you now, too. Because of me. He'll have been watching. He'll know you mean something to me."

Something flickered in her gaze. "Ren . . ."

"No, I'm not going to let you put yourself at risk. Fuck that. Andre, don't you dare let her go after this guy."

Andre frowned and glanced at Cora.

"The police aren't going to help you with this," she said, a ferocity to her expression. "I can. And I know how to be careful. I'm not going to show up on his doorstep. I know how to cover my tracks."

"Benning—" The word was a plea.

She stood. "I'm tired of people telling me what I can and can't do. I'm good at this. And I'm not that fragile. I'm not incapable of protecting myself or being careful."

"I didn't say—"

She stepped around the table and stood in front of him, arms crossed. "Plus, in case you haven't noticed, I might kind of care about you, too. And this whole thing could be kind of amazing if we have a chance."

His chest squeezed tight.

"And I have no idea how y'all feel about me, but there it is. Cora unfiltered. So I'll be damned if I'm going to stand by and let some psycho stalker with a God complex fuck up my chance to see where this goes with you two. I've had enough dating tragedies. Having the two guys I like end up in jail is not an option. Plus, if my ass was sitting in here, I'd expect you two to do everything you could to get me out. So don't expect less from me. Got it?"

Andre's eyebrows shot up behind her.

Ren stood, wishing he could reach out to her, pull her to him. He knew how much that must've cost her to lay her feelings out like that. But he couldn't get past the idea of her going anywhere near Gordon. "Please. It's not that I expect less of you. I'll go nuts in here knowing you're out there poking at Gordon. He's danger-ous. This just proves how much. I can get a private investigator again now that I know where to point him. I've already lost Hayes once. I just got him back and I've just found you. I can't handle it if either of you end up hurt in all this, especially because of me."

She leaned forward, cupped the back of his head, and kissed him. "You were a kid, Ren. This is not your fault. And if I can't get enough on him, you can call your PI. But for right now, I'm all you've got. A pissed-off hacker girl."

"And I'll watch her back," Andre added.

Cora peered over her shoulder, no doubt giving Andre a petu-lant look. "I'm not going in guns a-blazing, Medina."

Andre shrugged. "Doesn't mean I'm not going to look out for you. Ren's right. I don't know who this guy is that you're talking about. But if he's capable of framing someone not just once but twice and drugging the police captain's daughter, the guy's fearless and on a mission. And he's smart enough to have protected himself well for this long. You don't know how far he'll go." He looked to Ren. "If he's into hurting people Ren cares about, you fit the bill and could be next on the list."

Ren's jaw clenched. He wished he could grab Cora and drag her back to the cell with him. At least then he'd be assured she was safe.

But when she turned around, he could tell by the set of her stance that there was no chasing her off this hunt. She would do it whether he asked her to stop or not. So when she pulled a notepad out of her purse and sat down again, he answered her questions about Gordon.

And when she left, he let his head lower to the table and banged it there.

Andre's hand landed on Ren's shoulder. "I'm going to ask Grant if we can borrow some of his private security from The Ranch. I'll put a detail on her and make sure someone is outside her house. She'll never be out of sight."

Ren looked up and let out a breath. "Thanks, man."

Andre smiled, though it held no humor. "Of course. I'm not going to let anything happen to her." He tilted his head. "Speaking of which, while I have you in handcuffs and locked in a room, what *are* your intentions with her?"

Ren frowned. "My *intentions*?"

Andre sat on the edge of the table, looking every bit the intimidating detective in his suit and tie. "I've known Cora since she was a teenager. She's like the kid sister of the station. And I've known you and Hayes long enough to know that you two have always been one-and-done players at The Ranch. That's your business. I'm not judging. But I saw how that woman just looked at you. She cares about the both of you enough to go on a crusade to clear your names. When Cora puts her heart into something, it's all the way. She comes across as tough, and in a lot of ways, she is. But I've seen guys use her before. She's been hurt. So if you're planning to be one-and-done with her, tell her now. She deserves that."

One-and-done? Moving on? That had always been the plan in the past. A little kink. A little fun. No big deal. This didn't feel like no big deal.

Ren stared at him and then sighed. "Honestly, I have no idea where the hell my head is at. I've only known her for a few weeks. And I originally planned for it just to be some fun between friends. But she's, I don't know . . . She's so . . . And last night . . . and . . . Fuck."

Andre's mouth curled into a smile and he patted Ren on the shoulder. "That's all I needed to know, brother."

"What?"

Andre shook his head, amusement in his eyes. "Come on, let's get you back to your cell before my boss finds out I'm breaking ten kinds of protocol. I'd like to keep my job."

Ren stood. "Why'd you do this, then?"

He walked Ren to the door. "Because your girlfriend is damn persuasive."

My girlfriend.

For the first time in his life, he didn't want to run at the sound of that.

It sounded . . . right.

But now he was going to have to go back to a cage and pull his hair out while his *girlfriend* went after the man who had tried to tear his life apart.

TWENTY-EIGHT

Cora stood at the bottom of the staircase of the apartment complex, her feet feeling like lead. She'd been to this apartment countless times. Had jogged up those stairs many a late night. But now dread sat heavy on her chest. God, she didn't want to ask for help.

This was her best option, though. She'd done all she could at the police station, breaking more laws than she'd ever admit to. But she'd gotten into the system and found the number the anonymous tip had come from. Unfortunately, it'd been an inside line from the bar. The guy was careful. But not careful enough. The photo he'd emailed to the station had come from a cell phone. And that cell phone was registered to G.D.T. Entertainment, a company that owned a few strip clubs around Texas and Louisiana. The owner: Gordon Davis Teller.

So Cora had their guy. But the problem was she had nothing on him. Her mother and the police would need hard evidence to do anything about it or even take her seriously. And it wasn't like she could just go to one of the clubs and start asking questions. If Gordon was following Hayes and Ren closely, he knew who Cora was. So she had to rely on what she knew how to do. Or more important in this case, *who* she knew.

Unfortunately, who she knew was exactly why she didn't want to be here.

She glanced over at the car that had tailed her—compliments of Andre Medina. The guy had turned off his lights, and the nondescript Ford was tucked away in the dark parking lot, but she still felt like it was glaringly obvious. And really, the last thing she needed here was backup. The only thing in danger right now was her ego.

With a sigh, Cora trudged up the stairs. She knew he was here. His Toyota was sitting in its usual spot and she'd texted him to let him know she needed to talk to him. But it still took him a while to come to the door after she knocked.

The door swung open and Kevin's lanky form appeared in the flashing TV light coming from inside. He braced a hand on the doorjamb and gave her a lopsided smile. "Well, hey, stranger. I was starting to wonder if you'd ever stop by again."

She let her eyes travel over him with a quick sweep. He hadn't changed in the months since she'd seen him. He'd always been cute in that floppy-haired, California boy kind of way. But she found the sight did zero for her now. "Can I come in?"

He slid his arm up the doorjamb and made room for her to step under. "*Mi casa es su casa.*"

She ducked under his arm, annoyed that he didn't just step out of the damn way, and went inside. Some superhero movie was on the TV and there was a pizza box on the coffee table. "Sorry to interrupt the Marvel marathon."

The door shut behind her. "No worries. It's nice to see you. You're looking . . . good."

There was a flirty undercurrent in his words, and she barely resisted the urge to spin around and punch him in the throat. Did the guy actually think she'd show up out of the blue for a booty call? Probably. She turned and pasted a tight smile on her face. "I look like shit. I got roofied last night and woke up in a hospital."

He grimaced. "Shit, Cora."

"Yeah, fun times."

He ran a hand over the back of his head, looking genuinely disturbed. "You okay? Did anything—"

"Nothing happened. Thank God." Some of the starch went out of her shoulders at his genuine show of concern. The guy had been a shitty non-boyfriend, but he wasn't a shitty person. She would focus on that. "I need your help with something. I know who did this to me but I need evidence."

His eyebrows lifted. "You're coming to *me* for help?"

Okay, so maybe she'd always made a point to be better at him on most things at work. She *had* been better at her job at Braecom. But that's because Kevin did his day job for the money. His passion was the gray-area stuff. He liked breaking in where others had failed. He liked to prove he could. His specialty? iThings.

She pulled a folded piece of paper from her pocket. "I've got the asshole's phone number and the email he uses for his mobile account. This is bigger than what happened to me. The guy's a seriously bad dude. So I need to get in and see if I can get any dirt on him."

"And how do you propose we do that?"

"Do you still have that malware you used to get into Carol's ex's phone?"

Last year, one of the assistants at Braecom had been threatened by her boyfriend. He'd been holding naked pics of her hostage. Cora and Kevin had tried to get into his system to help, but the only way they'd been able to get into his cloud was via his text messaging system with malware Kevin had developed. They'd deleted the stolen photos and put a few bugs in his phone just for kicks.

Kevin tucked his hands in his back pockets and frowned. "Shit, Cora. I haven't used that in over a year. You know how many security patches they've had since then? Unless his phone's been jailbroken, it's going to be next to impossible. They have companies offering million-dollar prizes for people who can develop that kind of remote hack. Even the FBI took forever to get into that terrorist's phone. I'm good, but I'm not that good."

"Can we at least try and see if it's jailbroken? He thinks he's above the law, maybe that translates to his phone. If I can get into his cloud, I know I'll find something. This guy's hands are in too many things. He's got to mess up somewhere."

Kevin sighed. "Well, what have we got to lose, right? You know I love a challenge."

She cocked a brow. "I'm not sure I know that."

"I dated you, didn't I? No one's more challenging than you."

She crossed her arms. She hadn't come here for this. She didn't have time for it, but she couldn't help the words from coming out. "Oh, no. I distinctly remember we weren't dating. We were FWB. Or as you so quaintly referred to me—a bro with a vagina."

He frowned. "I meant that as a joke and a compliment. All I meant was that you're a cool chick to hang out with. I didn't have to put on a show with you. We could just be. We were chill."

"No, I was convenient and put out and that worked for you. Let's just call a spade a spade."

He stared at her, taken aback. "Are you serious right now? You put out, but so did I. That's what we did for each other. Don't pretend you wanted more or make it sound like I was using you. If you had thought of me as your boyfriend, you would've let me in—at least a little. You never trusted me like that. I found out from someone else that when you took off for a few days, it was because your grandfather had died. You didn't even look to me to help you through that."

She sniffed. "Like you would've wanted me to cry all over you for days."

He held out his hands. "I would've been there for you, Cora. I cared about you. But you always had the tough-girl thing going. You're a Mac."

"What?"

"You're a closed system. You never let me see behind the curtains. Even when we slept together, you kept that wall up. I wasn't invited past a certain point. So don't pretend you ever wanted a real relationship with me. You closed that door before I could ever try to open it."

She frowned.

"Both of us stuck around all those years with each other for the same reasons. It was easy. We got along well, the sex was decent, and it saved us both from dealing with the drama of the dating world. We were both guilty of the same crime."

The words weren't what she expected, but she couldn't muster up a good argument against them. She thought back to all the time she'd spent with Kevin. It had always been about activities. Hanging out. Playing video games. Watching movies. Sex. She couldn't think of one time that they'd had a heart-to-heart. Hell, she'd told Ren more on that first night at the taco shop about her past than Kevin knew after three years. "Oh."

Kevin smirked and shrugged. "You just weren't that into me. A major personality flaw, by the way. Because I'm freaking adorable. That's what my eighty-year-old neighbor tells me every morning, and she's very wise."

She snorted. "No way Mrs. Meyerson says *freaking.*"

"You're right. She goes full f-bomb but I was trying to be attuned to your delicate sensibilities."

Cora laughed. And in that moment, she remembered why everything had started with Kevin in the first place. She *liked* him. She'd just labeled it wrong. She hadn't known the difference at the time between a friendship connection and more. Now that she'd met Hayes and Ren, she knew what gut-level, bone-deep attraction felt like, that need to be with someone, to open up to them and show them the real you. She'd never had that with Kevin. But she'd had this. That comfortable vibe, easy humor.

"I can't believe you just called me a Mac. You're such a dork," she said, some of the tension draining out of her.

"One of my best qualities. Which is why you're here, right? To get a piece of my big, sexy-ass brain?"

She rolled her eyes. "How about your hot, dangerous malware?"

"Don't talk dirty to me, C. I've been working long hours. And there's no bro with a vagina in residence anymore."

"I swear to God, if you ever utter that phrase out loud to anyone again, I'm going to nut punch you. Take it out of your vocabulary, Watkins."

He lifted his hands, palms out. "Consider it deleted." He tipped his head to the left. "Come on, I've moved all my good stuff into the office. Let's see if we can take this asshole down."

Cora nodded, switching back into mission mode. "Let's do this."

TWENTY-NINE

Ren had finally fallen into a fitful sleep at some point in the middle of the night. But early the next morning, a cop was calling his name. He rolled over, every muscle stiff, and shook the fog from his head. "What?"

"Your bail's been posted. I need you to sign a few things and then you're free to go."

He sat up, relief moving through him. "Thank God. And Hayes?"

The cop shook her head. "The judge denied bail for him."

Fuck. That meant they really did have some kind of solid evidence. Wrong evidence. But solid. "Once I'm out, can I visit him?"

"Only lawyers for now."

He groaned. He didn't want to think about Hayes behind bars for another minute much less another day or however long it took to figure this shit out. Being locked up had nearly broken Hayes the first time. A second time would kill him. Ren wasn't going to let that happen.

He'd track Gordon down himself. Though the thought made his stomach turn. That old fear was permanently tattooed on his psyche—with Ren always being the helpless kid and Gordon being all-powerful. He knew that wasn't the case anymore, but it was an impossible feeling to shake. For that brief moment when he'd thought he'd seen Gordon in the bar, the teeth of panic had snapped at him, his teen self surfacing. But he'd deal with it. No one was sending Hayes back to prison, especially not one of Ren's mistakes.

Ren went through the procedure for getting released in near silence, his brain already formulating a plan, and got his stuff back. His phone, wallet, and his keys. He didn't have his car, but his lawyer could give him a ride to the house.

"Where's Jim?" Ren asked when he'd signed the last page.

"Who?" The cop looked up from stamping the document.

"My lawyer. The guy who posted my bail."

He cocked his head toward the door. "He said he needed to take a call outside."

"Great."

Ren tucked his things in his pockets and headed to the front. He pushed open the door, more than a little thankful to see the morning sun, and squinted in the bright light, looking for his attorney. But there was no one outside except an older couple walking their dog across the street. He jogged down the steps of the station and scanned the area.

"Well, shit."

He lifted his phone to call Jim and see where he'd gone off to, but his phone was dead as hell. Fantastic.

He glanced at the station. He didn't want to step foot back in that place, so he headed down the street toward the Starbucks on the corner. He needed coffee and could use their phone to call for a ride and to check in with Cora. Andre had promised he'd have someone keep watch over her, but Ren wasn't going to feel better until he talked to her and heard her voice. She'd left the station with a mission. If she'd found something, she would've sent word or come to see him. She was probably at her place on her computer doing her detective work. She was probably fine.

But for some reason, his heart had started to pound harder, a bad feeling making his skin prickle. He pressed the power button on his phone again on the off chance he could get a burst of juice from it, maybe at least send a text, but the black screen mocked him. He shoved the useless thing in his back pocket and took a breath. It would only be a few minutes before he could call her. He needed to stop being paranoid.

He picked up the pace of his walk. But he wasn't a block away from the police station when a man stepped out from between buildings and blocked Ren's path.

Ren pulled up like a horse getting its reins yanked, an automatic reaction, but when his brain registered the face in front of him, everything went still inside him.

The man was older, more lines around his eyes, and his hair was deep brown instead of blond, but the pale blue eyes were as familiar as ever. Gordon's mouth spread into a smile. "Hello, Renny."

Just the sound of the old pet name was enough to snap Ren out of his frozen state. He'd had nightmares where that word was whispered into his ear. His fists balled, his body ready to fight off the threat before his brain even registered everything. But he couldn't make words come out of his mouth.

"I see everything went smoothly at the jail," Gordon said conversationally. "Idiot cops. They had no evidence to hold you. You didn't give the girl the drink. I'm sure I did a better job than your overpriced lawyer would've."

Ren swallowed, reality crashing over him. "You posted bail."

"You're welcome." He cocked his head in that way he used to do when he wanted Ren to fetch something for him. "You can thank me by taking a drive with me. We have a lot to catch up on."

The easy way he said it, the absolute confidence, made black, bitter hatred well up in Ren. This was the man who had used him, who had convinced him that he loved him, then loaned him out like he was a commodity to be rented. And now this left no doubt. This was the man who had put Hayes behind bars for what Ren could only figure was some twisted punishment of Ren. "So all this time it was you. You sick fuck."

Gordon smirked and straightened his suit coat, ever the polished businessman. "Sick, huh? I believe that's what you used to love best about me. Or have you forgotten?"

Ren fought to keep his cool. He wanted to punch the fucker to the ground, beat him until he was broken, put him through some of the shit Ren had endured from him. Ren was bigger than he was now, much more muscular than he'd been at sixteen. He could take him down. But he kept his fists at his sides. This was the man who had put Hayes in prison, but right now, he was also the only one who could get him out. The police station was a block back. A few words from Gordon could clear Hayes's name. If he knocked Gordon out, that wouldn't happen. "I haven't forgotten anything."

Gordon smiled like that pleased him. "Glad to know it was as memorable for you as it was for me. I hate that it turned out the way it did. A lot of misunderstandings, and your big friend got in the way of me apologizing to you for how things went down. I got a little carried away back then. Love does crazy things to people."

Ren gritted his teeth. "That wasn't love, Gordon. You don't manipulate and force the people you love to do things against their will. You don't fuck with their lives after they leave you."

Gordon frowned. "You were too naive back then, didn't understand what I was trying to do for you. I see that now. I threw you into the deep end before you were ready. That was my mistake. And when you left, it left you vulnerable to be manipulated by someone like Hayes Fox. You always needed someone to take care of you, and he knew how to take advantage."

Now Ren really did have to breathe through the need to start swinging at him. "Keep his name out of your mouth. If you have a problem with me, fine. Here I am. But you're going to go into that police station first and tell them you made a mistaken report. Clear Hayes."

A black Buick pulled up to the curb next to them. Gordon glanced that way and then gave Ren a patient smile, like he was tolerating Ren's outburst. "I have no idea what you're talking about. But we can chat more in the car."

"Fuck you. I'm not going anywhere. We've got nothing to say that we can't say right here."

Gordon tucked his hands in his pockets like they were just two men on the street discussing the weather. "All those years ago you didn't just embarrass me and bring the police sniffing around, Ren. You *hurt* me. I had looked a long time for someone like you, someone who was so perfectly made for submission. You promised me you'd stay with me forever, you gave yourself to me, and then you walked. You walked to be someone's sidekick, someone's *project*. What the fuck is that? You're more than that. I would've made you more than that."

Ren stared at him, the layers of crazy just too much to take in. "I was a *kid*. And confused and lonely. You sold me a bill of goods that wasn't true and then threatened me when I wanted to leave. That's not love, asshole. It's abuse."

Gordon's gaze slid to a spot behind Ren, probably people coming close enough to hear the conversation. "Get in the car."

"You have zero chance of that happening."

Gordon's expression smoothed and his eyes went flinty. "You'll do it because if you don't, not only is your boyfriend going to rot in jail, your latest plaything is going to have a very bad day. I wonder how much Rohypnol is too much in a week."

Ren's stomach clenched. "What?"

"I was hoping you'd come willingly. Be a man about it. But I had a feeling you'd be difficult. I realize the girl is a passing whim. You never stay with women long. Probably because the dom act is such a laughable farce on you. But I doubt you'd want her hurt just because you don't know how to take responsibility for your mistakes."

Fear like Ren had never felt before filled him—bright, sharp stabs of it. Gordon had Cora.

Visions of Gordon's hands on her, hurting her, holding her down, filled Ren's head and he wanted to vomit. He'd seen what Gordon could do to people, had experienced it. The man used BDSM as a front but he was no dominant. He was just a cruel, controlling man hiding his sickness beneath the veneer of kink. Ren had found that out the hard way when Gordon had started pushing lines Ren wasn't comfortable with. There were no safe words with him. And he didn't care if consent was there or not. He would hurt Cora and not flinch, especially if he knew it was hurting Ren at the same time.

Ren swallowed past the tightness in his throat, searching for that calm place inside him, that piece that could shut out the emotions and deal with this. If Gordon had Cora, Ren would go with him. He would do whatever it took to get to her. "What do you want from me? What could you possibly want to go through all this trouble?"

Gordon reached out and opened the car door. "You. One more night. A proper good-bye."

Bile rose in the back of Ren's throat. A proper good-bye. Such a civil term for what he suspected Gordon really wanted. Ren's utter and merciless humiliation. A final punishment for walking away. Proof to Gordon that he was still in charge, that Ren never had any power. He would try to break him.

Fuck him. Anger bright and blinding rose up in him. Gordon knew what Ren's answer would be, knew he wasn't going to let Cora suffer. The smile on his face said as much—*I've already won, Renny. Don't bother arguing.* But let Gordon try to get into his head, let him try to play those games. The smug bastard looked so sure of himself, so positive that he could take his place over Ren again, pull his strings like a puppet and make him beg. But he didn't know this Ren Muroya. He knew a shadow of the person he was now. Ren wasn't that kid anymore. Let Gordon try. Ren would not be broken. He would fight.

But first, he had to get to Cora.

Ren gave one last look to the police station down the block and then he climbed into the car. He didn't greet the driver. He didn't react when Gordon slid in next to him.

And he never saw the needle in Gordon's hand.

The world went black before Ren could say another word.

THIRTY

Cora hadn't slept. She and Kevin had spent all night trying everything they knew how to do to break into Gordon's phone. They'd lucked out that the phone was jailbroken, but Gordon had a third-party security app installed and Kevin's malware wasn't designed for that.

So Cora had been coding on the fly, tweaking Kevin's program, and Kevin had been trying to find another way in. He'd managed to get into the system at one of Gordon's clubs, but there'd been nothing of note in there besides payroll stuff, financial documents, and employee records. On the off chance she'd hit pay dirt, she'd had Kevin search for the name of the woman who'd accused Hayes all those years ago, hoping maybe she'd been a stripper employed by Gordon's company, but nothing had come up.

Cora took a big gulp of coffee and stared at the program she'd written. Her eyes burned. All the letters and numbers were blending together. But she thought maybe she had something. "Let's try to run this. I think I found a workaround that won't trigger the security app."

Kevin leaned over, looked at her screen, and scanned through what she'd done. "Oh, so you . . . Yeah. That's— Damn, that's good. That could work."

"As long as he has his phone on and doesn't delete the message, it should get us in."

Kevin smirked. "You sure you're not slipping a black hat on in your off-hours? You've got some evil genius in you."

"Only to take revenge on ex-boyfriends," she said mildly. "Good thing you weren't my boyfriend."

That earned her a snort.

"All right, let's give this baby a go."

Fifteen minutes later, the message went out as she'd designed it and, somewhere in the city, lit Gordon's screen with a notification.

She and Kevin barely breathed, waiting for the wall to slam down, the blocks to slide in place. But no alarm bells were triggered. Instead, the open road rolled out before them.

Cora clicked, and there it was. Gordon's phone.

Text messages. Emails. Photos. All at her fingertips.

Cora's heartbeat picked up speed. "Gotcha, motherfucker."

Working fast just in case they got interrupted or the message got deleted, she opened up his photos and started scanning through. She confirmed the shot sent to the police was from him. But there were a lot more shots from the bar, the lens firmly focused on her, Ren, and Hayes. Talking. Dancing. Singing.

All time-stamped and proving that she was there willingly with the guys before Hayes handed her any drink. She took screenshots of each one. Then moved to the next.

A shot of her in a passionate kiss on the dance floor, both guys caging her between them.

Kevin coughed behind her.

"Shut up, Kevin."

"I didn't say a word." She could feel him smiling even without looking his way. "But I'm happy to know it took two dudes to replace one of me."

She groaned. "A nut punch is still on the table, just so you know."

"It's always on the table with you. But keep scrolling. He could delete you at any time."

"Right." She jumped back a few days in the photo stream, not sure what she was looking for but going on instinct. The pictures filled the screen, and a creeping cold moved through her. It was shot after shot of Ren. Getting out of his car at work. Walking into a restaurant for lunch. And farther back, him walking next to Cora outside of the Mexican restaurant. "Jesus."

"Whoa," Kevin said as she continued to click through pictures. "Stalk much?"

She scrolled back even farther. Hayes walking out of prison, Ren waiting for him. The two men embracing. Their house. Hayes's SUV. Then screenshots from Hayven of Master Dmitry and Lenore. Records of their private chat conversations. She quickly closed those, not wanting Kevin to see the content.

She rubbed the goose bumps from her arms. "He's been watching the whole damn time."

"This is freaky, Cora. You need to bring in the police. This guy is obviously unhinged."

"I know." She took a few more screenshots and then scrolled back to the ones at the bar to make sure she didn't miss any. But after she clicked through the last one, the scene jumped to something new. A place she recognized because she'd just been there yesterday. The police station. And Ren was walking out.

"What the hell?"

He gaze scanned to the photo's information. Time stamp: a little over three hours ago.

Her heart jumped into her throat. "Oh no."

"What?"

"I need to call Ren." She looked around the cluttered desk, trying to find her phone, her movements frantic. When she found it under a pile of papers, she hit Ren's number, her fingers shaking. It went straight to voice mail, no ring. "Fuck."

She shoved her chair back and stood. "Kev, I know it's a lot to ask, but can you keep looking through this to see what you find? And forward me all those screenshots. I need to show them to the police."

"Yeah, no problem." Kevin's brow furrowed, genuine concern on his face. "But, Cor, you really need to turn all this over to the cops. I mean, people don't stalk someone to never make a move. This guy's got something planned. You could get hurt."

Dread curled around her, making her feel light-headed. She didn't want to think too far ahead or overreact, but she couldn't shake the feeling that this was all coming to a head. That something had happened. Another thought struck her. "Wait, can you get me a location? Open up his Maps."

Kevin rolled his chair to the spot where hers had been and clicked through to a few screens until he got the Maps app to pinpoint the phone's current location. The address didn't mean anything to her, but she took a picture of it with her phone.

Kevin spun around and grabbed her hand. "Hey, I'm serious. Be careful."

The worry in his voice touched her. She leaned down and kissed his cheek. "I will. And thank you for this. Nut punches are officially off the table, all right?"

He smirked, though the sarcasm didn't reach the rest of his face. "Good to know. I'll send you what I find. And call me and let me know you're okay."

"Deal."

Her phone was already to her ear when she jogged down the stairs and out to her car. Her mother answered on the second ring.

"Coraline, where the hell are you?"

"Mom, I need you at the station now."

"What? Why?"

"We've got a bad guy to catch."

THIRTY-ONE

Ren's knees ached and the rope around his wrists and ankles had rubbed his skin raw. There wasn't a place on his body that didn't hurt. When he'd woken up from whatever drug Gordon had given him, he'd found himself in a garage of some sort—bound, naked, and lying at Gordon's feet. Gordon had smiled down at him, welcomed him back to the world of the conscious, and then had kicked him hard in the ribs and told him to get to his knees.

That'd been the easiest part. The pain. The beating. The cuts Gordon had carved into his skin with his pocketknife.

He could handle that. He'd learned to take that a long time ago. Pain was just pain.

But when Gordon had tried to touch him, had put his hand around Ren's cock, his palm slick with Ren's blood, and told him all the things he was going to do to him, Ren hadn't been able to shut it out and take it. He'd snapped and fought back. Had spit in Gordon's face and thrashed around and had told him what a pathetic excuse for a man he was. How disgusting he was, how shitty the sex had been with him.

Gordon had backed off at that and Ren had thought maybe he'd won. He might die but at least he'd gotten the last word.

But then Gordon had said that since Ren was being less than

accommodating, he would entertain himself with Cora until Ren had a change of heart. Ren had instantly protested, but it'd been too late. Gordon had seen how the threat had affected him. That fear was more of a turn-on to him than anything else.

He'd blindfolded and gagged Ren, left him on the floor to bleed, and then went into the room next door, leaving doors open. Ren had heard every moment of the beating and rape, every muffled scream from her, every groan from him. Ren had nearly broken his hands trying to get himself free and his voice had given out from the shouting he'd done from behind the gag. He could feel the blood running down his wrists and his fingers had gone numb, but there was nothing he could do except listen to the anguished sounds and die on the inside.

She was suffering because of him. This was happening because he'd always been too impulsive, too reckless. Too cocky. He'd gotten in that car like he was going to be some kind of superhero. And when it'd come down to it, he hadn't been able to bear what Gordon dished out. If he'd been able to take it, Cora wouldn't be going through this. He'd never forgive himself. And the second he was free, he would kill Gordon with his bare hands. Rip him apart and watch him die.

But the sounds had quieted a while ago and there was no sign of Gordon. He had no idea if Cora was still here or how badly hurt she was or if she was alive at all. If Gordon knew she was the daughter of the police captain he wouldn't let her leave. How could he?

And that's when Ren realized exactly what this was. Gordon had promised to break him. This was how he'd do it. He'd tried to do it by putting Hayes behind bars. But Ren had fought back, fixed it. He wouldn't be able to fix this.

This time Gordon had made sure of it. He would win. Gordon would always win.

Tears dampened the cloth over Ren's eyes, mixing in with the sweat and making his eyes burn. He could feel his mind starting to break, the need to scream and scream and not stop pushing at him. She couldn't be dead. He couldn't let that thought enter his head. But in his gut, he didn't know how things could turn out any other way.

Cora had been right. Gordon knew the ultimate torture—hurting and taking away the people you loved. That was what was worse than death.

Footsteps sounded against the concrete and Ren braced himself for the cool blade of Gordon's voice, the words that would officially kill Ren for good.

But when the sound came, it wasn't what he expected.

"Get an ambulance," the female voice called out.

A male voice responded and a radio squawked.

Ren lifted his head.

"Mr. Muroya, I'm Captain Benning of the Dallas PD. You're going to be okay. Just stay calm and we're going to get you some help."

Instantly, his voice scraped past his throat in protest, and he started to shake his head. No. *No.* Things were not okay.

"Please, sir, calm down. I'll get the gag and blindfold off. Just try to be still. You're hurt, and I don't want you making it worse."

Cool hands touched him. He jumped instinctively but tried to take a breath to keep ahold of his panic. Captain Benning wrapped something around him—a blanket, maybe—and carefully removed the blindfold.

Her expression was businesslike as she tucked the blanket around him, but her eyes were tense, worried. She unhooked the gag.

"Cora," he gasped, once he could find his voice. "He has Cora. She's . . . hurt. Please."

The woman's eyebrows dipped and she shook her head. "Cora?"

Ren closed his eyes, anguish rising up again. "He hurt her. *Please.* Help her. Find her."

A gentle hand landed on his shoulder and squeezed. "Ren, take a breath. It's okay. Cora's okay." Her voice had slid from business-like to a soothing, motherly tone. "She's the one who helped us find you. I made her stay at the station, but she'll be at the hospital as soon as we get you there."

The words didn't make sense. He opened his eyes, searching her gaze. "But I heard . . ."

Her expression turned grim. "There was a woman here at the house. She was roughed up, but tried to block us from coming inside. We believe she worked for the suspect. Officers have cleared the house. She was the only other person who was here. I swear to you, my daughter is safely at the station, worried sick about you and pissed at me for not letting her come along."

Relief welled up inside him and he felt the cracks go through him like a sheet of ice in spring. He couldn't hold it together anymore. Cora was safe. Gordon had mindfucked him one last time. But she was okay.

They would all be okay.

He bent his head and let the exhaustion and the pain and the stress pull him under. Cora's mother stayed by his side until the EMTs came and started working on him. He heard their voices, talking about blood loss and broken things and shock. They kept saying his name, but he couldn't respond, couldn't do anything but let them handle him.

The pain became a thing he could only recognize from a distance. A hum.

He closed his eyes and let the relief of oblivion take him.

THIRTY-TWO

Cora leaned into Hayes, his big arm gathering her next to him, and she put her head on his shoulder. It'd been hours since they'd first seen Ren wheeled in, and the doctors weren't allowing visitors. All they'd gotten word of was that he was hurt and needed a blood transfusion but was not in critical danger.

That'd been a relief, but the not knowing and not being able to see him for themselves had put both her and Hayes on edge. When she'd gotten to the police station with the photos, she'd been worried about Ren, worried that Gordon was somewhere watching him. What she hadn't considered was that Gordon would *kidnap* him. But when Ren wasn't home or at the office, true fear had set in. And her mother, thankfully, had finally believed her and taken action.

She'd told them to release Hayes from his cell and had him watch the surveillance tape of Ren's "lawyer" coming inside. The guy had been smart. Had worn a hat and had kept his face angled away from the camera, but Hayes had been able to identify at least one thing—it wasn't their lawyer.

So without wasting any more time, her mom had gone along with two squad cars to the location Cora had pinpointed from Gordon's phone. They hadn't expected to find what they'd found.

Ren bleeding out and tied up in the garage. Cora didn't want to think about what would've happened if they'd been delayed any longer or if her mom would've questioned her again. The possibilities would give her nightmares for a long time.

Hayes rubbed his hand along her arm, chasing the goose bumps. He'd been quiet, his thoughts probably running the same routes hers were. Despite his stoic expression, she could feel the quick pound of his heart against her cheek.

She blew out a breath. "He's going to be okay. That's what we need to keep reminding ourselves."

Hayes gave a stiff nod. "As okay as you can be after the person you fear the most beats you, tries to kill you, and . . . whatever else he put Ren through."

She shivered. That was hovering at the edge of her thoughts, too. They didn't know details. But she couldn't imagine Gordon would have left any lines uncrossed. Her stomach twisted. Sexy, funny, lighthearted Ren. What kind of monster would want to hurt someone like that? But she knew the answer. Someone who couldn't tolerate that kind of joy in a person unless he was the owner and controller of it. "He would've killed him."

The words slipped out, her scariest thought escaping the confines of her mind. She knew enough about obsession. Gordon would've been satisfied by only two conclusions. Owning Ren's love. Or killing Ren so that no one else could have him.

"I know." Hayes pulled her a little more tightly against him and kissed the top of her head. "You saved him. Saved us both. I'm not sure I would've been able to live in a world that doesn't have him in it."

She heard the catch in his throat, but when she looked up at him, he covered the chink in his armor quickly. He was trying to be strong for her. She turned in his hold and lifted her hand to brush along the stubble that had grown there. "Hey, it's okay that you're freaked out. You can lean on me, too. I care about Ren. But

I won't pretend to know what you're going through right now. What you guys have runs deeper than I'll ever know."

He met her gaze at that, his eyes softening. "I don't know if I'd say *ever*." He brushed her hair away from her face. "I'm not that old. We've got time. You know, to get deep."

"To get deep?" She smirked. "If Ren were here, he'd jump all over that one. *Let's go find a closet and get deep right now.*"

Hayes chuckled under his breath. "That's exactly what'd he say, the fucker."

She smiled but then looked down, the eye contact too much, her thoughts all over the place. "All I'm saying is that we've gotten thrown into serious shit really quickly. It feels intense. Emotions are high. But I'm one hundred percent aware that I'm the third wheel in this picture. I don't want there to be, like, this obligation to continue things just because I got involved in all this. I would've tried to help regardless of how I feel about you two because it's the right thing to do."

"So you think in exchange for your concern about our well-being and use of your brilliant hacking skills, we'll feel the need to repay you with dates and sexual favors?"

She sniffed. "You make it sound ridiculous when you say it like that."

"Because it's ridiculous."

She looked up.

He gave her a soft smile. "You know what kept me from losing my mind in that jail cell this time?"

"Hmm?"

"I kept thinking about the other night. Replaying it in my head. There were so many great things about that night, but most of all I remembered standing in the shower and listening to you and Ren teasing and horsing around in the bathroom as you dried each other off. Y'all were loud, the laughter bouncing off the walls, everything so silly and light. And I found myself smiling like an idiot. I couldn't believe that after everything I'd been through in the last few years, I'd somehow found not just one but two people who lit me up. Each of you alone is more than I deserve. But both of you? It was like the universe was somehow paying me back with interest. And that if it took three miserable years in prison to be able to get what I had right there in that moment then it was worth it. That I'd do it all again."

Cora's breath caught.

"You're not obligated to us. That street goes both ways. And Ren will have his own feelings and thoughts on all of this." His hand slid to the back her neck, a light touch. "But I fell for Lenore a long time ago. Not her body or her image, but her words, her humor. *You*, Cora. And after the other night, how right everything felt?" He shook his head. "I knew then that even though part of me knows we've just met, the other part is already gone on you. I don't want you to walk away. I want this to be the beginning for all of us. Not the end. But only if you want that, too."

Cora didn't realize she was crying until he wiped a tear off her cheek with the back of his hand. The words were so big, open, and heartfelt from such a stoic man that she could barely breathe them in. What he was suggesting was so much more than sex or kink or even friendship. He was inviting her into his life, his relationship with Ren, his heart.

It was a lot. Everything she wanted but terrifying at the same time. Her whole life, she'd plodded along so carefully. Every move had been calculated. Even looking back now, she realized why she'd stayed with Kevin so long. Not because of insecurity or convenience or hope it would turn into more. None of the labels she'd put on it. She'd stayed because it was safe. She and Kevin would've never fallen in love. They didn't fit that way. She could get hurt, but only a little. A surface scratch.

But with this, with Ren and Hayes, this would be tearing open her collar and offering her throat up to a sword that could slice right through her. She didn't remember all of their night together. But she remembered the feeling of it, the utter sense of rightness, that sense of finally finding a place in the world that didn't require her to adjust or tweak anything about herself. These men wanted her just as she was. And if it didn't work out, if the two of them decided they just wanted each other, that this kind of complicated relationship wasn't worth the trouble, she'd be flayed by it.

That was the risk. That was the danger.

She dipped her head, pressing her forehead to Hayes. But before she could say anything else, a throat was cleared somewhere behind her. A familiar throat-clearing. Cora lifted her head and turned.

Her mom stood there, her gaze darting between Cora and Hayes but offering no clue as to how she felt about what she was seeing. "The doctors said you can both go in now. He's stabilized, but is on painkillers so may be in and out."

Cora got to her feet, Hayes right behind her. Her heart began to pound. She'd only seen a glimpse of Ren when they'd wheeled him in. She needed to brace herself for how he might look, try not to let her worry show on her face. Ren didn't need to see her freaked out.

Hayes put a steadying hand on her lower back and they walked down two hallways to get to the room. The lights were low when they went in and the nurse who'd been adjusting Ren's IV gave them both a nod. "You can only stay a few minutes. He needs rest."

"Of course," Hayes said, his voice library-quiet.

But Cora couldn't respond. Instead she froze in the doorway, her focus glued on the bruised and battered man lying on the bed. Ren's face was pale, his cheek swollen and bruised and his lip cut. The sheets covered him to his shoulders, so she couldn't see the extent of his injuries, but just the bits she could see sent her stomach into a tumble. *Ren.*

She wanted to cry, wanted to run to him and curl her arms

around him, take the pain from him. The rush of emotion was so thick and blinding that it almost took her knees out from under her.

Hayes grasped her around the waist, obviously sensing the shift in her. "Easy, now. It's okay. He's okay. We need to be strong for him."

Tears jumped to her eyes. "I'm sorry, I don't know what's— I'm sorry."

Hayes squeezed her side, but a tremor went through him. "I know. I'm right there with you."

She glanced over, saw the anguish in his face, knew it reflected what she was feeling. She'd known she'd be upset, but this . . . this was something different. This was how you felt when someone you loved was hurt.

The realization stole the breath from her. And she knew without a doubt that if roles were reversed, she'd have the same reaction if Hayes were lying in that bed. She didn't know how to fully explain that feeling or justify it after such a short time of knowing these men, but there it was. The beginnings of love. Something real and scary and undeniable.

"Are you assholes just going to stand there and gawk or actually come and visit me?"

The hoarse voice broke through Cora's pounding heart and tore her from her thoughts. Relief moved through her. She stepped inside. "We didn't want to wake you."

"No way to sleep through that nurse poking and prodding at me. I think she's a closet sadist." Ren turned his head, his eyelids lifting halfway. "Hey, gorgeous."

Cora's lips rolled together as she tried not to start crying again. "Hey, yourself."

"Sounds like they're giving you the good stuff," Hayes said, his gruff voice belying his emotion.

Ren's mouth curled into a lopsided half smile. "Man, I'm super high right now. The only bonus of getting bested by my psycho ex."

"You weren't bested," Hayes said, his tone brooking no argument. "Captain Benning said you went with him to save Cora. You were a hero."

"What?" Cora blurted, turning to look at Hayes. Her mother hadn't told her anything about that.

Hayes nodded at Ren. "Gordon made him think he had you."

Ren closed his eyes, a flicker of pain flashing there. "I thought he'd hurt you, killed you."

"Jesus," she whispered. She reached out and gently brushed Ren's hair away from his forehead.

Ren trembled beneath her touch as he took a shuddering breath, but then he opened his eyes again. "I don't want to talk about it. Maybe not ever."

"That's fine," she said, her heart hurting for him. "But thank you for trying to save me."

"Some superhero I am. I get myself kidnapped and you weren't even there. My comic book would suck." Some of the light came back into his eyes. "But yours wouldn't. I heard you helped find me."

She smiled, trying to keep the mood easy even though imagining what'd he'd been through kept running through her mind. "Yeah. Turns out my ex-boyfriend is good for something."

"Ex-boyfriend?"

"She spent the night over there," Hayes added.

Ren's gaze narrowed. "It's not fair to make an injured man jealous when he can't do anything about it. Fox, go put the fear of God into this ex-boyfriend."

She laughed. "Not necessary."

"I've been informed all hands were kept on keyboards," Hayes said with a faux-businesslike tone.

"Oh, I have no doubt. Like what's-his-face could compete with this?" Ren swept a hand in front of himself and winced at the effort. "But seriously, thank you, to you and to whatever that shit-head did to help."

Hayes poured a cup of water and brought it to Ren's lips for him to sip.

Ren groaned. "Fuck, it feels like I swallowed razor blades."

"Maybe you shouldn't talk," Hayes suggested.

"Always trying to shut me up." He sent Hayes a smirk. "But I can at least use the sore throat as an excuse to delay the grilling by the police a little longer. I'd rather not talk to the good captain ever again."

Cora's eyebrows lifted. "Why? Was my mom rude to you?"

"Your mom was amazing. But she's the one who found me. I was hoping to meet her over Thanksgiving dinner or something. Not tied up and naked and freaking out."

Cora frowned. "My mom's been a cop for a long time. She's seen more naked people freaking out than you can count. And once you get to know her, you'll see that when she's on the job, she's all business. She won't let it be awkward."

"Oh, it's going to be awkward." Ren's gaze turned sly. "But does this mean I've landed an invite to Thanksgiving dinner?"

She crossed her arms and cocked her head. "Are you fishing, Ren Muroya?"

"With big-ass bait."

She shook her head and smiled. "Once my mom gets over the fact that her upstanding daughter has gone to the dark side and is falling for not just one but two kinky-ass men, *maybe* you'll get a turkey invite. Maybe."

Ren's eyebrow arched at that. "Falling for us, huh?"

Cora's cheeks heated. Hayes had expressed how he felt about her, but she had no idea where Ren stood. And once again, her mouth had gotten ahead of her good sense and she'd blurted out feelings all over the place.

"Well, thank God for that," Ren said finally and reached for her hand. His wrist was bandaged and his fingers battered, but he brought her hand to his mouth and kissed it. "Because frankly, everything else is broken on me right now. I don't want to add my heart to the pile. I want you in my life. Both of you."

All the breath sagged out of her. They were words she'd never heard before today. Big words. Scary words.

She'd never realized how much she'd ached to hear them. She didn't know where this would lead. Everything still felt so new. But something deep in her bones told her to leap. That the universe didn't reward cowards. That this was right. And that she'd waited long enough.

Hayes put his hand over the top of hers, the three of them joined. And everything settled inside her.

These were dangerous men.

But dangerous in ways she'd never considered before.

And it was time to be brave.

She leaned over to brush her lips over Ren's, savoring the knowledge that he was here and alive and safe, and then she turned to Hayes. Those green eyes held hers, hope and sweetness and promise there. She pressed her mouth to his and then smiled, answering his question from the waiting room. "I want this to be our beginning, too."

Hayes let out a breath, like he'd honestly been worried she would bail, and he touched his forehead to hers, all three of their hands still joined. "Once upon a time . . ."

EPILOGUE

six months later

Cora sipped her drink as partygoers cruised by her table in tuxedoes and fancy dresses. The policemen's ball was in full swing, and the band was starting to get more takers on the dance floor. Cora watched in amusement as her mother was escorted onto the dance floor by Andre's husband, Jace. Her mom was laughing and waving a dismissive hand like she really didn't want to dance, but the flush high on her cheeks said she wasn't immune to the man's charms.

"He's going to get me fired."

Cora peered up to find Andre standing behind the empty chair at her table, eyeballing the dance floor and looking dapper in his tux. His wife, Evan, was hooked on his arm in a sparkly green dress that set off her dark hair and creamy skin.

Cora smiled. "Or promoted. He's treating her like the belle of the ball. I say let him do his thing."

Evan smirked. "I think he's just trying to make us jealous. Your mom's gorgeous."

"Thanks," Cora said, though it wasn't like she could lay claim to her mom's good looks.

Evan nodded toward Cora. "And I adore your jumpsuit."

Cora glanced down at the black halter-style jumpsuit she'd

worn. Ren had bought it for her when he'd heard there'd be a ball, and she'd fallen in love with the outfit. She'd been oddly touched that Ren had known exactly what she'd like. Those guys got her. She wasn't sure she'd ever felt prettier or sexier at a party. "Thanks."

"I wish I would've thought of wearing one," Evan said, smoothing the hem of her dress. "I haven't been able to sit down in this thing all night without risking Andre's co-workers knowing far too much about me."

"Sitting's overrated," Andre said, looking down at his wife with a sexy smile.

Evan rolled her eyes. "Boys."

Andre nodded toward the empty seats at Cora's table. "So where are your dudes?"

Cora shrugged. "I think they weren't sure if I was ready to out my relationship to all my co-workers yet, so they told me not to feel obligated to bring them. I could've brought one but that feels a little weird, you know?"

"I totally know," Evan said, peering at the dance floor toward Jace and then back to her. "It's hard to be in the closet about the whole thing. I remember how tough that was."

"It is. And to be honest, my mom knows and is . . . dealing. That's really all that's important to me. I mean, I'd hope the people in the other precincts I'm working in now wouldn't judge me, but I'm not all that concerned if they do. I'm over putting on masks for others' benefit. But I wasn't sure if the guys would be cool hanging out with a ballroom full of cops. No offense, Medina."

"None taken. And I don't blame them. But my guess is they would happily be here for you, especially with you looking so hot, Junior. That really shouldn't be wasted."

She groaned. "Please don't tell me that. It feels like my big brother telling me I'm hot."

Andre chuckled. "Just calling it like I see it. It's nice seeing you come out of your shell and doing you. And I'm damn glad they finally hired you full-time. I'm not sure we would've solved that Driskoll case near as quickly without all your help."

"Thanks." She took a long sip of her drink, letting his words settle in and press those happy buttons inside her. She loved that she'd been able to help.

"Well, I'm about to take this hot woman in the too-short dress out on the dance floor. I'll catch you on the other side."

"Have fun." Cora gave them a little wave and then leaned back in her chair. Her table was empty yet again, but somehow it didn't feel awkward like it had at that party all those months ago. She was content to sit here and enjoy the goings-on and do some people-watching. She didn't need someone to sit down and prove she was worthy enough to talk with. She already knew that. Plus, watching cops get tipsy and attempting to dance was more than a little entertaining.

Her phone buzzed in her purse, making the silverware on the table vibrate. She pulled it from her bag.

Dmitry: I've been thinking about you all day.

Cora smiled at the screen, at the old, familiar words. Her thumbs moved over the screen.

Lenore: Same here. Long, lonely night.

Dmitry: Such a shame. Don't your men take care of you?

Lenore: No men tonight. Stuck at a boring work thing.

Dmitry: Boring? Since when is doing high-level hacking work for the police department boring?

Cora glanced around at the crowd, at all of her co-workers, at her mom. This was her world now. A world she hadn't been sure she wanted but now couldn't imagine anything else. She'd liked the idea of running her own business, but when her mom had told her she should try to apply with the department again, Cora hadn't been able to resist. Tracking down Gordon had been terrifying because of who was at stake if she was wrong, but the detective work itself had been like finding a new piece of her internal puzzle. *This* was what she was meant to do.

It didn't pay as much as working for a big company and it didn't pay as much as she could've made signing on to be permanent at FoxRen, but this had never been about money. So she'd applied and with her mom's blessing (and her long lecture about safety and privacy and not putting herself at risk), she'd landed a full-time position helping multiple precincts. She was helping catch bad guys for a living. Nothing had ever felt as rewarding.

Well, almost nothing.

Lenore: No hacking tonight. Just a lot of drinking and watching people dance.

TheRen: Heavy drinking? I knew I should've gone.

Lenore: I'm starting to regret not taking you two. I've never seen y'all in tuxes. And I *am* looking particularly hot tonight. I had a rookie cop try to flirt with me. I think he may have been a few days over twenty-one and a little drunk, but hey, I'll take it.

TheRen: Is she trying to make us jealous?

Dmitry: She is.

TheRen: Unacceptable.

"Agreed."

The spoken word made her startle and clutch her phone to her chest. She spun around in her chair, almost bumping her knees into the man behind her. The broad, beautiful tux-wearing man behind her. Warmth rushed through her. "Hayes."

He put out his hand, green eyes sparkling. "My girl should never be left alone at boring work things."

She took his hand and let him pull her to her feet. His gaze slid over her with slow, appreciative heat.

"You like?" she asked.

"I like. Spin around." His voice had dropped a register, husky. That sexy tone he got when he slid into dom mode. "Let me see all of you."

Slowly, she turned around, letting him see the backless state of the jumpsuit. He put a hand on her shoulder to pause her spin and then dragged his knuckles lightly over her spine, sending goose bumps over her skin.

"Damn. No wonder you didn't let us see you before you left. You never would've made it out the door with that in one piece." He turned her back to face him, illicit promise in his gaze. "You might not make it now."

She smiled, her skin growing warm and sensitive from the way he was devouring her with his eyes. She put her hands to his chest under his jacket. "You look damn fuckable yourself."

"You say the most romantic things," he said with a sly grin.

She pushed up on her toes and pressed her mouth to his. It'd become so easy with him and Ren, so natural. She didn't care that her co-workers might be looking her way—or her mother for that matter. Let 'em look. She was kissing that guy who'd gone to prison. So what. She loved that guy.

But when Hayes clasped her waist and she felt herself taking the kiss to a more heated place, she had to reel it in. This was still a work event even if her body suddenly had no qualms about that. "You're going to get me in trouble looking this tempting. Stop being so irresistible."

"I'll try, but no promises." He brushed a hair away from her face. "Wanna dance?"

She licked her lips, still tasting him there. "Not really."

"Wanna drink?"

"Nope."

"What do you want to do?"

"How about get the hell out of here?"

He lifted a brow. "You sure? I didn't show up to try to rush you out."

"I've done what I needed to do here. I even managed to mingle a bit. But I think I've hit my socializing limit. I'd rather join my party of three instead."

"You're definitely not going to hear any complaints from me

on that. Let's go." He lifted his phone to type something, probably to let Ren know they were on their way home, and then took her hand. She grabbed her purse, dropping her phone inside.

She didn't bother saying good-bye to anyone. Hayes had sat down with her mother and had a long conversation after everything had happened. They were on good terms. But she knew being around a bunch of cops was still uncomfortable for Hayes. So she let him lead her through the crowd, under the sparkling chandeliers, and behind the bar on the far side of the room.

She peered over her shoulder when she realized which way they were headed. "Where are we going? The door to outside is that way."

"You go where we tell you."

"We?"

"Yep." He tugged her into an alcove off the main ballroom and then they slipped through a half-opened door.

Cora squinted in the low light. A coatroom, but there were no coats in this weather. It was just rods and shadowed darkness. For a moment, she felt like the naive girl in a horror movie. This looked like the place where monsters hung out. But before she could get her bearings or question Hayes, an arm clamped around her waist from behind. She automatically yelped, but it got caught in her throat.

"Shh." His scent hit her before her brain registered anything else, a hint of aftershave and fresh laundry. *Ren*. His lips landed on her bare shoulder. "Holy fuck, you look hot."

She closed her eyes and groaned. "What are you boys up to?"

"No good. Always no good." He planted kisses along her skin, making a trail of tingly heat track down her spine.

The sound of a lock turning over was loud in the quiet space but only made her heart beat faster. All of her co-workers and her mother were only a few yards outside that door. Somehow that was terrifying and hot all at once.

Hayes stepped in front of her, his heat registering before she even opened her eyes. He'd clicked on a bare bulb and soft yellow light filled the small room, bringing into view carpeted red walls and more empty space.

Hayes gazed down at her and cupped her chin. "No one saw us come in here. And Ren bribed the bartender for the key. No one can get in."

She licked her lips. "Y'all are very bad men."

"The worst," Ren said, turning her toward him. His gaze ate her up as she took her own fill of seeing him in his tux. *Goddamn*, he looked good. He brushed the back of his hand over her breast, the lack of bra making her nipples go hard and sensitive instantly. "But you're no angel yourself."

"Definitely not." His face was half in darkness and it reminded her of the first time she'd seen him, that air of dominance and mystery swirling around him. But now he was hers. She got to be the one to know his secrets. And he knew hers. "So why did y'all drag me into a dark closet? Finally decided you're done with me and need a good place to hide the body?"

Ren's lips curled. "Such a cop. Always thinking about bodies."

"I'm thinking about bodies," Hayes said from behind her, his fingers teasing at the base of her spine. "Two in particular."

"I wanted to bring you here," Ren said, his eyes holding her gaze. "Because I once was at this boring party. And there was this amazing girl who watched me do bad things in a hallway. Who looked at me with such honest, naked intensity that I couldn't turn away. I wanted her so much. So much more than anything that was happening at the moment. But she was my Cinderella who ran without even leaving a glass slipper behind. I thought I'd never see her again. Then she walked into my office. I'm not sure I believed in fate until that day. Or if I did, I thought fate was a sadistic bastard."

Cora's chest squeezed tight.

"And I promised myself when she walked back into our lives that I wouldn't let her slip through my fingers again. That if she'd let me, one day I'd answer that plea she'd had in her eyes that night in the hallway. That I'd have her just like that. Sneaking away at a party and giving her all the things I knew how to give." He slid his hand around her hip and pulled her to him. "But I realize now that she wasn't the one needing things. I was. *We* were. And she gave those things to us. Somehow in all the chaos, fate decided to make us the luckiest bastards around."

"Ren . . ." Her heart swelled in her chest and before she could respond further, Ren leaned down and kissed her. Long and deep and like they had all the time in the world. Maybe they did. The party outside didn't exist. Nothing else mattered but this moment. These men. Their love. And she felt herself falling into the swirl of sensation. Ren's mouth, his hand kneading her neck, and Hayes not far behind her, holding her waist, his breath warm against her hair.

When Ren moved down to kissing her neck, Cora tipped her head back and Hayes unfastened the hook holding her top together. She didn't startle or falter or entertain any worries. The trust was absolute. They would protect her. She was safe. The halter fell to her waist, the belt on the jumpsuit the only thing holding the outfit on, and cool air moved over her exposed breasts, making everything hypersensitive.

"So beautiful," Hayes murmured as he slid his hands around her and cupped her breasts, plumping them for Ren's mouth.

Cora couldn't help but glance down, seeing Hayes's hands holding her, Ren's tongue gliding along her flesh and kissing the tips of Hayes's fingers. The two men in sync, always. Just the sight was enough to make her squirm in need, her temperature spiking.

"She needs to stay still," Ren said against her skin. "Fasten her wrists."

Hayes's hands slid away from her breasts and grabbed her wrists. "Hands over your head, L."

Her blood pumped hot as she lifted her arms. Hayes messed with something behind her, a bag, and then hooked leather cuffs around her, securing her to one of the coat rods. She tugged at the bindings. The rod was solid as steel, not some flimsy thing from a home closet. This one was meant to hold many heavy winter coats. Or a woman.

The state of things sent a thrill through her, making her skin prickle with awareness. They'd played a lot in the months they'd been together but always at the house or her place. And rarely with bondage. The new elements were ratcheting up her arousal.

"Safe word," Hayes said, tracking his hands down over her ribs.

"Red."

"Good girl." His voice had gone low and rumbly. "Strip her the rest of the way."

Ren gave her a wicked smile and unfastened her belt. Then, he carefully slid her jumpsuit down over her hips and off. He laid it over a stool shoved in the corner before coming back to dispose of her panties.

Before long, she was cuffed to the bar and bare, standing under the lone light bulb. The bar was high and she had to rock onto her toes a bit to maintain her balance. She swallowed hard. "Y'all plan on interrogating me? Who's going to play bad cop?"

"No need to interrogate. You'd give up all your secrets, L." Hayes pressed his clothed body to her, letting her feel his thick erection, and then reached around to slide his fingers between her legs. He grunted in satisfaction. She was slick and hot already, the touch lighting her aflame. "All I'd have to do is promise to touch you right here or taste you, and all the information would be mine."

She groaned at the touch, pushing higher onto her toes with the force of the need going through her. "Good thing I really wasn't an international spy."

He kissed the side of her neck and tucked his fingers deep inside her, rocking against her ever so gently, making her ride his touch. "Good thing. Then you wouldn't be here with us right now."

Ren moved back to the place in front of her, his hand joining

Hayes's but focusing on her clit with slow, almost tortuous circles. Two hands but full coverage of all her hot spots. The combination was going to blow her head off. She jerked in the cuffs and tried to move away to get a breather so she wouldn't go over too quickly, but the guys were having none of that. They'd locked her in place between them and continued to stroke and fuck her with their fingers.

"Breathe through it, L. Self-control," Hayes murmured.

She made some unintelligible sound of protest, but she knew it wouldn't matter.

They had a plan and they weren't going to let her control it. And the plan seemed to be to drive her out of her ever-loving mind. While their fingers took turns teasing her, they put their other hands and their mouths everywhere, one kiss and bite blending into the next until her entire body was shaking with need. Nipples were pinched, her clit was licked, her pussy filled with fingers, with tongues.

Then when she thought she couldn't be driven any higher, both of them lowered to their knees and went down on her, their tongues tangling with each other as they tasted her. Hungry. Dirty. And obscene. Arousal coated her thighs and her body pulsed with pounding need to come. All she could do was watch and cling to the edge of her self-control by a thread.

But soon it was all too much, and when Ren pumped fingers into her and Hayes licked over them and every bit of her, the darkness behind her eyelids burst into a white light. She cried out, gasping through the rush and trying not to make too much noise as she came with the force of a freight train.

The bar clinked with the cuffs above her, and the men made those sexy grunting noises as they drove her onto another plane, and she let it all go. No more holding back. She let it take her. Let them have her. She was no longer in the driver's seat and she couldn't care less. This was what oblivion felt like. What love felt like.

And when she drifted down from the high, she didn't attempt

to make a joke or adjust her position or take back the reins. She just sagged in the cuffs and let Hayes hold her up.

Without words, they unhooked her from the bar and rolled out a thick blanket Ren had pulled from the bag they'd apparently stashed in the corner. The room had plush carpet but she was grateful for the extra padding when she automatically sank to her knees.

Hayes and Ren were still fully dressed, buttoned up in their tuxedos. But their hair was mussed from her grabbing at it and their flys were distended with their very obvious interest in the proceedings.

She reached for the two of them, her movements a little drunk. "Come here. Let me touch you."

Ren was the first to step forward. He caressed her hair. "I love the sound of that, but not yet."

"We had something to ask you first," Hayes said, joining Ren and gazing down at her in that stoic way he had.

She lifted her brow. "So you got me blitzed with an orgasm first?"

Ren grinned. "We are very smart men."

"Devious, really."

She smiled. "All right. Well, now you've got me curious."

Hayes dipped into his pocket and pulled out a key. Not the one for the coatroom door. This one was normal sized. Shiny. New. He got down on his knees to meet her eye to eye. Ren put his hand on her shoulder.

Cora stared at the key.

"Move in with us," Hayes said, the soft rumble of his voice rolling over her like warm ocean waves. "We know it's soon and we know you like your place . . ."

"And there's no pressure," Ren added, his gaze tender on her. "But we're fucking gutted every time you have to go home. The house doesn't feel right without you in it."

Hayes pressed the key into her palm and she felt the weight of it in her hand, the weight of the question. She'd spent her whole life fighting to be independent, wanting to be on her own, only feeling truly comfortable when she was alone, her true self only emerging when no one was watching. But this time, when she considered the question and looked at these two men, she realized there'd never been an easier answer. She'd kept her place like a safety blanket and because it seemed logical, practical. She didn't want to put any undue stress on a new relationship, but she was just fooling herself. Safety blankets were overrated.

Her fingers curled around the key and her lips curved. "We're gonna need a bigger bed. And a better Internet connection."

Ren laughed and got to his knees next to Hayes. "Done. So very done."

She reached out and put her hands to both their faces. "God-damn. What did I do to deserve you two?"

Hayes smiled, this brilliant warm thing that seemed to fill the dark room. "You were you."

"And we were us. And somehow that just fit," Ren added. "Fate is a brilliant bastard."

She closed her eyes. That was exactly it. Somehow in this universe of chaos, they'd found the combination that worked just right. Found exactly where they were supposed to be.

One day, she needed to thank Grace for dragging her to that God-awful party. That had been the first night she was with both Hayes and Ren, where fate had reached down and laid its hands upon her. She just hadn't known it yet. Good thing she hadn't bothered to mingle.

She lowered her head, all three with their arms around one another, and inhaled all that goodness and rightness. "I love you."

"We love you back," Hayes said.

Ren pulled away first and brushed tears she hadn't known she'd shed from her cheek. "You ready for us, Benning? Because we're more than ready for you."

She gave a nod. And as if deciding against whatever else they had planned, they picked up the blanket, got her dressed in silence, and then ushered her out. But instead of leading her out to the parking lot, they led her into the hotel that was holding the ball. Apparently, there was another key in this night. A key card that led to a luxury suite on a high floor.

There were no more words as they led her into the bedroom and stripped her and themselves free of everything. Then Ren was climbing on the bed and beckoning for her. He kissed and touched and caressed her until the fires were burning hot again, and then settled her over him. They'd ditched condoms a month back, so there was nothing between them but heat as she slid down onto his cock. The feel of him so deep inside her sent a hot shudder through her and she peered back over her shoulder.

Hayes was watching from the foot of the bed, his desire a palpable thing. She smiled at him. "Going to join us, Master Hayes?"

"Always," he said, climbing onto the bed with them.

And with that, he got in position behind her, kissed her neck and touched her breasts as she rode Ren. And just when she thought she was nearing her edge again, he bent her forward.

Ren gripped her wrists to his chest and held her gaze, his expression full of pure sin. "We're all yours, Benning. And you, ours."

She knew what was coming before it happened. They'd done this separately but hadn't gone there together yet. But the feel of the slippery fluid against her backside had her toes curling and her heartbeat picking up speed. Fear and arousal twining together.

And when Hayes pushed against her opening with gentle pressure, she let out a low, gritty groan.

"Stop me if it's too much," Hayes said, his voice tense, like it was taking every bit of his restraint not to pound her into the bed.

"You two are always too much," she said between panted breaths. "And I love it."

Hayes let out a loud breath at that and then sunk home, sliding into her body and making everything feel impossibly full. Both men made sounds of hot pleasure, but her groan trumped them both. Everything felt alive and intense and absolutely perfect. She was between them, every part of their bodies and hearts shared. This was exactly where she was meant to be.

She rocked back against Hayes, giving him the silent go-ahead, and the two men made love to her slow and careful at first and then with the passion that seemed to ignite between them anytime they were together.

And when they were done and curled up in a naked mess, she found that old urge from their very first night together bubbling up. She tried to stop it, tried to press her fingers to her lips, but it burst out of her. Laughter. Loud and long and full-throated. The kind that brought tears.

And almost simultaneously, Hayes and Ren joined in.

None of them could help it. Because they all knew. It was impossible not to feel it.

They'd found something none of them had ever believed they could have.

And now they knew exactly what to do with it.